12/07
5-12

W9-BUX-233
0 00 30 043766Y Y

HAYNER PUBLIC LIBRARY DISTRICT
ALTON, ILLINOIS

OVERDUES .10 PER DAY MAXIMUM FINE
COST OF BOOKS. LOST OR DAMAGED
BOOKS ADDITIONAL $5.00 SERVICE CHARGE.

THE TALE OF
HAWTHORN HOUSE

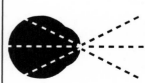 This Large Print Book carries the
Seal of Approval of N.A.V.H.

THE COTTAGE TALES OF
BEATRIX POTTER

THE TALE OF
HAWTHORN HOUSE

SUSAN WITTIG ALBERT

WHEELER PUBLISHING
An imprint of Thomson Gale, a part of The Thomson Corporation

THOMSON

GALE

Detroit • New York • San Francisco • New Haven, Conn. • Waterville, Maine • London

HAYNER PUBLIC LIBRARY DISTRICT
ALTON, ILLINOIS

THOMSON

GALE™

Copyright © 2007 by Susan Wittig Albert.
Map by Peggy Turchette.
Frederick Warne & Co Ltd is the sole and exclusive owner of the entire rights titles and interest in and to the copyrights and trademarks of the works of Beatrix Potter, including all names and characters featured therein. No reproduction of these copyrights and trademarks may be made without the prior written consent of Frederick Warne & Co Ltd.
Wheeler Publishing, an imprint of The Gale Group.
Thomson and Star Logo and Wheeler are trademarks and Gale is a registered trademark used herein under license.

ALL RIGHTS RESERVED
This is a work of fiction. Names, characters, places, and incidents either are the product of the author's imagination or are used fictitiously, and any resemblance to actual persons, living or dead, business establishments, events or locales is entirely coincidental. The publisher does not have any control over and does not assume any responsibility for author or third-party Web sites or their content.
The recipes contained in this book are to be followed exactly as written. The publisher is not responsible for your specific health or allergy needs that may require medical supervision. The publisher is not responsible for any adverse reactions to the recipes contained in this book.
Wheeler Publishing Large Print Hardcover.
The text of this Large Print edition is unabridged.
Other aspects of the book may vary from the original edition.
Set in 16 pt. Plantin.

LIBRARY OF CONGRESS CATALOGING-IN-PUBLICATION DATA

Albert, Susan Wittig.
  The tale of Hawthorn House : the cottage tales of Beatrix Potter / by Susan Wittig Albert.
    p. cm.
  ISBN-13: 978-1-59722-617-2 (hardcover : alk. paper)
  ISBN-10: 1-59722-617-3 (hardcover : alk. paper)
  1. Potter, Beatrix, 1866–1943 — Fiction. 2. Women authors — Fiction. 3. Women artists — Fiction. 4. Foundlings — Fiction. 5. Haunted houses — Fiction. 6. Country life — Fiction. 7. England — Fiction. 8. Large type books. I. Title.
PS3551.L2637T348 2007b
813'.54—dc22   2007033769

Published in 2007 by arrangement with The Berkley Publishing Group, a member of Penguin Group (USA) Inc.

Printed in the United States of America on permanent paper
10 9 8 7 6 5 4 3 2 1

S
F
ALB

6179857904

*To Linda Lear,
with grateful thanks for her sustaining
friendship*

The most wonderful and the strongest things in the world, you know, are just the things which no one can see. There is life in you; and it is the life in you which makes you grow, and move, and think: and yet you can't see it. And there is steam in a steam-engine; and that is what makes it move: and yet you can't see it; and there may be fairies in the world, and they may be just what makes the world go round to the old tune of

C'est l'amour, l'amour, l'amour
Qui fait la monde à la ronde:

and yet no one may be able to see them except those whose hearts are going round to that same tune. At all events, we will make believe that there are fairies in the world. It will not be the last time by many a one that we shall have to make believe. And yet, after all, there is no need for that. There must be fairies; for this is a fairy-tale: and how can one have a fairy-tale if there are no fairies?

Charles Kingsley, *The Water Babies,* 1863

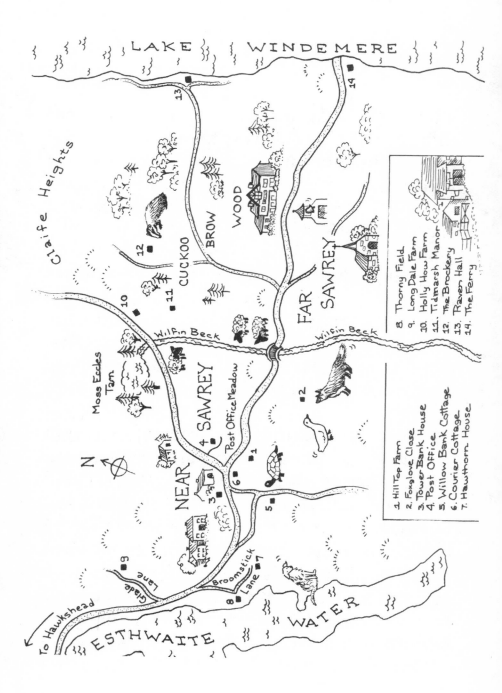

CAST OF CHARACTERS

(* indicates an actual historical person or creature)

PEOPLE OF THE LAND BETWEEN THE LAKES

Beatrix Potter* is best known for the series of children's books that began with *The Tale of Peter Rabbit* (1902). She lives with her parents in London and owns Hill Top Farm, in the Lake District village of Near Sawrey. *Mr. and Mrs. Jennings* live in the Hill Top farmhouse with their three children: *Sammy, Clara,* and *Baby Pearl.* They manage the farm while Miss Potter is in London.

Sarah Barwick (also known as Sarah Scones) lives in Anvil Cottage, at the corner of Market Street and the Kendal Road, where she operates her bakery.

Captain Miles Woodcock is Justice of the Peace for Sawrey District. He lives in

9

Tower Bank House with his sister, *Dimity Woodcock,* who has assumed temporary care of *Baby Flora,* a foundling child. *Elsa Grape* keeps house and cooks for the Woodcocks.

Major Christopher Kittredge is the master of Raven Hall and an admirer of *Dimity Woodcock.*

Will Heelis, * Captain Woodcock's friend, is a solicitor who lives in the nearby market town of Hawkshead. He is the captain's choice for a husband for *Dimity Woodcock.*

Lucy Skead is the village postmistress. She lives at Low Green Gate Cottage and dispenses gossip with the post. Other notorious village gossipers: *Mathilda Crook,* of Belle Green; *Hannah Braithwaite,* of Croft End Cottage (wife of the village constable); *Lydia Dowling,* of Meadowcroft Cottage (the village shop), and her niece and helper *Gladys;* and *Bertha Stubbs,* who works at Sawrey School.

Mr. and Mrs. Barrow operate the village inn and pub, the Tower Bank Arms, where they live with their children.

Jane Crosfield, a weaver, lives at Holly How Farm, on the Tidmarsh Manor estate. Her nephew, *Jeremy Crosfield,* fourteen, attends boarding school in Ambleside.

Mrs. Graham, a midwife, lives with her

husband and children at Long Dale Farm, on Glade Lane. Her old mother, *Mrs. Frost,* a former weaver, lives with them.

Mrs. Janet Allen lives at Willow Bank Cottage on Graythwaite Farm. She keeps exotic pets, including a pair of leopard tortoises named *Hortense* and *Horatio.*

Deirdre Malone, thirteen, lives with *Mr. and Mrs. Sutton* and their eight children at Courier Cottage. *Deirdre* takes care of the children, and *Mrs. Pettigrew* cooks and keeps house.

Emily Shaw was formerly a maid at Tidmarsh Manor, then employed by *Miss Rowena Keller* at Hawthorn House, and lastly by *Miss Pennywhistle,* at Miss Pennywhistle's Select Establishment for Young Ladies, in London.

Caroline Longford, thirteen, lives with her grandmother, *Lady Longford,* at Tidmarsh Manor. She has a new governess, *Miss Cecily Burns.* Also at Tidmarsh Manor: *Mrs. Beever,* the cook-housekeeper, and *Mr. Beever,* the gardener and coachman.

Mrs. Overthewall is one of the Thorn Folk, who were evicted from the hawthorn trees at Hawthorn House.

Tabitha Twitchit, who lives with the Crooks at Belle Green, is the senior village cat. A calico with an orange and white bib, she expects respect and sometimes gets it.

Crumpet is a gray tabby who makes her home with the Stubbses in Lakefield Cottage, and believes that she is next in line for senior cat status.

Rascal, a Jack Russell terrier, lives with the Crooks at Belle Green, but spends most of his time organizing and managing village affairs.

Jemima Puddle-duck is the maternally minded duck in Miss Potter's book, *The Tale of Jemima Puddle-Duck* (1908). *Mr. Reynard Vulpes, Esq.,* of Foxglove Close (who also appears in Miss Potter's book), is her ardent admirer.

Kep,* a collie, is the new Top Dog at Hill Top Farm. *Mustard,* an old yellow dog, helps out when he is feeling fit. Other barnyard animals include *Aunt Susan* and *Dorcas,* the Berkshire pigs; *Kitchen* the Galway cow and *Blossom,* her calf; *Win-*

ston the pony; *Boots, Shawl,* and *Bonnet,* the superfluous hens assigned to hatching ducklings; and various *Puddle-ducks. Tibbie** and *Queenie** and their Herdwick lambs enjoy the freedom of Hill Top Farm.

Jackboy the Magpie carries tales, but his Cockney rhyming slang makes it hard to understand them.

Bosworth Badger XVII lives in The Brockery on Holly How with an ever-changing variety of residents and guests. Bosworth maintains the *History of the Badgers of the Land Between the Lakes* and its companion work, the *Holly How Badger Genealogy.*

Professor Galileo Newton Owl, D.Phil., is a tawny owl who conducts advanced studies in astronomy and applied natural history from his home in a hollow beech at the top of Cuckoo Brow Wood.

PROLOGUE:
HAWTHORN HOUSE

Thursday, 20 August, 1908

From the very beginning, Emily had been uneasy at Hawthorn House.

Granted, she was an imaginative girl whose fancies sometimes ran away with her common sense. But her feelings about Hawthorn House went beyond fancy — or so it seemed to Emily. The house was secretive, as if it were keeping a great many things to itself, things that ought to be revealed. It sat on the side of a hill overlooking the lake, but not proudly, the way a hillside house ought to sit. Instead, it seemed hunched and huddled, as if it were too troubled by interior matters to look out across the lake.

Or perhaps it was merely that Hawthorn House did not want anybody to look at it. It was, after all, very ugly. The walls came together at the wrong angles, the slate roof was studded with towers and turrets and chimney pots and gables, the windows were in all the wrong places, and the garden was overgrown with nettle and thistle. No one had lived in Hawthorn House in years and years, for one very simple reason.

It was haunted.

Oh, not in the usual way. No long-dead ladies dressed in white, or headless monks or bearded gentlemen without arms. It was worse than that — oh, much, much worse. Hawthorn House was haunted by dead dreams. It had been cursed by its evicted tenants, who vowed that the house would never again —

But we'll come to that later. The baby is crying, and we must get on with our story.

In fact, Baby Flora (who was generally quiet and well behaved, for one so young) had been crying steadily in her cradle for the past hour, ever since Mrs. Graham had brought her back. It was now one in the afternoon, and not even her bottle had brought her any comfort.

And Emily — who was pacing up and down the kitchen, biting her lip and wringing her hands — was crying, too, mostly in sympathy with Baby Flora, but also in vexation and disappointment. At this very hour, she should have been at Windermere Station, boarding the afternoon train for London, where Miss Keller was waiting. Instead, she was marooned here at Hawthorn House, which (even if nothing had gone wrong) would have been a very unpleasant prospect, for the place was gloomy and isolated and ugly. And haunted.

Emily shivered at the word, pushing it away, out of her mind. The situation was bad enough without thinking about that, for everything *had* gone wrong. She was here by herself, with no hope at all of getting away. At the thought, the tears came even more freely — tears, it must be admitted, of self-pity.

Now, before you think too ill of our Emily, I must tell you that she believed little Flora to be the dearest thing imaginable. While Emily was waiting for the baby to be born, she had knitted tiny caps in baby colors: pink for a girl, blue for a boy, yellow for both. She had been the first to cradle the newborn in her arms, to kiss the corner of her sweet rosebud mouth and whisper a welcome into her tiny pink ear. She had slept beside Flora's cradle and got up in the night when Flora fretted. And in the fortnight since the baby's birth, she had willingly learnt all sorts of new and necessary motherings, from changing baby's nappies to administering bottle and bath.

But I must also tell you that Emily was scarcely sixteen and still a girl, for all that she had the form and face of a young woman. And even though she had understood what she was letting herself in for (as much as one can be said to understand a new situation before one finds oneself in it up to one's pretty chin), Emily's romantic mind had painted the prospective experience in unmistakably rosy hues. But she had made mistakes, some of them quite regrettable.

For one thing, she had trusted the gypsy lad to whom she had given her heart when she met him at market some months before. But he did not love her as faithfully as he had promised. He had gone to the south of England to work in the hops fields without a goodbye and she had not had a letter from him since, not even so much as a ha'penny postcard.

And for another, she had trusted Mrs. Graham, who had agreed to take the baby when Miss Keller returned to London, so that Emily could follow. Emily would much rather have taken Flora with her, of course, but Miss Keller said that was out of the question. So Emily had no choice, and really, when you stopped to think of it, Flora would be happier growing up in the country, rather than the city. But London — well, London was Emily's dearest dream. London, and the blue velvet dress that Miss Keller had mentioned, and the smart blue boots that would go with the dress, and the white fur muff. Oh, such joy!

But Mrs. Graham had let her down, just like the gypsy lad. The City seemed as far away as the moon, and the dress, boots, and muff might as well be on Mars. Emily felt terribly betrayed, as you would, too, I daresay, if you had your heart set on going to London and learnt, at the very last minute, that you could not go.

So I'm sure you can understand why Emily was crying. Miss Keller had already left for London, and was expecting her. Mrs. Hawker, the cook, had gone away, too, to take care of her sister. Mrs. Hawker was deaf as a doorpost and could not be counted on for ordinary conversation, but at least she had been another presence in the house. Deirdre Malone hadn't dropped in lately, either. Deirdre was too young to be a true confidante, but she had been a willing listener, even if Emily couldn't tell her the whole truth.

Emily could scarcely blame her employer for the way things had turned out. All the arrangements had been completed before

Flora's birth, and Miss Keller had left believing everything satisfactorily settled. Mrs. Graham, the midwife, had undertaken to foster the child: the best of possible outcomes, Emily agreed — although sadly, as I said before, because she truly wanted to take the baby with them. The Grahams already had three little girls of their own, and Mr. Graham's earnings as a lorry driver provided a comfortable cottage, two good milk cows, and three pigs. Little Flora would grow up happily there, a prospect that had reconciled Emily to the pain of giving her up.

But it was Mr. Graham who had thrown the spanner into the works. When he learnt that the baby was another girl, he flatly refused to have her. " 'Tis boys we wants," he had said to his wife. "Give us a boy and you can keep 'im. But doan't give us nae more worthless girls."

So Mrs. Graham had brought little Flora back to Hawthorn House just as Emily was ready to leave, and now the baby wouldn't stop crying, and Emily had got to her wits' end, which, according to her former employer, was not very far.

"You are a silly girl," Lady Longford had scolded whenever Emily had committed some minor infraction of a Tidmarsh Manor rule. "A foolish, spoilt girl with no more brains than a ha'penny bun, and wretchedly conceited into the bargain."

Of course, we can't permit Lady Longford to have the last word on Emily, but it is certainly true that the girl was thinking less about Baby Flora and more of her own disappointments: of her portmanteau packed and ready, of the train ticket Miss Keller had bought her, of the shilling for the hansom cab she was to hire when she arrived in London. She wrung her hands and fresh, hot tears pooled in her eyes and ran down her cheeks. Miss Keller was expecting her, and she must go to London, she really must!

But how, now that Mr. Graham had sent Flora back? Take the infant with her on the train? That might be the only alternative. But Miss Keller had made it very clear that their life in London would not permit her to care for an infant and —

BANG!

The kitchen door flew violently open and a woman stepped inside, although it might be more accurate to say that she *blew* in on a gust of sudden wind that lifted her bodily over the threshold and deposited her in the middle of the kitchen, her clothing tossed and tumbled and twisted about her. This was curious, since the August day had, up to that moment, been sultry and very, very still, without the slightest whisper of wind, and since country people never, ever came into a kitchen without pausing at the door to knock and yoller.

Emily stared, shocked into open-mouthed silence, as her visitor shook herself. She was shorter than Emily by a full head, and roundly plump, with untidy gray hair and soft features, like a sweet-faced cloth doll. But her expression was as keen as a knife, her chin was firm, and her blue eyes piercing. Despite the warmth of the summer's day, she was dressed in a rag-bag jumble of bright plaid and paisley woolen scarves and knitted shawls, with layers of pinafores, some white, some yellow, some printed with flowers and decorated with rows and rows of buttons, on top of a bright red petticoat. Peeking out from under all this were heavy wood-and-leather pattens, and on her arm hung an old-fashioned woven reed basket covered with a blue-checked cloth.

"Who —" Emily faltered.

"You might call me Mrs. Overthewall," the woman said cheerfully, "but then again you might not." Her voice was creaky, like a hinge that wants oiling. She set down her basket and unwound a paisley scarf, then a plaid one, then one allover green. "I've come to visit."

"Very kind, I'm sure," Emily said, in a formal tone, "but Miss Keller is away and —"

"Flora is crying." Mrs. Overthewall pulled her scant gray eyebrows together in a stern frown. "She has been crying for several hours. Sev-er-al," she repeated with forbidding emphasis.

"I'm afraid so," Emily said guiltily, so taken aback that she did not think to ask how Mrs. Overthewall knew the baby's name. "She has been . . . well, cross. I was just going up to see to her."

"Allow me," Mrs. Overthewall said, and went toward the stairs, still carrying her basket.

Alarmed, Emily put out her hand. "Oh, no, really, please! Don't trouble yourself!" But Mrs. Overthewall paid no attention, and Emily's eyes grew round as she watched the woman go up the stairs — not walking, not running, but *twinkling* smoothly and gracefully, which was all the odder because it is virtually impossible to twinkle in wood-and-leather pattens, as you will know if you have ever worn them. They are something like the Dutch wooden shoes, except that the tops are leather. You are far more likely to *clomp* than *twinkle.*

And then, before Emily could draw in another breath, Mrs. Overthewall was twinkling down the stairs again.

"The matter is taken care of," she announced with a calm authority. "You have missed today's train, my dear Emily. But the next one leaves at nine o'clock in the morning. You shall be in London by teatime."

Emily stared, an uncomfortably insistent idea elbowing itself into her reluctant awareness.

"Are you a —" She bit her lip. She could not bring herself to say the word.

"Don't be impertinent," said Mrs. Overthewall, in a tone remarkably like that of Lady Longford. "I advise you to take the earliest ferry, so as to be at the station on time."

Emily gulped. "But I . . . but you can't possibly . . ."

"Of course I can," said Mrs. Overthewall, with extraordinary firmness. She stood on her tiptoes and kissed Emily on the forehead. Her voice softened. "And so can you, my child. And so you must, and that's an end to it. Now, I'm off."

And exactly as if it had been waiting on her word, the door flew open, slamming so violently against the wall that the dishes danced. The wind hurtled in and gathered up Mrs. Overthewall, twirling her twice so that her shawl and mufflers wrapped themselves firmly around her and her basket. And then it whirled her out the door and slammed it shut behind her.

Emily stared at the closed door, her heart thudding in her chest. She turned and ran as fast as she could up the stairs to Flora's cradle. It was empty.

Now half sick with fright, Emily ran to the window and flung it open. The nettles along the garden path were bent nearly double by the wild wind, and the neglected roses flung their petals into the blustery air. Mrs. Overthewall twinkled swiftly over the gravel, her mufflers and shawls and pinafores and petticoats swirling about her in a kaleidoscope of magical colors. When she reached the stone wall at the back of the garden, she rose to the top, where she turned, looked up at Emily, and blew her a kiss.

"Don't worry," she called. "And don't miss your train, dear girl!" And with that, she flew off the wall and was gone.

Emily blinked, closed her eyes, and looked again. Of course, it might have been a trick of the light or cloud or wind or an overwrought imagination. But even though she could plainly see the stile and the stone fence and the hillside beyond, Mrs. Overthewall was nowhere in sight.

She and her basket and Baby Flora had utterly vanished.

1
THE VILLAGE GOES
TO A FÊTE

Saturday, 22 August, 1908
A century ago in the English Lake District,
late summer was filled, dawn to dark, with
hard work. There was more to do than could
easily be done: hay to cut and stack and
cure and cart; oats to cut and bind and
stook; sheep to wash and shear and full
fleeces to roll and tie; Damson plums and
red raspberries and blackberries to gather
and make into jams and jellies; and vegetables to harvest and lay by. If the weather
was fair and fine, the work went quickly and
the villagers were in general good spirits. If
it was cold and damp, the hay spoilt, rats
and birds got into the grain, fruit dwindled
on branch and vine, and everyone felt low-
spirited and cross.

But all through the August in which our
story takes place, the weather had been fine.
Much too fine, I fear. The sky was relent-
lessly blue and cloudless, and the winds

blowing down from the western fells and up from the broad midlands were so hot and dry they might have blown in from the Sahara. Across Esthwaite Water, a heat haze veiled the shoulders of Coniston Old Man. The Galway cattle and Herdwick sheep would have been glad of green grass, the currants had shriveled into hard knots, and everyone in the twin hamlets of Near and Far Sawrey lamented the sad state of their flowers and vegetables, especially since the Summer Fête was upon them.

This annual event was held in Post Office Meadow and attracted not only the local folk but visitors from as far away as the market town of Hawkshead to the west and Bowness and Kendal to the east. The Sawrey fête had earned quite a reputation around the Lake District, for it featured a garden show. The villagers were known for their remarkably green thumbs, with dahlias, cauliflowers, and roses numbering among their specialties, and they all looked forward to displaying their prize specimens. The hot rainless summer had made gardening difficult, but as usual, the village gardeners remained undaunted.

The Summer Fête is always held in Near Sawrey, for Far Sawrey has the October Fête. If you're wondering how these hamlets came by their names, it is very simply explained: Near Sawrey is nearer the market town of Hawkshead, while Far Sawrey (which is nearer Lake Windermere) is farther away by a half mile or so. Although their residents might not own to it, both hamlets are of nearly equal size and importance. Near Sawrey boasts the pub, the bakery, the smithy, and the joinery; Far Sawrey prides itself upon St. Peter's Church and the vicarage, the village school, and the Sawrey Hotel. Each has its own post office, and each feels itself much superior to the other, as of course it is.

The posters announcing the Summer Fête had been displayed for weeks: at the ferry landings on both sides of Lake Windermere, in shop windows in Hawkshead and Bowness, on notice boards and gateposts and tree trunks. The week before the event, the cottages on Market Street were blazoned with bright bunting, and a Union Jack was hung over the door of the Tower Bank Arms. On Friday, village children had erected a flowery arch at the entrance to the meadow, and streamers and ribbons and banners fluttered everywhere.

And by the time the sun rose over Claife Heights early on Saturday morning, curious to see what was going on, it beamed down on a meadow in which stalls and booths and tables had sprung up like mushrooms around the large white central tent, where the exhibits were displayed and the judging took place. At the far end, a wooden platform for dancing, singing, and reciting was in the final stages of completion. And everywhere there was such a cheerful noise — men hammering, children shouting, women singing, birds calling, hens cackling, dogs barking — that I shouldn't wonder if the sun had put its hands over its ears until it had risen high enough to be above it all.

For the people who pinned their hopes on a prize, the exhibits were the entire reason for the fête. They were entirely devoted to scrubbing, polishing, grooming, arranging, and otherwise perfecting their entries. But others had more to do.

Grace Lythecoe was managing the cake stall, Hannah Braithwaite the jellies-and-jams, George Crook the vegetables, and Lydia Dowling the jumble.

Dimity Woodcock and Major Christopher Kittredge had overall charge of the event, the major taking responsibility for sports, games, and entertainment and Miss Woodcock the stalls, the judging, and the evening dance.

Music was provided by the Village Volunteer Band (Lester Barrow on trombone, Mr. Taylor and Clyde Clinder on clarinet, Lawrence Baldwin on coronet, and Sam Stern on the concertina). The Hawkshead Morris Men, kitted out in gay vests, ties, sashes, and hats, would be dancing twice during the afternoon and once in the evening.

Everyone had something to do. And everyone benefited in the end, for the proceeds would be used to complete (at last!) the repairs to the Sawrey School roof.

Throughout the morning, the trio of judges moved from table to table inside the Exhibit Tent, sniffing, tasting, poking, and pinching. At two o'clock, the prizes were announced. Betty Leach's golden pompoms took the honors, as did Joseph Skead's cauliflower and Henry Stubbs's honey. And the Barrow children's rabbit — a flop-eared bunny named Rhubarb — was pronounced the best of the best and a blue ribbon was proudly pinned upon his cage.

Mrs. Lythecoe's cake stall was the first to sell every item. Sarah Barwick had generously donated seed wigs and sponges, while other village ladies sent shortbread, gingerbread, and tea cakes, every last crumb of which had vanished by three in the afternoon, to the disappointment of those who arrived at five minutes past.

The jams-and-jellies stall was next to clear out, with Bertha Stubbs's gleaming jars of marmalade and Elsa Grape's chutney (made from a recipe Captain Woodcock brought back from India) going first. Agnes Llewellyn's green gooseberry jam, which is too tart for most people's taste, went home with Vicar Sackett, who bought it to spare Agnes the embarrassment of having to take it back, unsold, when Hannah Braithwaite closed the stall.

It took a bit longer for George Crook at the vegetable stand to unload the last of Roger Dowling's Brussels sprouts. And it was after four by the time Lydia Dowling got rid of the last two bits of jumble: a beaded egg cozy donated by Annie Nash and an emerald-green scarf knitted for Captain Miles Woodcock by his former nurse, Mrs. Corry, whose eyesight was not of the best. I regret to say that Henry Stubbs bought it to top off his scarecrow.

"Well!" exclaimed Lydia, surveying the ravaged jumble table. "Though I says it as shouldn't, I'd call it a right success." She rattled the box of coins as she handed it to Miss Woodcock. "Haven't counted it yet, but must've took in all of four quid."

"That's grand, Lydia," Dimity said, taking

the box. "You've done splendidly. I always say that jumble is hardest of all. Just pricing it is a challenge."

Lydia rolled her eyes. "T' biggest job is fendin' off t' stall workers 'til we open for business. Let 'em at it early, and they'll grab all t' good stuff afore anybody else has a chance."

Christopher Kittredge hurried up. "Pardon, Miss Woodcock, but you're wanted at First Aid. One of the Banner boys bloodied his nose in the potato sack race, and his mother can't be found."

Dimity always turned pink when Major Kittredge spoke to her. But she only said, "Oh, dear. The poor child!" and hurried off, tucking the coin box into the string bag she carried over her arm.

The major surveyed the empty jumble table. "Well done, Mrs. Dowling," he said with a smile. "I wouldn't have wagered that we'd get rid of that green . . . er, that we would sell *everything.* You must be very persuasive."

Major Kittredge had only one arm and one eye and his face was visibly scarred — war wounds suffered in a skirmish with the Boers in '01 — but Lydia thought he was still quite the handsomest man in the village, even if his reputation wasn't all it should be. She ducked her head, muttering a pleased "Thank'ee, sir."

The major had no idea that anyone, least of all a woman, considered him handsome. In fact, when he looked into his mirror, he looked quickly away again, feeling that he was ugly enough to frighten children and horses and that he should become a hermit after all. But he was determined not to yield to this unhealthy impulse, so when the Vicar asked him to give Miss Woodcock a hand with the annual fête, he'd agreed. One hand was all he had, he said with a rueful chuckle, but perhaps one would do.

He was glad he'd said yes. The fête gave him a chance to involve himself in village matters, as his father and grandfather had always done. It was an opportunity to try to redeem himself, for he knew that most in the village disapproved of him. And it gave him a chance to spend some time with Dimity Woodcock. His face might be altered almost beyond recognition, but if Dim found him repugnant, she was kind enough not to let on.

With a goodbye to Lydia Dowling, the major walked over to see whether Lester Barrow had finished setting up the dartboards for the evening's tournament. All looked in good order, but to the west, the blue sky had turned dark and thunderheads threatened the fells. They'd be in for a good soaking shortly — a boon to fields and farmers, but hardly welcome to fête-goers. Bad news if it poured with rain on the one day when every villager hoped for clear skies, and none more than the major. It was his first fête since he'd come home to Raven Hall after the war, after that long stay in hospital and that blasted business with —

The major broke off with a shudder. Losing his heart, and his common sense, to that woman had been a disaster.

A damned, downright, undeniable disaster.

2
VILLAGE AFFAIRS, FROM OTHER POINTS OF VIEW

The major was too busy with his thoughts to notice the two cats — one a calico, the other a gray tabby — sitting side by side on a wooden bench. But they certainly noticed him.

"Major Kittredge is remembering that woman he thought was his wife," Tabitha Twitchit observed in a condescending tone. *"He should never have married her."*

"A sad bit of business," returned Crumpet, although she couldn't help feeling that Tabitha might show a little more sympathy toward the major. It hadn't been his fault that the woman wasn't the person she pretended to be.

"An actress, a beautiful woman, but dangerous," Tabitha went on, as if Crumpet didn't already know all the facts of the case. *"Lucky for him, she turned out to be someone else's wife, so their marriage was never a legal one. He is well rid of her."*

"It was an expensive lesson," remarked Crumpet. A smooth gray tabby with a red collar and a golden bell, she was younger and sleeker than Tabitha. It was her opinion that Tabitha's age (she was fifteen, which is seventy-eight cat years) was slowing the older cat down. It was high time she retired from her position as president of the Village Cat Council — but of course, Tabitha would never do that of her own accord, not while she felt so superior to every other animal in the village.

"Expensive?" Tabitha said, licking her paw. *"I think not, Crumpet. The woman's attempt at theft was a complete failure, thanks to our Miss Potter."*

A small tan-colored dog, sauntering past, paused to add his opinion. *"You're right, Tabitha,"* Rascal barked. A Jack Russell terrier, he lived with the Crooks at Belle Green but devoted himself to the task of overseeing village affairs. *"The Kittredge jewels are safe, and the credit is entirely due to Miss Potter."*

Miss Beatrix Potter, of Hill Top Farm, had asked the major not to disclose her part in the unhappy business of some months past. But one might as well try to hide a thunderstorm under a thimble. Word of the adventure spread, and it was not long before everyone knew that the woman who called herself Mrs. Kittredge was an imposter and that she and her co-conspirator would have succeeded in making off with the family jewels, had not the intrepid Miss Potter thwarted their escape by the simple expedient of —

But I shan't rob you of the pleasure of reading this story for yourself. It is related in *The Tale of Cuckoo Brow Wood,* which tells what happened when Miss Potter went with three young people — Jeremy, Caroline, and Deirdre — to Cuckoo Brow Wood on May Eve, in search of fairies.

"You've completely missed the point," Crumpet said impatiently. *"The major's foolish marriage cost him dearly. Folks in the village have not forgiven him. And he and Dimity Woodcock would be married by now if that other business hadn't happened."*

"Too true," Rascal conceded, thinking that Crumpet, as usual, had got it right. *"Miss Woodcock won't have him now."*

Tabitha's eyes popped open. *"The major would have married Dimity Woodcock?"* she cried. *"How do you know?"*

Crumpet smoothed her whiskers with a fine gray paw. *"You're not the only animal in the village who keeps her ear to the ground, Tabitha."*

Rascal barked a laugh. Tabitha was an old dear, but she did put on airs. It was good to see her taken down a peg or two.

"Well!" Tabitha made a loud harrumph. *"If that is true, I am sorry for it. But what makes you think she won't have him, now he's free?"*

"Why, because of the scandal, of course!" Crumpet replied in a catty tone.

Rascal nodded regretfully. *"Miss Woodcock would never consent to be the wife of a man who lost his head and married a London actress on a fortnight's acquaintance."* For that is what Major Kittredge had done. Not usually an impulsive man, he had allowed his fancy to run away with his common sense, and in consequence had suffered all sorts of ills and evils. He had lost the respect and admiration of the village, and he had lost Miss Woodcock.

"Perhaps." Tabitha paused delicately. *"But if Miss Woodcock truly loves the major, she might forgive him."*

"If *she were left to her own devices, she might*," Crumpet acknowledged. *"But Captain Woodcock has made up his mind against it, and she would never oppose her brother in something as important as the choice of a husband."* And then, with the air of a cat who knows a great deal more than she is at liberty to tell, she added, *"There's something else, but it is highly secret. If I tell you, you must promise not to tell a soul."*

"I promise," Rascal said eagerly.

Tabitha's mahogany ears pricked forward. Every fiber of her feline being was screaming out to hear the secret, but promising was an admission that Crumpet knew something she didn't.

"Oh, all right," she said at last, crossly. *"I promise."* But she crossed her forepaws under her furry white bib, as the Big Folk crossed their fingers when they told a lie.

Crumpet purred, feeling that she had finally got the best of Tabitha. *"Captain Woodcock,"* she said, *"has already chosen his sister's husband."*

"But who?" Rascal asked, puzzled. *"The major is the only suitable candidate in the village. And Miss Woodcock would never leave. Who would do all the things she does?"* Miss Woodcock was never too busy to knit stockings for the poor or take food to the sick. Without her, everyone said, the parish would simply fall apart.

"Yes, a husband," Crumpet said authoritatively. *"And I shouldn't be surprised if the engagement were to be announced within the fortnight."*

Tabitha abandoned her efforts to appear nonchalant. *"Who is he?"* she cried. *"Who? Who?"*

Crumpet gave a hard, triumphant laugh, the laugh of a cat who has the upper paw. She leaned forward and whispered a name, just loud enough for Tabitha and Rascal to hear — but not loud enough for us, I'm afraid. (I suppose we might have moved closer, but I shouldn't like to be accused of eavesdropping.)

Rascal blinked. *"Really? Are you sure, Crumpet?"*

Tabitha tossed her head. *"I suspected it all along,"* she said airily.

"You didn't!" Crumpet snarled, arching her back.

"I did!" Tabitha hissed. Her tail puffed out.

"Now, now, ladies," Rascal soothed, raising a cautioning paw. *"Let's not fight."*

But the cats paid no attention. Crumpet's claws flashed. Tabitha bared sharp teeth. And then, in a fine fury of fur and fierce whiskers, they tumbled off the bench, biting and scratching and shrieking and slashing. Tabitha escaped and ran yowling through the crowd, the furious Crumpet snarling at her heels. They were last seen disappearing over the stone wall.

■ ■ ■ ■

In a village, it is naturally ordained that nothing, not even the smallest bit of business, escapes attention. The cats' quarrel was witnessed by Misses Potter and Barwick, who happened past at that moment.

"Just look at that," Sarah Barwick said. "Tabitha and Crumpet after each other, hammer and tongs. Wonder what it's about."

"A difference of opinion about mice, perhaps," replied Beatrix Potter with a chuckle. In London, where she lived with her parents, quarrelsome cats were beneath notice. But in Sawrey, small doings like this one merited comment, and villagers found them endlessly amusing.

Sarah nodded. "Like good friends who get into rows. Or family members." In honor of the fête, she had forsaken her usual corduroy trousers (you can imagine what the village had to say about those trousers!) for a neat gray serge skirt of practical length.

"Indeed," Beatrix agreed regretfully. "Family squabbles are every bit as fierce as cat fights."

At least, hers were. She had just left her parents at Stock Park, their holiday house, some fifteen miles away at the southern end of Lake Windermere. Her brother Bertram had joined them for a fortnight, but it had not been a happy time. Their parents had constantly nagged and grumbled at their son about his decision to leave London and live year-round on a farm in Scotland. It had been quite tiresome. Quarreling made Beatrix unhappy.

"P'rhaps it's better not to have any family," Sarah mused. "No family, no family rows — although one does hit a lonely patch now and then."

Sarah, whom the villagers called "Sarah Scones," operated a bakery out of her kitchen at Anvil Cottage. Old enough to be considered a spinster, she always said she doubted she would ever take a husband. She would have to put up with his going to the pub and spending weekends with gun or rod. He would have to put up with her cigarettes and trousers, her business hours (up before dawn to bake, and open to customers on Sunday), and her habit of saying exactly what she thought. Neither would be suited.

"To tell the truth, I shouldn't mind a little loneliness," Beatrix replied wistfully. "It's tedious to continually explain where one is going, or where one has been, and with whom and why." She made a rueful grimace. "When one is a fully grown adult, one can surely be counted on to find one's way without losing parcels or being run over by cabs." She looked up at the western sky, which had grown quite dark and ominous. "Do you suppose it's going to rain?"

"Of course not," Sarah declared staunchly. "It can't rain today. Not with all these trippers about, and the foot races still to be run, and the dance tonight."

As if in answer, a bolt of lightning flashed, thunder rumbled, and the scent of wet grass sweetened the rain-cooled breeze. A few large drops splatted onto the warm ground, creating dust cones like tiny volcanoes. Ladies put up their parasols and stall-keepers scurried to cover their wares.

"I think I had better go home and close my windows before it doesn't rain," Beatrix said with a laugh. She had intended to stay for the Morris dancers, because she especially enjoyed watching Mr. Heelis. He danced with a grace and lightness that she admired. But someone mentioned that he had not been able to come, so she didn't mind missing them.

Sarah giggled. "And I should take my laundry off the line before it doesn't get wet. Goodbye, Bea." She picked up her skirts for the short dash to Anvil Cottage.

Beatrix hurried in the other direction, crossing the Kendal Road and climbing the path to the top of the hill above the Tower Bank Arms. She didn't mind the rain, for the plants and animals needed it and the coolness was refreshing. And best of all, she was going to Hill Top Farm. She was going home, and the thought of it swept her, as it always did, with a sweet wonder.

She was going *home.*

3
"No More Babies!"

Deirdre Malone, who worked for the Suttons at Courier Cottage, had been eagerly looking forward to the fête, for she and her friend Caroline Longford had planned to go together. But I am sorry to say that their plans didn't work out.

Caroline sent a note saying that she was in bed with a summer cold and couldn't leave Tidmarsh Manor, where she lived with her grandmother. So when Mrs. Sutton asked Deirdre to take Libby, Jamie, and Nan, the three older Suttons, Deirdre agreed. The other five Suttons were too young for such excitements, and would have to stay at home.

By the time Deirdre had combed her hair and put on her hat, the children were waiting at the door, hands scrubbed and faces shining, hair ribbons and shoelaces neatly tied, pocket money knotted into handkerchiefs. "We're ready!" they chorused, dancing up and down.

"Off we go, then," Deirdre said cheerfully, and marched her troops down the path in the direction of Post Office Meadow.

I daresay you're thinking that Deirdre's cheerfulness must be pretended, but I am glad to tell you that it is entirely genuine. An orphan and just thirteen, Deirdre had worked for the Suttons at Courier Cottage for nearly two years, and felt very lucky to have a comfortable place with a congenial family. It might just as easily have been otherwise, of course. If someone else had come to the orphanage and chosen her, Deirdre might have found herself on an isolated farm where she did double duty in the nursery and in the kitchen, or in a large manor house where she was the most junior of the nursery staff, charged with lighting fires and carrying hot water for baths and ironing endless ribbons and ruffles for a tyrannical head nurse. Instead, she had a good place where the work was shared, the grownups were civil, the children were reasonably well mannered, and she could go to school.

Courier Cottage was large but not fancy and was always in something of a state, owing to there being so many little Suttons. But Deirdre loved the children dearly. And now that Mrs. Sutton had hired Mrs. Pettigrew as cook-housekeeper and Deirdre had finished her studies at the village school, she could spend all her time with them, serving as nursery-maid, minder, and nanny. For their part, the children viewed Deirdre as something akin to an older sister, which didn't mean that they always did what she told them, just that they always felt very sorry afterward, and promised to do better.

There were enough Suttons to keep Deirdre on her toes, especially because they were all so adventurous. The eldest, eleven-year-old Libby, had dark eyes and raven hair and a fiercely independent spirit. Jamie, at ten, was always thinking up larks that got his sisters into trouble. Nine-year-old Nan (whom everyone called Mouse) was next, and after her came Lillian. The younger ones weren't in school yet: the twins, Andrew and Phillip, whom only Deirdre could tell apart; Edwina, not quite three; and Gillian, whom everyone called Baby. As Margaret Nash (head teacher at Sawrey School) occasionally pointed out, there were enough Suttons to fill their very own classroom.

The fête was even more exciting than the children had dared hope. Libby scraped both elbows when she tumbled off the whirligig, but was rewarded with a lollipop by the operator, for refusing to cry. Jamie got into a scuffle with Jack Braithwaite and managed to do enough damage to his opponent's nose to feel that he had come out on top. Mouse lost her best yellow hair ribbon, but dried her tears when Deirdre gave her the stuffed bear she'd won at the ring-toss — especially gratifying, because she had beaten Harold Beechman, who always teased her about her red hair and Irish accent.

These excitements were followed by others. The children took a rattling ride in the pony cart, until the pony decided it was too hot to work and went to stand in the shade of a tree. Mouse got her finger nipped when she stuck it in front of Rhubarb the prize-winning rabbit, who nearsightedly mistook it for a carrot. Libby spent sixpence on a beaded egg cozy for her mother (one of the last items on the jumble table), an embroidered bookmark for her father, and jacks for herself. All three children ate so much candy that Jamie went behind a bush and was sick, and Mouse put some of her caramels into the pocket of her apron, where they melted into a gooey mess. And if this sounds rather tedious to you, I can only say that it was great fun for *them*, perhaps because there were so many things to do and see and no grownup to tell them that they couldn't do and see *everything.*

That is, until Deirdre heard an ominous rumble of thunder and noticed that the sky had suddenly gone very dark.

"It's time we started home," she announced in a grown-up voice. "There'll be rain soon."

"But the egg race is just starting," Jamie protested.

"I want to buy more candy!" Mouse said, digging the last caramel out of her pocket.

Libby pushed out her lower lip. "Let's stay until the Morris dancing is over."

There was a jagged flash of lightning. This time, Mouse, who was always nervous about storms, edged close to Deirdre.

"I'll tell you what," Deirdre said, taking Mouse's hand. "On our way home, we'll stop at the Hill Top barn and look in on Jemima Puddle-duck. How does that sound?"

"I say," said Jamie excitedly, "I'd like that, rather!"

"Yes, let's," Libby agreed. "Jemima's eggs must have hatched by now. It's been days and days!"

If anything could have lured the children away from the fête, it was the promise of a visit to Jemima. And although Miss Potter did not encourage the other village children to make free of the farm's barnyard, she allowed Deirdre to bring the older Suttons, as long as they didn't harass the cows or annoy the sheep. So, shooing Libby and Jamie in front of her and holding Mouse by the hand, Deirdre shepherded her little group through the crowd.

You might have smiled at the sight. Deirdre wore a plain brown dress that had been let down several times but was still too short and tight around the middle, and a straw sailor hat with a ragged brim that had once belonged to Mrs. Sutton's sister. Her red hair was pinned up, but it was thick and heavy and preferred to hang in damp tendrils down her neck. Her hat was askew, and dust smeared her freckled cheek.

But such niceties as tidily pinned-up hair and a clean face did not much matter to Deirdre Malone. Her previous life in the orphanage had taught her to do without things other girls might count as necessities, such as pocket money and Sunday shoes. Hers was not an easy life, for Mrs. Sutton (while kind and doting) was a somewhat casual mother who liked to read books even more than she liked to direct the household. Dr. Sutton, a veterinarian and an amiable person, regrettably paid more attention to other people's animals than he did to his own boys and girls. Deirdre, who had very nearly made herself indispensable, got up early, managed the children all day, and went to bed late at night.

But you must not feel sorry for her, oh, not at all! She was allowed to read as many of Mrs. Sutton's books as she had time for. And every night before bed, Deirdre read aloud to the children — *The Back of the North Wind* and *Alice in Wonderland,* and *The Wouldbegoods,* and (of course) Miss Potter's books. Their favorite just now was *The Tale of Jemima Puddle-Duck,* because they were acquainted with Jemima, admired Kep the collie (who had saved the foolish duck), and had even met the fox one evening as they were coming home from the lake.

And while it might be hard to be cheerful when the twins were shying pillows at one another, Jamie had knocked over the coal scuttle, and Edwina was smearing mashed peas in Baby's hair, Deirdre did her best. She was gifted with an unusually energetic and fertile imagination that allowed her to transform quite ordinary events into exciting adventures, and to make up stories that distracted the children when they were otherwise inclined to be bored and tiresome.

So since it was rather poor fun to be leaving the fête before the egg race was run and the dancers had performed, Deirdre made up a story. "Here are the four brave explorers," she said, as they went through the throng and across Post Office Meadow in the direction of Hill Top Farm. "They are fighting through the ranks of savage natives to reach the buried treasure before the flood comes and sweeps everything away."

"Jolly good," Jamie said approvingly, and picked up a stick to use as a weapon against the natives.

And when they had crossed Kendal Road and were climbing the stone wall on the other side, Deirdre said, "The four courageous climbers make their difficult way up the dangerous rock face, while the angry tribesmen far below rattle their spears and shout violently."

This Libby amended, in ringing tones: "They're not tribesmen, they're awful cannibals, and they'll eat us alive if we fall!"

Which made Mouse cry, until Jamie pointed out that they were safely over the mountain and nobody had been eaten alive just yet, and Deirdre added that they had better press on through the jungle as quietly as they could so as not to attract the lions and tigers.

The jungle wasn't really a jungle at all, of course, but only the lilacs and ferns along the edge of Miss Potter's garden. The lions and tigers were Miss Potter's Herdwick sheep and Galloway cows, and the great mountain peak, which seemed only a stone's throw off to their right, was really the slate roof of the Tower Bank Arms. However, it was just as well to be quiet. Miss Potter had given her permission to bring the older children to the farm, but Deirdre didn't like to call attention to their visits, in case Miss Potter was working at one of her books or having a lie-down in her bedroom overlooking the garden.

The valiant band of explorers crawled out from under the lilac bushes and went along the path to the barn, where they said hello to Kep and Mustard, the two Hill Top dogs, and lay down on their stomachs to have a look at Jemima, who was sitting on a clutch of eggs under the feedbox. In fact, as Libby pointed out, the duck had been sitting there for quite some time, far longer than the twenty-eight days usually required to hatch a duckling.

"I wonder what's taking so long," Jamie said worriedly.

"Do you suppose the eggs have spoilt?" Libby asked.

Jemima gave several soft quacks, and Mouse smiled. "She promises they'll hatch soon," she said, and stroked Jemima's snowy white feathers with a soft finger.

"Before we go back to school, I hope," grumbled Jamie, and at the mention of school, the three of them groaned.

After a few minutes, Deirdre said, "We'd better get home before the rain starts." The second time she said it, the children clambered reluctantly to their feet, brushed the straw off their clothes, and followed Deirdre out of the barn. They had gone only a little way on the path toward home when there was a clap of thunder so loud it made all of them jump, and a gust of wind so fierce it nearly bowled them over.

"My goodness," gasped Deirdre, as Mouse grabbed for one hand and Libby for the other, while Jamie tried to pretend he wasn't at all frightened, only just taken aback for a moment.

They had barely got their breaths when they looked up and saw an odd-looking person standing directly in front of them, a basket over her arm. The old woman was no taller than Libby, who was the tallest of the Suttons, and dressed in layers of pinafores, one on top of another, with knitted shawls and woolen scarves wrapped all around.

"Who . . . who are *you?*" Deirdre managed at last. She had the distinct impression that the lady had been blown there by the wind, which of course was entirely impossible.

"I am Mrs. Overthewall," the lady said cheerily. "Who else would I be? And you are Deirdre, of course." Raising one finger, she pointed to each child in turn. "And Libby, Jamie, and Mouse, adventurers all. I congratulate you on scaling that last mountain, cannibals notwithstanding."

They stood with their mouths open. No one said a word.

"A magpie will get your tongues," said Mrs. Overthewall, and all four of them snapped their mouths shut.

"You startled us," Deirdre said. "We . . . we didn't see you."

"Of course you didn't. People don't. They're not supposed to." She gave Deirdre a benevolent look. "I have something for you." And with that, she thrust the basket into Deirdre's hands. It was so unexpectedly heavy that Deirdre nearly dropped it.

"What is it?" Libby asked uncertainly, bending over to look. They all heard a small cry, and she jumped back, startled. "Why, it's a *baby!*" she exclaimed.

"I knew you'd like it," said Mrs. Overthewall smugly. "It's a nice baby. It never cries." She pulled her scanty gray brows together. "Well, almost never. Only when it wants its nappy changed. Her nappy," she corrected. "She's a girl. Her name is —" She scowled and began looking through her shawls. "Where did I put that? Where — Ah, here it is." She took out a scrap of paper. "Her name is Flora," she announced, and dropped the paper into the basket.

Deirdre pulled the cloth back. It was — yes, it was unmistakably a baby! She looked up, her eyes wide. "But what are we to *do* with it?"

Mrs. Overthewall was adjusting her shawls. "*Do* with it?" she repeated in surprise. "Why, raise it, of course. And love it, and kiss it when it wants kissing. What else do you do with babies?"

"But we already have several babies at home," Jamie said with great firmness. "We don't need any more babies."

"It's true," Libby said, in an apologetic tone. "Our house is full. I overheard Mama saying to Papa just the other day that we have more than enough children."

"Not that Mr. or Mrs. Sutton could bear to give up any they already have," Deirdre added, with a comforting glance at Mouse, who had put her thumb in her mouth and was trying not to cry. "The Suttons are very, very, *very* fond of all of their children."

"I know they are," said Mrs. Overthewall, beaming. "That's exactly why I thought of you. You're the perfect family for this baby, precisely because there are so many of you. You can all pitch in to help." She paused. "This baby *needs* you. It has no family, you see."

Mouse took her thumb out of her mouth. "But doesn't its mother want it?" she cried, suddenly struck with pity for a baby without a family.

Mrs. Overthewall was stern. "Its mother," she said, "is too busy to be bothered with babies."

"Too busy?" Deirdre asked incredulously.

"We have no room for another baby," Jamie growled. "All the beds are full. And there are no chairs for a baby to sit in."

Libby sighed. "In fact, there's hardly room to step without knocking a baby over."

"That's right," Jamie said. He scowled. "No more babies!"

At this, there seemed nothing more to say. Regretfully, Deirdre handed back the basket. "You are most kind to think of us, Mrs. Overthewall," she said in a formal tone.

"And I am sure that Flora is a perfectly delightful baby. But the children are right. We can't accept her."

"Oh, dear," cried the lady, sounding quite aggrieved. "You're sure you won't reconsider?"

"Quite sure," the children chorused.

"But what am I to *do* with it?"

"You could give it back," Libby suggested.

"I can't," Mrs. Overthewall replied crossly. "There's no one to give it back *to*. Everyone's gone." (Of course, you already know this, since you heard Mrs. Overthewall tell Emily to catch the early train to London.)

"But where did it come from?" Deirdre asked, thinking how very odd it was that the baby's mother had gone away and left it behind. But then the whole thing was odd, top to bottom.

"Never mind," said Mrs. Overthewall. "The question is, where is it to go, if you won't have it?"

Libby ventured, "Perhaps Miss Potter would like to have it. She draws pictures and writes stories for children."

"Miss Potter doesn't have any babies," Mouse said, around her thumb. "I'm sure she's very lonely."

"She would take good care of it," Jamie said helpfully. "She likes animals."

Mrs. Overthewall brightened. "Out of the mouths of babes," she exclaimed. "Why, Miss Potter, of course! Why didn't I think of her?" She flung her scarves around her neck and took the basket. "There you are, then. That's settled, and quite agreeably, too, I'd say. Now go along and climb mountains or crawl through jungles or whatever else you've a mind to. Cheerio!"

With that, there was another clap of thunder, a gust of wind, and a sheet of blinding rain. When it cleared, the path was empty. Mrs. Overthewall was gone.

Libby frowned. "Did we . . . did we make that up?"

"I don't think so," Deirdre said doubtfully. "Did we?"

"She was a fairy," Mouse asserted with confidence, around her thumb.

"Mouse is right," Jamie said. "Fairies sometimes bring babies."

"Storks bring babies," Libby said, for that was the tale her mother always told them when the arrival of another little Sutton was imminent. "She wasn't a stork."

"It doesn't matter," Jamie said firmly. "We are not having any more babies." He shook his fist at the sky and roared, "Do you hear that? NO MORE BABIES!"

The wind flurried the bush beside the

path. Deirdre took Mouse's hand. "See the four valiant explorers," she said, "struggling through the hurricane to reach their base camp in time for tea."

"Miss Potter will like the baby," Mouse predicted comfortably, and they went home.

4
MISS POTTER IS
ASTONISHED

The village had not been pleased when Miss Potter of London purchased Hill Top Farm. The women (those who hadn't met her when she came on holiday with her parents) thought she would be much too grand for their little village. The men were offended by the idea that an off-comer — a spinster, without a brain in her head about farming — had bought the nicest farm in the district straight out from under their noses. They snickered when they learned that she had paid more than it was worth ("Took for a reet fool, she was," as George Crook put it). They even laid wagers on her success.

"Won't last t' year out," Mr. Llewellyn predicted. "I'll put a half-crown on't."

"Not six months," said Mr. Barrow complacently.

"Gone by Christmas," said Clyde Clinder. "And then t' place'll be up fer sale agin. Me brother-in-law says he'll buy it off her, but not fer what she paid."

The villagers' attitudes changed somewhat when Miss Potter not only lasted, but began making very needful improvements to the neglected farm buildings. What's more, she used local labor, bought local materials, and insisted that things be done in traditional ways, just as any of them would have done. And upon acquaintance, she proved, as Bertha Stubbs said approvingly, "as common as any t' rest of us, and more so." Still, many in the village continued to doubt that a woman who dressed fictional frogs in mackintoshes and galoshes would know how to deal with real cows and pigs and sheep, and that someone who could go about as she liked in London society would be content with theirs.

But Beatrix was not troubled by the villagers' opinions, for the farm fulfilled her heart's dearest wish. She had paid for it from the royalties from her dozen books: among them *Peter Rabbit, Squirrel Nutkin, Mrs. Tiggy-Winkle,* and *Jemima Puddle-Duck,* recently published. She still felt a private, wondering amazement that the little books should have earned enough to enable her to buy a farm. To buy her very own farm, among the fields and fells of her beloved Lake District! It still seemed unbelievable, impossible. She couldn't help thinking that some sort of good fairy had been waiting in the wings, magic wand in hand, to give her exactly what she wanted.

The house was a seventeenth-century, two-story North Country farmhouse, plain and so simple that it might be called severe. The farm had thirty-four acres when she bought it, although she had since purchased several more fields. And to accommodate the Jenningses, the family who took care of things when she was in London, she had added on several rooms and other improvements, including a detached kitchen at the edge of the garden and the water that was to be laid on this week.

She had made a great many changes to her own part of the house, too, but mostly with an eye to restoring its original simple beauty. The exterior was plastered with a pebbly mortar painted with the traditional gray limewash. The steep roofs were covered with local blue slate. The chimneys wore the familiar peaked slate caps, like school-boys lined up in a row. And the porch was constructed of four very large blue slate slabs: one for each side and two more for the peaked roof.

She had restored the interior as well, upstairs and down. In the main living area

— the "hall," as North Country folk called it — she had pulled down a rough partition and opened the room to its original generous size. She papered the walls in an airy green print, installed an antique oak cupboard for her collection of dishes, and put down a sea-grass rug and a smaller, shaggy blue one in front of the cast-iron range. With red curtains at the window and a pot of red geraniums on the table, the room was comfortable and homey. And all the other rooms suited her, too: the downstairs parlor with its marble fireplace and richly paneled walls; her very own bedroom upstairs, with its window overlooking the garden; and the treasure room she had created for her collection of favorite things. Indeed, Beatrix's artist's eye told her that the house was perfect in every way, and her heart told her that this was home. It was a great pity that she could not get away from London more often.

But you must not think that Beatrix allowed herself to feel sad about something she could not change. If that had been the case, she must have been very melancholy indeed, for the same fairy godmother who had given her the farm had not given her everything she wanted. Not by any means! She had thought that happiness might be within her reach, but her fiancé, Norman Warne, had died suddenly, unexpectedly, and very tragically in 1905, just a month after their engagement and only a few months before she took possession of Hill Top.

Even her engagement was not the happy, uncomplicated event it should have been, for her parents had strenuously disapproved. Her mother and father, both of whom became more difficult as they grew older, took great pride in the knowledge that their daughter should never have to marry a man who worked for his living. And although Norman was certainly respected and respectable enough — he was Beatrix's editor, in his family's publishing house — he didn't belong to their social class. He wasn't "good enough," in their terms, for their daughter, who ought not to marry "beneath her." They refused their permission, quite selfishly, we would say now, although perhaps they didn't think it was selfish, at least not consciously. They were behaving as many parents in their position behaved. They were keeping their beloved daughter from making an appalling mistake.

But Beatrix thought it *very* selfish. She loved Norman and she insisted on accepting his ring, which of course provoked a huge family row. Still, she owed a duty to her parents, so it was agreed that she and Norman would keep their engagement a secret and postpone their marriage to some indefinite future time. The prospect of postponement was painful, because every year that passed would make it less likely that they would have children. And Norman, boyish, ebullient Norman, was born to be a father. Coming from a large and happy family, he delighted in his nieces and nephews, loving nothing better than to build dollhouses for them and play games with them and read stories to them — *her* stories, of course. When Beatrix saw him with little Winifred and Eveline and Fred, she knew how much he wanted children and how much she wanted that for him.

Three years had gone by since Norman's death — an infinity of time, it seemed. The day of his death seemed a terrible sword, cutting her off from her past and from her future, leaving her, alone and lonely, in some interminable present. What would have happened had he lived? The question had no answer, but when she forced herself to think of it truthfully, she had to admit that they might not have been happy. Norman would have urged their marriage, and her mother and father would have resisted.

She would have been dreadfully torn, longing to marry Norman and leave her parents, yet feeling she could do neither. There would have been one awful argument after another, until she was thoroughly miserable and Norman had repented of his devil's bargain.

She hated to think it, but perhaps things had turned out for the best. Anyway, this was the way it had turned out, and nothing she thought or did could change it. She would never have a husband. She would never have a child. But she had a farm, and she would make the best of it.

By the time Beatrix reached her front door, the storm clouds over the lake had turned a deep, greenish mauve and the air seemed to have a weight and texture of its own. The trees were waiting anxiously, leaning toward one another and whispering in leafy apprehension as they looked over their shoulders toward the darkening fells and braced themselves against the coming storm. The birds had gone quiet, and all that could be heard was the distant rattle of the whirligig at the fête and the happy shouts of the children running their egg race. But the rain still held off, only a few large drops splattering here and there on the dusty path.

Beatrix went inside and shut the windows, feeling quietly happy. Upstairs in her bedroom, she changed her clothes, deciding that she would skip tonight's dance. She would rather spend the evening alone, reading and knitting — and anyway, she had plenty to keep her busy. Her brother Bertram was coming up from Ulverston in a day or two, and she would take him to all her favorite places. He had visited the village, of course — the Potters had spent several holidays in a large house on the road to Kendal. He had even visited Hill Top. But he had not been here since it became *her* farm, and she was looking forward to showing him all she had done.

Beatrix was tidying her hair when she heard a strange sound over her head, as if a hundred straw brooms were brushing across the slate roof. Stepping to the window, she saw the trees twisting and tossing and leaves and dry grass flying in wild flurries. In the barnyard, the three red hens — Mrs. Bonnet, Mrs. Shawl, and Mrs. Boots — briskly shooed their chicks to the shelter of the barn, while four white Puddle-ducks lifted their heads and opened their beaks, glad for a drink. Downstairs, the heavy oaken door banged sharply against the wall. She must have left it unlatched, and she hurried downstairs to close it before the rain could blow in.

But just outside the door, on the porch, sat a large woven basket, covered with a hand-woven blue-and-white-checked cloth.

How kind, Beatrix remarked to herself, thinking that someone had left her some squashes or an eggplant — a natural assumption, since this sort of thing happened often. Several of the villagers felt that Miss Potter (who had no husband to take care of her) wanted looking after. They liked to share their garden bounty, especially when there was a surfeit of squashes.

Now, you have been reading this story, so you know what the basket contains (at least I hope you do!) and who put it there, and why. But Beatrix was not present when Mrs. Overthewall encountered Deirdre and the three young Suttons, and she lacks your advantage. She put the basket on the table and lifted the blue-checked cover, expecting to uncover an eggplant or some zucchini or cauliflower, or more happily, a loaf of fresh bread and a pot of raspberry jam — a large pot, judging from the basket's weight.

But what she uncovered instead was a baby doll, wearing a cleverly knitted pink cap and securely wrapped in pink flannel. And then the doll opened its very blue eyes, waved a tiny fist, and yawned, the prettiest, most perfect little round O of a yawn that anyone has ever seen.

Beatrix gasped in sheer astonishment. "A baby!" she cried.

She stared down at the baby for a moment, her heart beating fast. Of all the things in the world that might have been in that basket, a baby was the very last thing she would have thought of. And then, suddenly recollecting herself, she ran out onto the porch, hoping to catch a glimpse of whoever had left it.

And what did she see?

Why, exactly what you might have predicted. A small, round, gray-haired old lady wrapped in an untidy bundle of scarves and shawls was climbing over the garden wall. At the top, she turned and waved at Beatrix. Then she vanished.

And at that moment, the heavens opened and it began to pour with rain.

5

The True Tale of
Jemima Puddle-duck

Listen to the story of Jemima Puddle-duck, who was annoyed because the farmer's wife would not let her hatch her own eggs.
Beatrix Potter, *The Tale of Jemima Puddle-Duck*

The downpour delighted the ducks, annoyed the hens, and prompted Kep the collie and Mustard, the old yellow dog, to seek refuge in the Hill Top barn. They sprawled on the earthen floor just inside the door and watched the rain pelting in gusty, wind-spun sheets across the garden. They also took notice of the old woman who was just going over the wall.

"Haven't seen that one in quite a while," Mustard remarked in his broad country dialect. *"Those Hawthorn Folk mostly keep to themselves on Broomstick Lane. They moved house when they was evicted, back some while ago."*

"Hawthorn Folk?" Kep asked curiously. A brown collie with a shawl of white fur around his shoulders, four white paws, and a white tip to his full tail, he had been brought from Low Longmire by Farmer Jennings to help Mustard with the herding. The older dog was getting on in years. He was fine with the cows (who were slow and deliberate) but no longer spry enough to go after Miss Potter's nimble-footed sheep.

"Thorn Folk are like t' Oak and Beech and Willow Folk," Mustard replied, licking a paw. *"Fairy folk tree dwellers, y'know. This lot was evicted from t' hawthorns at Hawthorn House when t' trees was chopt down."*

"Chopt down!" Kep barked, aghast. *"Where I come from, taking down a thorn is the worst sort of luck. Unless it's done right,"* he added. *"With proper notice and apologies. And even then, the Folk may take offence."*

" 'Tweren't done right at Hawthorn House," Mustard replied. *"An Army man bought t' place. Arrived one day, ordered t' thorns chopt down t' next. Said they stood in the way o' his lookin' out o'er t' lake."* He shook his head darkly. *"Gave t' Thorn Folk no notice, no by-your-leave, not even 'I'm sorry.' T' thorns was chopt down and carted off, with t' Folk running after, cryin' and sobbin' as if their hearts 'ud break. Not that t' Army man noticed, o'*

course. *Some humans doan't, worse fer them."*

Kep was somber. *"I've heard people say that Hawthorn House is haunted."*

"Worse 'n haunted," Mustard said with a sigh. *"Curst. T' garden won't grow, t' well's dried up, and there's to be no babes."*

"No babes? That's a sad thing."

"Aye. If a babe is born in t' house, t' Folk are bound to carry it off."

Kep whistled softly and cast a glance at the spot where the woman had scaled the wall and disappeared. *"And that was one of them?"*

"Aye. Wonder what she's doin' here at Hill Top."

Not having heard Mrs. Overthewall's conversation with the children or seen what she left on Miss Potter's doorstep, the dogs were at a loss. So we shall turn our attention to another creature in the barn: the would-be mother duck whose misadventure with a certain fox was chronicled in Miss Potter's story *The Tale of Jemima Puddle-Duck.* I'm sure you have read it but perhaps a long time ago. So that you can understand what Jemima is doing in the barn, I will relate the tale to you here, although the story will include some details Miss Potter omitted from her book, perhaps in deference to the youthful innocence of her audience.

When *The Tale of Jemima Puddle-Duck* begins, we learn that the farmer's wife has been thwarting the duck's desires to fulfill her maternal destiny. Each day, Mrs. Jennings sends her son, young Sammy, to collect the duck eggs and give them to the hens to hatch. (You may see a picture of Sammy taking Jemima's eggs from under the rhubarb on page 12 of *The Tale of Jemima Puddle-Duck.* You will also see the box-hive that Miss Potter placed in an alcove of the garden fence. The box was built for a swarm of bees that were knocked out of a tree by a storm. Miss Potter found the swarm, brought them home, and installed them in the box, where they have lived happily ever after.)

But back to Mrs. Jennings, who did not think much of ducks as mothers. "Ducks is lazy sitters," she told Miss Potter. "We gets more ducklings wi' less bodderment when t' chickens is put in charge, and that's a fact."

This arrangement met with the enthusiastic approval of most of the female ducks. (The drakes had no opinion, since their part of the business was already done.) Rebecca

Puddle-duck, Jemima's sister-in-law, was delighted to leave the hatching to the chickens, and advised Jemima to do the same.

"I don't have the patience QUACK to spend twenty-eight days on a nest," Rebecca said. She shuddered. *"Not to mention the danger from weasels and QUACK! stoats."* (Ducks, as you may know, have a habit of nesting away from the civilized safety of the barnyard, in wild places where they are vulnerable to ambush.) *"Let the Bonnet and Boots and Shawl hatch the duCKluCKlings,"* she added, with a careless flip of her wing. *"I have no laCK of things to do with my time, Jemima. I am content to sit baCK and let the hens taCKle it, and so should you be."*

But Jemima felt deep in her heart that motherhood was both a duty and a privilege, and scorned the suggestion that the hens could do a better job. So she hid her eggs as cleverly as she could, under a rhubarb leaf, in the middle of a blackberry thicket, or among the ferns on the bank of Wilfin Beck. But she was never quite clever enough, for Sammy Jennings stole each one. And twenty-eight days later, a smug red hen was parading around the barnyard with Jemima's ducklings quacking along beside her.

It was enough to drive a duck to distraction!

Which is why Jemima, desperate to start her family, put on her best blue poke bonnet, tied her paisley shawl over her shoulders, and flew across the fields, searching for a nesting site so far away that Sammy couldn't find it. She landed on a neatly clipped lawn where, to her surprise, she came face to face with a sporting gentleman with a narrow, sharpish face and the handsomest sandy whiskers she had ever seen. Dressed in smart green tweeds and a salmon-colored waistcoat with brass buttons, he was lounging in a wicker chair, sipping a cup of fine coffee, smoking a fat Manila cheroot, and studying the racing form in the *Times.* (These last few details, reported to me by Jemima, are not in the book. It must be assumed that Miss Potter omitted them so as not to corrupt the morals of her youngest readers.)

This sporting gentleman, who seemed to be of a cheerful and sympathetic temperament, lived in a summer-house built of faggots and turfs in a casually elegant style, like the holiday home of a Turkish pasha. (Miss Potter was apparently not impressed by the house, calling it "dismal-looking.") Its name, and its owner's, were engraved on a small gold plate under the bell-pull beside the door:

Foxglove Close
R. V. Vulpes, Esq.

When Jemima explained that she was looking for a place to begin her family, Mr. Vulpes (who spoke in an accent that you or I might think of as phony-French, but certainly impressed the duck) was eager to help. He showed her to a chamber at the rear of his summer-house, sumptuously upholstered with feather bolsters spread with Turkish shawls.

"Eet eez a poor place," he said with a deprecating wave, *"but private and comfortable. I hope zat eet eez not unworthy of Madam's maternal dedication."*

Jemima was thrilled. The feathers were soft, the shawls luxurious, and the chamber was quite the thing. Quite the thing, indeed — and entirely safe, for Mr. Vulpes (who was the kindest and most courteous of gentlemen) generously offered to keep an eye on her eggs in her absence.

And when Jemima had finished what she came to do, Mr. Vulpes brought out a silver dish on which were arranged a half-dozen sugared pieces of Turkish Delight and

78

served them with tiny cups of very dark Turkish coffee, to which he added a great deal of sugar. The charming Mr. Vulpes was, as you can clearly see, a gourmet, and Jemima indulged in his dainties with great enthusiasm — as well she might, since laying such a fine, large egg had made her very hungry, and of course, she had to fly all the way home.

Now, I venture to say that if you found yourself in this situation, you might not have been so willing to leave your offspring in a stranger's care, or so eager to accept his offer of treats. But an inexperienced duck who has never before been so far from her barnyard can scarcely be faulted for yielding to the sophisticated temptations of confection, coffee, and feather bolsters. What Jemima's mother, Priscilla Puddleduck (who was brought up Presbyterian by very strict parents), would have said about her daughter's adventure, I daren't think. But if this simple duck is susceptible to the seductions of such a sweetly mannered host, who amongst us can blame her? Surely not I, nor you, nor anybody else.

So each afternoon, Jemima flew over the fields, landed on the lawn at Foxglove Close, and retired to her upholstered chamber to lay an egg. When there were nine altogether, it was time to begin hatching. She told Mr. Vulpes that when next she came, she would bring her knitting (she was planning nine dear little shawls, all in yellow wool) and a few romantic novels to pass the time. When her eggs had hatched, she would lead her nine fine ducklings back to the barnyard. And then those smug hens would learn who was the better mother!

Mr. Vulpes congratulated her, proposing that they celebrate the auspicious occasion with a feast. The menu might include a savory omelette, he said, as well as some delicious pâté de foie gras — *"Zat most delicious of delicacies!"* he exclaimed, kissing his fingers and rolling his eyes — if Jemima could contribute two onions and a few sprigs of sage, thyme, and parsley. Jemima was not familiar with pâté or omelettes (she had never learnt French), but she was sure that they would be every bit as delicious as everything else her host had served.

But alas! Jemima was not to enjoy her feast. When she went to the Hill Top kitchen to get two onions out of Mrs. Jennings's basket, Kep inquired what she was doing. Flattered by his interest, the duck told him. He listened, asked several thoughtful questions, and then went about his business, as did she, forgetting all about their conversation.

But she had scarcely reached Foxglove Close that afternoon when Kep appeared, accompanied by the two fox-hound puppies who lived at the Tower Bank Arms. The puppies chased Jemima's host away while Kep translated the words "pâté de foie gras" (a paste made from the liver of a fat goose or duck) and "omelette" (eggs whipped and fried) for a horrified Jemima. She burst into tears when Kep told her that R.V. Vulpes of Foxglove Close was actually Reynard Fox (the poor duck was as ignorant of Latin as French), and that her host intended to breakfast on her eggs and dine upon her person, in the form of roast duck, with herb-and-onion stuffing and fois gras on the side.

Ah, poor Jemima. She felt betrayed, a betrayal that was made worse — oh, much, much worse! — by the fact that she had begun to feel something more than friendship for Mr. Vulpes. Naively, she had even hoped that, over the time they would spend together while her eggs were hatching, the gentleman might come to return her feelings. And now, in the light of Kep's explanation, she saw herself for exactly what she was, an unwary, unsuspecting, gullible duck who had been duped by a bold deceiver. A duck with no more brains than a ha'penny bun (as Lady Longford once said about Emily). Her heart was broken.

But at that moment, another tragedy occurred. Having got rid of the fox, the puppies ran straight to Jemima's nest and gobbled up all nine of her beautiful eggs, proving that foxes and fox-hounds have similar appetites, and that neither are to be trusted.

Distraught over her betrayal and hysterical over the loss of her eggs, Jemima allowed Kep to escort her home. And Kep, who wanted to spare her feelings as best he could, promised that he would tell no one about her disgrace, a promise that he honored.

But the perfidious puppies had no such consideration. Back at the Tower Bank Arms, they confided the tale to Tabitha Twitchit and Crumpet, who went straight out to tell all the other animals. News travels fast in a village, and it took only a short while for the word to spread to every Sawrey household and across the Hill Top barnyard. Jemima was deeply chagrined.

And then things got worse.

Miss Potter put the story into a book, portraying Jemima's humiliation to the whole, wide world. In fact, Miss Potter was overheard to say that twenty thousand copies of her book had been printed, with the likelihood of one or two additional printings before the holiday season, as grandmothers bought them to read aloud to their little grandchildren on Christmas morning.

Twenty thousand copies! Jemima had no head for numbers, but it sounded as if every single person on this earth would soon know that she was a miserable failure as a mother. On the very last page of the story, Miss Potter had drawn her with four ducklings, but that was a fictitious happy ending, so that the children would not be disappointed. And even so, the last seven words of Jemima's book were like seven knives plunged right into Jemima's heart:

She had always been a bad sitter.

There.

Now that you have heard the full story, perhaps you can appreciate Jemima's desire to redeem her reputation.

Perhaps you can understand why she was determined to have another go at motherhood, this time in the safety of the barn, as far away as possible from fox-hound puppies, foxes, and one particular fox.

And there was the rub.

The duck had tried with some success to put that particular fox out of her mind, for she knew that harboring any sort of friendly feeling toward such a crafty creature was the worst sort of romantic folly.

But alas! She had not been able to put him out of her heart. In spite of all she knew about him, in spite of Kep's stern warnings and the Puddle-ducks' worried remonstrations, she had still remembered how much she had enjoyed Mr. Vulpes' witty conversation, his charming manners, his intriguing accent, and yes, his Turkish Delights. And even though she knew what a feather-brained fool she had been to trust him, she had to admit that, deep in her heart, she still cared for the fellow, for her sandy-whiskered gentleman, as she had come to think of him. She was afraid that if she met him, she might fall under his spell once again.

So she found a secret place for her eggs behind the feedbox, where nobody could see her. The ducks' nesting season was over, so Sammy Jennings was no longer dispatched to look for eggs. Boots, Bonnet, and Shawl had done their duty as surrogate mothers, and Mrs. Jennings was already considering which of their fat young ducklings ought to be invited to holiday dinner.

(I hope that you, as I do, consider it a cruel irony that everyone should go to great trouble to keep the ducklings safe from foxes, only to eat them at the holidays!)

So Jemima had every reason to believe that her nest was secret, and thus far, she had been right. Not even Kep knew. The Sutton children sometimes stole into the barn to say hello and stroke her feathers and whisper encouragement, but there had been no other visitors or intruders — except for an annoying Cockney magpie named Jackboy, who had recently flown up from London and hung around the barnyard, chattering incessant nonsense. He couldn't be trusted to keep her secret, but his magpie jabber was so full of rhyming slang that it was impossible to know what he was saying.

"Apples and pears, kick me upstairs," he chortled, peering at her with one glittering black eye. *"Still here, ducky dear?"*

"Go away, JaCKboy," Jemima said, with great dignity. *"I am QUACK a busy duCK."* To prove it, she took her knitting out of the basket beside her. It was the tenth little yellow shawl, for the last of her ten ducklings — a good thing, too, since she was almost out of yarn.

"Busy lizzie, buzzie loozie," Jackboy warbled gaily. He hopped from one foot to the other.

"Rub-a-dub-ducky, chuck-a-luck-dabble-duck. Wot can I give ye, me fine Puddleplucky?"

"You're giving me a headACHe," said Jemima. She looked down at her knitting. Had she dropped a stitch in the previous row?

"Kiss me a-miss," chirped Jackboy impolitely. *"Miss me a kiss. Why ain't yer eggs hatched, cluckie-duckie?"*

"BeCAUse they haven't," Jemima snapped. She had dropped not one stitch but two, two rows back, not one — which I daresay wouldn't be a problem for you, but for a duck of limited intelligence, it posed a puzzling dilemma. Should she rip out two whole rows and repair it, or simply go on and pretend it hadn't happened?

"Bad batch!" Jackboy cackled maliciously. *"Dropt stitch won't fix, broke lock won't latch, watched pot won't boil, spoilt egg won't hatch."*

"TaKe that baCK!" Jemima cried in dismay. *"My eggs are not QUACK spoilt! They are the very finest of duCK eGGs!"*

"Bad eggs," Jackboy sang gaily. *"Mad eggs, sad eggs, plaid eggs."* He twirled around on one foot. *"Eggs begs, bandy legs, hat pegs, beer kegs!"*

Jemima gave the bird a cold look. *"PaCK it up, JaCK. I have important worK to do."*

"Kegs 'n' kettles, kettles 'n' hobs!" Jackboy shrieked madly. *"Foils 'n' fobs! Foxes 'n' clockses! Watched clockses never boil! Boiled eggses never spoil."* And with that, he flew away.

Jemima settled herself back onto her nest, trying to concentrate on her knitting. Boiled eggs, spoilt eggs! Now she wouldn't be able to get the phrase out of her mind. How many days had it been since she began to sit? Quite a few, she thought wearily, more than twenty-eight. More than thirty-two, more than thirty-five! Her brain was growing fuzzy, her thoughts were in a muddle, and her posterior had gone numb.

What in the world was keeping these eggs?

Why hadn't they hatched?

Was something *wrong* with them?

But Jemima could not bear that thought, so she pushed it out of her mind. Anyway, they were bound to hatch soon. That very evening, or tomorrow. Certainly no later than the day after.

But wait! I hear you say. If the nesting season is over, where did our duck get those eggs? Did she hold back as long as she could and lay them very late, in hopes of keeping them safe from Sammy Jennings? Or did she —

But even though you are quite right to

raise these questions, and I very much hope they are answered at some point in the future, we must not anticipate. So let us leave our duck sitting patiently on her nest under the feedbox in the Hill Top barn, and open another chapter of our story.

6

MISS POTTER MAKES
A SPECIAL DELIVERY

It was Sunday morning and the Woodcocks, sister and brother, had breakfasted an hour ago. Miles Woodcock, wearing his slippers, was enjoying his pipe and newspaper beside the library fire. Saturday's rain had persisted, and Dimity Woodcock was wondering whether she should brave the drizzle to go to morning service at St. Peter's, or stay at home and finish the argyle stockings she was knitting for Miles. She had decided in favor of the stockings and was looking for her knitting basket when the doorbell rang.

"If that's the constable, tell him to go away," Miles said from behind his newspaper. "It's Sunday. I worked hard at the fête yesterday, and I am taking a holiday."

Dimity knew he didn't mean it. Miles was the Justice of the Peace for Sawrey District. It was his job to certify deaths, investigate accidents, and generally help in maintaining law and order. He was called out at all hours, in all weathers, and he always went willingly wherever he was needed.

But when Dimity opened the door, the person ringing the bell was not Constable Braithwaite. She was Miss Beatrix Potter, wearing a gray mackintosh and a droopy woolen hat. She was carrying a large basket.

"Why, good morning, Bea!" Dimity exclaimed with pleasure. She stepped back, holding the door open. "How very nice to see you! Come in and take off your wet things. I'll have Elsa bring us some tea."

Dimity and Beatrix had grown to be close friends, although in Dimity's view they could never spend enough time together. Beatrix's parents, elderly and demanding, insisted on having her with them in London most of the time. Bea couldn't escape very often, and when she did, she was busy with the farm.

Which was a great pity, Dimity thought. For the past year, she had harbored the secret idea that Miss Beatrix Potter — attractive, capable, with a genuine kindness and sharp intelligence — was ideally suited to her own dear brother Miles, who (it went without saying) would make an ideal husband. He was good-looking, with regular features and fine brown hair, and was possessed of a pleasant and steady temperament. Beatrix's parents, who had strenuously objected to her engagement to Mr. Warne, could hardly object to Captain Woodcock, a gentleman who commanded the respect of every single person in the parish. It would be a perfect match.

Of course, Dimity was wise enough to hug this romantic plan strictly to herself. Miles was fond of Beatrix in a neighborly sort of way, but like most bachelors, he was fixed in his habits and needed a bit of encouragement — whilst Beatrix remained devoted to the memory of her dead fiancé. It might be some time before they could see how well suited they were to each other.

Beatrix relinquished her mackintosh and followed Dimity into the sitting room, still carrying her basket. "It's Miss Potter, Miles," Dimity said.

"Good morning, Captain Woodcock," Beatrix said. "I hope I'm not disturbing you."

"Miss Potter!" the captain exclaimed, putting aside his newspaper. "No, not at all. How kind of you to call."

"I am sorry to intrude on a Sunday morning," she said, "but I have something to show you." She put the basket on the sofa and folded back the blue-checked covering.

Dimity stared at the pink-wrapped bundle.

"Why, it's a baby!" she cried in great astonishment. She clapped her hands excitedly. "Such a pretty little darling! But where in the world —"

"She was left at Hill Top Farm yesterday evening," Beatrix said soberly.

"Left!" Dimity exclaimed.

"The devil you say!" Miles jumped to his feet, came to the sofa, and leant over the basket. "Left at Hill Top?" He took his pipe out of his mouth and bent closer, peering. "By Jove, it really is a baby," he muttered, as if he had doubted Miss Potter's word.

Beatrix pulled off her gloves and folded them into the pocket of her gray tweed jacket. "I found the basket on my doorstep last evening, just as it began to rain. Mrs. Jennings supplied a bottle and my cow supplied the milk, so she has been fed." She looked down at the baby with a fond smile. "Several times, actually. I have heard that young babies do not sleep the night through. Flora certainly proved the truth of that, although her crying was never very loud."

"Flora? That's her name?" Dimity knelt down, putting out a tentative finger to touch the velvety pink cheek. The blue eyes opened and a tiny hand grasped her finger and held it tightly. She felt herself smiling. What a pretty little thing the baby was, with that dark hair curled in masses all over her head and that cunning little nose and rosebud mouth.

But whose baby *was* she? And why in the world would her mother abandon her on somebody's doorstep?

"Yes, her name is Flora," Beatrix said, "according to the note I found in her basket." She took a folded paper out of her pocket and handed it to the captain. "There was a sprig of hawthorn, as well," she added.

The captain put his pipe back in his mouth and unfolded the paper. " 'See that Flora has good care, or I shall come and fetch her,' " he read aloud, around the stem of his pipe. "No signature." He looked up, one eyebrow cocked. "A bit cheeky, I'd say."

"I am sure it must be a crime to abandon a baby," Beatrix said. "That's why I've brought her to you, Captain Woodcock. I very much hope you can find her parents."

"Find her parents?" Miles grinned. "I should think that would be your department, Miss Potter."

Dimity had to repress a smile. Bea had already gained a reputation amongst the villagers as something of a sleuth. She had retrieved a stolen miniature painting, had helped to identify old Ben Hornby's killer, and had managed to unmask that frightful woman who had tricked Christopher Kittredge into marrying her — and keep her from making off with the Kittredge family jewels.

At the thought of Christopher, Dimity felt at once a deep sadness (the appalling business had been so painful for him) and a quick joy (it was over now, and he could get on with his life). She also felt a warm, abiding gratitude, for if Bea had not found out that the dreadful woman was already married to someone else, Christopher might still be married to her. There would be no chance that —

She blushed and pulled her mind away. It was impossible. She would not think it. To cover her confusion, she said, "Abandoning a baby must be a crime. Mustn't it, Miles?"

"Most certainly it is a crime, although it's rarely prosecuted." Miles pursed his lips. "It might be hard to locate the parents. And if they were found, would one want to force them to take back a baby they had abandoned out of desperation?"

Dimity's maternal spirit was aroused. "But that's appalling!" she exclaimed hotly. "A mother who abandons her baby ought to be put in gaol!" She appealed to her brother. "Miles, you *must* arrest this person!"

"Easier said than done, my dear Dim,"

Miles replied. "Any idea who left the child, Miss Potter?"

"As a matter of fact, I saw the person," Beatrix said. Her mouth turned up at the corners. "I caught a glimpse of her as she was scaling the wall along the side of my garden."

"Scaling the *wall?*" Dimity asked doubtfully. The wall at Hill Top was brick, and something over five feet high.

"Yes. A plump creature," Beatrix said. "She was wearing a red woolen petticoat, blue-and-white-striped stockings, and pattens. But I don't think she was the baby's mother."

"Oh?" Miles asked. He put his pipe into his mouth. "Why not?"

"Because she had gray hair," Beatrix replied with a small smile. "She was certainly nimble — she seemed to sail over the wall in quite a remarkable way — but I had the impression that she was rather old."

Pulling on his pipe, Miles looked down at the basket. "We may have two crimes, then. Kidnapping and child abandonment."

"Two crimes and a mystery," Beatrix said.

"Yes, a mystery," Miles replied. "Whose baby is this?"

"I don't know of anyone in the village who fits your description," Dimity said. It sounded very odd indeed, but she did not doubt her friend, whose powers of observation were quite remarkable. Bea noticed things that other people did not, which came of being an artist, Dimity supposed. Sometimes she almost seemed to see *through* people, into their insides. It could be disconcerting, especially if you were thinking something you didn't want her to know.

"There's old Dolly, of course," she added. "But she always wears black, and she gets around with a cane. The poor old thing would never be able to hop over your wall. In fact, I can't think of anyone who is that spry."

Elsa Grape appeared in the doorway, a brass-handled tray of tea and scones balanced across her ample middle. "It'll be a gypsy," she remarked in a matter-of-fact tone. "Them and their ponies and caravans are camped at t' foot of Broomstick Lane. Gypsies is bad to steal babies, and that's t' truth."

"That'll be all, Elsa, thank you," Dimity said hastily. Once Elsa got on about gypsies, there was no stopping her.

Elsa set the tray down and bent over the basket to look at the baby, clucking sadly. "Wee poor bairn! Left all by her lone in t' cold, uncarin' world." She straightened. "T' butcher's boy only had lamb chops on t' cart yesterday, mum, so it's lamb fer dinner today, instead of beef." She pulled down her mouth. "And Molly broke t' upstairs hallway lamp chimney again."

"Oh, dear. I hope she didn't cut herself," Dimity said distractedly. This was the second broken lamp in a fortnight. And lamb today would make it lamb three times since last Sunday, although she didn't suppose there was anything to be done. Elsa put in their order, but by the time the cart reached Tower Bank House, there was not much left.

Miles frowned. "Where on Broomstick Lane, Elsa?"

"Thorny Field. Been camped there near a fortnight now." Elsa pursed her thin lips disapprovingly. "Mathilda Crook's lost her best settin' hen and a nest of eggs. Hannah Braithwaite's missin' a pair of young Jack's green corduroy trousers. And Bertha Stubbs says they pinched Henry's wool underdrawers from t' bush where she put 'em to dry in the sun."

"That's all for now, Elsa," Dimity interrupted hurriedly, picking up the teapot. "Thank you."

Where gypsies were concerned, the villagers already knew what they thought, and it was never kindly. The itinerant Romany people were a regular feature of Lakeland life, traveling through the countryside in their brightly painted wooden wagons, selling horses, peddling pots and knives and baskets, telling fortunes, and working as seasonal farm laborers. There was always a nasty quarrel of some sort when they came to the district. And when the villagers talked about them, it was usually in whispers and usually had to do with something that had recently gone missing, like little Jack's trousers or Mathilda Crook's setting hen, or Henry Stubbs' wool under-drawers.

Miles turned to Beatrix. "Could the person you saw have been a gypsy, do you think, Miss Potter?"

"It's possible," Beatrix said. She glanced at Elsa and said, not unkindly, "However, I do think we ought to withhold judgment until there's a proper investigation."

Elsa made a harrumphing sound. "Old er young, gypsies is fast as pure lightnin'. Thieves, ever' one. Stole t' babe fer a ransom, most like, and then decided it was too dang'rous to keep her."

Dimity poured. "Bea, will you have a cup of tea?"

"And John Braithwaite's t' constable," Elsa said crisply. "I told Hannah if she wanted Jack's trousers back, she ought to send her husband down Broomstick Lane after 'em. All he has to do is watch fer a gypsy boy wearin' green corduroy trousers and yank 'em right off." She made a face. "Harder fer Mathilda to git her hen back, I'd say. T' old biddy's stewin' in some cookpot by now. And Lord knows what's become of Henry's —"

"I'd be glad of a cup, thank you," Beatrix said, and sat down on the sofa beside the baby's basket.

Elsa, on her way out of the room, remarked, over her shoulder, "One thing's sure. T' bairn's not a village babe. T' last babe was born to Mrs. Hopkins, at Easter. His name is Jeremiah, and he's got hair t' color of boiled carrots. Mrs. Crawley's due next, but not 'til Guy Fawkes." And having delivered this definitive pronouncement, she left the room.

"P'rhaps I'll go to the encampment myself," Miles said, taking the cup Dimity handed him and helping himself to a scone. "Won't hurt to have a look around." He grinned. "I can keep my eyes peeled for Jack's trousers and Mathilda's hen, but I doubt I'll see anything of Henry's missing undergarment."

Beatrix fingered the blue-and-white-checked cover on the basket. "This fabric has a distinctive pattern," she said thoughtfully. "It appears to be hand-woven. If we found the weaver —"

"If there are no infants of this age in the village," Miles said, turning to Dimity, "this baby must have come from the district at large. What've you heard, Dim?"

Feeling helpless, Dimity shook her head. "Not a thing, Miles. And if a mother had lost her baby, we would certainly have heard of it immediately." The families of Near and Far Sawrey were bound by close ties of kinship and friendship. Babies were welcomed with a great deal of enthusiasm, and provided much happy gossip among relatives and friends.

"What about the Mums' Box?" Beatrix asked, sipping her tea. "Has anyone borrowed it lately?"

"Only Mrs. Hopkins," Dimity replied. "She's still using it for Baby Jeremiah." The parish Mums' Box was filled with infant garments and necessities and lent out to mothers and babies in need. As the volunteer-in-charge, Dimity had possession of the box between babies.

"I happened to see Dr. Butters on my way here," Beatrix said. "I took the liberty of asking him. He said that the last girl baby was born at High Loanthwaite Farm two months ago, the other side of Hawkshead. At a quick glance, he guessed that Flora is a fortnight old. If she was born in this area, he knew nothing of it."

"I'll make inquiries," Miles said. He cast a concerned look at the basket. "But in the meantime, what's to be done with the child?"

"I should be very glad to keep her," Beatrix said, "if only for a little while." Dimity saw that her friend's blue eyes were filled with longing and her mouth was sadly wistful. It was a revealing look, Dimity thought with a pang. Beatrix's life must be a lonely one. Another reason, if one were needed, to encourage the match with Miles! They were still young, and Beatrix might yet have the baby she so obviously wanted.

"By all means, then, do," Miles said, smiling warmly. "I'm sure she would be in very good hands with you, Miss Potter."

Beatrix gave him a regretful look. "There's nothing I should like better, Captain Woodcock, but I can't. I'm expecting my brother today, and I want to be free to take him around the district. And I must go back to London later in the week — Wednesday, I think — to see to a business matter with my publisher. It's just for a day or two, but —"

She made a gesture. "I would suggest Mrs. Jennings, but little Clara has a very bad cough. I'm afraid we shall have to think of something else."

Dimity understood. Beatrix had to look after her books — although when she married Miles, that sort of thing would certainly be less important than it was now. She smiled to herself, thinking how good it would be for her brother to have a wife who would make him the center of her world. And how wonderful it would be for Bea to have a husband to take care of her.

"Well, then," Miles said, "we shall have to give her over to the parish authorities. If her parents cannot be found, they'll send her to the workhouse at Ulverston, to be cared for there."

"The workhouse!" Dimity cried, horrified. "Oh, surely not, Miles! Not the workhouse!"

"But something has to be done with abandoned children," Miles replied reasonably. "That's the law, Dimity. Don't worry — she'll be looked after. I don't know how many foundlings Ulverston has at any given time, but I'm sure it's several."

Beatrix leant over to smooth the pink knitted cap. "Perhaps she might be kept in the village until her parents are found."

"Yes, Miles, yes," Dimity said urgently.

Miles frowned. "Whom would you suggest? The Braithwaites, perhaps? Would they have room for another child?"

At that moment, the baby stirred, raised her tiny fists, and began to squirm and fuss. Dimity was surprised by her own sudden surge of longing. If only things had worked out differently with Christopher, they might have had their own children by now. If only —

She gave herself a little mental shake. "I should like to keep the baby here, Miles. For the time being, of course," she added hastily. "Just until you've found the family."

Miles raised both eyebrows. "Wouldn't it be better if she were given to someone with children, Dimity? You have no experience. Perhaps Mrs. Sutton would be willing, or —"

"Mrs. Sutton has a houseful. Miles, I *want* to keep her!" Dimity took Flora out of the basket and held the baby to her shoulder. Almost at once, she stopped fussing and snuggled her face against Dimity's neck. Dimity's heart leapt, and she took a deep breath.

"It won't be for long, I expect," she said, steadying her voice with an effort. "You'll find her mother quickly, I'm sure. And Elsa's had children — she can help me.

Between us, we will manage quite easily."

Miles studied her for a moment. "Well, then," he said finally, "keep her if you like." He frowned down his nose in mock severity. "She won't cry in the night, I hope."

"She doesn't cry loudly," Beatrix put in. "I'm sure she won't disturb you, Captain." To Dimity, she added, "Mrs. Jennings could supply you with milk and a baby bottle."

"We'll need nappies, too," Dimity said, cuddling the baby happily. She brushed her lips across the soft hair. "And infants' clothing. Perhaps Mrs. Hopkins will be willing to share out of the Mums' Box." She frowned. "Was anything left with her, Beatrix? Any clothing or supplies?"

"Oh, dear," Beatrix said, "I almost forgot!" She reached into her bag, took something out, and put it into Miles' open hand. "There was no clothing, just the note and the hawthorn sprig. And this. A scarab ring."

Dimity saw that Beatrix had given Miles a ring, a heavy signet ring, set with a large cornelian, the color of blood.

"It is indeed," Miles said, turning it in his fingers. "See the Egyptian carving?" He held the ring up. "Lends credence to Elsa's gypsy theory, I'd say. This is the sort of jewelry the Romany people favor."

"Both the stone and the setting seem quite

unique," Beatrix said. "It occurred to me that it might be traced to its owner, which —"

"Which might lead us to the baby's parents!" Dimity exclaimed excitedly. "Of course, Bea!"

"It's certainly most unusual," Miles said. "Yes, p'rhaps it can be traced." He glanced at Beatrix and shook his head ruefully. "You've done it again, Miss Potter."

She looked at him, her blue eyes wide. "Done what, Captain Woodcock?"

He chuckled. "Brought us a mystery. This is getting to be a habit, you know."

"But surely this one won't be too hard to solve," Dimity said, feeling the baby's warmth against her. "The mother must be simply frantic. She must be moving heaven and earth to find this precious child."

I am sorry to tell you, however, that this was not the case.

7
WHERE EMILY WENT
AND WHAT SHE
FOUND THERE

Stories that involve quite a number of
people (as this one does), may not always
progress in a chronological order. To learn
why Flora's mother was not moving heaven
and earth to find her daughter, we must
turn the calendar from Sunday back to
Friday, and follow Emily Shaw as she took
the up train from Windermere Station.

Emily had never before ridden on the
railway, and the prospect was thrilling. The
trip, however, was not. The train was noisy,
smoky, and crowded. The ten-hour ride was
punctuated at random intervals by frightening bumps and lurches, and when they went
round a curve, the car shook itself and
threatened to tip right off the rails. A person
(Emily could not call him a gentleman) had
made unwelcome advances in the carriage,
and if it had not been for the intervention
of a kindly clergyman, she did not like to
think what might have happened.

She also did not like to think what had happened the day before, when Mrs. Overthewall (whoever or whatever she was!) had come into the house and snatched up Baby Flora. As she recalled it, Emily remembered herself shrieking "No, no, no!" and chasing the old lady until her breath gave out and she collapsed from exhaustion. Of course, that was not at all the way it happened, as you very well know and could testify if the magistrate called you as a witness. But perhaps you, too, have had the experience of remembering an event in an entirely different way than it actually transpired. Sometimes we have compelling reasons for not recalling the truth — and Emily no doubt had her reasons.

In any case, the trip was long and wearisome, Emily's eyes were red with weeping, and her heart was sore. She was relieved when at last (after several confusing changes of trains), she reached Earl's Court Station and the beginning of her exciting adventure in London. London, the place she had been longing for. London, her heart's dream! Now that she was here at last, things would be better.

But like the railway journey, London was not at all what Emily had expected. She imagined it as a fairyland of twinkling lights and lilting music, peopled with fine lords and beautiful ladies. But the streets were full of ordinary people, scurrying along with their heads down and their shoulders hunched. The air was a sulfurous, stinking yellow, thick and heavy with coal smoke and filled with the deafening roar of motor lorries — ten, hundreds, *thousands* of them, all speeding recklessly only inches away from the kerb, so that she had to cling to the buildings for safety, lest one jump the kerb and run her down. And when at last she was able to summon a hansom and climbed in and gave the address, the driver whipped up the horse and they flew along the streets so fast she was sure they'd all be killed, she and the driver and the horse as well. By the time they'd got where they were going and she was let out, her knees were like noodles and her fingers were trembling so that she could scarcely get the fare from her purse.

The address Miss Keller had given her, on Lime Tree Place, was in an area of South Kensington called Bolton Gardens. The name of the street had conjured up images of pleasant houses surrounded by lacy-leaved lime trees and pretty gardens filled with blooming flowers. But the dull, dark brick house before her stood in a long, stolid row of identical dull, dark brick houses, and there was not a lime tree to be seen, much less a garden of blooming flowers. Her eyes widened as she read the words engraved on the brass door plate:

No.3 Lime Tree Place
Miss Pennywhistle's Select Establishment
for Young Ladies of Excellent Family

Select Establishment? Oh, dear. The cabman had let her out at the wrong address! She put down her carpet bag and looked anxiously at the slip of paper on which Miss Keller had written the street and number.

No, here was where she was meant to be, although by this time Emily felt so confused that she scarcely knew where "here" was or what business she had with it — as I daresay you would feel, if you were plucked out of a hamlet in the country and plunked down on an unfamiliar street in one of the largest cities in the world, without the least idea of what to expect. She took a deep breath, lifted the heavy brass doorknocker, and let it fall. Why in the world had Miss Keller given her this address?

She was still asking herself that question when Miss Keller herself opened the door. Saying nothing at all, only putting a finger to her lips, she pulled Emily inside. Emily began to speak, but Miss Keller shook her head violently and motioned to her to bring her valise and follow. They went up a carpeted flight of stairs and then another, narrower and uncarpeted. The third and fourth were was so steep that Emily was quite out of breath by the time they reached the top, where they went down a long hall and entered a chilly garret room. It was completely bare except for two narrow cots, two black trunks, one green-painted wooden chair, and a broken scrap of mirror on the wall beside the window.

Miss Keller shut the door behind them. "Put your things in the trunk," she said shortly. "You are to share this room with Dora, the head housemaid. She will show you your duties. I believe you are to take the third floor."

The head housemaid? The third floor? It sounded as if Emily herself was meant to work as a housemaid here! She looked around, aghast. She had thought she would be Miss Keller's maid in Miss Keller's own home, and take care of Miss Keller's hair, clothes, and jewels. To be sure, Miss Keller had not gone quite so far as to promise all this, but —

"You must be tired," Miss Keller said. She

frowned and added uneasily, "I trust all went well with the arrangements."

The arrangements. Emily took a deep breath. Now was the time to say that Mr. Graham had refused to take Baby Flora because she was a girl, not a boy, and that something else — something truly incredible — had happened at Hawthorn House. She opened her mouth to say all this, but the words wouldn't come. How could she possibly describe Mrs. Overthewall? Wouldn't Miss Keller think she was lying?

She cleared her throat and tried again, knowing that if she didn't tell the truth now, she might not have another opportunity. But again her voice failed her.

Miss Keller, taking silence for assurance, seemed relieved. "Well, then, that's all right," she said, and put her hand on Emily's shoulder. "You're a strong, resourceful girl, Emily. I knew it would be hard for you to do what had to be done — especially since you had grown so fond of the child. But I was sure you could manage it. And I am sure you will do well here. It is a new beginning for you."

Emily tried again to speak, but the weight of Miss Keller's hand, once so reassuring, now seemed heavy and oppressive. If she had been thinking more clearly, she might have stopped to wonder why Miss Keller had asked her to come to London — had, in fact, quite insisted on it. But she wasn't thinking at all clearly. In fact, it was all she could do to keep from bursting into tears.

Miss Keller squeezed her shoulder, just a little too hard for comfort. "Very good, my girl," she said, in a more kindly tone. "Now, wash your face and tidy your hair and take yourself down to the kitchen. Cook has saved a bowl of soup and a cup of tea for you. In the morning, you shall meet Miss Pennywhistle, and Miss Carew, who teaches music, and Miss Mapes, who instructs in literature and needlework. I myself teach French." She gave a careless wave of her hand. "The teachers like to know the servants — because of the girls, you understand. The boarders who are our pupils." She met Emily's eyes with a direct look. "*Their* moral characters must be protected, at all costs."

"Yes, miss," Emily said, and gulped.

Miss Keller turned to the window, which showed only a bleak array of soot-streaked roofs and a grainy patch of gray sky. Not looking around, she said, "I am sure you understand that it would be terribly unwise to speak of what transpired at Hawthorn House. That is in the past now, and must stay there. No one must know, and especially the other servants, such as the one who shares this room." She turned back to look directly at Emily, and now her eyes were hard, her voice cold. "You may be tempted to speak of it, but I assure you that it would not be in your best interest to do so. Do you understand me?"

Our Emily wasn't the cleverest of girls, perhaps, but she was certainly clever enough to hear the veiled warning. If she spoke about Baby Flora, it would go badly for her. Well, she didn't intend to say a word. She might be turned out, and then what could she do? Without a character, no one would hire her. She would never find another place in London.

And she daren't go back to the village, either. Once it was known what had happened at Hawthorn House, her reputation would be blackened. Worse, the constable would come into it, and she might go to gaol! So she had to carry on, even though London was not at all what she had expected, and Miss Keller did not seem like the same person she had known.

"Yes, miss," she said humbly. "I understand."

"That's a good girl," said Miss Keller. Her face softened. "Off you go, now."

8
JEMIMA COUNTS TO TEN

"I wish to hatch my own eggs; I will hatch them all by myself," quacked Jemima Puddle-duck.
> Beatrix Potter, *The Tale of Jemima Puddle-Duck*

Back in the Hill Top barn, Jemima Puddle-duck is still sitting on her nest, counting the hours until her beautiful eggs finally hatch. Is there any progress to be reported? None yet, I regret to report. But eggs being eggs, we know that something is bound to happen soon — don't we?

Of course, if this had been your nest and your eggs, I am sure that you would not have settled down to the tedious business of hatching without taking some thought as to how to mark the time. You might have pinned a calendar to the wall in order to know what day it was and calculate how many were left until your eggs hatched. You might also have brought postage stamps and envelopes, for writing to your friends so they would be informed of your absence and would not bother to call on Thursday afternoon, as usual. And your pocket watch, so as to know when it was teatime.

But while our Jemima is devoted and dedicated, she is not the most discerning of ducks. She had brought her knitting and a few lending-library romances and several crossword puzzles to help her pass the time. To make things neat and cozy, she had put up a peg for her bonnet and shawl, spread a nice little red rug beside her nest, and hung a picture of dear old Queen Victoria (she was not fond of King Edward, who was quite the playboy). But she had not thought of a calendar (much less a pocket watch and postage stamps), so she had no idea of what day this was, or when her eggs would hatch. And she had not told any of the other creatures what she was doing. She intended her beautiful new family to be a surprise.

Unfortunately, however, Jemima's project was about to be revealed, for Jackboy, the loudmouth magpie, was shouting the news to all the animals in the barnyard. But Jackboy was a clown, and his speech was so odd that few could understand him.

"Plucky ducky missy sitzie long time,"

chirped Jackboy, hopping along the top of the fence.

"*Pardon* moi?" Aunt Susan, Miss Potter's fat black Berkshire pig, looked up from her muddy wallow in a corner of the pig sty. *"I didn't quite catch that."*

Miss Potter was fond of saying that Aunt Susan had such full, round cheeks that she looked as if she had the mumps, although I think it is doubtful that pigs catch the mumps. More likely, Aunt Susan had been stuffing herself again. She was Miss Potter's favorite pig and had come to live at Hill Top when she was a tiny piglet, small enough to fit into one of Miss Potter's pattens. She was quite the pet, sleeping in a basket beside Miss Potter's bed and drinking milk from a baby bottle until she was big enough to look after herself.

Now fully pig-size (and then some), Aunt Susan still enjoyed kitchen privileges: biscuits and brown bread and beans and rice pudding from the Hill Top table, all stirred together in a bucket and moistened with warm, fresh milk from Kitchen the cow, and one or two eggs added to the mix. Which is why Aunt Susan was the fattest, laziest pig in the Hill Top barnyard, and why she was always thinking ahead to the next meal.

"Eggsie-peggsie in a nestie-pestie," Jackboy

remarked informatively, stretching his black wings.

"I think," hazarded Dorcas, *"the fellow is babbling about eggs."* Dorcas was a clever, enterprising pig, slimmer, speedier, and not nearly so docile as Aunt Susan. Whenever she could, Dorcas pushed her way under the fence and darted into the woods (if you have ever seen a pig run, you will know that "dart" is exactly the right word). When she was safely out of sight in the woods, she always trotted straight to her favorite oak tree to root for acorns until someone fetched her home to tea.

"Eggs?" Aunt Susan murmured. She rolled over onto her right side, setting in motion a muddy tidal wave. *"I am very fond of eggs. I have been known to eat them raw, but I prefer fried or scrambled."* She closed her eyes, grunting dreamily. *"Poached eggs are very good, too. And shirred eggs, and soft-boiled and baked. And creamed with chipped beef on toast, and deviled, and smothered and —"*

"Ducksie-wucksie," remarked Jackboy in a confidential tone. *"Quacksie-hatchie-missie-blissie."* And with that, he flew away.

Dorcas scratched her piggy ear with one hind hoof. *"I always imagine that there is some great significance in Jackboy's tales,*

117

but they are probably just nonsense. It sounds as if he is talking about ducks and eggs."

"There is no nonsense about eggs," said Aunt Susan firmly. *"They are extremely significant. Chicken eggs, duck eggs, goose eggs, guinea eggs, partridge eggs — delightfully tasty, each and every one of them."* She shuddered. *"Except, of course, when they are served with pork sausages or bacon. Then they are incredibly inedible."*

As you can see, some of the barnyard animals had other things on their minds than the absent Jemima. But there was someone else who cared, and who listened closely to the magpie's maniacal chatter. This was Kep the collie, who was deeply troubled by the duck's disappearance.

For centuries, collies have been bred as herding dogs. Their job is to keep all the barnyard creatures safe, to ward off predators, and assist the shepherd in rounding up wayward animals. Kep, like other collies, took his work very seriously. He was on the job day and night, paying close attention to the comings and goings of every animal on the farm. Not an easy task, I'll warrant, but one for which he was suited by nature and training.

Collies are different from all other animals in this regard, you see. Most creatures have learned to pay no attention to the sudden disappearances of friends, who may be here one minute and gone the next. In fact, there's an important reason for this apparent nonchalance. It cannot be comfortable to think that one's missing comrade — a chicken or a pig or a goose or a duck, or even a cow or a sheep — might reappear in a day or two on the Hill Top dinner table, roasted and basted or steamed, seasoned, stewed, sauced, or stuffed. Oneself might be next! So one learns to turn a blind eye and a deaf ear, to bury one's head in the sand. One cultivates the fine art of ignorance.

But Kep was constitutionally unable to do this, and had been deeply troubled by Jemima's absence. He suspected that she harbored a certain fondness for the fox, and feared that (foolish duck that she was, so easily beguiled) she might have agreed to run away with him. He had already spent quite some time searching, so when Dorcas happened to mention that Jackboy might (or might not) be chattering about ducks and eggs, he cornered the magpie beside the barn.

"Jemima Puddle-duck has been absent without leave for some weeks," Kep said, fixing Jackboy with a stern stare. *"She is of average height and weight, with white feath-*

ers, a yellow beak, yellow legs, and orange-colored webbed feet — last seen wearing a shawl and poke bonnet. If you have any information concerning the whereabouts of this missing duck, it is imperative that you inform me at once."

Jackboy spread his iridescent black tail into a glossy fan. *"Bat and wicket, wot's the ticket?"* he chuckled. *"Wot'll ye give me t' spill me bill?"*

"The ticket?" Kep bared his teeth. *"What'll I give you, snitch? I'll yank out all your tail feathers, that's what I'll do, bird-brain. You won't look so smart then, will you, nincompoop?"*

Jackboy took two giant hops backward. *"Wot?"* he cried, his bright magpie-eyes anxious. *"Me whistle and flute? Me weasel and stoat? Me black tail-coat?"*

"Yes, your whistle and flute," Kep growled. *"Every fine feather in that fashionable magpie tail of yours."* He narrowed his eyes and flexed his claws. *"And I'm big enough and fast enough to do it, too. If you value your feathers, you'd better squawk, stool pigeon!"*

Jackboy gave a lurid shriek. *"Stranger ranger under-the-manger! Spy with yer mince pies!"* And off he flew.

Jackboy's directions might seem incoherent to us, but Kep was a clever collie. He put his head under the feedbox and spied the duck. She was standing over her nest, tenderly turning her eggs, counting them with the counting rhyme that country children used in those days to count birds on a roof. Perhaps you will recognize it:

One for sadness, two for mirth;
three for marriage, four for birth;
five for laughing, six for crying;
seven for sickness, eight for dying;
nine for silver, ten for gold.

She stopped, turned, and settled herself on the nest, gently quacking the last line to herself: *"Eleven a seCRet that will never be told."* And then she tucked her head under her wing, in preparation for a nap.

"What do you think you're doing?" a voice asked severely.

Startled, Jemima pulled her head out from under her wing and her eyes flew open. She was frightened until she realized that it was Kep. *"I am QUACK hatching my duCKluCK-lings,"* she said, with as much dignity as a duck can muster. *"Please go baCK to whatever you were doing so I can CArry on."*

Ducklings! Kep thought in surprise. *"But you've been gone for nearly two months,"* he replied, in a more kindly tone. *"It shouldn't* take that long to —"

"*Two months!*" quacked Jemima. "*Alas, alaCK, I am thunderstruCK! I had no idea! Why, I COuld have hatched two CLutches in that amount of time!*"

Kep frowned. He did not like to alarm Jemima, but he didn't have to be Sherlock Holmes to know that something was obviously wrong here. Chicken eggs took twenty-one days to hatch, give or take a day or two. Goose eggs took thirty. Duck eggs took twenty-eight. Why were these eggs taking twice as long to hatch? It was time to find out what was going on.

"*Is it possible that they are . . .*" The word he wanted was "infertile," but it seemed a very indelicate word to use in conversation with a lady. "*Is it possible that your eggs have no ducklings in them?*" he asked gently.

"*No duCKluCKlings?*" Jemima squawked indignantly. "*Of COurse there are duCKluCKlings! I have been feeling movement in them for some time now.*"

But there was another question to be asked. Hesitantly, he said, "*Well, then, are they* your *eggs, Jemima?*"

"*My eGGs? Indeed they are my eGGs!*" Jemima quacked, flapping her wings in high dudgeon. "*In faCT, I have been sitting on* them for such a protraCTed time that a certain part of my anatomy — it would be improper to name it — is thoroughly numb. These eGGs belong to me and to no one else. Are you QUestioning my ownership?"

Kep sighed. This was clearly a sensitive issue. *"I shall rephrase,"* he said. *"What I mean to say is — what I want to know is —"* This sort of thing was not at all up his line, and he was at a loss as to how exactly to put it. He took a breath. *"That is to say, did you, er, did you lay these eggs yourself?"*

"Did I QUACK lay these eGGs?" The duck's eyes flashed and she ruffled her feathers in a great show of outrage. *"Did I lay them myself? What sort of unKIndly QUestion is that, sir? You should be ashamed, asking a lady QUACK such a thing."*

Kep was ashamed. But the question had to be answered. He waited until the ruffled feathers had subsided, then, very humbly, he lay down and put his nose between his forepaws. *"Well?"* he asked. He wagged his tail gently. *"Did you?"*

Jemima gave him a sulky look. *"Did I what?"*

"Did you lay them yourself, Jemima?"

Jemima preened a feather, ignoring him. But her silence told him the answer. She had taken the eggs from another bird's nest. Stolen them, if you like. She was guilty of

123

egg-napping. But while Kep was fully aware that one must pay for one's crimes, he could also understand why Jemima had done it. A mother duck could scarcely be blamed for longing to do what ducks had done since ducks had been put on this earth with the instruction "Be fruitful and multiply" in their pockets.

However, there were other considerations. The mother from whom the eggs had been stolen, for one, who must be frantic about their loss. What mother bird would not worry if she came back to her nest and found her entire clutch gone, vanished without a trace? And just as importantly, he had to think what sort of bird that would hatch from these eggs. What if they weren't duck eggs? What if Jemima had somehow managed to collect the eggs of some predatory bird, thereby introducing nearly a dozen dangerous strangers to the barn lot? The idea turned him cold from the tip of his nose to the tip of his tail.

Trying to hide his apprehension, Kep said, very quietly: *"I know that maternity is a delicate subject, and must be approached with respect and consideration. But you do want to clear up the mystery, don't you?"*

"Mystery?" Jemima shot him a defensive look. *"What QUACK mystery?"*

"The mystery of your eggs, my dear duck, and why it is taking so long to hatch them." Kep managed a reassuring smile. *"If you could tell me where they came from, I might do a spot of detective work and tell you when you may expect the blessed event."*

Once he knew the location, Kep thought, it should not be difficult to locate the real mother. Whether he should then have to restore the eggs to their rightful owner, he wasn't sure, but he was confident that he would sort it out somehow. Of course, if you know anything about collies, you know they are always exceedingly confident about *everything.* There is no puzzle that is too difficult for these self-assured, self-reliant dogs to solve, no challenge too formidable for them to meet. Give them a simple task, such as fetching the newspaper, and they will fetch tea and toast and a bucket of coals and a shawl in case you are cold. And then they will go belowstairs to make sure that the cook has ordered the fish and that there will be hot water for your bath.

But even among collies, Kep stands out. It is no wonder that he could speak with such confidence to Jemima.

There was a long silence. Finally, Jemima quacked, in a tentative way, not quite rejecting, not quite accepting, *"Do you aCTually*

125

thinK that's liKely? That you could tell me . . . when?"

Kep smiled with that calm, encouraging demeanor that makes collies such pleasant dogs to have in one's life. *"Yes, it's possible. But to be of the greatest help, I should need to see your eggs — that is, if you would be so kind as to show them to me."*

Another silence. *"Oh, very well, then,"* the duck said finally. She heaved a heavy sigh, resigned. *"TaKe a looK, if you feel you must."* Her face averted, she stood up and lifted her wings so that her eggs were clearly visible.

Kep leaned over to look. He counted. There were ten. And even though his experience of eggs was rather limited, they looked right to him. They were not stones or croquet balls or figments of a duck's fertile imagination. These eggs were smallish, nicely rounded, white, and — to the eye, at least — perfect in every respect except one. They had not yet hatched. And they should have done, had they been duck eggs.

"Thank you," said the dog respectfully, recognizing how difficult it had been for the duck to show him her treasures. He waited until she had rearranged her feathers and was settled back on her nest. *"Now, if you*

will be so kind as to tell me where you got them —"

"Must I?" she whispered.

"I fear so," he replied softly. "Otherwise, how can I investigate?"

Another silence. Then, in an even lower voice, she said, "I don't fancy QUACK all the other duCKs knowing. They'll want some for themselves, you see."

"I promise not to say a word to anyone." He held up his right paw. "Collie's honor, Jemima."

Persuaded at last, Jemima leaned forward and whispered her secret into Kep's ear. But because she did not mean anyone else to hear, you and I will retire a discreet few paces and turn our backs. And I hope, as our story continues, that you will not think too unkindly of Jemima. For even though she has perhaps been too eager, and has rushed too quickly into a situation she did not understand, she intended neither malice nor harm, which is a good deal more than can be said of every human in this unhappy world.

Our Jemima may be a very foolish duck, even (by some standards) a criminal duck. But at bottom, I think we must agree that she is a duck with a very good heart.

9

IN WHICH MISS POTTER LEARNS A SHOCKING TRUTH

Beatrix had hoped her brother might arrive on Sunday afternoon, but Sunday came and went and he did not appear. This was not altogether a surprise, unfortunately. He was at Stock Park, with their parents, and once you were in their clutches, it was difficult to get away. It wasn't that they meant ill, of course. But Mama kept finding tiresome little chores for one to do, and Papa simply kept talking, so that one could not even leave the room.

It was not until midday on Monday that Beatrix finally opened the door to Bertram's knock. She saw on the porch a thin-faced, dark-haired man, dressed in a gray tweed suit and vest, with a blue tie, an umbrella hung over his arm. He set down his bag and took off his tweed cap.

"Hullo, Bea. Had you given me up? I meant to come yesterday, but Mama and Papa put up a devil of a fuss." He sighed wearily. "You know how it is."

"No matter, Bertram," Beatrix said happily, stepping back to let him in. "I'm just glad you could get away." She would have liked to fling her arms around him, but the Potter family preferred handshakes and brief brushes of the cheek to warm embraces. It was one of the many differences she always noticed when she visited Norman's boisterously affectionate family. The contrast made her own parents seem cold and distant. "Did you leave them well at Stock Park?"

"Leave them well?" Bertram raised one dark eyebrow and his mouth took on a cynical slant. He was taller than she, with a full, dark mustache and delicate good looks. "Of course not. They were just as unhappy as usual. Nothing I do suits them." He chuckled. "But I'm in good company. You don't suit them much, either, Bea."

"We're a pair," Beatrix agreed with a rueful laugh. "They're disappointed in both of us."

Beatrix, who was almost six when Bertram was born, had grown up loving to play Big Sister to Bertram's Little Brother. The two lived together in the third-floor nursery, and when Bertram was old enough, he joined Beatrix for lessons with her governess, Miss

Hammond. In those days, the Potters spent the long holiday — August, September, and most of October — at Dalguise House, in Perthshire, in the Scottish highlands, where sister and brother shared a deep, delighted interest in the out-of-doors. Together, the children went on expeditions through the magical woodlands along the River Tay, catching rabbits and hedgehogs and voles and bats to take back to London, identifying wild birds and searching out their nests, and sketching everything they saw. Both youngsters were seldom without their painting supplies, and as they grew older, both became deeply serious about their art, Beatrix in watercolor, Bertram in oils. And both were nature artists: Bertram painted large landscapes, while Beatrix thought of herself as a miniaturist, painting plants and the small animals she loved to collect: rabbits, mice, guinea pigs, frogs, and more.

Bertram was small for his age, and delicate. But the Potters packed him off to school at the age of eleven, while Beatrix stayed behind to continue her studies at home. Beatrix always felt that she got much the better of the bargain, for Bertram was miserable at school. He could never stand up for himself against bullies, and seemed to have few friends. He had little direction, preferring painting to Latin, Euclid, and most especially to rugby. The headmaster's reports made Mr. Potter mutter and scowl furiously, while Mrs. Potter dabbed her handkerchief to her eyes and refused to distress herself by discussing the matter.

Very little changed as Bertram grew older, the Potters continuing to be disappointed in his lack of interest in anything they thought suitable for him. At twenty, with a great family fanfare, he went off to Oxford. But he didn't stay long, and when he came back to London, he was desperately unhappy and far too fond of the bottle. Bertram's drinking might have been caused by the family failing that seems to have hastened the end of poor Uncle William Leech ("The story is so shocking I cannot write it," Beatrix once confessed to her journal). More likely, it was his way of rebelling against his eternally disappointed mother and the carping, critical father whom he could never please. Beatrix, always intensely aware of the emotional climate in the family and continually feeling that she ought to be able to do something to make things happier for all of them, did what she could to shield Bertram from the worst of their parents' displeasure.

After the failure at Oxford, Bertram simply stayed away. First, he went abroad.

Then he began taking long sketching trips to the Scottish border country where he and Beatrix had spent so many happy weeks and months as children. And finally, about the same time that *Peter Rabbit* became popular and Beatrix began escaping into her little books, Bertram escaped, too. He bought a small north country farm called Ashyburn, where he could spend most of his time painting.

As the years went on, Bertram saw less and less of the family, joining them only at the holiday, and then for only a few days. Mr. and Mrs. Potter loudly lamented his neglect, but Beatrix understood, all too well. If she had been their son, instead of their daughter, she might have done just what Bertram did. In fact, in one important way she had. Bertram defied their displeasure by buying Ashyburn and going there to live. Beatrix bought Hill Top, and spent as much time there as she possibly could.

Bertram cast an approving look around the room. "For one who is such a disappointment to her parents," he said lightly, "you seem to have done quite well by yourself. I like it, Bea. I like it very much."

"Thank you," Beatrix replied modestly. "Shall we have a cup of tea?"

"I had rather have the grand tour of your

farm, starting with this marvelous old house."

"You were here when Mama and Papa were at Lakefield a few years ago, weren't you?" Beatrix asked, hanging his cap and umbrella on a peg. The Potters had taken a holiday house on Esthwaite Water and had boarded their coachman (Mrs. Potter liked to take the carriage out in the afternoon) at Hill Top Farm.

"Yes, I was here," Bertram said with a chuckle. "Remember the day we found Hortense and heard all about those blasted fairies?"

"Of course," Beatrix laughed, too, remembering. Mrs. Allen, who lived at Willow Bank Cottage on Graythwaite Farm, kept exotic pets, among whom was a pair of tortoises named Hortense and Horatio. Hortense had escaped to the lake, where Beatrix and Bertram had found her blissfully sunning herself on a rock. Mrs. Allen had been so pleased at the return of her wayward tortoise that she had invited them in, served them tea and scones, and regaled them with stories about the various Tree Folk who lived thereabouts, in whom she wholeheartedly believed.

"I know you've made a great many changes in the old place," Bertram said. "I want to see them all. From top to bottom, if you please — barns and fields, as well."

"Come along, then," she said. "Bring your bag upstairs and I'll show you where you'll sleep. Then we'll begin our tour at the top, with the attics."

So for the next hour or so, sister and brother went through the house, Bertram saying all the right things in all the right places and in general approving of the changes his sister had made. After that, they went out into the barnyard, where Bertram looked over the Galloway cows, the Berkshire pigs, the farm horses, and various chickens and ducks and geese, pronouncing them all quite fit, well fed, and extraordinarily handsome.

Then, accompanied by the two village cats, Tabitha Twitchit and Crumpet (who had made up their quarrel and were once again the best of friends), they toured the garden, the orchard, and the meadow. When they got to the top of the hill, they paused to survey Beatrix's Herdwick sheep, which were scattered like so many puffs of white cotton across the green grass all the way to Wilfin Beck.

"So he's Miss Potter's brother," Crumpet said thoughtfully, studying the pair. *"I can't say they're much alike."*

"Not in looks," Tabitha agreed, *"although there is something similar in their manner. And they do seem to get along."*

"I say, Bea, you have a jolly good place here," Bertram said, leaning back against a tree, the cats sitting nearby. He took out his pipe and began to fill it from a leather pouch. "Close enough to London to be convenient, remote enough so that Mama and Papa aren't likely to come."

Beatrix made a face. "It's not as remote as all that, I'm afraid. They threaten to come back to Lakefield, as they did before. But happily, they prefer a place with more society. Sawrey boasts only Lady Longford, and Mama can call on her only once a week." She chuckled. "And poor Papa can find no one at all to listen to him here. Stock Park suits them better."

"Mrs. Potter complains that Ferry Hill is hard on their horses," Tabitha confided to Crumpet. *"The Potters take their carriage and pair on holiday, you know."* She gave an amused laugh. *"They hire an entire railway car."*

"They must have pots of money," remarked Crumpet, but without envy. Animals always feel they inhabit the best of all worlds. While they may be jealous of their own kindred, they never envy other species — particularly humans, on whom they mostly take pity.

Tabitha nodded. *"Yes, but you'd never know it to look at our Miss Potter. She prefers plain to fancy, and if she has a loose shilling in her pocket, she spends it on the farm."*

Bertram scrutinized his sister. "I must say, Bea, this place agrees with you. You're looking pink and pretty." He tamped the tobacco into his pipe and found his matches. "You've gained weight, too. You were too thin, I think."

"I love it here," Beatrix said, from the bottom of her heart. "The village is infinitely interesting, like the world in miniature. And there is such a wonderful largeness and silence in the fells that I can scarcely get enough of it. I only wish that Norman might be here to share it with me." She had long ago forgiven Bertram for not taking her side in the awful family row over her engagement, but she couldn't hold back a sigh. "I'm sure he would have loved it every bit as much as I do."

"Poor Miss Potter." Tabitha gave a romantic sigh. *"So alone. She needs someone to take care of her."*

"Yes, she does," agreed Crumpet. She gave Tabitha a knowing glance. *"Miss Woodcock has a plan."*

Tabitha leaned forward. Her eyes glinted with interest and her tail twitched. *"What sort of plan? How do you know?"*

Crumpet smiled mysteriously and only shook her head, for Bertram was speaking.

"I agree," he said. "Norman would have enjoyed being here — or anywhere, if you were there." He pulled on his pipe, blew out a stream of smoke, and looked off into the distance. "Being with someone you care for — someone who cares for you — makes all the difference."

Beatrix nodded, trying to swallow. Her throat hurt too much to speak.

After a moment, Bertram said, very quietly, "I'm sorry about leaving you stuck with Mama and Papa, Bea. It's not fair to you, and I know it."

"If that's what he's doing," Crumpet said tartly, *"it isn't at all fair. He ought to do his part, and not leave it all to his sister."*

"What is Miss Woodcock's plan?" Tabitha asked eagerly.

"I —" But Crumpet stopped because Miss Potter was speaking.

"I don't suppose men are generally of much help with aging parents," she said, pulling off her straw hat and fanning herself with it. "There isn't a great deal you could do for Mama when she goes to bed with one of her sick headaches. And no one can please Papa — not you, not I, not the

137

government, nor God in heaven." She chuckled wryly. She tried to make light of things she couldn't change, and she had long been accustomed to make excuses for her brother's absences from home. But she was glad of Bertram's words, and even gladder of the genuine apology she heard in his voice. She would remember it on those horrible days when resentment got the better of her.

"I suppose," Bertram went on, "that between the parents, the farm, and your books, you are kept too busy to think about things much. It's good you've had so much success with your art." He puffed on his pipe. "A kind of consolation prize, as it were, for having to look after Mama and Papa. And of course richly deserved, on the merits," he added hastily.

Beatrix slanted her brother a look. His large landscapes, while very fine in their way, had not yet found an enthusiastic public. But she saw nothing in Bertram's face that made her uncomfortable. You and I might have considered his remark unforgivably condescending — "consolation prize," indeed! — but it did not trouble her. She knew he was entirely happy for her success, which was all that she asked.

"Who would have thought that the world

would make so much out of a few foolish bunnies?" she mused. "It all seems very odd, when I stop to think of it, especially the sideshows. The rabbits are doing well, and soon there will be a Puddle-duck doll, if the manufacturing problems can be sorted." She chuckled. "The tea sets are in demand, too, which is amusing. Just think of all the little girls serving pretend scones on Peter plates."

The little books had resulted in a great many merchandise offshoots, and each sale earned Beatrix a royalty — individually quite small, but taken together, it all mounted up in a surprising way. It might mount up to a good deal more, if only her publisher would pay the proper attention to the licenses, and not muddle so many of the opportunities. But Mr. Warne, Norman's brother, rarely listened to her suggestions.

"Everything I earn goes into the farm, of course," she added. "I've rebuilt the barn and bought more sheep, all thanks to those ridiculous rabbits."

"But rabbits aren't ridiculous!" Crumpet cried, lifting her head. *"They're very good exercise!"*

"Her rabbits only run as far as the edge of the page," Tabitha said. *"You'll not get any exercise out of them."* She batted a paw at

Crumpet. *"I want to hear about Miss Wood-cock's plan, Crumpet!"*

"Later," Crumpet said. *"Later."*

"To think that your farm is built on books and bunnies." Bertram's dark eyes crinkled at the corners. "It's good that you have such a head for business, Bea. Much better than mine, of course." He puffed on his pipe. "You're planning more books, I suppose."

"Two for next year," Beatrix replied. "There's to be a sequel to the bunnies, and a tale about the village shop. *Ginger and Pickles.*"

"Wait!" Crumpet frowned. *"Why is it Ginger and Pickles? Why not Crumpet and Tabitha?"*

"Tabitha and Crumpet," Tabitha snarled.

"You might call it *Two Bad Cats,*" Bertram said, with a glance at the quarrelsome pair. He lapsed into silence, smoking and looking off into the distance.

Beatrix fell silent, as well. She felt comfortable with her brother. Even when they didn't talk, the silence was easy, for each of them knew what the other was thinking. To Beatrix, Bertram had seemed more content these days, and not so perpetually out of temper. Healthier, too. He had put on weight and his color was better. Living in Scotland must agree with him, although it was too bad that he had to be alone. That must have been what was behind his oblique remark: "Being with someone you care for — who cares for you — makes all the difference."

But Beatrix had no more congratulated herself on knowing what was in her brother's mind than he said something that not only astonished her, but proved her completely and utterly wrong.

"I say, Bea." Bertram cleared his throat uncomfortably. "I must tell you something. But I . . . that is, I — Well, I don't quite know how to begin."

Beatrix was alarmed. Had he got himself into some sort of serious trouble? Did he need money? There had been a great many scrapes and difficulties in the past, and like a big sister, she had always stood up for him. She would do that now, no matter what.

She tried to laugh. "Remember what Miss Hammond used to say when we were children. 'Truth is the beginning of every good thing, both in heaven and in earth.' " She swallowed. How stiff that sounded, and priggish, and older-sisterish. She wished she could take it back. "Come, Bertram, tell me," she said, more lightly. "Is something wrong? What can I do to help?"

"No, there's nothing wrong. Actually,

things are perfectly all right. But I —" He folded his arms, not looking at her. "I will tell you, but first you must promise not to tell the parents."

"Uh-oh," Tabitha said softly. *"Doesn't sound good."*

"That's the thing about humans," Crumpet replied. *"They keep secrets."*

"Animals do, too," Tabitha retorted with a nasty look. *"When are you going to tell me about Miss Woodcock's plan?"*

Beatrix looked at Bertram, feeling the apprehension rising inside her. Her brother had that guilty, defensive expression he always wore when he had to confess and apologize for something he had done. It was a familiar look, and it brought back unhappy memories of past misdeeds and penitent confessions. But she would promise.

"Yes, yes, of course, dear. I won't say a word."

The silence stretched out between them — uneasily now, as Beatrix thought of all the terrible things he might be about to say. He was in debt and needed money. He had lost his farm and would have to come back to Bolton Gardens to live. He had been caught cheating at cards. He was desperately ill with some dreadful —

"I'm married, Bea." He let out his breath

in a rush. "I'm married."

"Married!" Beatrix whispered. The world seemed suddenly to have stopped turning.

"Married?" Crumpet meowed sarcastically. *"Is that all? From the look on his face, I thought he was going to say that he'd murdered somebody."*

Bertram squared his shoulders. "I am telling you because I feel that someone in the family should know, in case anything should happen to me. But the parents are not to know. Not yet."

"I . . . I hardly know what to say," Beatrix managed at last. The only son, married without his father's consent, his mother's blessing!

"I know what's in your mind, Bea," Bertram said unhappily. "But Papa and Mama would not have given their consent, so there was no point in asking for it. And no point in telling them after the fact, either. Mary — my wife — is a wonderful person, but they could never allow themselves to recognize her worth." He pulled on his pipe, his voice laced with bitterness. "She doesn't belong to their social class, you see. She isn't a lady. No fine carriage, no silk dresses, no servants to fetch and carry." He stared down at his pipe, then knocked it against the tree, emptying it. "We met when she was working as a serving girl in her aunt's hostelry, where I had taken rooms."

"A hostelry?" Beatrix asked weakly.

Tabitha's eyes widened. *"A Potter has married a barmaid? No wonder he doesn't want to tell his parents."*

"The barmaid at the Tower Bank Arms is one of my best friends," Crumpet remarked. *"She understands my fondness for steak and kidney pie."*

Tabitha rolled her eyes. *"But gentlemen don't marry barmaids, Crumpet. If the Potters knew, it would destroy them."*

"Yes, a hostelry," Bertram said angrily. "And she's worked in the textile mills, as well." He hit his pipe once more against the tree, and broke it. He stared down at the pieces in his hand, then tossed them away. "You're not going to look down on her, too, Bea? You, of all people?"

Beatrix put her hand on her brother's arm. Astonished as she was, she understood how he felt, and shared his pain. Their father could be scathing in his remarks about the "lower classes." And their mother looked with scorn at people she thought beneath her. She had been disagreeable enough about Norman and his family, who were "in trade." She would be unspeakably disagreeable about Mary. Bertram was right to spare himself — and of course, his wife.

His wife. Suddenly Beatrix felt cold and alone. Until this minute, she hadn't understood how much it had meant to feel that Bertram was . . . was with her, at least in some way. Now he wasn't. He was with his wife.

She mustered all the assurance she could. "If you love her, I am sure that Mary is truly worthy. I only wish I could have been at your wedding. When did it take place?"

He didn't look at her. "Mary and I met the year you came up to Scotland with me, to see the farm. We married not long after."

She stared at him blankly. "But that was . . . good heavens, Bertram, that was six years ago!"

"Yes, six years, almost." He hunched his shoulders. "I . . . I meant to tell them when you . . . when they made such a fuss about you and Norman Warne. I thought if I told them about me, they might have to let you marry him."

Beatrix pressed her lips together mutely.

"I even tried, once," Bertram went on miserably, "when we were all on holiday in Wales, after Norman's proposal. They were still furious at you, of course. Remember?"

"Yes, I remember," Beatrix whispered. She would never, ever forget. It had been an agonizing time. Her mother wouldn't speak to her, her father —

But that pain, awful as it was, had been erased by an even greater agony. Norman had fallen sick and died, in the space of a few weeks. She was left with nothing. Nothing.

"Papa and I went out walking together," Bertram continued, "and that was the only thing he could talk about — this marriage you wanted to make, and how unsuitable it was for you. I tried to tell him about Mary, but I couldn't get a word in edgewise. And the longer he went on about you and Norman, the harder it was for me. I knew how furious he would be, and I was . . . I was afraid."

His voice broke and he swallowed hard, his bony Adam's apple bobbing against his collar, and Beatrix thought how young he looked, and how utterly wretched.

"I . . . I'm weak, Bea. I can't tell you how much I admired your courage, standing up to them the way you did, insisting that you would accept Norman's proposal, that you would wear his ring. But that made me feel even worse. I . . . I was a coward. I promised Mary I would tell them, and I failed her. I failed myself. I failed . . . you. If I had told them, it might have changed things."

Beatrix blinked away the tears. "No, Bertram. St. Peter and all the angels could not have persuaded them." She gave a sad little shrug. "And anyway, things would still have come out the same." She let out her breath in a long, sad sigh. "Norman would still be . . . gone."

"I suppose you're right," Bertram said gloomily. "Anyway, that's what I told myself, after Norman died. But that didn't make me feel better then, and it doesn't now. I could have done the right thing, for once in my life. I didn't. I was a coward then. I am still a coward."

"Six years," Beatrix said softly, and asked what she dreaded to know. "Do you . . . do you and Mary have children?"

"Not yet," Bertram said shortly. "When that happens, I suppose I shall have to break down and tell Papa." He chuckled sourly. "His only son, married to a commoner, bringing common children into a common world onto a common farm! It will send him into an apoplectic fit."

Beatrix looked down at the gold engagement ring she meant to wear forever and chuckled sadly. "It might at that. He stumped around for weeks after our quarrel, red as a beet and muttering under his breath. And Mama went right on sulking even after Norman died and I was out of danger."

"That's because it wasn't just Norman," Bertram growled. "The danger, I mean."

Beatrix frowned. "What did you say?"

"It wasn't just Norman, of course," Bertram said again. "It wouldn't matter if the Prince of Wales offered for you, Bea — Mama means you to stay at home until both she and Papa are dead, so you can take care of them. Didn't you know that?"

"I suppose I did," Beatrix said slowly. "I just didn't —"

"You just didn't think of it that way. You're too sweet-natured to see how unreasonably selfish Mama is. And hypocritical. She says 'He's not the right man for you,' when what she really means is, 'I don't intend you to marry.' "

"Such a wicked old lady!" Tabitha exclaimed. *"How can Miss Potter go on in the face of such selfishness?"*

"Some Big Folk are very good at making their families miserable," Crumpet replied with a sigh.

Beatrix did not say that Bertram was changing the subject, although he was. She only put on a smile and said, determinedly cheerful, "Anyway, you've proved my point, Bertram. Telling them about your marriage wouldn't have made any difference. Whatever Mama's reasons, you couldn't have changed her mind."

But that wasn't to say that it wouldn't have made a difference to him, she thought. If he had told the parents three years ago, he wouldn't be carrying the guilty burden still. It had to eat away at his happiness, and Mary's. But there was no point in telling him something he already knew. She put on her hat and took his arm.

"And all that's over and done with, dear. Water under the proverbial bridge. You are a married man and I am an old maid, and so we shall forever be. You have your Mary, and I have my books and my farm. Now, let's go back to the house and have a cup of hot tea and one of Sarah Barwick's scones. I want to tell you about the baby I found on Saturday —"

"A *baby?*" Bertram exclaimed with an incredulous laugh. "Did you say 'baby'?"

"I did indeed. I shall tell you all about her, and you shall tell me all about Mary. I want to know *everything* about your wife. Is she pretty? Does she like farming? Is she a cheerful person?" She paused, surveying him with a mock-critical look. "She must be a very good cook, for you have fattened up nicely."

Bertram threw back his head and laughed. "You certainly know how to make a fellow feel better, Bea." And then, for the first time since they were children, he put his arm around her shoulders and hugged her. "You're a brick, d'you know? The fellow who gets you will be counting his lucky stars."

Her brother's arm warm across her shoulder, Beatrix laughed, too. She pushed away the pain and said, in a very clear, very firm voice, "That's not going to happen, Bertram. You're the only one in this family lucky enough to marry."

"It seems amazing to me that she can laugh over such a thing," Tabitha said in a wondering tone.

Crumpet gave Tabitha a wise look. *"She might be wrong, you know. If Miss Woodcock has her way, Miss Potter might yet have a husband."*

Tabitha shot out a frustrated paw. *"Miss Woodcock! Miss Woodcock! When are you going to stop hinting and tell me what you've heard?"*

"Oh, I don't know," Crumpet said in a superior tone. *"Maybe today, maybe tomorrow. Maybe never."*

This, of course, completely enraged Tabitha. With a furious yowl, she struck out at

Crumpet, catching her claw in an ear. Crumpet bit down hard on Tabitha's paw. And then they were rolling over and over on the ground, spitting and snarling and shrieking.

"Those cats can't seem to get along," Beatrix remarked as she and Bertram walked away. "I wonder what set them off this time."

If Beatrix had known, she would have found the idea very funny, for Miss Woodcock's scheme was something to which she had not given a moment's thought.

10
THE FOX AND THE BADGER

When we last glimpsed Mr. Reynard V. Vulpes, he was being pursued across the fells by a pair of enthusiastic fox-hound pups. Of course, they couldn't catch him, but like good fox-hounds, they were always up for the game — as was Reynard, who liked nothing better than leading the pack on a merry chase through the fields.

And where was he now, this fugitive fox?

He had taken an extended holiday in the remote fells, as far away as Sea Fell and Dunmail Raise and Loughrigg — names almost as wild and glorious as the mountains themselves. His days and nights had been enlivened with sportive adventures, mostly involving unsuspecting lambs and wayward voles and naive rabbits. And vixens, too, generous, seductive creatures with amber eyes and red-gold fur as soft as silk. But even with all the distractions of holiday travel in exotic places, he couldn't get

Jemima out of his mind. He'd somehow got . . . well, rather fond of the duck. She was so sweetly innocent, so wide-eyed with wonder at the various little offerings he placed before her, so grateful for his attentions. He found himself hoping that, one day, their paths would cross again.

By the time Reynard returned to Foxglove Close, he was feeling rather better. He aired the cottage, washed the linens, restocked the larder, and began to sort the post that had accumulated in his absence. Amongst the advertising flyers and out-of-date announcements and such, he found a copy of *The Tale of Jemima Puddle-Duck,* which had been sent to him by his old uncle Vulpes. Enclosed was a tart note, suggesting that if Miss Potter had accurately represented the facts in this latest book of hers, the affair reflected badly on foxes in general (who are supposed to be clever and crafty) and Reynard in particular (who was made to look quite ridiculous). Miss Potter even wrote that "nothing more was ever seen of that foxy-whiskered gentleman," which implied that the fox had been so frightened that he had quit the district forever. How, inquired Uncle Vulpes, did Reynard intend to redeem himself?

When Reynard read the book, he was appalled at his unflattering portrayal, and no end annoyed at Miss Potter. If he had known what she was going to make of the affair, by George, he would have eaten that dratted duck the day she tumbled out of the sky and landed on his lawn. He was a fox, wasn't he? Foxes ate ducks, didn't they? No one would have blamed him if he had served her up à la orange that very night. And no one, not even Miss Potter, could have made a story out of roast duck.

But oh, no, he had to be clever. He had played Jemima along, plying her with exotic food and drink, with the intention of adding one more daily egg to the ultimate, inevitable omelette. He was, in a sense, feeding the duck that laid the golden eggs, and in the end he expected to dine on both eggs and duck, all at one glorious banquet.

But he had outfoxed himself, for Jemima (while she might not be the brightest of birds) was certainly the most delightful of companions, and over the nine days of her visits, he had developed a taste for her company.

And now, trying very hard to be honest with himself, Reynard had to admit that Jemima had become an obsession. She was the duck who had got away, which quite naturally whetted his appetite. But if he were to be completely and utterly honest, Reynard had to admit something else. He had grown far too fond of Jemima, not as the source of duck-egg omelettes and not as a roast duck upon his table, but as a companion by his side.

He shuddered as he heard the words echoing in his mind. A fox growing fond of a duck? It was unorthodox, unnatural. It was unaccountably unfoxlike. It was —

It was true. Reynard closed the book, held it between his paws, and gazed at the color portrait of Jemima on the cover, decked out in that foolish blue bonnet and shawl, on her way to their rendezvous. She was so pleasingly plump, so delectable. His heart yearned for her. He must see that duck again. He must!

He was still considering how best to go about this when he discovered, quite by accident, that Jemima had been confined to quarters. He learnt this news from a manic magpie named Jackboy, whom he met one warm afternoon in the lane. The magpie was glad to tell him where the duck was penned, but as to why — well, at the end of a half hour of listening to Jackboy's prattling, the fox was no wiser than he had been in the beginning, and certainly a good deal more frustrated. It is not easy to understand a magpie, let alone a Cockney magpie.

This news gave our fox something to think about, but at the moment, he was occupied with the business of moving house. Male foxes have well-established territories with several dens along the boundaries, some summer dens, some winter dens, some in-between. Foxglove Close was Reynard's favorite den, but he always spent several weeks in August at Sandy Place, a comfortable den that his grandfather had dug under the hawthorn hedge at the foot of Broomstick Lane. He chose August, for that was when the gypsies came to camp in nearby Thorny Field.

Reynard enjoyed his stay at Sandy Place, not only because it was amusing to watch the dark-eyed gypsy children at their ball-and-stick games and the crafty old gypsy grandmothers at their fortune-telling cards, but because the gypsy fathers took large numbers of rabbits and birds from the nearby fields and the gypsy mothers stewed them with dumplings and plenty of paprika in large pots over open fires. The fox found it easy to get a tasty meal without going to the trouble of catching and cooking it for himself. Afterward he stretched out in the grass to listen to the gypsies' songs and stories, feeling as you might feel if you lived next door to a Hungarian restaurant that featured a fine goulash and the best in after-dinner entertainment.

Sandy Place was located on the southern boundary of Reynard's territory. On the northern boundary was an animal hostelry known as The Brockery at Holly How, where Reynard had stayed from time to time. The fox always enjoyed himself at The Brockery, for the proprietor, Bosworth Badger, set an excellent table and poured an outstanding wine. And since the hostelry was a convenient stopover for animals traveling through the Land Between the Lakes, it was always a good place to hear the most recent gossip — such as news about a certain duck. It was with these things in mind that Reynard decided to visit his friend. And it was no accident that he dropped in just at dinnertime.

If you have ever examined a badger sett (that is what a badger's house is called), you know that it is an extensive arrangement of underground living, sleeping, and eating chambers, linked by tunnels leading to various exterior entrances and exits, strategically placed for emergency escape. A sett is the work of not one but many generations of determined badgers who are very experienced at this earth-moving business, excavating astonishingly large amounts of soil without any shovels or spades or scoops or steam-powered diggers. All they have is a badger's strong claws, a badger's indomitable spirit, and a badger's dedication to duty.

At The Brockery, this habit of continuous daily industry is honored in the badger family emblem:

De parvis, grandis acervus erit

which is inscribed upon the famous Badger Coat of Arms (twin badgers rampant on an azure field) hanging over the fireplace in the library. In English, this Latin motto is translated as "From small things, there will grow a mighty heap." This motto says a great deal about the digging skills and the dogged (so to speak) perseverance of Bosworth Badger's family, whose story is set down in twenty-four leather-bound volumes of the *History of the Badgers of the Land Between the Lakes* and its companion work, the *Holly How Badger Genealogy,* all of which are shelved in orderly fashion in The Brockery's library.

And that is exactly where we find Bosworth at this moment in our story, in front of a pretty fire of sticks brightly ablaze in the fireplace. But he was not lolling in a chair, toasting his toes. No, indeed, he was hard at work at his writing table, his pen in his hand and his tongue fast between his teeth. He was making an entry in the *History,* which has evolved over the years from a mere compendium of badger doings into a comprehensive and authoritative account of all important activities, animal and human, in the Land Between the Lakes.

As Badger-in-Chief (a title conferred upon him by his father, together with the Badger Badge of Authority), the *History* and the *Genealogy* were Bosworth's responsibility. He had many other obligations, of course — maintaining the security of the sett, overseeing the staff, and ensuring that his guests were well fed and well taken care of. But the *History* was his most significant duty and Bosworth performed it with enormous seriousness, often pausing as he worked to look up at the portraits of his badger ancestors that hung on the library walls. He imagined that they were smiling down at him and approving his diligence and accuracy.

Bosworth had just laid down his pen and taken a sip from his evening sherry when he heard the brassy *clang clang clang* of The

Brockery's front door bell. This was followed by the scurry of feet, the opening of the front door, and the murmur of friendly voices. Bosworth relaxed, for as Chief Badger he was always wary, always bearing in mind the Seventh Badger Rule of Thumb: *One may hope for friends at the door, but one is well advised to anticipate enemies.* He glanced at the sherry decanter. Yes, there was enough for another glass or two, since this promised to be a friendly call.

The door was opened by Flotsam, one of the twin rabbits who were in charge of hospitality. *"Mr. Reynard Vulpes to pay his respects, sir."* And with that, she withdrew and a sandy-whiskered gentleman in green tweeds entered the library.

"Hullo, Fox!" exclaimed Bosworth in hearty welcome, taking his friend's green tweed cap and hanging it on the peg beside the door. *"Good to see you, old chap! Do come in and warm yourself. It's damp out."*

"Kind of you, Badger," said the fox, going to stand in front of the fire. *"I've been staying down at Thorny Field for the past few days. But I was up this way and thought I'd just pop in and say hello."* He lifted his coat-tails to warm his backside. *"Trust I'm not intruding on your dinner hour, old man."* (If

160

you have noticed that our fox is no longer speaking in that French accent he used in the company of the duck, you are correct, although I regret the impression this must create.)

"Not in the slightest," Bosworth said hospitably, handing his guest a glass of sherry. *"In fact, we'd be pleased if you'd join us for dinner."*

"Delighted." The fox lifted his glass. *"Cheers."*

"Cheers to you," said the badger, and they sat down on either side of the fire. *"I must say, dear fellow, you're looking well."* In speaking thus, Bosworth was observing the Thirteenth Badger Rule of Thumb, which asserts that it is impolite to inquire about missing ears (or parts of ears), torn fur or feathers, missing paws, and other injuries. Animals are prone to accident and the world is full of traps, snares, and hunting parties. Most would agree with Bosworth's mother, who always liked to remind him, *"Least said, soonest mended."*

"I've been on a bit of a holiday," the fox allowed, swirling his sherry. *"Nothing like a change of scene to renew the old spirit, what?"*

"Glad to hear it." Bosworth gestured diffidently toward a table, whereon lay a copy

of Miss Potter's book, *The Tale of Jemima Puddle-Duck*. *"I was a bit concerned that perhaps you had suffered some serious damage when you made good your escape."*

"Oh, blast," said the fox disgustedly. *"You've read it, then?"*

The badger nodded.

"A wretched book, of course," the fox went on in an irritable tone. *"The author may know a thing or two about ducks, but she has not an idea in her head about foxes."*

Bosworth might have protested, for he thought Miss Potter's story quite amusing. She'd got the fox to a T. But he could see why Reynard might have taken offense, so he said nothing.

There was a moment's silence, as the fire cracked and popped. *"Speaking of ducks,"* remarked the fox, *"I don't suppose you've heard what's happened to that one, have you? Jemima, I mean."* He said this with such a studied carelessness that Badger immediately understood that it was the very question he had come to ask.

"As a matter of fact, I have," said the badger slowly. *"I understand that she is beginning a new family."*

"A new family?" exclaimed the fox, and the badger heard the consternation in his

162

voice. But nothing further could be said, for at that moment the door opened, and Jetsam, Flotsam's twin, put her head through.

"Parsley's just dishing up, sir. She says it's sausage and potato pancakes tonight and hopes you won't mind coming right along, for she doesn't like the pancakes to go soft."

"We're on our way," Badger replied heartily, pushing himself out of his chair. *"Tell Parsley we'll need another plate. Fox will be with us."* To the fox, he added, *"Come along, Reynard, old fellow. Everyone will be glad to see you."*

The other animals — Primrose Badger and her daughter Hyacinth and son Thorn, a pair of itinerant hedgehog brothers, Old Templeton Toad, and an assortment of mice — had already gathered in the dining hall, a capacious chamber, which boasted a large table, a roaring fire, and a mantle hung with twinkling brasses and decorated with drinking mugs and bits of interesting moss and pretty rocks collected by various visiting youngsters. The ceiling soared up into the dusky darkness (badgers like to construct high-ceilinged rooms for their social gathering-places) and tunnels shot off in various directions, most of the entries hung with heavy draperies to keep out the drafts.

Badger made introductions, and everyone exchanged pleasant greetings. And in case you are concerned, I must tell you that when animals are gathered together under the aegis of comradeship and hospitality, predator and prey restrain their appetites (on the one hand) and their terrors (on the other), and get along quite nicely, which I daresay ought to be a lesson to us all.

When Parsley (The Brockery cook) had served up the sausages and potato pancakes, with mushrooms and mashed parsnips and slices of hearty brown bread and butter, everyone fell to the food with such good appetite that conversation lagged. But with second helpings and glasses of elderflower lemonade, the conversation became animated, and all were eager to trade stories of the day's experiences.

Thorn, a handsome young badger whom Bosworth hoped might grow up and take his place someday, said that he had come across a large wasp nest in a hollow tree beside the brook in Penny Wood and reported its location so that the other badgers, who are exceedingly fond of wasp grubs, could go and have a picnic.

The hedgehog brothers hesitantly (hedgehogs are shy and want prompting) told of having been at the village fête on

164

Saturday. They reported that the sudden afternoon rain scattered the fête-goers and muddied Post Office Meadow so beautifully that a great many earthworms actually swam to the surface to keep from being drowned. After the dancing was over and everyone had gone home, the brothers had had a jolly good feast. They recommended the Post Office Meadow earthworms highly, in case others found themselves in the neighborhood on a damp night.

Primrose said that she and Hyacinth had been in the Tidmarsh Manor garden and had seen young Caroline Longford out for a walk with her governess and Caroline's guinea pigs, Tuppenny and Thruppenny. Hearing this, Bosworth brightened, for little Tuppenny had played a brave role in the Great Raid, and it was good to have word of him. (If you haven't read about the animals' rescue of Primrose and Hyacinth from the badger-baiting, known thereafter as the Great Raid, you'll find the story in *The Tale of Holly How.*) Primrose noted that it was especially good to know that little Tuppenny had a friend, and would no longer have to go on adventures alone. A single guinea pig must, in her opinion, be a very lonely creature.

Bosworth, always eager for news of the

district, turned to the fox. *"You said you'd been staying at Thorny Field, Fox. Are the gypsies still there?"*

"They are," said the fox, buttering a slice of brown bread. *"As it happens, I was there this morning when Captain Woodcock stopped for a talk with Taiso Kudakov, the chief. Official business."*

"The captain is the Justice of the Peace," Bosworth explained to the table at large, in case any did not know. To the fox, he said, *"Official business, eh?"*

Reynard nodded. *"There was some excitement in the village at the weekend, I understand."* He eyed the near-empty platter in the middle of the table. *"My dear Parsley, your pancakes and sausages are first-rate. My compliments."*

Parsley colored prettily. *"Thank you, sir. Are we ready for rum cake, then? The sauce is keeping warm on the cooker. I'll just pop out to the kitchen and get it."*

"Excitement?" Thorn asked curiously. *"Besides the fête, d' you mean, sir?"*

"Had to do with a baby," said the fox. *"If nobody minds,"* he added apologetically, and helped himself to the last potato pancake.

"A baby?" chorused Primrose and Hyacinth, in wide-eyed unison.

166

"An abandoned baby," said the fox, and took the last sausage as well. *"A human baby,"* he added, to clear up any confusion. *"A girl child, a fortnight old or so, I understand."*

"Oh, dear!" chorused the hedgehogs. They themselves had been orphans from a young age, their mother having died under a wagon wheel on the Kendal Road in front of the Sawrey Hotel. They left flowers at the spot several times a year, which suggests that animals, like humans, do mourn their losses.

"And p'rhaps stolen, as well," the fox added. *"The child was left in a basket on the doorstep at Hill Top Farm on Saturday."*

"Left in a basket!" Primrose cried. *"How can anyone do such a thing?"* Primrose herself was a careful mother, always looking out for the health and well-being of Hyacinth and Thorn.

"Indeed," the fox said. He looked reprovingly down his long nose. *"But Miss Potter doesn't fancy babies, it seems. She handed the infant off to Captain Woodcock's sister."*

"Ahem," said the badger, feeling that Reynard was being unkind to Miss Potter, perhaps in retaliation for his treatment in her book. *"Well, in defense of Miss Potter, she has a farm to manage and elderly parents*

in London. I expect Miss Woodcock has more time to spare for babies."

"*And I don't see how Miss Potter could* not *like children,*" Thorn said, with a very grown-up air. "*She certainly understands what they want in the way of stories. That latest book was jolly good.*" He stopped, seeing the look on the fox's face. "*Well, I thought so, anyway,*" he said, trying to cover his confusion. "*But then, I'm not a —*" He bit his lip, realizing that he was only getting in deeper.

The fox gave a nonchalant shrug. "*Be that as it may. In the event, Miss Woodcock is keeping the baby whilst the captain investigates the crime. Perhaps two crimes,*" he amended. "*Kidnapping and abandonment.*"

"*Kidnapping!*" squeaked one of the hedgehogs excitedly.

"*Abandonment!*" shrilled the other, rising half out of his chair.

" *'Twas gypsies done it,*" said old Templeton Toad, groping blindly for his lemonade. Primrose put the glass in his hand and he drank thirstily. "*Bad 'bout babes, them gypsies. As soon steal one as look at it. Why, when I was a lad, gypsies nabbed a babe right out of its pram in Kendal High Street whilst its mother was buying apples.*"

"What happened?" asked Hyacinth apprehensively.

"A world of fuss was made, but t' poor babe was never got back. Disappeared right off t' face of t' earth. Ever 'body said 'twas gypsies pinched it."

He put down his glass and immediately knocked it over, requiring Primrose to dam the lemonade puddle with her napkin.

"D-d-d-disappeared!" wailed the littlest mouse, who had lost her twin sisters to a cat when she was very young. She began to cry. *"How d-d-d-dreadful!"*

"There, there, dear," Primrose said soothingly, applying her lemonade-damp napkin to the mouse's eyes. *"I'm sure it was got back. Babies may be gone for a time, but they're always got back in the end."*

"This 'un never 'twas," the old toad said stoutly. *"T' Big Folk said that gypsies put it to work, 'long with t' other babes they stole. Slav'ry, y'know. They pinch ponies, too."*

The mouse broke into fresh tears. The hedgehogs looked as if they would like to cry, as well, but the fox frowned sternly at them and they subsided into hiccups.

"The usual suspects, gypsies and foxes," the fox said darkly. *"Big Folk always have to have someone to blame when a criminal act occurs. In case you haven't noticed,"* he

added, with a significant look at the toad, who fell into a fit of coughing.

"What did the gypsies tell the captain about the baby?" asked the badger. He had the uncomfortable feeling that the serious crimes they were discussing were not fit for younger animals' ears.

"That they knew nothing about it," the fox replied. *"That's what they told the captain to his face, and that's what they said 'mongst themselves after he left, so I suppose we can take it as truth. For once, the gypsies didn't do it. Nor foxes."* He slanted another dark look at the hiccupping hedgehogs, who stuffed their napkins in their mouths and slipped down in their chairs so that only their little black eyes could be seen above the cloth.

Parsley appeared with the rum cake on a platter and a dish of sauce. Primrose, catching Bosworth's meaningful glance, got up from the table.

"I think," she said in a motherly tone, *"that the youngsters will have their desserts in the kitchen. You, too, Mr. Toad. Your feet must be cold — you can put them up on the fender."*

"There's tea in the kitchen, too," Parsley added helpfully. *"And everyone may have an extra spoonful of cream. Come along, now."*

Suddenly recovered from their grief by the

anticipation of cream, the little animals trooped out, and the toad groped after them. The badger, the fox, and young Thorn were left with the rum cake, and elderflower wine succeeded the lemonade.

Badger, now very serious, said, *"But whose babe can this be, Fox? I've not heard of any born in the Land Between the Lakes in the past fortnight. I'm usually told, for the record."* By the record, he meant the *History,* of course, which included births and deaths.

"Ah, whose? That's the mystery, isn't it?" said the fox, leaning back in his chair.

"Might be an off-comer's child," Thorn suggested.

"Next thing you know," the fox added bitterly, *"Captain Woodcock will come looking for me, wanting to know whether I did it."*

Badger chuckled. *"Oh, come, now, Fox. If it were a chicken or duck gone missing, they might think of you. But I don't suppose anyone will imagine that a fox stole that baby and left it on Miss Potter's doorstep."*

The fox laughed and changed the subject. *"With regard to ducks — you mentioned earlier that Jemima Puddle-duck is starting a new family. I understand from another source that she's been confined to quarters — probably that collie is keeping her close. Any idea where she might be?"*

The badger shifted uneasily. While in his view it was not a crime for a fox to eat a duck (such was, after all, the nature of foxes and ducks), he was not inclined to be an accessory before the fact. On the other hand, there was the Third Badger Rule of Thumb, generally thought of as the Aiding and Abetting Rule: *One must be helpful to one's fellow creatures, large and small, for one never knows when one will require help oneself.* (We humans observe a similar maxim, although mostly in the breach. We call it the Golden Rule.)

And the badger did have some information, as it happened, for a pair of mice had recently dropped in for tea on their way to Tidmarsh Manor, where they had been invited to move in with friends. At the table, they mentioned that they had spent the previous night in the Hill Top barn, where a certain misguided duck had been sitting for weeks and weeks on a clutch of eggs that showed no signs of hatching.

But as Bosworth hesitated, trying to frame a diplomatic reply, Thorn took the matter into his own paws. *"You might have a look in the Hill Top barn,"* he suggested helpfully.

"The barn?" the fox asked eagerly. "Where *in the barn, exactly?"*

Bosworth cleared his throat. *"Could be any-*

where," he replied. *"The mice who told us didn't have any specific information."* Under the table, he gave Thorn a warning kick in the shins. *"And if I were you, Fox, I'd keep a sharp eye out for that collie. Kep is said to be a first-rate watchdog. That old yellow dog still has some life in him, too."*

Thorn dropped his head quickly, coloring, and the badger knew that he understood. And later, when Reynard had gone and Bosworth had returned to the library to have a quiet smoke before bed, the young badger tapped on the door.

"I'm sorry, sir," Thorn said. *"I just didn't think."* He sighed. *"He's such a pleasant fellow. I completely forgot that he's a fox. He probably has designs on that duck."*

"I understand, young Thorn," Bosworth said sympathetically. *"But there's some truth in what he says about foxes and gypsies. When something happens, they're always blamed first. I doubt Fox intends any harm. I shouldn't worry about it, if I were you."*

Thorn bit his lip. *"But it was my fault. If anything happens to that duck, I shall be very sorry."*

"I understand your feelings, dear boy," Bosworth said. *"They testify to your honorable spirit. But you must remember the Eighteenth*

Badger Rule of Thumb: If a fox (or any other predator) is intent on helping himself to a sitting duck (or any other prey), there's nothing of consequence a badger can (or should) do about it."

"I suppose," Thorn said dubiously. He paused. *"Are the Rules of Thumb always right?"*

Bosworth frowned, for he had never considered the question. *"Well, it is only a rule of thumb, I suppose — that is, a method derived from practice or experience, without any basis in scientific knowledge."*

"So it could be wrong?" Thorn persisted. *"Not to be disrespectful, sir, but if you had obeyed this rule, you would never have organized the Great Raid, and my mother and sister would both be dead."*

Bosworth was a simple badger, and had no head for moral conundrums. In a soothing voice, he replied, *"That may be, my boy. That may very well be. But this is not something we're going to solve tonight. So pull up a chair and I'll read a chapter from the* History *while you roast a few chestnuts in the fire."*

And that's what they did, Bosworth and Thorn together, in a cozy, companionable sort of way. But while they said nothing more about the fox or the duck, a cloud of gloom seemed to have settled over the both of them, and the joy had gone out of the evening.

Each of them felt that Jemima Puddle-duck's death warrant had been signed and sealed at their dinner table that evening, and both of them felt very sorry.

11
CAPTAIN WOODCOCK CONSULTS

The next day (that would be Tuesday) dawned clear and fair, with the promise of a bright summer morning and a fine afternoon. Miles Woodcock drove his Rolls-Royce along the narrow road to Hawkshead. It was a short trip and uneventful, except when he pulled his motor car onto the narrow verge to allow the horse-drawn brewery wagon from Ambleside to pass. His right front wheel struck a sharp rock and the air went out of his tyre. This dismaying event became even more dismaying when the captain opened the boot and discovered that he was not carrying a spare.

It was a warm day, and by the time Miles had patched the punctured tyre and pumped it up with his hand pump, his shirt and waistcoat were drenched with sweat and he wished fervently that he had ridden his horse. The trouble was the road. There was a great deal more traffic these days, and the right-of-way should be widened and paved. But that would require removing several stone walls and hedges and any number of trees. There was considerable opposition to that. Most of the local people resisted the cutting of trees, an attitude that Miles attributed to their general resistance to any kind of progress.

As the captain resumes his journey, I will take a few moments to tell you about his destination: the quaint little market town of Hawkshead. If you visit today, you will find it much as was on the day of our story, and several hundred years before that. It was established by a Norseman named Haukr in the ninth century, which makes it a true medieval village.

And like other medieval villages, Hawkshead is not built around a green. Instead, its narrow streets dart off in all directions, higgledy-piggledy, under the beneficent gaze of St. Michael and All Angels, the church that crowns the hill overlooking the town. One of these streets bears the descriptive name of Rag, Putty and Leather Street, so called for the tailors, cobblers, and painters who had businesses there. It is also called Wordsworth Street, for the poet William Wordsworth boarded in Anne Tyson's home there, whilst he was attending the local grammar school. The cottage is now a bed-and-breakfast, but at the time of our story (or shortly before) it housed Tyson's Shop, where our Miss Potter once bought two striped petticoats.

Miles drove across the bridge over Black Beck, left his motor car near the old grammar school, and made his way along the cobbled main street to Red Lion Square, to the office of the legal firm of Heelis and Heelis. The two solicitors, cousins, handled a great many of the legal transactions in the district, and could be counted on to know what was going on at any given moment.

Miles was just approaching the Heelis office when the door opened and Will Heelis stepped out, his bowler hat on his head and a leather briefcase in his hand.

"Why, hullo, Miles," Will said with a grin. He was a tall, athletic, good-looking man, a bachelor, and although he was painfully shy with women, he was less so with men and not at all with longtime friends. "You're out and about early this morning."

"I've come to see you, Will," Miles said. "Have you time for a cup of tea? P'rhaps we might go to the tea shop round the corner."

A few minutes later (it takes only a few minutes to get anywhere in Hawkshead), the two men were settled at a table beside a white-curtained window looking across a cobbled street to Thimble Hall. The proprietress brought them two china cups, a pot of tea, and a plate of seed wigs — small, sweet cakes covered with caraway seeds — hot from the oven.

"Well, Miles," Will said, stirring his tea. "How did the fête go on Saturday? I wanted to come and dance with the Morris men, but the Hawkshead bowlers had a match in Appleby, and I was obliged to take part."

"We got a good drenching," Miles replied. "No one complained but the trippers who forgot their umbrellas. The rest of us were glad of the rain." He paused. "Who won the match?"

"Oh, we did, of course." Biting into his seed cake, Will added, "Haven't been in Sawrey for some time. Your sister is well, I trust."

Miles nodded, brightening. "Yes, Dimity is well, indeed. In fact, we are having a small dinner on Saturday night. We'd both like you to come."

"Saturday night," Will said in a thoughtful tone. "I'm rather afraid that I have a prior —"

Miles picked up his cup. "Miss Potter is coming, as well. It will be a small party, just the four of us."

"I believe I'm free, after all," Will said. "I should love to come."

Miles was pleased. For the past year or so, he had been trying to arrange things so that his sister and his best friend would fall in love. He couldn't understand why Dimity was so slow at recognizing what a comfortable life she would have with Will Heelis. She couldn't argue that Will was unattractive. Athletic, fit, and trim, he had firm features, fine eyes, and thick brown hair that fell boyishly across his forehead. His character couldn't be faulted, either, for his good judgment, his amiability, and the steadiness of his temper were remarked by everyone who knew him. He was keen on fishing, bowling, golf, and cricket, and followed the local hunt as often as he could spare the time. (All of this endeared him to Miles, of course, who loved nothing better than an afternoon with gun or rod.) All round, in all ways, no man in the district was more respected or better liked than Will Heelis. Christopher Kittredge couldn't hold a candle to him.

Miles frowned when he thought of that wretched Kittredge, who had so completely monopolized Dimity at the dance on Saturday night. Kittredge, whose family had lived at Raven Hall for a great many years, had lost an eye and an arm and got his face badly scarred in the war. Miles could scarcely object to that, of course — Kittredge was brave enough. What he objected to was the man's appalling want of judgment. He had had the bad sense to marry a woman (an actress!) who turned out to be the worst sort of adventuress, and the cloak of scandal had clung round him ever since. No sensible woman — Dimity most of all — should have anything to do with him after such a disgrace. To ally herself to this fellow would be to associate herself with his shame. It was, of course — of course! — entirely out of the question.

With this in mind, after the dance, Miles had spoken to his sister about the impropriety of Kittredge's attentions. She had listened thoughtfully, and to his relief, had not raised any objection. But then, he had always found Dimity sweetly compliant. There had never been a serious disagreement between them, and there never would. So, in a celebratory mood, he had proposed a dinner party, with Will Heelis and Miss Potter as their guests. It was high time his sister found herself a suitable husband.

Will, for his part, had not a clue that his friend had it in mind to turn him into a brother-in-law. He was happily enjoying his tea and seed wig when Miles put his hand into his waistcoat pocket.

"I want you to have a look at something, Will." He took out a small object, wrapped in a bit of tissue, and handed it to Will. "Ever seen anything like this?"

Will put down his cup, unwrapped the tissue, and was surprised at the weight of the signet ring he held in his fingers. The ring was gold, with a setting of twisted gold wire. The stone was a large orange-red cornelian, carved with strange-looking hieroglyphics.

"I've seen other pieces of jewelry made from Egyptian scarabs," he said, studying it, "but none nearly so fine." He held it up so that the sunlight through the window gave the cornelian a mysterious glow. "How did you come by it?"

"It came from Miss Potter," Miles said. "It was in the basket with the baby."

Will stared at his friend incredulously. "Miss Potter has a *baby?*" He was accustomed to surprises from Miss Potter, whom he liked very much — but a baby was rather shocking, especially since he had not heard that the lady was married. He had not seen her for some months, though, and he supposed that anything was possible. He was conscious of a sharp disappointment, but only barely. Will Heelis, like many other British men, was not always aware of his feelings.

Miles chuckled dryly. "Yes, the lady has done it again," he said, and told about the baby girl Miss Potter had found on her doorstep and brought to Tower Bank House on Sunday morning. "Dimity is having the time of her life," he added, with a significant look. "My sister likes nothing better than playing mother, you know. Pity she has no children of her own."

Will was not thinking of his friend's sister's maternal ambitions. He was thinking of Miss Potter and (although he was only vaguely aware of this) feeling very relieved to learn that she was not married, after all. In his estimation, she was observant, forthright, and very sensible. — Pretty, too, with a shy, quiet softness that he found unusually appealing, although there was no point in thinking that way about her. (If we were to look deeply into Will's thoughts at this moment, however, we would most likely find that he had no clear idea of what "that way" meant. He was not even aware that he regretted the fact that Miss Potter's heart still belonged to the fiancé she had lost a few years before.)

He pulled his attention back to the ring.

"You said this was found in the basket. Any idea where it might have come from?"

"Miss Potter caught a glimpse of the old lady who left the baby at Hill Top. Might be one of the gypsies camped at the foot of Broomstick Lane. And the child is dark-haired and dark-eyed — she could easily be a gypsy baby. With that in mind, I spoke yesterday with Taiso Kudakov, the Romany chief."

Will nodded. "Ah, yes, Kudakov. A shrewd man. Very able."

"You know him, then?" Miles glanced up. "Is he truthful?"

"I know him. As to truth —" Will chuckled. "Perhaps it's best to say that he's true to his purposes, whatever they may be."

Will was acquainted with the gypsy bands that traveled through the district in their wooden caravans, mostly in the summer, camping in vacant fields, selling horses and other wares and offering itinerant labor. They found this traditional way of life much harder these days. Many of the farmers who had once eagerly bought their horses or relied on them for help with harvesting or shearing now regarded them as nuisances or worse, and no longer welcomed them as laborers. Men like Kudakov were finding it harder to locate work to support their families — a shame, Will thought, for there was certainly work to be done and families to support.

"Perhaps it wasn't to Kudakov's purpose to tell me the truth," Miles said. "He claimed total ignorance where the infant was concerned."

Will glanced at the ring. "Yet this piece is certainly something a gypsy would favor. What did he say when you showed it to him?"

"I didn't, since he denied knowing anything about the child. I was hoping he would say she was theirs — although why they would abandon one of their own has me mystified. That's not like them. They are especially affectionate toward their children — as well they might be," he added dryly, "since they raise them to work. Even their daughters."

Will could have pointed out that the local folk raised their children to work, boys and girls alike. But he only said, "The baby doesn't belong to a local family?"

Miles shook his head. "Dimity says not, and she would know. She has charge of the Parish Mothers' Box." He gave Will a pointed look. "Dimity is certainly enjoying herself with this infant, even though she has only temporary custody. I'm sure she will be a wonderful mother to her own brood. She's awf'lly domestic, you know."

Will had a dim suspicion that he was missing the point, which seemed to have something to do with Dimity and infants. "The Mothers' Box?" he hazarded tentatively.

"Clothing, nappies, that sort of thing. A sort of traveling infant-kit. Dimity sees that it goes wherever there's a new baby. She's very good that way. I tell her it's because she's frustrated about not having one of her own."

"Ah," Will said. "You're telling me that there are no new babies in the parish."

It must be observed in justice to Will that he had never knowingly been the target of anyone's matchmaking, and so entirely failed to notice that he was supposed to imagine Dimity as a potential mother for his own children. He merely wondered whether there might be something more to the remark about the box and let it go, feeling that if Miles had anything very important to tell him, he would say it straight out, rather than beating about the bush.

"Right-o." Miles put down his cup with what seemed to be disappointment. "And if Kudakov is to be believed, there are no infants among the gypsies, at least none that they've lost track of. So we must look elsewhere." He paused. "I was hoping you could suggest how we might identify the ring."

Will pushed back his chair, happy to have something concrete to deal with. "Let's drop in on Mr. Aftergood, shall we? He does a fair bit of pawning. If he's seen the ring, he'll remember it."

The door to Mr. Aftergood's tiny shop was located up a narrow stone stair behind the Crown and Mitre Hotel, under a painted sign that read KURIOS & KNICK-KNACKERY. Crammed to the ceiling with dusty treasures, strange carvings, and odd lots of furniture, the place reminded Miles of the Old Curiosity Shop in Dickens's novel by that name. The light inside was dim and opalescent, and the air seemed filled with a perpetual, dusty twilight.

Mr. Aftergood came toward them with jerky, shuffling steps as if he were one of his own mechanical curios, wound up and set into motion. He was a tiny old man in a coat and trousers of rusty black that were much too large for him, with a dirty red silk kerchief knotted under his chin, gold-rimmed glasses pushed up on his head, and deep wrinkles that nearly hid his eyes. He peered at them as Will explained why they

187

had come, then took the signet ring and looked at it for a very long time.

"Mmm," he said at last, in a hoarse, cracked whisper, addressing himself to Will. "Oh, aye, sir. I may've seen it before, may have. Curious, isn't it, sir? And very fine. Oh, yes, very fine, sir, very." He gave it another appreciative look. "Likely to've been brought back from Egypt, I do believe, sir."

"My friend and I couldn't quite make out the engraving on the scarab," Will said. "Will you have a look?"

"On the scarab, sir?" Mr. Aftergood picked up a jeweler's loupe, fastened it over his head, and peered at the ring. "Indeed, sir, I can make it out, but it's hieroglyphics, sir, and I don't speak Egyptian." He gave a crackly chuckle. "Bless me, I don't speak Egyptian, now, do I, sir?" This seemed to tickle his funny-bone. "Don't speak Egyptian, no, sir," he chortled. "Never have, sir, never will."

"No, nor I, Mr. Aftergood," Will said amiably, and joined in the laugh.

Still chortling, the old man brought the ring close to his eye, turning and squinting. "Howsoever, I can read the engraving on the *back* of the stone. Plain English, it is, sir, although I don't hold with scratchin' mod-ren names on ancient stones. I don't for a fact, sir, don't for a fact. Not respectful, sir. Not respectful of fine old stones, sir."

Miles frowned, annoyed with himself for failing to look on the back of the stone. "What does it say?"

Mr. Aftergood put the ring on the counter. "Says the same thing it said the last time I saw it." He scowled. "Says 'To R.K., Forever,' sir. That's what it says, sir. What it says, for a fact. 'To R.K., Forever.' "

Will picked up the ring, examined the engraving, and handed it to Miles.

"R.K.," Miles muttered, rewrapping the ring and putting it into his pocket. Now they were getting somewhere! These had to be the owner's initials.

"You say you have seen this ring before, Mr. Aftergood," Will said. "Do you recall the circumstance?"

The old man tapped a yellowed fingernail against a tooth, looking doubtful. "The circumstance. The circumstance," he whispered. He scratched his head, as if he were trying to locate the spot in his brain where the fact was stored. "The circumstance."

"You saw it here, at the shop?" Will prompted.

Mr. Aftergood pondered, squinted,

scratched, and finally nodded, very slowly. "May have, sir. May have."

"Recently?" Miles asked, feeling a bit like charades. "Or long ago?"

"Not that long ago, sir, not that long ago," the old man said. He closed his eyes, as if he were consulting an inner calendar of dates but could not quite recall the page on which the occasion had been jotted down.

Miles sent Will an interrogatory glance, and Will gave a quick little nod. Miles reached into his pocket. "P'rhaps this might help you remember." He put a shilling on the counter. "A small consulting fee."

The old man's eyes opened slightly. "Why, I b'lieve 'twas brought in by a girl, sirs." He paused significantly.

"A girl?" Miles asked in some surprise. He added another shilling to the one on the counter.

"A girl, sirs. A girl." The old man scratched his head again, and then brought forth the fact as if it were one of his curios, blowing off the dust, rubbing it up with his sleeve, and laying it on the counter in front of them. "Left for a week, sirs, and redeemed," he said, with a note of triumph. "Redeemed with interest, I'm pleased to say. Redeemed!"

"Well, then," Will said cheerfully, "you will

be able to show us your pawn book, won't you? It will have the girl's name in it, and an address."

Mr. Aftergood hung his head apologetically. "Don't keep a pawn book, sir," he whispered. "Don't do much pawning these days. Just now and then."

Miles bristled, about to say that perhaps a trip to the magistrate would persuade the pawnbroker to observe the law requiring him to keep his pawn book. But Will signaled silence and turned back to the old man.

"Well, then, Mr. Aftergood, perhaps you can describe the girl, and tell us where she was staying."

"Yellow hair, young, pretty," the old man said. He slid both coins off the counter and clinked them into his pocket. "A lady's maid, I'd say. Respectable, as you might say, sirs, rather than otherwise." He peered over his glasses. "If you take my meaning, sirs."

Miles leaned forward, frowning darkly. "It did not occur to you that the ring might be stolen?"

The old man shrugged his thin shoulders, as if to say that whether the ring was stolen or not was no business of his, now, was it?

"Well, then," Miles said, "do you have any idea where this girl might live?"

The old man shook his head. "Left the ring and said she'd call back t' redeem it. And so she did, sir. So she did." A bell rang in the back, and he lifted his head, listening. "That'd be my Anna. My wife. Wants her tea, I'm afraid." He grinned, showing two gold teeth. "A right terror without her tea, Anna is, sir. I daren't delay." And without another word, he turned and shuffled off.

"A right terror," Miles snorted disgustedly, as they made their way through the dusty aisle to the door. "We didn't get much for those two shillings, did we?"

"He pointed out the initials," Will said, "which I'd missed. And there's the bit about the girl."

"But we don't know where she lives," Miles said.

Something stirred in a heap of rags by the door, and a pair of bright eyes emerged out of the shadows — bright eyes in a dusty, lively face, under a mop of uncombed hair. It was an urchin, boy or girl, Miles could not make out which. She, or he, was accompanied by the largest black cat he had ever seen, with eyes like glowing green fire.

"I'll tell ye where she lives," said the child, and stuck out its grubby hand.

Miles frowned down at the dirty face.

"How do you know that?"

"Carried her parcels there m'self, din't I?" chirped the child. He jumped out into the light, and Miles saw that he was a boy. At least, he was wearing trousers, of some sort of sacking material, held up with a pair of red braces. Under the wrapping of scarves, his shirt was marginally clean, and he was barefoot.

"Carried her parcels right the way home, din't I? Right to t' door, though it was a far way t' go 'n a far way t' come back." He picked up the cat, which draped itself across his shoulder like a furry black stole, purring loudly. "Give me thruppence, too, din't she?"

"Did she?" Miles put his hand in his pocket and took out a thrup'nny bit. He held it up. "Yours, if you'll tell us where she lives. Truthfully, now."

The boy reached for the coin, but Miles held it just out of reach. "Where?"

The boy put his head on one side. " 'Tween Hawkshead and Near Sawrey, down Broomstick Lane, left at t' corner. Hawthorn House."

"Done," Miles said promptly, handing over the coin.

"Well done," said Will with a grin, and added another to it.

They left the boy jubilantly pocketing the coins and went down the stairs. "Hawthorn House," Miles said, when they reached the street. "That's near the gypsy encampment."

"Right," Will said. "The boy earned his pence, I'd say. It's a good three miles there and back."

"But I thought the place was vacant," Miles said, as they walked along the cobbled street. "I hadn't heard it was let." Which was odd. When someone moved into a house in the district — especially an important house — word got out. If someone was living at Hawthorn House, they had kept their residence secret.

"Nor had I," said Will. "The place is no longer in good repair. Had a rather unfortunate appearance, I always thought, with all those silly towers and turrets and pepper pot chimneys. Originally built for a gentleman from Bristol, as I recall, back in the 'forties. When he died, it was sold to an Army man." He thought a minute. "Villars, wasn't it?"

"Ah, yes," Miles said. "Villars. Major Rodney Villars. I met him a time or two, although he didn't live there long." He chuckled dryly. "Just long enough to cut down the hawthorns that gave the place its name

— which scandalized the villagers, of course. You know how they feel about trees. They predicted dire events, at least one of which came to pass. Villars went off to India and lost a leg in a carriage accident there. He's not been back since, and the place has developed a reputation for hauntings."

"And that's where the boy delivered the parcels for the girl with the ring," Will remarked. "I wonder how she came by it. And how it got into the basket with the baby."

"I wonder, as well," Miles replied. "I think I shall go there this afternoon, when I've finished my business, and see what I can learn."

Will grinned. "Intending to motor, are you? The last time I went that way, the lane wasn't fit for an automobile. Best to walk, if you value your tyres."

"Blast," Miles muttered. "I should have brought my horse." He paused. "Don't forget — Saturday night. Dimity will be *most* glad to see you, old chap. Most glad."

"Right-o," Will agreed cheerfully, and went on his way.

And just between you and me, if Will thought of Dimity Woodcock at all, it was only to wonder why her brother brought up

her name so often, and with such an odd
emphasis.

12
BEATRIX SAYS
GOODBYE

On Tuesday morning, Beatrix got up before dawn to give Bertram a hearty breakfast of sausages and eggs and drive him to the Windermere ferry in the farm's pony cart, pulled by Winston, the farm pony. At the landing, she bade Bertram safe journey and watched as the steam ferry, belching black smoke and heavily loaded with a charabanc, six passengers, and four horses, carried him across the lake. For a long time, he stood at the stern, waving.

She watched him go with a huge, hard lump in her throat. Bertram was the only one in her family — the only one in the whole, entire world — who truly understood her. They were alike in so many ways, the two of them, and it had always been comforting to know that they were of one mind when it came to dealing with Mama and Papa.

But now they were no longer quite alike.

Bertram was married. Beatrix could barely comprehend what he had done — not just marrying, but marrying someone of whom his parents would not approve and keeping his marriage secret. More, she could not ignore the sharp pang of envy she felt. Her brother now had a life of his own, separate, independent, apart from the family, apart from her. It might be a life based in secrecy and veiled in falsehoods, which must surely compromise the sweet innocence of its pleasures. But Bertram enjoyed love every day of his life, and companionship, and someone to share the work, the joys, and the pain. He had all these, and she did not. They were no longer alike.

Still, Beatrix couldn't bring herself to resent him, or even to judge him harshly for his refusal to face their parents' disapproval. Yes, perhaps he had been cowardly. And yes, it would have been better to stand up to the parents like a man, own that he was married, and take the consequences. But Papa was formidable, and Mama could be appallingly disagreeable. All Bertram wanted was what she herself wanted: peace and quiet and relief from the constant bombardment of their parents' likes and dislikes. What he had done, he had done, and she would not fault him for it.

Beatrix lifted Winston's reins. Bertram's situation, while dramatically changed from what she had imagined, changed nothing of her own. Norman was dead, and she would never have someone to share her life. She would never have love — but she had her farm, her books, and her animals, all of which together made up for a very great deal of everything else.

No, nothing had changed. Yet, at the same time, everything had changed, the whole world had changed! Bertram had found someone to love, someone to care for and be cared for in return. He was married. She felt suddenly bereft, as if a chapter had ended in her life, one that could never be reopened.

But Beatrix was not a person to dwell in the past. There was work to be done at the farm. She clucked to Winston, who put his shoulders into the harness willingly, although Ferry Hill was notoriously challenging. (Many unprincipled ponies refused to pull their load up its steep slope, and even Captain Woodcock's motor car had difficulties.) Winston stopped only once, near the Sawrey Hotel, where Miss Potter pulled him to the side of the road to allow a faster-moving trap to pass, heading in the direction of Near Sawrey. The pony took the opportunity to investigate a fresh bit of green grass, nibbling for a moment, exchanging a friendly greeting with a robin who happened by, and then getting on with the job.

It was a beautiful morning in the Land Between the Lakes, and there were a great many things for a pony — and a farm lady — to do.

13
MAJOR KITTREDGE
TAKES A MAJOR RISK

The trap that went speeding past Miss Potter and her pony belonged to Major Kittredge. He was driving faster than he ought for a reason — a very good reason. We are about to find out what it was.

Christopher Kittredge was no fool. He had seen Captain Woodcock's narrowed eyes and darkening expression as he and Dimity were waltzing at the fête on Saturday night — dancing to the romantic "Blue Danube," which Christopher had particularly requested the band to play as a change from the country dances that filled the program. If the captain's look could have killed, Christopher would have been dead by now, although he would have died a happy man, he thought, remembering how lightly and gracefully Dimity had moved and how warmly and sweetly she had smiled.

Now, a sensible man, or one less brave,

might have been daunted by the captain's obvious disapproval. But as he had proved during the war, Christopher Kittredge was exceedingly brave, and he had been emboldened by the experience of holding Dimity in his arms. His heart was now telling him what to do: "By Jove, Kittredge, it's time to buck up and be a man!"

His heart also told him that he should act upon his convictions, seize time by the forelock, and strike while the iron was hot. (Odd, how hearts always seem to speak in clichés.) So he got his horse and trap and was driving as fast as he could up the road to Near Sawrey and Tower Bank House. He hoped to find the captain out and the captain's sister in, because he had something important to say to her that he did not want her brother to hear. He had composed a carefully reasoned speech of apology and entreaty, and his heart was telling him that there was no time like the present to deliver it.

To Christopher's joy, the captain was indeed out. (As you know, he was at this very moment in Hawkshead, eating a seed wig and hinting unsuccessfully to Will Heelis that Will ought to marry Dimity.)

The lady in question, on the other hand, was very much in at the present moment, for she was tending happily to the needs of the newest lady of the house, Baby Flora. As a matter of fact, Dimity was engaged in pinning on the baby's fresh nappy. Her face was flushed and smiling with this necessary effort, her sleeves were rolled to the elbows, and her light brown hair was in a charming disarray, kissed by the sun that shone through the window for just this purpose. She was, in short, as delightfully and desirously lovely as a dairymaid in one of Thomas Hardy's novels.

Once Christopher got over his surprise at seeing Dimity Woodcock with a baby in her arms, he was struck by how entirely natural and altogether fetching she looked. The sweet sight so warmed his heart (which as you have probably guessed was already pretty warm) that he forgot every word of his carefully planned out speech and blurted his feelings right then and there, with no preamble or preface or other sort of silly introduction. He did just manage to avoid falling down on his knees, but otherwise, he said most of the words that men have been saying to women ever since the whole foolish business of formal marriage proposals began.

"Dimity, what a fool I have been, what an utter, total, complete, unredeemable fool! I know how presumptuous this must sound, after all that has happened. But I love you, dear. I love you with all my heart and soul. I love you to the very breadth and height my soul can reach." (Christopher had been reading the poetry of Elizabeth Barrett Browning and could have spilled out the entire business, all the way down to "I shall but love thee better after death" if it had been necessary.) "I know you need time to consider, and I daren't press you for a decision now. But I beg and implore you to tell me that you return my feelings, if only just a little bit."

Dimity's face was pink, her eyes cast down. In a very low voice, she said just one word: "Yes."

Christopher blinked. Of all the things Dimity might have said to him, this single word was the last thing he expected. He was so taken aback that he was nearly speechless.

"Y-y-yes?" he stammered.

She raised her eyes, searching his. "Yes," she said, barely above a whisper. "I feel as you do, Christopher."

And then our brave major proved his mettle. He stopped saying anything at all and got busy with doing something, which in this case involved taking Baby Flora away from the lady and placing her back in her basket, and then putting his own arms (or rather, his arm, since he had only one) around Dimity and kissing her soundly and at length. Not just once, either, but several times, with passion, until both of them had to break away to catch their breaths.

And then he spoilt it all by dropping his arm, hanging his head, and saying, in a muffled voice, "I'm so sorry, Dimity. Really, I am. I don't know what came over me. I —"

Dimity put her finger to his lips. "Don't apologize, Christopher. I'm glad you kissed me. I've been wanting you to."

The major blinked, astonished. But of course. He should have known that Dimity would speak her heart. That was the sort of woman she was, honest and true and spunky — yes, above all, spunky. That was why he loved her.

"And that business about forgiving you," she went on, now very pink indeed. "It's really not necessary. Not a bit of it. There is nothing at all to forgive."

The major set his mouth. He had come to say something, and even though the lady already seemed on the verge of agreeing to his proposal, he was going to confess to the whole bloody business and get it off his chest, once and for all.

"Yes," he said urgently, "there is something to forgive, Dimity, and I've got to get it out. I've been a beast. I should have come straight back here to you after the war, never mind how I looked. I should have thrown myself at your feet and told you straight off that I loved you and needed you, instead of going off to London and losing my head and marrying that woman." His voice broke. He had got to the hard part, the risky part. "I've been all kinds of a fool, Dim. But all I want now is for us to spend the rest of our lives together. I want to make you happy. I want to take care of you. I want us to be married. Please say yes."

"No," Dimity said sadly.

"No?" Christopher stepped back in some confusion. "But if you love me —"

"Loving you is one thing, Christopher," Dimity said, in a voice clearly meant to be sensible but marred by a sad quaver. "Marrying you is another. My brother does not —"

"I know," the major said. "He's made it quite clear that he doesn't approve of me. He thinks I'm quite unsuitable." He leaned forward and seized her hands eagerly. "But you — you aren't bound by his wishes, are you? Can't you — can't you be guided by your own desires?"

"I've made my home with Miles for over ten years," Dimity said. "I owe him a certain respect, a certain —" She broke off, turning her head away. "I must take his feelings into account, Christopher. I cannot go against him."

"But you must speak to him," he urged. "You'll tell him how we . . . how you feel."

She repossessed her hands. "I don't know, Christopher. I need to think."

"I don't want you to think," Christopher said. "Thinking muddles everything. I only want you to *feel.*" He put his hand on her shoulder, bent forward, and kissed her, gently. "May I call again? Tomorrow?" And then he remembered. "Oh, blast. I need to go up to London. I won't be back until late on Thursday."

"That's just as well." Dimity managed a smile. "You've given me a great deal to think about while you're gone."

He nodded distractedly. Looking at her made him positively woolly-minded. He was about to kiss her again when Elsa Grape appeared in the doorway, a note in her hand.

"From Miss Potter, mum," she said, with an inquiring glance at Christopher. "Brought from Hill Top by the Jennings boy. He's waitin' fer an answer."

Dimity read the note, then went to the desk, took out a piece of stationery, and wrote a reply. "Send that to Miss Potter with the boy, Elsa." The baby began to fuss, and she added, "Oh, and heat a bottle for Flora, will you, please?"

"Yes, mum," Elsa said, and with another, even more curious glance at Christopher, left the room.

Christopher looked at the baby in the basket. "Whose baby?" he asked.

"Well, that's the thing of it, you see," Dimity said, picking the baby up and holding her against her shoulder. "She was abandoned on Miss Potter's doorstep on Saturday afternoon, while we were all at the fête. Miles has been looking for her mother, but he's had no success yet."

"Abandoned!" Christopher exclaimed. "That's appalling!"

Dimity nodded. "She doesn't belong to any of the families in the village — we know that much, at least. And not in the district, as near as we've been able to discover."

Christopher took in the baby's dark hair and eyes. "A gypsy baby?" he hazarded. "They're camped on Broomstick Lane."

"Perhaps, although Miles asked yesterday, and they said they're not missing a baby. Wouldn't you think they'd claim her, if she were theirs? I know I would."

Dimity rested her cheek against the baby's hair, and Christopher thought how beautiful she looked, how sweet and motherly. He touched Dimity's cheek with his finger.

"Marry me, Dimity," he said urgently, "and if the baby's parents aren't found, we'll keep her. We'll give her a good home — her, and our own children. You'll be a wonderful mother."

Dimity raised her eyes, and Christopher saw that they brimmed with tears, and that her mouth was trembling. This time, he didn't bother to take the baby from her. He enfolded both of them in his one-armed embrace.

And that's how Elsa Grape found them, when she came back into the room with the baby's bottle.

14
THE VILLAGE IS FULLY INFORMED

It's a good thing that Major Kittredge and Dimity Woodcock were not able to hear the conversation in the kitchen at Tower Bank House that afternoon, after the luncheon washing-up was done. They would have been amused, embarrassed, enlightened, and irritated by turns, but mostly irritated.

The conversation involved three village ladies: Elsa Grape, of course; Hannah Braithwaite, the wife of the police constable; and Bertha Stubbs, Elsa's sister-in-law and custodian at the Sawrey School. Tabitha Twitchit and Crumpet were there as well, for the cats always accompanied Bertha on her summertime gossip rounds, at which tea and the hostess's specialty sweets were served. Bertha always dropped in first at Elsa's (jam tarts), then went through the hedge to Agnes Llewellyn (honey cake) at High Green Gate, and up the hill to Belle Green, where Mathilda Crook (gingersnaps) lived. Tabitha Twitchit usually stopped there, for Belle Green was her house, too.

"I've somethin' to tell," Elsa Grape announced with an air of barely suppressed excitement. She went to the door, looked both ways in the hall, and closed the door behind her securely. Then she sat down and reported what she had seen in the sitting room that morning.

"He kissed her?" Hannah Braithwaite exclaimed.

"He kissed her!" Bertha said, scowling. "That's a fine piccadillio!"

"Peccadillo, she means," translated Crumpet, who lived with Bertha and understood her when nobody else could. Crumpet did not even consider it an irony that she always understood Bertha when Bertha almost never understood *her.*

"He kissed her," Elsa said. "And then he kissed her again." She gave a gusty sigh. "It was seein' her with t' babe in her arms what did it Fair drove him out of his mind with love, it did."

When Elsa was not working, she was reading romantic novels. Her favorites were those in which the hero and the heroine were madly in love with each other, but their union was prevented (until the last chapter, sometimes even the very last paragraph) by some awful external force. The kiss she witnessed had completely overturned Elsa's views on the subject of Miss Woodcock and Major Kittredge. She had been as opposed to the match as one could possibly be, on the grounds of the major's scandalous past. Now, she was all for it.

Tabitha Twitchit, having already had all the jam tart she was likely to get, was sitting on the stone doorstep, washing her whiskers. *"But you said Miss Woodcock wouldn't have the major,"* she reminded Crumpet. *"And that Captain Woodcock had someone else picked out for his sister."* She gave a little purr of satisfaction. *"You see, Crumpet, you were wrong. Wrong, wrong, wrong."*

Beside her, Crumpet scowled. *"The captain will be livid when he hears about this,"* she predicted, and Bertha Stubbs agreed.

"T' captain will put a hard foot down on t' bus'ness," said Bertha, in an authoritative tone. "He woan't have his sister a-marryin' that man." She picked up her cup of tea and took a sip. "It'd discombooble t' whole village."

"Discombobulate," said Crumpet.

"Well, if he does put his foot down, I'll think it a pity," said Hannah, reaching for another jam tart. Elsa was known to make the best jam tarts in the parish, better even than Sarah Barwick, who sold hers, and had people queued up to buy. "Miss Woodcock ought to marry whosomever she likes and be happy."

"Even if t' major went and married an actress who was a'ready married?" Bertha asked with disdain. "That's bigamminy, that is. No sens'ble lady'll marry him after that bungalow."

"Bigamy," said Crumpet. *"You see, Tabitha? That's exactly what I said. No sensible lady will have him."*

"But love isn't sensible," Tabitha replied. She sighed. *"At least, not for me. I never let sense stand in the way of love."*

"Yes, I know," Crumpet said dryly. Tabitha had had more than one husband, and more litters of kittens than she could count. Crumpet enjoyed her freedom and saw no future in being tied down with kittens, even if only for a few months.

"Bungle, not bungalow," said Elsa. "Have another tart, Bertha."

"A bungle's only a bungle, not a crime," Hannah observed, taking a bite of tart. She could never bear to think ill of anyone. "Miss Woodcock 'ud make a fine mistress of Raven Hall."

Elsa frowned, not having thought that far

ahead. "But then who'd be mistress here?" she asked, getting up to replenish the plate of tarts from the store in the cupboard.

"Why, tha wud'st, Elsa," Hannah said, widening her eyes innocently. "And tha cud'st boss young Molly all tha lik'st, and choose t' menus all by thisel' — until t' captain takes a wife, o' course. And then she'll be mistress."

Bertha's smile had something of malice in it. "Speakin' of the captain takin' a wife, what dust tha think of Miss Potter, Elsa? Wud she do fer t' captain?"

Elsa put the plate on the table and sat down. "Miss Potter?" She narrowed her eyes. "Nae, Bertha, nae! Miss Potter's too sharp and bossy by half. T' captain needs a sweet, soft wife, like his sister."

Bertha laughed. "What Elsa means," she said to Hannah, "is that she wudn't be able to wrap Miss Potter around her finger t' way she wraps our Miss Woodcock. Ain't that right, Elsa?"

"I wudn't put it that way, Bertha," said Elsa stoutly. "I kin deal with Miss Potter, if I hast to."

"I agree with Bertha," Crumpet said with a chuckle. *"Miss Potter would never stand for Elsa's back talk, the way Miss Woodcock does. Elsa would have to change her tune."*

"That's the truth." For once, Tabitha agreed.

"What of t' baby?" asked Hannah, tactfully changing the subject. She did not enjoy it when Bertha and Elsa bickered, as they frequently did.

"What about her?" Elsa shrugged. "No diff'rent from any other babe — eats and sleeps and dirties her nappies." She smiled. "Sweet lit'le thing, though. And good."

"What do you mean, no diff'rent?" Bertha demanded indignantly. "She come from t' Folk, di'n't she?"

"The Folk?" Tabitha sat up straight, blinking. *"Which Folk?"*

"The Hawthorn Folk," Crumpet replied smugly. What luck! Once again, she knew something Tabitha didn't. *"Mustard told me. He saw one of them going over the wall in the Hill Top garden, the same afternoon the baby was delivered."*

"But where did the Folk get the baby?" Tabitha asked in a wondering tone.

Crumpet was glad that Hannah was speaking, for she didn't have an answer to Tabitha's question.

"Doan't tha be sae goosy, Bertha." Hannah rolled her eyes. "T' Folk are only old wives' tales."

"Shh!" Bertha spoke with real alarm, putting a warning finger to her lips. "They'll hear!"

Hannah gave a skeptical glance around the kitchen. "I doan't see nae Folk." She made a great show of peering beneath the table. "Nae Folk under here, neither." She appealed to Elsa. "Dust'a see 'em, Elsa?"

"Ta canst'na see 'em," Bertha said darkly, "but that doan't mean they ain't here. They're indivisible."

"Invisible," Crumpet said. *"The Folk can be anywhere."*

"So tell me," Hannah said with a disbelieving look, "where t' Folk got t' babe from in t' first place. Whose babe is she?" And then she answered her own question. "She's a gypsy babe, that's who, Bertha. Comes from t' gypsy camp. That's what my husband says, and he should know." And on that unassailable authority, Hannah sat back, triumphant.

But Elsa leant forward. "Your John doan't know ever'thing, Hannah, even if he be constable." She lowered her voice to a whisper. "I'll tell tha whose this babe is, 'cause I know fer sure. She belongs to —"

But at that moment, the upstairs bell rang. Elsa stood up and straightened her apron, all business. "Ta, ladies," she said loftily. "Miss Woodcock needs me."

"Elsa!" Bertha wailed.

"Elsa!" Hannah protested, "tha was tellin' us who —"

"Aye, I was," Elsa agreed. There was a glint in her eye. "But now I've work to do, so tha'll just have to wait. Come back tomorrow." With that, Elsa went off to do her duty.

Hannah made an unhappy noise, but she had no choice. Anyway, she had left a pot of vegetable soup simmering on the back of the kitchen range, so she went straight home to make sure that the children hadn't pulled it down and scalded the dog and made a mess on the floor.

But Bertha had time for more gossip. Trailed by the two cats, she went across the garden and through the hedge to High Green Gate Farm, where Agnes Llewellyn put the last spoonful of Earl Grey into the teapot. Whilst it was brewing, Bertha reported that Elsa Grape had with her very own eyes seen Major Kittredge kissing Miss Woodcock, who was holding the gypsy baby in her arms (the gypsy baby who had been stolen by the Folk and left on the doorstep at Hill Top Farm), and that unless the captain put an immediate stop to the business, there would be a wedding in the very near future. And of course, if that happened,

Tower Bank House would be without a mistress and Captain Woodcock without a wife. Which would leave the field wide open for Miss Potter. She would make a fine (if firm) wife for Captain Woodcock but would put Elsa Grape's nose quite out of joint.

Then Bertha put down her cup, looked at the clock, and remembered that if she didn't go straight home and put the tatie pie in the oven, there would be no dinner on the table that night, and Henry Stubbs would be quite out of patience with her.

The minute Bertha was out of sight, Agnes Llewellyn took off her apron, put on her straw hat with the pink ribbon roses, and walked across the street to the village shop, which was run by Lydia Dowling and her niece Gladys, who helped on Tuesdays and Thursdays. Agnes bought a tupp'ny twist of Earl Grey tea and a packet of hairpins.

As she was paying over her money, she told Lydia and Gladys (on their solemn promise not to tell another soul) that Miss Woodcock and Major Kittredge were planning to marry and adopt the gypsy baby as their own, which was dangerous (in Agnes's opinion) because the baby had been in the hands of the Folk since her birth, but no doubt a natural thing to do since the baby had dark hair and eyes, like Major Kittredge.

But Agnes for one was all in favor of the match, because she understood that Miss Potter had it in mind to marry Captain Woodcock, which meant that there wouldn't be room for Miss Woodcock at Tower Bank House, so it was good that the poor dear was going to Raven Hall. There wouldn't be room at Tower Bank for Elsa Grape, either, since she and Miss Potter would certainly not get along, so Elsa had better pack her bags.

A few minutes after Agnes had delivered this stunning news and gone home, Lydia asked Gladys if she would mind running to the post office to post a letter to Lydia's aunt in Portsmouth. Gladys, who always liked the opportunity to walk past the smithy, where Charlie Hotchkiss was helping Mr. Crook at the forge, was only too happy to oblige. (And happy to smile and wave to handsome Charlie Hotchkiss when he lifted his hammer in a salute, which made Gladys' heart beat very fast and her feet want to skip in an entirely unladylike way.)

And when Lucy Skead, the postmistress, happened to ask Gladys if she had heard any interesting gossip lately, Gladys was happy to oblige again. She related to Lucy (and Rose Sutton, who happened to be in the post office at the same time) that the baby Miss Potter had found on her doorstep looked enough like Major Kittredge to be his very own, and that Miss Woodcock had agreed to marry the major and be a mother to the little girl, and that Miss Potter and Captain Woodcock would be announcing their engagement in the next few days. As a consequence, Elsa Grape would no doubt be looking for different employment.

To which Rose replied this was all very interesting, and she was glad that Elsa would not have to look very far, because Mrs. Thompson, the vicar's cook-housekeeper, was going to Ambleside to take care of her mother. Elsa would be perfect for the vicar, who needed taking in hand. So, when Gladys got back to the shop, she was happy to tell Lydia that Elsa didn't have anything to worry about, since she could have a place at the vicarage when Miss Potter pitched her out.

And all of these various contributors could breathe more easily for the rest of the day, having sorted everyone's business to their satisfaction.

There is nothing like a village for managing affairs.

15

MISS POTTER AND MISS WOODCOCK GO CALLING

Quite unaware that her marital destiny was on the minds of the village, Beatrix went calling on Tuesday afternoon. She changed from her working dress into what she thought of as her "calling costume" — a ruffled shirtwaist, striped in blue and violet, a gray tweed skirt, and a straw hat with violet silk flowers — and drove Winston over to Tower Bank House, to collect Dimity Woodcock. The two of them had arranged by note that morning to drive the pony cart to Tidmarsh Manor at two o'clock, to call on Lady Longford.

Beatrix's visits to Hill Top were never as long as she liked, and she did not like to spend precious time making social calls. But she had a special reason to call at Tidmarsh Manor. Lady Longford had hired Miss Cecily Burns, the governess Beatrix had recommended for her ladyship's granddaughter, Caroline. Caroline had written to say that

221

she liked Miss Burns very much, but Beatrix wanted to see firsthand how the arrangement was working out. Dimity was coming along to return a book on Lake District birds she had borrowed from her ladyship.

"Well," Beatrix said with a smile, as Dimity answered her knock at the door. "How is our little Flora this afternoon?" She noticed that Dimity's eyes were sparkling with something like excitement, but that she was wearing a puzzled frown. Her friend had the look of someone who has just learnt a bit of very good news, but is completely at sixes and sevens about it.

"Elsa has just put her down for a nap," Dimity said, picking up her hat. "She didn't quite sleep through the night, but she fussed very quietly."

"Any word yet on her parents?" Perhaps that was Dimity's puzzle, Beatrix thought. If Dimity wanted to be Flora's mother, she might be secretly hoping that the baby's real mother would never be found.

"No word that I've heard," Dimity replied, pinning on her hat in front of the hallway mirror. "Miles went to the gypsy encampment on Broomstick Lane, but they couldn't tell him anything. He's in Hawkshead now, making inquiries about the ring." She gave herself another look, patted her hair, and pulled on her gloves.

"I've been thinking about that hand-woven coverlet on the baby's basket," Beatrix said. "Since we won't be far from Holly How Farm, I thought we might ask Jane Crosfield to have a look at it. I'm sure she knows the work of all the weavers in the district."

Dimity nodded without a great deal of enthusiasm, and went to get the coverlet. From the look on her friend's face, Beatrix knew she was right. Dimity hoped that Flora's mother would not be found — but she couldn't say it out loud without appearing mean-spirited.

She was back in a moment with the coverlet, wrapped in brown paper and tied with string, and the two ladies went out to the pony cart, where they were greeted by a fawn-colored terrier with a polite grin on his face. He was wagging his tail.

"Good afternoon, ladies," Rascal barked. *"I should love to ride up to Tidmarsh Manor, if you've the room. I haven't seen Caroline for much too long."*

Winston turned his shaggy brown head to frown at the dog. *"Bit cheeky, aren't you?"* he inquired dryly.

"Never ask, never get," the dog replied.

223

"Never try, never taste. Never taste, never enjoy."

"Rascal wants to ride in the cart, I think," Dimity said, bending down to pet the dog, who was a village favorite. "Shall we take him with us to the manor?"

"Jump in, Rascal." Beatrix got into the cart and picked up the reins. "But you'll have to promise to mind your manners when we get there. No nipping at Dudley."

Rascal showed his teeth. *"Dudley wants a swift nip in the backside to get him moving."* Dudley, Lady Longford's spaniel, spent most of his time on the hearthrug, eating cheese and biscuits. *"Fellow's too fat by half and twice too rude. When I see him, I'll —"*

"You'll do nothing of the sort." Miss Potter scowled down at him. "And if you are uncivil to Dudley, I will not take you to the manor again. Is that understood?"

"Ha!" snorted Winston, with a triumphant flick of his brown tail. *"Miss Potter has her eye on you, puppy!"*

Rascal put his ears back and looked contrite. *"Yes, miss. I'll try, miss."*

"Trying isn't good enough, sir." Miss Potter sniffed, and rattled the reins. "You will *do* it. Shall we go, Winston?"

Winston picked up his neat pony feet and they rattled through the village and up the lane. In the cart, Rascal made himself small. He could never quite make out how it was that amongst all the humans in the village, Miss Potter was the only one who understood what the animals were saying. Of course, it might have to do with the fact that most Big Folk paid no attention. If they took the time to listen and observe as carefully as Miss Potter, perhaps they would understand, too.

Whatever the reason, Rascal had to agree with Winston. When Miss Potter had her eye on you, you'd better not try to get away with anything.

Tidmarsh Manor was a gloomy stone house at the edge of Cuckoo Brow Wood, shadowed by ancient yews and pines. It wore the same cheerless, sullen look as did its long-time owner, Lady Longford — which might lead us to wonder whether her ladyship was cross and ill-tempered because she lived in the house, or the house was cross and ill-tempered because her ladyship lived in it. It is not a question to which we can expect an answer, so we shall just have to leave it there.

But there is a story to be told, and we shall not neglect to tell it. Not long after old Lord Longford died, her ladyship had a disagreement with her only son, who refused to wed his mother's choice and took himself off to New Zealand, which was the only way he could think of to get out from under his mother's thumb. He fell in love with a New Zealand girl and married her and was happy for a little while, but his wife died and he himself was killed in a train accident, leaving their only child, Caroline, an orphan. Lady Longford, still nettled by her son's impertinent wish to choose his own wife, was not anxious to give her granddaughter a home. But Vicar Sackett and Will Heelis (her ladyship's solicitor) finally persuaded her to do the right thing, and Caroline came to live at Tidmarsh Manor.

Now, a sensible person might think that a young girl — who was likely to laugh and sing and play games — would brighten a dark old house and lift the gloom of its inhabitants. But if that's what you thought (being the sensible person you are), I am afraid you would be wrong, at least insofar as Lady Longford was concerned. She had been a gloomy old woman for years and she intended to stay that way. It gave her a perverse pleasure to ignore any sort of subversive cheerfulness.

Caroline, on the other hand, was just as stubborn as her grandmother and just as determined not to be reduced to a cheerless state of mind. She did all she could to keep herself busy and happy. She played with her two guinea pigs, Tuppenny and Thruppenny. She wrote daily in her journal, a practice encouraged by Miss Potter, who gave her a blank book bound in Moroccan red leather. And she planted some flowers behind the kitchen garden — snapdragons and petunias and dahlias for herself and flowering thyme for the bees — which she tended every day.

During her first year at Tidmarsh Manor, Caroline had happily attended the village school. She liked the village children, especially Jeremy Crosfield (who lived with his aunt in the Holly How farmhouse, on Lady Longford's estate) and Deirdre Malone (who worked for the Sutton family, in the village). But Jeremy had gone away to school, and Lady Longford had decided that Deirdre was not an "appropriate" acquaintance. What her granddaughter needed was a governess who would teach her French, art, and music, and tame her rebellious spirit.

Caroline was not at all happy with this turn of affairs (she already spoke French pretty well and did not want her spirit tamed). Thankfully, however, Miss Potter had found someone Caroline truly liked,

Miss Cecily Burns, a friend of Miss Potter's own former governess, Mrs. Annie Moore.

Lady Longford had hoped to find an older lady — at twenty-two, Miss Burns was objectionably young. But no suitable older candidates appeared, so Miss Burns was hired. She had pale yellow hair, sparkling blue eyes, and a lively expression. She spoke French even better than Caroline, drew and painted handily, played the piano and sang in a clear, pleasant soprano, and read poetry aloud with a dramatic flourish — all positive aspects, in Lady Longford's view. On the other hand, Miss Burns was too young, too pretty, too athletic, too modern, and far too willing to indulge Caroline's appetite for games. Moreover, she did not wear a corset and her skirts were two inches too short. Her ladyship accepted the new governess on sufferance and went on hoping to find an older, sterner lady, one who did not encourage *romps.*

On this particular afternoon, Caroline and Miss Burns were playing a rather rowdy game of croquet on the lawn, with Dudley looking on. Caroline had just knocked Miss Burns's ball out of bounds when a pony cart pulled up and Miss Woodcock and Miss Potter got out. Miss Woodcock was carrying a book, Miss Potter a basket, and they were accompanied by a small brown terrier.

"Miss Potter!" Caroline exclaimed happily, skipping to them. "And Miss Woodcock, and Rascal, too! How nice of you to come!"

"I've been wanting to see you, Caroline," Rascal said earnestly. *"It's been awf'lly lonely since Jeremy went off to school."*

"Miss Potter!" Miss Burns exclaimed, striding forward. "I say, it is good of you to come!"

Miss Potter smiled. "Hello, Caroline. Good afternoon, Miss Burns. I plan to see Mrs. Moore in a few days, and she's sure to ask for a report. I hope I can tell her that you are liking Tidmarsh Manor."

"You may tell Mrs. Moore that I am well and quite happy," Miss Burns said. "And you can take her a small package from me, if you don't mind. I'll get it before you leave."

Miss Potter introduced Miss Burns and Miss Woodcock, and Caroline invited them in for tea. "Grandmama is napping," she confided, "so we shall have cake with our tea."

They laughed at this, for Lady Longford's bread-and-butter teas were infamous, and many callers considered her ungenerous. (Beatrix was not one of these, for it was her opinion that all one really needed for tea was brown bread with fresh-churned butter and a bit of cheese.)

Dudley scrambled to his feet. *"Cake?"* he barked hopefully. *"In that case, I'll come, too."* He gave Rascal a superior glance. *"I've no mind to stay out here with the village riff-raff, anyway."*

"Thought I'd chase you around the manor house a time or two," Rascal said in a taunting tone. *"Do you good, you flat-footed fatty. You must get tired, dragging that belly around."*

"Rascal!" Miss Potter said sternly. "Remember what I told you."

"He started it," Rascal muttered, aggrieved.

"Never mind," Miss Potter said. "Go lie down under the cart. We shan't be long."

"Yes, miss," Rascal said, adding under his breath, *"Eat cake, you stupid dog, and die of a fatty liver."*

But no one ate cake that afternoon. Lady Longford had already awakened from her nap and was sitting in the drawing room, reading a book. A small fire had been laid but not lit. Her ladyship was frugal with fires.

"Well," she said in a disagreeable tone, "you have been out walking, I see. Tramping through the woods, no doubt, getting your feet wet." She put her book aside and scowled down at Caroline's feet. "Shoes do not grow on trees, young lady." To Miss Burns, she said, "You should know better, Miss Burns. Caroline has had a bad cold, and now it will get worse. We shall have to have the doctor."

"Caroline and I were playing croquet on the lawn," explained Miss Burns. "I believe it was suitably dry."

"Miss Potter and I just this minute arrived, Lady Longford," Dimity said, in a soothing tone. "I am returning the book you lent me. It was very informative."

"And I've brought you some cheese from the Hill Top dairy," Beatrix remarked briskly. She set down a basket. She smiled at Miss Burns, who she thought looked fit and happy. "And I did especially want to hear how Miss Burns and Caroline are getting on."

"Very well indeed," said Miss Burns. "Caroline is a bright young lady, with a decided interest in literary pursuits. Her piano is coming along nicely, too. She might spend more time in practicing, but she seems to have a talent for it."

"Young persons should not be praised in their hearing," said her ladyship, pursing her lips and frowning at Caroline. "They

231

will come to think too highly of themselves."

"On the contrary," Beatrix said. "It has been my experience that most young persons, particularly girls, do not think highly enough of themselves." She gave Caroline a slight smile. "I trust that Miss Burns will help Caroline to develop a sound opinion of her abilities, neither too high nor too low."

"Rubbish," snapped her ladyship. She rang the small bell at her elbow, then rang it again, violently. The maid appeared, a nervous-looking young woman wearing a ruffled afternoon apron and cap. "Bring us some bread-and-butter with our tea, Rachel." She looked down her long nose at the cheese. "And a knife for Miss Potter's cheese. I do not care for it, but others might." She looked up. "Well, what's keeping you, girl! Fetch the tea!"

When poor Rachel had scurried out of the room, Dimity remarked, "I'm not acquainted with your new maid, Lady Longford. Emily Shaw is no longer with you?"

Lady Longford waved a dismissive hand. "Emily is even more foolish than I thought," she said shortly. "She took another post."

"Another post?" Dimity asked in surprise. "Why, where did she go?"

It was a reasonable question, for Emily could hardly have expected to find a better position than the one she had held at Tidmarsh Manor. Better, that is, in terms of status and prestige, not compensation. Lady Longford did not pay her staff well.

"She went to Hawthorn House," her ladyship said in a sour tone.

"Hawthorn House?" Dimity asked, looking up with some surprise. "Why, I had no idea anyone was living there! The old place is so inconvenient — and so ugly. And it is not in good repair."

"I myself have not seen the house," her ladyship said, her tone implying that it was not fit to be seen. "However, I understand that a lady — a Miss Keller — came up from London to spend several months there. Emily knew the position was temporary, but she was in a state of great excitement about it. It seems that her employer promised to take the girl back to London with her." She sniffed. "It is so trying when one's servants leave one."

"Emily will be going to London, then," Beatrix remarked, in a musing tone.

Caroline leaned forward eagerly. "Actually, she —"

"Children do not speak until spoken to." Lady Longford was brusque. "Emily Shaw is a naive, giddy young girl who gave up a good place here in the vain hope of a better one someplace else. Where she is now and what she is doing is of no interest to me."

"But Grandmama," Caroline protested, "I only wanted to say that —"

"Horrid things happen to giddy young girls, Caroline," Lady Longford said darkly. "They will happen to Emily. Mind they don't happen to you."

And with that gloomy admonition hanging over their heads, Beatrix and Dimity finished their bread-and-butter and cheese, drank their tea, and took their leave, all in somber spirit. While Miss Burns went to get the package for Annie Moore, Caroline, who clearly had something to say, walked with them to their pony cart.

"Emily *has* gone to London," she said, when they were safely out of Lady Longford's hearing.

"Really," Beatrix said, with interest. She did not share her ladyship's low opinion of Emily. She had met the girl during the unfortunate experience with Miss Martine, who had intended to get her hands on Lady Longford's fortune. Emily was inexperienced and easily taken in, but when she learned to trust her own judgment, she would do well.

"Yes," Caroline said. "I saw her riding in Mr. Puckett's cart, on her way to the ferry landing. Miss Burns and I went out to sketch very early on Friday morning. We were crossing Kendal Road when Emily and Mr. Puckett happened along. I asked her where she was going. She said she was off to London. She was very excited. She said it was her heart's dream."

Dimity shook her head. "She will find the city a very different place than the village."

"Yes," said Beatrix. "I am not at all sure she will be happy there."

At that moment, Miss Burns hurried out with the package for Mrs. Moore, Beatrix promised to deliver it safely, and they all took their leave.

16
AT MISS PENNYWHISTLE'S SELECT ESTABLISHMENT FOR YOUNG LADIES OF EXCELLENT FAMILY

If Emily Shaw had heard Lady Longford's remark — "Horrid things happen to giddy young girls" — she would have been compelled to agree, at least in part. She might not have thought of herself as giddy, but it was certainly true that horrid things were happening to her.

And Miss Potter's prediction was sadly accurate. Emily was not at all happy. Now that she had time to reflect on what had happened, she felt that she had betrayed Baby Flora by allowing her to be carried off (although she could not think exactly how she might have prevented it). And she could not help feeling that she herself had been betrayed by Miss Keller, who had promised her an exciting life in London, and fine clothes and expeditions and pleasures.

Or at least Miss Keller had seemed to promise these things, although Emily, trying to remember exactly what had been said to

236

her, was no longer quite sure. Had Miss Keller deliberately deceived her? Or had she been too eager to believe in such good fortune, and hence deceived *herself?* However that might be, Emily now understood that not a single one of the promises Miss Keller had made (or seemed to make) would come true. Miss Keller was only a lowly teacher in Miss Pennywhistle's Select Establishment, and could promise nothing at all.

Emily understood this the day after her arrival, when Miss Keller took her to the parlor to be introduced to Miss Pennywhistle.

"This is Emily," Miss Keller said. "She comes to us from —"

"Thank you, Miss Keller," Miss Pennywhistle said in a prim, dismissive voice. "I believe you have other duties. You may leave us now."

"But I thought —" Miss Keller began. She looked anxiously at Emily, then back at Miss Pennywhistle. "I feel I should stay and explain —"

"I am perfectly capable of making all necessary explanations, thank you," said Miss Pennywhistle, with a do-not-argue-with-me look. Miss Keller hung her head and went away, leaving Emily with the distinct impression that of all the select personages at Miss Pennywhistle's Establishment, Miss Keller was among the least select.

"You are a fortunate young person," said Miss Pennywhistle, looking down her nose and curling her *R*'s with a royal flourish. She was a very tall, very thin, very dark woman with a long face and cold dark eyes. "Miss Keller has told me that you proved useful as a maid-of-all-work whilst she was on holiday in the Lakes, and that you are particularly good with a smoothing iron." She sat down behind the table that served as her desk. "This is altogether unusual, you understand. Our girls ordinarily come to us through one of the London agencies. But since Miss Keller is so eager to vouch for your suitability, I am willing to give you a trial."

And then, without stopping to ask whether Emily had any questions or objections or any feelings at all on this subject, Miss Pennywhistle began to rattle off Emily's duties.

"The maids are up at five a.m. Before breakfast, you will carry coals and ashes, clean grates, and lay fires. You will fetch hot water for our third-floor young ladies' baths, and towels and linens. After breakfast, you will assist Dora in the making of beds and the cleaning of floors. On Wednesdays and Fridays, you will assist Mrs. Hodge in the laundry, and particularly with the ironing. We have twelve young ladies in residence at the present time, so you will appreciate that there is quite a lot of fine ironing to do. As for the rest of the day, your duties will be distributed where they are needed. The young ladies are to have their hot water again at six. Your tea is at five. Your supper is at eight, after which you will turn down the young ladies' beds and arrange their night-things."

She gave Emily a critical look. "Your hair is not suitable. Pull it back and pin it. And straighten your shoulders. You look as if you are tired already and the day has scarcely begun. The clothing you have received — your dress, apron, and cap — will be charged against your account. You will take your instruction from Dora." She picked up her pen and a sheaf of papers. "That is all. You may go now."

Emily stared at her. Lady Longford had not been a kind employer, but Emily had never been asked to carry coals and ashes or help in the laundry. And Mr. Beevers, who looked after the garden, had always fetched the hot water because her ladyship thought the buckets too heavy for Emily to carry.

"You may go," Miss Pennywhistle repeated. And when Emily did not move, she threw her pen down on the desk. "What is wrong with you, girl?" she demanded. "Why are you staring at me like that? Have you no manners?"

And then, answering her own question, she said in an acid tone, "No, I expect you do not, coming from the Lakes. No breeding, and none to be expected." She rolled her eyes in exasperation. "Why Miss Keller is so eager to have you here with us, I don't know. I don't know how long you will last, either, if you persist in standing around with your hands dangling at the ends of your arms and your mouth hanging open in the middle of your face." She waved her pen. "Off with you, girl! Dora is waiting to show you your tasks."

And even though Emily had meant to ask such questions as "When is my half-holiday?" and "Am I required to attend worship?" and "What shall I be paid?" — normal, everyday questions that you or I would be sure to ask anyone who proposed to employ us — she found herself standing in the hall, outside the closed parlor door, with Miss Keller hovering at her elbow.

"I trust you said nothing about what transpired at Hawthorn House," Miss Keller said in a very low voice.

"No, miss," Emily said.

Of course she hadn't. She could not even begin to think about what had happened at Hawthorn House, let alone speak of it. She could still feel the warm weight of Flora in her arms, smell the baby's sweet-sour scent, hear her tiny milky sigh. Emily's arms felt achingly empty, her heart desperately hungry.

She looked at Miss Keller, tears springing to her eyes. "Don't you ever wish —"

"No, I do *not,*" said Miss Keller, taking her arm very firmly. "And neither do you, Emily. We are both grownups, you and I. We do what we must in order to get on in the world. What we must do now is go forward, not back. However much we may regret our mistakes, we must soldier on."

Emily shook her head in despair, feeling that Miss Keller did not understand, could never understand all she was feeling. And I daresay that Miss Keller was wrong about Emily being a grownup. For although she had worked for her living since leaving the village school at thirteen, some three years before, Emily was still a very young girl. She lacked the experience of life that might

241

have helped her to keep these horrid things from happening. She did not yet know enough to cope with the gypsy lads and the Miss Kellers and the Miss Pennywhistles of this world. She only knew enough to measure what she had lost.

And if we were to look into Emily's heart, we would see that it was filled with sadness and grief and confusion — and a great many anguished recriminations.

What had she done? Oh, oh, oh, what *had* she done?

How could she have done it?

And what would happen to her now?

17

THE HAND-WOVEN
COVER: PART ONE

When Beatrix and Dimity left Tidmarsh Manor that afternoon, they drove a little way up the road to Holly How Farm, where Jane Crosfield and her nephew, Jeremy, lived. Rascal could hardly restrain his excitement. He and Jeremy had enjoyed many tramps through the woodlands and meadows, up and down the fells — but that was before Jeremy went away to school. He must be home on holiday now, and Rascal was eager to see him again.

They were greeted at the door by a small, dumpling-shaped woman with a cheerful face and fly-away brown hair. "Why, if it isn't Miss Potter and Miss Woodcock!" she exclaimed, a faint Scottish brogue coloring her speech. "And Rascal, too. How nice. Sit ye down and have a cup of tea, do." She bent down to stroke the dog's ears.

"You're very kind," Rascal barked politely, and made a little bow to Snowdrop, Miss

Crosfield's white cat. Snowdrop, who was not partial to dogs, went to sit on the windowsill beside the pot of red geraniums.

As they entered the kitchen of the traditional farmhouse, Beatrix looked around with pleasure, thinking what a pleasant contrast it was to Tidmarsh Manor. The house was built like many others in the district, with a pebbly mortar on the outside, blue slate on the floors and the roof, and roses growing over the front door. But what set it apart from the others were the beautiful pieces of weaving that hung on every wall and the large wooden loom in the corner of the kitchen. In fact, it was on that very loom that Jane Crosfield had woven the tweed for the woolen skirt Beatrix was wearing at this moment, from fleeces donated by Tibbie and Queenie, the Herdwick ewes who lived at Hill Top Farm.

"Thank you, Jane, but we've just had tea at the manor," Dimity replied, in answer to Jane's invitation.

"That's every reason to have another, wouldn't ye say?" Jane retorted, with a merry grin.

At that, they all laughed. As they sat down at the table and Jane poured tea from a steaming pot, Beatrix said, "How is Jeremy, Jane? He's on holiday, is he?"

"School holidays, aye," Jane replied, going to the oven in the old-fashioned cooker that was set into one side of the large fireplace. A pan of currant buns, looking as if they had recently come out of the oven, sat on top. "But he goes back Monday fortnight. And just now, he's stayin' in Hawkshead to help Dr. Butters with his rounds. He will be sorry to have missed the both of ye."

"Oh, no!" Rascal exclaimed, disappointed. *"I so wanted to see him."* To Snowdrop, he said, with just a touch of anxiety, *"Is he much changed?"* Jeremy was a pupil at Kelsick grammar school in Ambleside, some fifteen long miles away. Most of the year, Jeremy boarded near the school.

"He's a young man now," Snowdrop said, washing a spot of dust from her white paw. *"I suppose that's what school is for,"* she added, sounding resigned. *"Changing a boy to a man."*

"I wish it wouldn't do that," Rascal said, aware of a keen sadness. Somehow he had never considered the question of growing up. In Rascal's mind, Jeremy would always be a happy boy browned by the summer sun, sharing his bread and cheese with a small brown terrier beside a tumbling beck high on a rocky fell, the wide world spread invitingly at their feet, the future endless

and bright and always exactly the same as the present.

"Wishing won't make it so, one way or another," remarked Snowdrop philosophically. She jumped down from the sill and went outside to say hello to Winston.

"I hope your nephew did well in school last term," Beatrix said. Jeremy was an artist and lover of nature, and a great favorite of Beatrix's. She had helped to persuade Lady Longford that it would be a good idea to send him for more schooling to prevent him from being apprenticed to Mr. Higgens, the Hawkshead chemist. And she had provided some of the money he needed for books and art supplies, as well. She was always eager for news of his progress.

"I'm pleased to say he's doin' beautifully," Jane replied happily. "Both of us are truly grateful for your help." She transferred the currant buns to a china plate and set them on the table. "His school marks are as high as anybody could wish, Miss Potter. Ye'd be that proud of him, indeed ye would!" she added, and put a bit of bun on a plate for Rascal, who gobbled it down.

"We're all proud, Jane," Beatrix said, adding sugar to her tea. "But I hope he's finding time to do some painting."

"Oh, aye," Jane said happily. "Just let me

show ye." She stepped into the next room and brought out a watercolor of a flock of sheep grazing in a green meadow beside a small stream. "Lovely, isn't it?" She sighed. "Fair makes me think I'm sittin' right beside Wilfin Beck, it does. And look — there's the wee dog. Rascal, that's you!"

Rascal stood up on his hind legs to inspect his painted self. He was sitting on his haunches, watching the trout swim round in the crystal water. He felt quite proud. *"Fancy me, in a painting,"* he said in wonderment. He would have to tell Tabitha, who was always lording it over him because Miss Potter had put her into a book.

"It's wonderful!" Dimity exclaimed.

"It is, indeed," Beatrix said, taking the painting and examining the way Jeremy had washed the color across the sky. "His work is coming along very nicely. Please give him my compliments, Jane, and say that I'm very pleased with what he's done."

"Me, too," Rascal put in, wagging his tail excitedly. *"Tabitha will be so envious!"*

"Just look at the beastie," Jane said, shaking her head at Rascal. " 'Tis for all the world like he knows it's him in the painting."

"Why, of course he does," Beatrix said. "Dimity, perhaps you could show Jane what we've brought."

Half-reluctantly, Dimity took out the brown paper parcel she had brought and opened it, unfolding the blue-and-white rectangle of cloth and laying it on the table. "We wondered what you can tell us about this, Jane."

"Well, now, this *is* lovely," Jane said, fingering the cloth. "Very fine work, I'd say, Miss Woodcock. Done by an expert weaver."

"The pattern is distinctive, don't you think?" Beatrix asked. "A twill, isn't it?"

"Aye," Jane said, picking it up for a closer look. "A dornick twill. Can ye see how the run changes direction? My old gran — she was Scottish, she was — used this sort of weave for tablecloths." She looked up, curious. "Where did this come from?"

Beatrix and Dimity exchanged looks. "We don't exactly know," Beatrix said. "We were hoping you might be able to tell us whether someone in the district is likely to have woven it."

"Well, if it was," Jane said briskly, "it could only have been woven here, on this loom, which it wasn't." She paused, smiled, and added, "O' course, old Sally Frost might've woven it."

Dimity folded the woven cloth and re-wrapped it in the brown paper. "Sally Frost.

Let's see — she's Mrs. Graham's mother, isn't she?" To Beatrix, she added, "Mrs. Graham is one of the local midwives — or used to be. I don't think she's working now."

Jane nodded. "Aye. Old Sally lives with her daughter and son-in-law, at Long Dale, on Glade Lane. The old dear is half-blind, though. Not weavin' now, I should think. But if she wove this, I'm sure she'll be pleased to own to it." She looked from one to the other, curiously. "Why are ye askin'?"

Dimity looked down and said nothing.

"It has to do with a baby," Beatrix said, and told the story.

Jane's eyes widened. At the end of the tale, she shook her head. "Babies are precious," she said sadly. "Babies are a gift of God." She looked up, her eyes filled with tears. "Who would give a baby to a stranger? Couldn't its own mother keep it?"

That plaintive question was still hanging in the air as Beatrix and Dimity took their leave.

18
THE HAND-WOVEN
COVER: PART TWO

By the time Beatrix and Dimity left Holly How Farm to go to Long Dale, the blue sky had darkened, Coniston Fell was draped in a cloudy veil, and a chilling breeze blew from the west. Rascal explained that he had decided to stay and see what sort of business the badger on Holly How was getting up to and barked a polite "thank you" before he ran off. Winston the pony explained that his bones predicted rain and he preferred to go straight home to the Hill Top barn. But Miss Potter explained that she and Miss Woodcock had other plans, and since Miss Potter held the reins quite firmly, Winston did what was asked. But he heaved a heavy sigh, letting her know that he wasn't to be held to account when all three of them got soaking wet.

For most of the afternoon, Dimity had been very quiet, and Beatrix remembered her earlier impression: that her friend found herself in the midst of an intensely private dilemma, and that it at least partly involved the baby. As they started back in the direction of the village, Dimity startled Beatrix by spilling the story of what had happened that morning: Major Kittredge's confession of love, his proposal (and his idea that they should adopt the baby), and her refusal.

"Miles will never consent to the marriage, Bea," she said disconsolately. "I had to tell Christopher that there's no point in even thinking about it."

Dimity and Christopher Kittredge?

Beatrix was taken suddenly aback. "But I thought you were interested in Mr. Heelis!" she exclaimed. Mr. Heelis was a frequent visitor at Tower Bank House, and she had assumed that he called to see Dimity. And since Beatrix knew that Mr. Heelis and Dimity's brother were the best of friends, she had thought it a perfect pairing. She had even envied Dimity, who was free to marry him, if she chose.

"Mr. Heelis?" Dimity managed a sad little laugh. "Whatever gave you that idea, Bea? He's just a friend, although a good one. And I daresay Miles would never object to *him*."

"I see," Beatrix said slowly. "I was wrong." And with that realization came another thought — not a thought, exactly, more like a feeling, and a rather disturbing one at that. It was a feeling of sudden lightness, as if a weight had been lifted from her shoulders. She felt . . . glad to know that she had been wrong. Why?

But Beatrix put the feeling away, for she didn't understand it, and anyway, it had nothing to do with Dimity. "Why does your brother object to the major?" she asked, and then answered her own question. "I suppose it has to do with his marriage."

Dimity nodded sadly. "Miles says that Christopher's reputation has been ruined, and that if I should ally myself to him, I would be tarred with the same brush."

"There's something to that, I suppose," Beatrix said, thinking that at least the captain's refusal was stated honestly. It wasn't hypocritical, like her mother's rejection of Norman. But why was it that people thought they could tell other people whom they should love? What gave anyone the right to dictate to someone else's heart? How could Captain Woodcock presume to rule his sister's life this way?

She turned to Dimity. "Do you love the major, then?"

Dimity sighed. "I've loved him since before he went to war, Bea. I've never loved anyone else. I never will." She laughed. "Not even Mr. Heelis, dear as he is."

Beatrix flicked the reins and Winston moved faster. If she had it to do over — if she had to decide between Norman and her parents — she would do the same thing. But Dimity's situation was very different. Captain Woodcock did not need Dimity in the same way Mama and Papa needed her. Dimity owed her brother a sister's respect and affection. She did not owe him obedience.

Beatrix took a deep breath, conscious that she was about to say something very important. "If you love the major, you must marry him, Dimity."

Dimity gulped down a sob. "But I don't think I could oppose Miles on this," she said. "I —"

Beatrix was firm. "But this is not your brother's business, Dimity. You and Major Kittredge are adults. You are obliged only to yourselves."

Dimity's eyes were suddenly bright and hopeful, and she put her hand on Beatrix's arm. "Oh, Bea, do you think so? Do you really?"

"I do, really." Beatrix sighed. "I do envy you, Dimity. You have the freedom to choose according to your own wishes. That is not to say that you mustn't consider your brother's feelings. But you must put yourself first — at least, I hope you will."

Dimity thought for a moment, and then the happiness dimmed. "I wish it were that easy, Bea." She shook her head. "I just cannot imagine myself going against Miles' wishes. It feels like . . . like a death, somehow."

"That's exactly it," Beatrix said softly. "A death." She paused. "But as you think about this, imagine living your life with the man you love — and then imagine your life without him. That's an even worse death, isn't it?"

After that, there was nothing more to be said.

Bordered by a stone wall on one side and an ancient hedge on the other, Glade Lane slanted steeply uphill toward Oatmeal Crag and Long Dale Farm, where the Grahams lived — and where Beatrix hoped to learn something about the blue-checked cloth that had been in the baby's basket.

"You said Mrs. Graham used to be a midwife," Beatrix remarked as Winston put his shoulder into the harness for the uphill climb. "She isn't working now?"

"She was ill for a time after her youngest daughter's birth," Dimity replied. "I don't think she's gone back to her work."

"A midwife, whether she's working now or not, might know about someone who has recently had a baby," Beatrix said thoughtfully.

"Not without Dr. Butters being involved, I should think," Dimity said, frowning. "The midwives in this area used to attend the births alone. But since Dr. Butters opened his practice, he's encouraged them to work with him."

"Still, it seems coincidental," Beatrix said, thinking about their mystery. "A new baby in a basket, with a cover that might have been woven by Sally Frost, and Sally Frost's daughter a midwife." She paused, reminding herself, "Of course, we don't yet know that Sally Frost wove the cover."

"We soon will," Dimity said. She pointed. "That's Long Dale Farm. I've met Mrs. Graham once or twice. I've never met her mother, though."

The Graham family lived in a two-up, two-down cottage built onto one end of a long, open barn. Several pigs could be seen in the pig sty, two cows were grazing in the meadow behind the barn, and an assortment of chickens were scratching in the yard. Pebbled with gray mortar like the other houses in the district but without any flowers to brighten its bleak severity, the house seemed to frown. The woman who opened the door was frowning, too. A little girl with smudges on her face hid behind her skirt, peeking out at the visitors, her thumb in her mouth.

"Yes?" asked the woman. Her dark hair was snugged into a bun at the nape of her neck, and her gray dress was completely covered by a white apron.

"I am Dimity Woodcock," Dimity said cheerfully, "and this is Miss Beatrix Potter, of Hill Top Farm. Perhaps you will remember me, Mrs. Graham. I have charge of the Parish Mothers' Box."

"Oh, aye," the woman replied. "What dust tha want?" The question was not asked graciously.

"We should like to speak to your mother," Beatrix said. "She was recommended to us as an excellent weaver."

"Her doan't weave now," said the woman firmly. "Her kin barely see, and her has no loom. If it's weavin' tha wants, see Jane Crosfield. None better round here." She began to shut the door.

"We don't want Mrs. Frost to do any weaving," Dimity explained hurriedly. "We want to ask her opinion about a piece of cloth. It won't take more than a moment, and we'd be ever so grateful."

"Gertie!" cried a shrill voice from inside the room. "Who's that knockin' at t' door, Gertie?"

"Good afternoon, Mrs. Frost," Beatrix replied loudly, standing on her tiptoes to peer over Mrs. Graham's shoulder. "We've come to see you."

"I said —" Mrs. Graham began angrily.

"Callers fer me, Gertie?" the voice cried. "Let 'em in, daughter! Let 'em in!"

Reluctantly, Mrs. Graham stepped aside and Beatrix saw a tiny, tottery old woman, her hair as white as snow under an old-fashioned white ruffled cap, her face lined and wrinkled, like apples a half-year after harvest. She wore a black dress, black mitts, and several knitted black shawls pinned around her shoulders.

"Come t' see me?" the old woman asked, sounding pleased, and Beatrix thought that she probably did not have many visitors. "Well, then, welcome. Gertie, fetch t' teapot, and we'll have a cuppa."

Scowling darkly, Mrs. Graham went toward the back of the house, the little girl trailing behind, glancing back, half-fearfully, over her shoulder. Beatrix and Dimity followed the old woman into a small, dark room, where a narrow plank table and two benches took up much of the slate-flagged floor. A coal fire sputtered sulkily in the fireplace, a wooden chair on one side, a high-backed settle on the other. Damp garments hung on a rack behind the settle, two pans of rising bread dough sat on the hearth, baskets and buckets were stacked in the corners, and a mantle over the fireplace held an assortment of bottles and jars and boxes.

Beatrix and Dimity seated themselves on the uncomfortable settle. The old lady sat down in the wooden chair and rested both feet against the fender. "Come about a piece o' weavin'?" she asked brightly. Her eyes behind wire-rimmed spectacles were snappy, her expression full of interest.

Dimity took the blue-and-white rectangle out of her bag. "Jane Crosfield says you might've woven this." She handed it to the old lady. "Is it yours, Mrs. Frost?"

Sally Frost took it in her fingers, turning it over to look at both sides, then bending low over it, examining it. "Dornick twill," she muttered. "T' blue is woad-dyed. And 'tis old, verra old."

Woad was not much used these days, Beatrix knew, with commercial dyes so readily available. "It's hard to find weaving like that now," she said, "when so much is done by machines."

"Aye. But this 'twas done by nimbler fingers than these old crippled ones," Sally Frost said, holding up an arthritic hand, the fingers bent at odd angles. "And sharper eyes than mine."

Beatrix smiled. "But it's yours?"

"Aye. Long, long ago, when I was a weaver." The old woman looked at them over her glasses. "T' last time I saw this piece, 'twas pinned to Gertie's clothes line. How didst tha come by it?"

Beatrix and Dimity exchanged glances. "It was . . . found," Beatrix replied, thinking that it was not perhaps a good idea to reveal too much.

"In the village," Dimity added helpfully.

"In t' village." The old lady gave them a sharp look. "Well, then, I'm glad to have it back, 'though I canna say how it got away. Cloths doan't have feet, now, do they?"

At that moment, Mrs. Graham came into the room with a teapot and four earthenware mugs on a tray. She set it down on the table, poured tea, and handed out the mugs. There was no sugar or milk.

"Look, Gertie," said the old lady happily, holding up the cloth. "This was found in t' village! T' ladies have brought it back."

Mrs. Graham gave the cloth a negligent

glance, then another, sharper. Beatrix could not see the expression on her face because she turned at that moment to pour herself a mug of tea. "Gypsies, most like," she said in a careless tone. "They're bad to steal things off folks' clothes lines. They've been camped at t' foot o' Broomstick Lane this past fortnight."

"So you think gypsies took it from your clothes line?" Dimity asked.

"Could be so," Gertie Graham said, and gave a careless little toss of her head. "T'was washed and hung out with t' last laundry. Dust'a think so, Mum?"

The old woman nodded.

"Aye, then," said her daughter. "Must be gypsies carried it off. Doan't know how else it'd get to t' village." She smiled thinly. "T' wind blows hard from t' fells, but nae so hard as that."

Beatrix thought that the gypsies were a very convenient excuse. But she only said, "Miss Woodcock tells me you do midwifery."

Gertie Graham nodded shortly. "Have done," she amended. "Not now."

"We were wondering," Dimity said in a tentative tone, "whether you might know something about the recent birth of a baby. A little girl. She was —"

Gertie Graham drained her mug. "Only boy babes lately, as tha well knowst, Miss Woodcock, seein' as how tha hast t' parish Mums' Box. Master Jeremiah Hopkins 'twas t' last." She stood and picked up the tray. "If tha'st finished thi tea, I've chores to do. And me mum allus has a bit of a lie-down this time of afternoon."

The old lady looked pained. "But I'm not —"

"Yes, tha art," her daughter said sternly. "Dust'a remember what Dr. Butters said, Mum? A nap ev'ry afternoon."

Reluctantly taking their cue, Beatrix and Dimity said goodbye and went out to the pony cart, where Winston was waiting with gloomy patience. He'd had nothing to do but count the chickens (thirteen foolish hens and one rude rooster), twitch his tail against the thunder flies (always fiercest before a rain), and listen to the Galloway cow, a silly creature who could talk of nothing but her new heifer calf. And to top it off, it was beginning to drizzle. He had been right about the weather.

Beatrix took out the big black umbrella she kept under the seat and Dimity held it over their heads as Winston pulled them down the hill, trotting much more nimbly than usual.

"Well, that was interesting," Dimity remarked.

"Not very, unless you're fond of chickens, flies, and cows," Winston muttered.

"Interesting, indeed," said Beatrix. "Mrs. Graham knows more than she wants us to know. I didn't believe that business about the gypsies for a minute. Did you?"

"No," Dimity said uncertainly. She moved the umbrella so that it would not drip in their laps. "But I do think we should go down to the camp and —"

"Nae!" Winston stopped dead in the middle of the lane, nickering sharply. *"We are NOT going to the gypsy camp. It is raining, and my mane and tail are very damp — or hadn't you noticed? Anyway, it's time for my tea."*

Dimity looked down at the watch pinned to her lapel. "Oh, goodness, Beatrix! Look at the hour! Flora will be wanting her bottle. I must get back to Tower Bank House."

"And we don't need to get any wetter." Beatrix lifted the reins and clucked to the pony. "Let's go home, Winston. The gypsies can wait."

Winston was very ready to oblige.

19
CAPTAIN WOODCOCK INVESTIGATES

Miles Woodcock had carried out his morning's business in Hawkshead, then enjoyed a late, leisurely luncheon at the Red Lion Inn, where the shepherd's pie, savory with veal and mushrooms and encased in a flaky pastry, was reputed to be the best in the Land Between the Lakes. It was half past two (just about the time his sister and Miss Potter arrived at Tidmarsh Manor) when he left the market town and motored along the Kendal Road, turning right at Broomstick Lane. This was as far as he could drive, so he parked and got out. He should have to go the rest of the way on foot. Glancing up at the darkening sky, he pulled a mackintosh out of the boot.

He followed a rutted lane that slanted away from the main road and down across a meadow, to the point where it forked. One branch struck off to the north toward the gypsy encampment, less than a half-mile away. The other branch curved back to the south, in the direction of Sawrey — and Hawthorn House.

This track, overgrown from disuse, grew even narrower as Miles walked along. Soon there were only the faintest of wheel marks to show that a cart had recently come this way. The land slanted down toward the lake, with willow coppices and patches of bracken and bog myrtle here and there. A mountain linnet, a graceful brown bird with a long tail, perched on a dipping spray of grass and poured his song into the scented air. Nearby, a cock grouse hunted caterpillars in the hay stubble, and over the water, gulls swung on the whirling wind. Somewhere along the shore, a dog barked furiously, and ducks scattered as if they had been shot.

If the captain had not been so keen on reaching his destination, he might have enjoyed the walk a great deal more. But he could feel the weight of the ring in his pocket and he was anxious to talk to the girl who had pawned it. She was likely a servant girl at Hawthorn House, he guessed. (He could not know what you and I do: that the girl — our Emily — has already gone up to London, where she is at this very moment lugging a heavy bucket of hot water up to the third floor of Miss Pennywhistle's

Select Establishment, as one of the young ladies of excellent family scolds her in a very unladylike way from the top of the stairs.)

In the distance, at last, Captain Woodcock saw his destination: a melancholy gray stone house, quite large, overlooking the lake, with a stone barn at the rear and a fringe of thin fir trees along a stone fence. It stood isolated and bleak on the side of its hill, its natural gloom deepened by the darkening skies. Clouds streamed in from the west, the sky had taken on a metallic hue, and the waves scudding across the lake were flecked with foam.

Hawthorn House was an architectural hodgepodge, and not a pleasing one, and I daresay that neither you nor I would be happy to stay there, not even for one night. It had what can only be called an enigmatic, furtive look, as if it were keeping secrets that ought not be revealed. The roof bristled with Tudor towers and turrets and chimney pots, Queen Ann gables poked up at oddly random angles, and Georgian bow windows bulged like ugly glass blisters from the stone walls. Unhandsome and inhospitable even in its best days, the place was now in sad need of repair. Roof slates were broken, stones had fallen from the walls, and two or three upstairs window panes were smashed.

The front garden, rank with weeds, showed no sign of recent tending, and splintered stumps marked the sites where the old hawthorn trees had been cut. The place wore an air of derelict vacancy and disuse, and Miles could easily understand its reputation for being haunted. It was not a pretty house. It was not happy.

But even though it looked deserted, this was the house where lived the girl who had pawned the ring, and Miles was eager to speak to her — and to her employer. So he braved the nettles that lined the narrow gravel path and made his way up to the front door, where he banged the brass knocker loudly.

There was no answer. The knocker's hollow echoes died away, bringing no sound in response — no voice, no step, nothing but the harsh cawing of a raven perched in one of the fir trees behind the house. Miles waited until the echoes had shivered into the dusty silence, then banged the knocker again. This time there was a flurry of wings, an alarmed clatter, and a trio of pigeons flew out of a broken gable window.

Miles went down the steps and around the side of the house. But now he tipped his hat on the back of his head and whistled jauntily, as if to cheer himself — or frighten away anything that might be lurking in the shrubbery, which was of course ridiculous. He was not given to wild imaginings, but even he had to admit that there was something about the house that invited apprehension. Perhaps it was its odd shape, its disrepair, its desolate ugliness. Or perhaps it was the tales of hauntings, and the uneasy sense that secrets were held here.

Or (speaking rationally) perhaps it was merely the house's isolated situation. The nearest neighbor was a half-mile to the east, along the lakeshore, and he knew there were two small cottages a hundred yards up the slope behind the trees. But these could not be seen from the garden. He might have been in the middle of a vast wilderness, populated by only a few birds and —

There was a terrified squeal in the shrubbery, followed by the crackle of breaking twigs and a muffled curse. Miles jumped, startled.

"Who's there?" he called shakily. He cleared his throat and summoned a braver tone. "Who's there? Step out where I can see you."

There was another curse, more dry crackling, and a man stepped around a large shrub, hastily coiling a wire. Miles was suddenly Justice of the Peace, feeling the two-edged stab of anger and sympathy, and the fellow was a poacher, getting a hare for his family's dinner table — although, judging from the curse, the hare had got away.

And this poacher was someone Miles knew: an old man nearing eighty, bandy-legged, slope-shouldered, scrawny-armed, but with bright, birdlike eyes that missed nothing. He was dressed in a sacking jacket, brown corduroy trousers held up with a rope belt, and leather boots nearly worn through at the toe.

"Hullo, Hawker," Miles said.

Even though he was responsible for upholding the law, Miles could not bring himself to blame — much less arrest — these fellows, especially the old ones. Hawker had labored well enough in his time, but his prime was past and he was no longer able to work. He still had himself and his old wife to support and no children to help, though, and what was he to do for food? A few potatoes, some green vegetables from the garden, and a hare or a pheasant every other day would feed him and his wife handsomely. And the owner of Hawthorn House — Villars, who was still in India, as far as Miles knew — would never miss the birds or rabbits Hawker put into his game bag.

Hawker thrust the wire coil into the pocket of his coat. "Hullo, Cap'n," he said with a toothless grin, and saluted, clicking his heels together like the old Army man he was. "Wasn't expectin' to see you."

"Nor I you," Miles replied dryly. "Having a pleasant walk?" He would say nothing about the wire and the bag, nor would Hawker. He glanced at the clouds blowing down from the fells. "Seems we may get some rain this afternoon."

"Aye," Hawker agreed, hitching up his trousers. He jerked his head toward the house. "To let again, is it? Tha'st come to have a look?"

Miles made a noncommittal sound. It wouldn't hurt to let Hawker think he was here on property business. "Has the recent resident gone?"

Hawker nodded shortly.

"What can you tell me of him?"

"Her," Hawker said. "A lady, 'twere."

"Ah," Miles said. A lady? In this decrepit old place? "A married lady, then?"

"Marrit?" Hawker shrugged. "As to that, I cudn't say. Alone, her was, 'cept for Mrs. Hawker and a girl to do fer her." He tilted his head, a crafty look in his eyes. "Tha'rt int'rested in knowin' about t' lady?"

Miles reached into his pocket, took out a

269

shilling, and held it up. When the old man reached for it, he pulled back his hand, making a fist. "When you've finished telling."

"Not much to tell." Hawker shrugged. "Her come from Lon'on and went back to Lon'on. Stayed here all by hersel', 'cept for Missus Hawker to cook and t' girl to keep house." He frowned up at the stone walls. "No kind of place fer a lady, is what I says. Haunted, 'tis."

"Old houses have their tales," Miles remarked.

"Aye. But t' tales are true, when it comes to this house," Hawker said in an ominous tone. " 'Tis haunted, fer sure."

"About the lady," Miles prompted.

"Aye. Stuck-up, her was. Stayed in her sittin' room. Wouldn't come t' kitchen." He spat disgustedly. "Wouldn't even talk to t' missus face-to-face. Allus sent a note."

Miles could understand the offense Mrs. Hawker must have taken at not being invited to discuss the menus, and it did seem queer that the mistress had never come to the kitchen. But Mrs. Hawker was deaf as a stone, and it might have been easier to communicate by note. "What was the lady's name?"

Hawker's shrug was eloquent. "T' missus just called her 'mum.' "

"How long did this mystery lady live here?" And how was it possible, Miles wondered, that the village hadn't found out about her?

"Not long." The old man shrugged. "Come at May-tide and left a se'nnight ago."

May through August. Make it nearly four months. "Do you know where in London she came from or returned?"

A firm shake of the head. "I only spoke to her onct, through t' window. I offered to do a bit of gardenin' and weed-cuttin'." He gestured at the derelict lawn. "Thought she might fancy t' place tidied a bit. But she said it wasn't hers and she wasn't payin' to keep it."

Which settled one question, Miles supposed. The house had been temporarily let. "What about the servant girl? Did she come from London with this mystery lady?"

Another head shake. "Local, she was."

Ah. They were making progress. "Her name?" Since the mistress had gone back to London, the girl would be looking for another post. She was obviously the one who had contact with the mystery lady, and most likely, the one who had pawned the ring. He'd talk with her and get her to tell all she knew.

Hawker scowled. "I doan't know all t' gals in t' village, now, do I? All of 'em looks alike to me. T' missus called her 'girl.' That's what she was, and that's what I called her. Didn't see her but onct or twice."

Feeling frustrated with the difficulty in getting any substantial information out of the fellow, Miles glanced up at the house. Its vacant windows reflected the lowering sky, and the unkempt weeds around it were dry and dead. "Seems an isolated place for a London lady's holiday," he remarked thoughtfully. City ladies avoided remote country houses as they would the plague. They feared being alone, and feared loneliness above all other ills of the human spirit. "Did she entertain many visitors?"

"Visitors?" Hawker shook his head. "Never, so far's I know. Kept to hersel'. Never walked out. Sent me or t' girl to Hawkshead for t' needfuls."

"What about the post?" Ladies were devoted to their correspondence. A lady on holiday would normally write and receive any number of letters, all of which would be posted through the village post office.

"Post?" The old man gave a shrug. "Nivver saw a post. Only saw t' five shillin's a week t' missus was paid. Good money, fer cookin' two meals a day. 'Tis all I know," he added significantly, and thrust out his hand.

No visitors, no post — it all seemed very odd to Miles, especially given the condition of the house. It could not have been a pleasant sojourn for a lady from London. And there was one more thing —

"What do you know about a baby?"

"A babe?" Hawker pulled his chin. "Missus nivver said awt 'bout a babe." He looked up at the house and frowned. "A babe wudn't last long in this place. T' Thorn Folk 'ud carry it off."

"The Thorn Folk?" Miles asked, frowning. He thought of the gypsy band, camped not far away. Was "Thorn Folk" some sort of local name for gypsies?

Hawker stared at him, incredulous. "Nivver heard of t' Hawthorn Folk? They lived in t' hawthorns, which was cut down by t' major so he could see t' lake out his windows." He shook his head darkly. "Cruel, cruel business, to evict t' Folk."

"Nonsense," Miles said scornfully. "There are no such things as fairies."

The old man's face paled at such irreverence. "Nae, Cap'n!" he protested, aghast. " 'Tis truth! I've seen 'em with me very own eyes!"

Many people, even educated people, professed to be charmed by the fanciful folktales of the Land Between the Lakes, and evenings were spent telling and retelling the local legends. But Miles had never been one of that lot. As far as he was concerned, this was just another example of the ignorant foolishness of silly, superstitious people. Utter stuff and nonsense.

"I have reason to believe," Miles said crisply, "that a baby was born in this house. Is it possible that your wife would not have known?"

Hawker shrugged. "I s'pose 'tis. T' missus was only in for a few hours in t' afternoon, to cook lunch and dinner. And her doan't hear." He grinned. "Her doan't hear me, even." He held out his gnarled old hand. " 'Tis all I know, Cap'n."

"Thank you." Miles put the shilling into Hawker's hand. "And now I should like to speak to Mrs. Hawker." The old woman might be deaf, but she could not have worked in the house for four months without noticing something. Babies needed milk, nappies, blankets, bottles. They needed someone to care for them. It would be worth another shilling or two to hear Mrs. Hawker's account.

But the old man was shaking his head. "T' missus went to Liverpool," he said, thrusting the coin into his pocket. "Sister's dyin'." He grinned crookedly. "First time t' missus been away from home since we was married."

Miles read the old man's thought in his face. Hawker missed his wife, with whom he had no doubt lived some sixty or more years and who kept his table and washed his clothes and was company in the evening beside the fire, despite her deafness. But he was enjoying his solitude, and was none too anxious for her return. At that moment, there was a loud SNAP at the back of the shrubbery, and a thin, despairing squeal that shimmered into a sad silence.

Hawker smiled. "Ah," he said softly.

Miles shivered involuntarily. He was fond of the hunt, but not the kill. "Since I can't talk to your wife, perhaps I can find the girl — the servant girl who worked here. Any suggestions as to where I might locate her?"

"Can't say." Hawker pulled his thin gray eyebrows together. "But I can say where her's gone."

"Well, then, where?" Miles asked impatiently.

"Why, to Lon'on."

"London!" Miles exclaimed. A local girl going up to London — a highly unusual event. Unprecedented, to his knowledge.

"Aye." The old man did not look as if he

approved of what had happened. "Friday mornin', 'twas. Carried her bag up to catch Puckett's cart on t' Kendal Road. Said her was goin' to Lon'on." He spat. "Goin' to t' devil, is what I say."

And with that, they parted ways. Hawker returned to the shrubbery to tend his snare. Miles thought of going into the house, but in the end, shrugged into his mackintosh and walked back along the cart track, his head down and his hands in his pockets. Someone in the village almost certainly knew who among the local girls had gone off to London. He would stop at the pub tonight and see if he could learn her name. A suspicion was forming in his mind, as dark as the clouds that now hung over his head, spitting cold rain. It seemed likely to him that the missing girl was Baby Flora's mother, and that she had callously abandoned her infant daughter in order to free herself to go to the City.

Angrily, he clenched his hands in his pockets. What sort of mother could so far forget her maternal instincts as to abandon her child to the tender mercies of utter strangers? Granted, the mother herself was young, and no doubt overwhelmed by the troubles that must have seemed to engulf her. But there were those who would have been glad to help, had she only turned to them instead of running away to London. The vicar for one, he and his sister for another.

And she could not be allowed to get away with this. Child abandonment was a criminal act, the lowest, basest, most despicable deed imaginable. He would find her, by Jove, and see that she was brought to justice!

Captain Woodcock's passionate determination is altogether commendable and necessary in a man who is charged with maintaining law, order, and the King's peace. I daresay that you and I would be very glad to have him on our team, if we found ourselves in a ticklish situation.

The good captain does, however, have his blind side, although he wouldn't own up to it. For one thing, he cannot see the terrible wrong he would do his sister if he prevented her from marrying Major Kittredge, or the pain his action would inflict on the one person he cares most for in this world. For a second, he cannot see whether he is headed in the right direction or the wrong, as far as the investigation he is conducting is concerned.

And for a third, he cannot see that one of the Folk, amused by his rash and foolish denial of their existence, is dancing down the path beside him, tweaking at his clothing and his hair (he thinks it is the wind, yanking so), and laughing and making faces at him as he trudges along.

To paraphrase the Bard: There are more things in heaven and earth, Captain Woodcock, than are dreamt of in your philosophy.

20
THE HAWTHORN FOLK

Belief in elves and fairies, as well as in witches, wizards and the supernatural in general, remained strong in remote districts of the Lake Counties until well into the twentieth century.

Marjorie Rowling,
The Folklore of the Lake District

Now, if you do not believe in fairies, or if you have a great many important things to think about and do not wish to clutter your brain with idle fictions, you may wish to skip this chapter. It is about the life of the Folk and whether this has much to do with the actual plot of our story is not yet clear.

But if you believe in fairies (as did Miss Potter, from her childhood to the end of her life), or if you are willing to suspend your disbelief for the space of time it takes to read a few pages of this book, you are invited to continue reading, and good luck to you.

As you probably guessed, it is Mrs. Overthewall who is having a good laugh at the cynical Captain Woodcock. The poor man cannot see her at all, even when she pulls at his sleeve or his hair and sings in his ear and dances along the path beside him. And since we know that Emily and Deirdre and the three young Suttons have had a conversation with the creature, and that Miss Potter caught a glimpse of her as she went over the garden wall, I think we shall have to admit a certain corporeality to her being. That is to say, she is real, at least to those who do not doubt her.

And yet it is not surprising that, as far as the Captain Woodcocks of the world are concerned, Mrs. Overthewall and her kind do not exist. For it is an unfortunate truth that the more educated one is, and the more concerned one is with facts and laws and reputations and things one can hold and count and put in the bank, the less likely one is to be aware of elemental realities, such as the Thorn Folk, or the Beech or Oak Folk, or all the other Tree Folk at large.

But this cannot mean that these elemental realities do not exist. Take a simple analogy — the water in Wilfin Beck, for instance, the picturesque brook that flows along the eastern border of Hill Top Farm. In the summer, it sparkles in the bright sun, chuckling happily to itself about the delicious fun it will have when it reaches the wild freedom of Lake Windermere, whilst in the winter, it turns to solid ice, cold and silent under the leafless willows. Which of us, in the summer, would deny the existence of ice? or in winter, the fact of sparkling, chuckling water?

But that, alas, is exactly what Captain Woodcock is doing when he denies the existence of the Tree Folk. And that is why Mrs. Overthewall is laughing at his poor, pitiable foolishness, and teasing him and taunting him for his blindness. (I may as well tell you now that it is a good thing she is amused, for when she is *not* amused, she flies into a temper and hurls things about and — well, it is not something we should like to see!)

To a great many people, it has seemed entirely natural that the trees — which are, after all, of such vital importance to our life and well-being — were inhabited by nature sprites, who were generally kind-hearted and well intentioned toward humans. This ancient belief reaches back many centuries, to the times when people all over the world worshipped trees; celebrated them in legend and lore; burned their wood for fuel and used it for many necessities; employed their roots, bark, and leaves for healing; and found in trees the deepest and truest mystery and magic of the natural world. For the Lakelanders who lived so companionably with Nature and understood her so well, it seemed the most natural thing in the world that the trees were inhabited by Folk. They understood it to be indisputably true in the very same way that we understand the land to be inhabited by people and animals, the lakes and streams by fish, and the air by birds.

And just as there are all sorts of trees, there are all sorts of Tree Folk. In the Land Between the Lakes, three were most loved and respected: the Beech Folk, the Oak Folk, and the Hawthorn Folk. The beech was known as the "Magical Mother of the Woodlands," for it nurtured and sheltered smaller trees and its leaves, nuts, and wood were used in divining; its folk were respected for their ability to see far into the future.

The oak, the sturdiest and strongest of trees, was used for boats and bridge timbers and the rafters of houses; its Folk were regarded for their strength and resiliency. In fact, Miss Potter herself wrote a story about an Oak Fairy, for two little girls in New

Zealand. In the story, the Oak Fairy was dismayed when her oak was cut down and sawn into timbers to build a bridge. But when she saw what a fine, brave bridge her tree had built, and how it served the people who used it, she went to live there contentedly — "and may live there through hundreds of years," Miss Potter added, "for well-seasoned oak lasts for ever — well seasoned by trial and tears."

But it was the hawthorn, the symbol of fertility and new birth, that held a special place in the hearts of Lakelanders. The thorn bloomed at May-tide, when flower festivals and weddings were celebrated with the "gathering of the May," as the thorn's lovely white flowers were called. Thorns were planted beside the village well to protect its waters, and since a thorn could live for four hundred years, the villagers could be sure their water would be safe for a very long time. Planted beside a house, a thorn protected the dwelling from lightning. Its berries, brewed in a tea, were known to comfort and protect the heart. It was called the "bread and cheese" tree, for its leaves were thought to be as physically sustaining as a hearty meal and as spiritually sustaining as a prayer. And since the thorn presided over childbirth, a sprig was always hung over the cradle or in the byre where calves and foals were born. It was regarded as the protector of all newly born creatures, human and animal alike.

It is no wonder, then, that the people held hawthorn trees (and their Folk-dwellers) to be sacred, and cared for them and celebrated them at particular times of the year. They understood that a very high price would be exacted from any who cut down a thorn without a very good reason and without first asking permission, both of the tree and the tree-dwelling Folk. In this scheme of things, cutting down a living tree was the equivalent of committing murder.

But that is exactly what Major Villars had done — out of ignorance, of course, although that is certainly no excuse. When he bought Hawthorn House, there were three very old, very large hawthorns growing in front. The major decided to cut them down in order to have a wider view of the lake. Two men came in a pony cart loaded with saws and chains and bill-hooks and other instruments of destruction, and whilst the major looked on, giving orders, began their work. The Hawthorn Folk, who had been taking a nap (it was March, and still weeks away from bloom-time), were wakened by the sound of the trees sobbing and crying as the axes and saws bit into them. And then all three trees came down with a crash, and the Thorn Folk were out of a home.

And when the trees were gone — well, how would you feel if your house was pulled down suddenly around your ears, and when it was reduced entirely to rubble, you were left with no place to go? And not just your house, either, but your best friend! "Surely it's cruel to cut down a very fine tree!" Miss Potter wrote in *The Fairy in the Oak*. "Every dull dead thud of the axe hurts the little green fairy who lives in its heart."

Hurts? Why, of course it hurts! Imagine having your arms chopped off, and then your legs, and then . . . well, we don't like to imagine it, not at all, so we won't. But the Thorn Folk not only felt the pain of their trees but had to watch them being killed and then, enraged and saddened beyond the telling of it, took refuge in several younger hawthorns at the edge of Thorny Field, where they immediately began crafting their curses. And can we blame them? Their dear, familiar trees were gone, destroyed, murdered — yes, murdered! — without so much as an apologetic "I am very sorry I must do this, but it's all for the best, you know."

Now, while Tree Folk are generally benefi- cent, they can be spiteful and vindictive when the occasion demands. And since this occasion certainly seemed to demand retribution of some sort, the Thorn Folk rolled up their sleeves and set to work with a will. They cursed the house because they had never liked the ugly, ill-proportioned hulk. They cursed the garden, which had never grown anything worth eating, anyway. And they cursed Villars, the arch-criminal, the villain, the murderer.

And the sad fruit of their curses gratified them. The house sat vacant and derelict after Villars was recalled to the Orient. It became the Folk's favorite haunt, especially on moonlit nights, when they brought hammers and pot lids and willow whistles and rattles and made a great din, to discourage human habitation. Nettles and thistles and groundsel invaded the garden and (brutes that they are) elbowed out the roses and lilies. And when, some three years later, the Folk heard that Villars had been run over by a carriage in Bombay and had his leg cut off, they felt enormously gratified, as I daresay you and I might feel, if we were not such civilized and noble human beings.

Oh, but I've almost forgotten the most important thing! The Folk made a vow (which is different from a curse) concerning babies. Hawthorn trees are known to protect infants, so the Folk decreed that any baby born in Hawthorn House would come under their special protection. If they didn't like the way the child was being treated, they would fetch it and raise it as their own, or give it to a human of their choice, or even (since Folk magic can be quite powerful) turn it into something quite nice, like a baby hawthorn tree, and plant it where it would get plenty of sunshine.

And that is why, when Mrs. Overthewall heard Baby Flora crying for several hours on end, she came and took her out of her cradle. She intended to give her to the Suttons, since they were already experienced with babies. But when that idea was rejected by the unanimous vote of the three oldest Sutton children ("No more babies!") and by Deirdre Malone, their young nursemaid, Mrs. Overthewall agreed that Miss Potter was an excellent alternative choice. And even though she was saddened when she heard that Miss Potter could not keep the baby and had given her to Miss Woodcock, she knew she had done the right thing. Babies definitely did not belong at Hawthorn House.

There is more to be learnt about Mrs. Overthewall and about the Thorn Folk of the Land Between the Lakes. But I expect that you are anxious to be getting on with our story. And since it is about time for Deirdre to hear from an absent friend, that is what we shall turn to next.

21
DEIRDRE RECEIVES A LETTER

At ten every morning, rain or shine, Mrs. Sutton sent Deirdre across the village to the post office in Low Green Gate Cottage. This was an important task, as you might imagine, since Dr. Sutton was the only veterinarian in the district and sent and received a great many invoices, payments, and supplies by post. It was a pleasant chore in fine weather, and usually involved taking a small Sutton or two in the perambulator for a breath of fresh air.

On this day, which would be Wednesday, in case you're keeping track, the weather was as fine as it could possibly be. The Tuesday afternoon and evening rain had ended, the air was sweet, with a just-washed smell, and the houses and gardens looked as fresh and pretty as watercolor paintings under a blue sky flecked with whipped-cream clouds. There was no perambulator to push today, since the smallest Suttons had gone with their mother to visit a friend, but Libby had come along. And as the two girls swung down the hill past the Tower Bank Arms (playing Alice and the Rabbit), they were joined by Rascal (who had to become the puppy that Alice played with after she ate the cake in Rabbit's house and grew very small).

At the post office, Deirdre handed over the outgoing letters and waited while Mrs. Skead, the postmistress, collected the post for Courier Cottage. Libby stopped outside to see what was growing in Mr. Skead's garden (and whether there was anything they might pretend was Alice's mushroom), while Rascal had a brisk encounter at the door with Mrs. Skead's calico cat, Cleo, who reminded Rascal very much of the Cheshire cat.

"These fer Dr. Sutton," Mrs. Skead said, handing the bundle across the counter, and then a single envelope. She sniffed. "And this'n fer thi, Deirdre. All t' way from Lon'on, and marked 'PRIVATE,' as if a body 'ud snoop in t' mail." She frowned at Rascal. "Leave that cat be," she said crossly, "or tha'll get thi nose clawed proper."

Rascal, who had once experienced Cleo's sharp claws, felt that discretion was the better part of valor and followed Deirdre outdoors. Besides, he wanted to know about Deirdre's letter.

"Look what I have," Deirdre said, holding up the envelope so Libby could see it. "From London!"

"From London!" Rascal barked. *"Ripping!"*

"I wish someone would send me a letter," Libby said, forgetting all about Alice and the mushroom. "Who wrote it?"

Deirdre turned it over in her fingers. This was the very first letter she had ever received in all her life, and she had no idea who in the world might have sent it. Perhaps it was meant for someone else, and Mrs. Skead had given it to her by mistake. (Mrs. Skead had many fine qualities, but she was sometimes careless. The Suttons' post often included letters to someone else, and the Barrows and the Llewellyns were forever returning letters that should have come to the Suttons. People had got into the habit of going through their letters before they left the post office, so the wrong ones could be handed back.)

But there was no mistake this time. The handwriting and spelling were not of the best, but the envelope clearly bore Deirdre's name, with "Courier Cottage" written underneath and in the lower left corner "VERY PRIVATE." Which was probably meant to keep somebody from trying to read what was inside by holding the envelope up to the light, as Deirdre had seen Mrs. Skead doing once or twice before.

Deirdre opened the envelope carefully, not wanting to tear it, and took out a folded piece of thin notepaper. Glancing down at the bottom, she saw that it was signed *"Yrs. Friendley, Emily."*

Deirdre shivered with pleasure. Why, the letter was from Emily! And all the way from London!

Emily had worked as a housemaid for Lady Longford at Tidmarsh Manor, where Deirdre's friend Caroline lived. Emily sometimes had tea with Deirdre and Caroline in Mrs. Beever's kitchen at the manor — that is, until late last spring. One afternoon, when Caroline had been summoned to the drawing room to wind yarn for her grandmother, Emily told Deirdre that she had given in her notice. Glancing over her shoulder to make sure that Mrs. Beever wasn't listening, she whispered excitedly that she had a new place, at Hawthorn House.

"Hawthorn House!" Deirdre had exclaimed, shocked. "But it's been empty for years. And it's haunted!"

Emily shook her head pityingly, as if Deirdre had said something childish. "Haunted? Don't be silly." And then she had glanced at Mrs. Beever, who was beating eggs at the opposite end of the kitchen, to make sure she couldn't hear. "Promise not to tell," she had whispered. "The lady I'm to work for insists on bein' private."

Of course Deirdre had promised. In fact, the confidence had made her feel very proud, for Emily was already sixteen and quite grown up, as anybody could easily see. She had been a chubby girl, but she now possessed the curvaceous figure of a woman, and a pretty woman, at that. One afternoon in early spring, she had whispered to Deirdre and Caroline about a certain gypsy lad who loved her passionately and begged her to go off with him, which she might have done, if Mr. Beever had not chased him away.

"Oh, how sad!" Caroline cried and clasped her hands. Deirdre, though, was not so sure. She felt that sometimes Emily made things up, although she didn't hold it against her. Romantic fancies could be much more satisfactory than the bleaker realities of everyday life.

"Aye, truly," Emily said with a sorrowing look. "He was ever so fine and handsome. And he loved me ever so much."

When Mrs. Beever heard them whispering, she said that Emily should stop prattling and take the linens upstairs, for there would be plenty of time for lads when she had a wiser head on her shoulders and knew better than to trust a gypsy.

Still, Deirdre thought that Emily's head was quite wise enough, and felt closer to her than she did to Caroline, who was more nearly her age but seemed younger. Deirdre and Caroline had been friends when they both attended the village school, but Caroline would be a lady when she grew up and could do exactly as she pleased all day long. Deirdre and Emily, on the other hand, would never be ladies. They would have to work to get their livings, and doing what they pleased would have to wait on the half-holidays that they got only every now and then. Deirdre felt as if she had found a friend in Emily, and would've liked to hear more about the handsome gypsy lad, and how Emily felt after Mr. Beever chased him away.

So since Hawthorn House was not far away and Deirdre had always wanted to go inside (she had never before been in a haunted house), she had stopped in to visit one Saturday afternoon shortly after Emily began working there. She knocked with some trepidation, because the garden was so overgrown and the place so very dilapidated.

At first, Emily hadn't seemed all that glad to see her. She wasn't supposed to have callers, she said. But after a few minutes she relented and took Deirdre around the house, and then they went to the kitchen for a cup of tea and some biscuits.

The inside of Hawthorn House was something of a disappointment. It was not what Deirdre had imagined, which was something like Miss Havisham's house in *Great Expectations,* full of spiders and cobwebs and stopped clocks and decaying furniture covered with dust sheets, like ungainly ghosts. The house was certainly large and old but clean enough, and there seemed to be no cobwebs or stopped clocks, although massive, old-fashioned furniture crowded the rooms, with shabby draperies at the windows and worn rugs on the floors. Emily explained that her employer had taken the place as a holiday house on a temporary let and was not at all troubled by the unattractive furnishings or the derelict garden. And before Deirdre left, she had reminded her that she and Lady Longford were the only ones who knew where she was, and cautioned her not to tell.

"Your mother doesn't know?" Deirdre asked, surprised.

"Mum's dead," Emily replied shortly. "Dad, too. And my sister's gone to Carlisle. T' only fam'ly I have is my aunt, Mrs. Crook, and I stay away from her. She carries tales."

Since this was a fair description of Mrs. Crook, Deirdre understood. "And the gypsy lad?" she prompted eagerly, thinking of Emily's love and loss. "What have you heard from him?"

Emily made a short, dismissive gesture, which gave Deirdre to know that she was not to mention this again. "Remember now," Emily said, frowning, "not a word of where I am."

"I'll remember," Deirdre had promised, and then, impulsively, had hugged Emily. "Orphans have to look out for one another," she said, feeling very grown up indeed. She had hoped to get to Hawthorn House to see Emily again, but had not been able to — and here was a letter from her, from London, of all places!

"Well?" Libby demanded anxiously, standing first on one foot and then on the other. "What does it say, Deirdre?"

"Yes!" Rascal barked, jumping up on his hind legs. *"Read it, Deirdre. Read it!"*

Deirdre shook her head. "The envelope says 'VERY PRIVATE,' which means that nobody can read it but me."

"But at least tell me who it's from," Libby begged. "That's not private, is it?"

"It's from a friend," Deirdre said abstractedly, already halfway into the letter and shaking her head a little at Emily's spelling.

Dear Dierder,
I take pen in hand to inform you that I hav come up to London, where I am starting a new life in my employer's employ. It will be a good life, I am shure, once I get used to it. But I am sore trubbled by something that happened at Hawthorn House before I came away, and you are the only person I trust to tell. I want you to know it was not my falt that Baby Flora was took. If any evil is said about me in the village, please let them know I have always tryed to be good. Mistakes were made, but I'm not a bad person.

Yrs. Friendley,
Emily

P.S. Tell them don't bother to look, as they will not fine me.

Deirdre's eyes widened and she hurriedly

297

read through the letter a second time. Baby Flora? Why, that was the name of the baby that the old lady had offered to them — to her and the three older Suttons — on fête day, and that had afterward been left on the Hill Top doorstep!

Deirdre had learnt Flora's name just the previous afternoon. She had been in the Sutton kitchen when Elsa Grape dropped in to gossip with Mrs. Pettigrew, the Suttons' cook. Mrs. Grape had told Mrs. Pettigrew that Miss Potter had brought the baby to Miss Woodcock, and that much to everyone's surprise, a valuable ring had been discovered in the basket, and a note saying that the baby was called Flora. Baby Flora had dark hair and dark eyes and was the picture (Mrs. Grape said this several times, making a great point of it), the very *picture* of Major Kittredge of Raven Hall, although she was sure that a gypsy was involved in the business somehow.

Deirdre did not quite understand what that was supposed to mean. But Mrs. Pettigrew obviously understood, for she shook her head darkly and muttered that those to the manor born always thought the world was made for their enjoyment, which they took where and however they liked, regardless of the right or wrong of it.

And then Elsa Grape said that Captain Woodcock was making every effort like the kind-hearted gentleman he was (she stressed the word "gentleman") to get to the bottom of the affair. But he hadn't had any luck, for the gypsies wouldn't own up and he couldn't find anybody who would admit to knowing who the poor lorn bairn was or who her mother and father were or where she came from or how she got to Miss Potter's doorstep.

But now, as Deirdre read and reread Emily's letter, it seemed clear that Baby Flora must have come from Hawthorn House, and that her friend knew something about it. She pulled in her breath, a sudden, painful question echoing sharply in her mind. Was Flora . . . could she possibly be . . . was she *Emily's baby?*

Deirdre's first reaction was to scoff at the idea as ridiculous. Emily wasn't that sort of girl. A bit flighty, perhaps, and not always very prompt when it came to following Lady Longford's instructions. But she went to church every Sunday morning and —

Deirdre caught her lower lip between her teeth. How did she know what sort of girl Emily was — really? She only knew her from their snatches of teatime conversations in Mrs. Beever's kitchen, and from what

Emily said about herself. And as for going to church, why, all of Lady Longford's servants were required to go every Sunday morning, like it or not. As Deirdre knew from her own personal experience, sitting in the Sunday pew didn't mean that you were perfect, or that you didn't sometimes do things you were very sorry for afterward.

And like most girls who grew up in the country, Deirdre had never been shielded from the facts of life. Living with a veterinarian's family that produced a baby almost every year, she had gained a rather more detailed understanding of what was involved with bringing babies into the world than might be expected of a girl her age.

Catching her lower lip between her teeth, Deirdre thought back rapidly over what she remembered: Emily whispering excitedly about the gypsy lad who had loved her ever so much, Emily abruptly leaving Tidmarsh Manor, Emily working and living in seclusion at Hawthorn House. Much as she didn't like the thought, it was possible, she had to admit.

Deirdre read the last sentence of the letter again — *Mistakes were made, but I'm not a bad person* — and shook her head. Maybe Emily didn't like to think of herself as a bad person, but you were judged in this world by your deeds, not what you said. The villagers, when they learnt about this (as of course they would, since this sort of gossip flies like thunder through a village, being heard in every quarter at the very same instant) would be very quick to judge.

And Deirdre herself had some very strong views on the subject. It was her firm opinion that no loving mother would give up her baby under any circumstances, no matter how badly she wanted to go to London and start a new life. She would stay right here and do whatever was needed to give her child a good home. She would raise and love it, no matter what people said. Deirdre pressed her lips together, feeling the hot anger well up inside her. How *dare* Emily do this! It wasn't right!

Now, perhaps you are thinking that Deirdre may be leaping to conclusions, and that she shouldn't be so quick to judge Emily, since there are two sides to every story and the facts in the case are not yet entirely known. But please consider that Deirdre herself is an orphan who must make her way alone in the world, and that she often imagines how different her life might be if her own loving mother were walking beside her. I daresay you won't blame her too severely if she is angry with a young woman who seems to have thrown away something very precious, something that she herself would cherish.

And now that Deirdre knew this terrible thing about Emily (or thought she did), what should she do? She stood for a moment, frowning down at the letter in her hand. Perhaps she should ask Mrs. Sutton for advice. Or Vicar Sackett, who was a very kind man and knew lots of people in London whom he could ask to look for Emily. Or Captain Woodcock, who was Justice of the Peace and would know what the law had to say about such matters. Or —

Libby tugged at her sleeve. "What is it, Deirdre?" she asked, concerned. "Who is Emily Shaw? Did somebody die?"

"Did somebody die and leave you some money?" Rascal inquired hopefully. He always liked to look on the bright side of things. But right now, he was thinking that it was too bad he couldn't see that letter. He remembered Emily Shaw, who used to work at Tidmarsh Manor, and he wondered why she was sending a very private message to Deirdre.

Deirdre thought for a minute more. She didn't want to talk to Mrs. Sutton, or the vicar, or the captain. She would talk to someone who might have a very good idea of what to do. She pocketed the letter, tucked Dr. Sutton's post under her arm, and reached for Libby's hand.

"Come on, Libby," she said, setting off at a speedy pace. "Let's go and visit Miss Potter. You, too, Rascal. She's always glad to see you."

"Oh, good!" Libby exclaimed, skipping to keep up. "Maybe she's writing a new story!"

At Hill Top, Deirdre had been knocking for several minutes on Miss Potter's door when the door to the left came open, and Mrs. Jennings put her head out.

"Needn't knock," she said shortly. "Her's gone off to Lon'on. Woan't be back 'til Friday." And with that, she pulled her head back in and shut the door.

Deirdre sighed. Friday was two whole days away. What should she do in the meantime? Perhaps she should talk to Miss Woodcock, who had charge of Baby Flora. Or —

She stopped, suddenly discouraged. It was no good talking to anybody, really. Emily had not put an address on the letter, and London was a gigantic city. No matter how many people went looking, they'd never find her. And even if she were found, there was no guarantee that she could be made to tell the truth — whatever the truth was.

Deirdre sighed. There was not a thing that

anyone could do, not the vicar, not Captain Woodcock, not even Miss Potter (who sometimes seemed to be able to do quite magical things). And since that was the case, she would keep the letter to herself, and hope that Emily was able to find it in her heart to do the right thing. Whatever the right thing was.

She put her hand on Libby's shoulder and summoned a smile. "I'm sure Miss Potter wouldn't mind if we went down to the barn and visited Jemima Puddle-duck for a few minutes."

"Oh, let's!" Libby exclaimed excitedly. "Maybe her ducklings have hatched."

"And I'll just pop in and have a word with Kep whilst we're here," Rascal said, and trotted ahead of them down the path to the barn.

22
KEP TURNS
DETECTIVE

At the barn, Kep the collie was sitting on his haunches, basking in the sweet morning sunshine. He was also keeping a close eye on an unruly trio of piglets who were rooting along the fence, looking for a means of escape from their pen. He glanced up to see a small fawn-colored terrier trotting toward him, while Deirdre Malone and the eldest Sutton girl loitered along the path, admiring the flowers.

"Hullo, Rascal," he said pleasantly. *"Haven't seen you for a while. What's the news?"* Kep had a working dog's low opinion of most of the village dogs, lazy lay-abouts with little to do but eat, sleep, and bark at the village cats. Rascal, on the other hand, was a valued friend, since he always knew what was going on in the village — a boon to Kep, whose duties usually restricted him to the vicinity of the farm. And if Kep wanted to hunt rabbits, Rascal (rabbit hunter *par*

excellence) was always ready to lend a paw.

"Everyone is talking about Baby Flora." The terrier sat down beside the collie. He liked Kep very much, although he often wished that his friend wouldn't take everything so seriously. Did he ever smile, or go off on holiday? *"I s'pose you've heard that she's now in Miss Woodcock's care, whilst the captain looks for her mother."*

Kep nodded. Tabitha Twitchit, another valuable source of information, had already relayed what she had overheard in the village kitchens, so he knew something of what was going on. *"I can understand why a mother pig might lose track of her little ones,"* he said, with a reproving glance at the pig in question, who was blissfully napping in the mud. *"But the Big Folk ought to keep better watch over their babes."*

Rascal nodded, although he feared that Kep's stern sense of responsibility made him rather a severe judge. *"Speaking of mothers and babies,"* he said, *"how is our Jemima getting on? Any sign of those ducklings yet?"*

"She's still on her nest," said Kep. He dropped his voice. *"But I'm afraid there aren't going to be any ducklings."*

"No ducklings?" Rascal stared at his friend in shocked surprise. *"But why? Don't tell me*

the eggs are spoilt — after all the weeks she's invested in that nest!"

"No, not spoilt," Kep said. He shifted uncomfortably, as if he had said too much. He changed the subject. "You haven't by any chance seen that fox lately, have you?"

"That fox?" Rascal asked, frowning. "You mean —"

"Reynard, of course," Kep growled. "The one who tried to eat our Jemima. Filthy fellow has been lurking around." He pulled back his lips in a menacing snarl. "I have a little surprise in store for that fox. If you see him around, you'll let me know, will you?"

"I certainly shall." Rascal grinned, thinking that the fox, a natty dresser who always took care to look very smart, would hardly like to hear himself called a "filthy fellow."

But Rascal could certainly understand Kep's feelings. His friend was, after all, a collie, bred to take full responsibility for the farm's livestock and trained to be on the watch for any potential danger. And he himself was a terrier, who loved nothing better than to follow the hunt. He was bred to dig foxes out of their dens, however deep, and trained to follow the scent of fox up fell, down fallow. That foxy gentleman had better not brandish his brush anywhere in the neighborhood. Between Kep and himself, Rascal thought happily, Reynard didn't stand a chance.

He looked up and barked a greeting to Deirdre and Libby as they came into the barn. To Kep, he said politely, *"The girls have come to visit Jemima. You don't object, do you, old chap?"* When another dog was on duty at his home station, it was always a good idea to ask his permission. Not that Kep would deny it, of course. Still, it was his barn and his barnyard, and he was in charge of what went on in it.

"Object? Not at all. The duck needs company." Kep looked concerned. *"I worry about her state of mind, you know, sitting there all alone, day after day. She is simply obsessed with those eggs, which is not at all good for her, I fear."*

The dogs watched as the girls knelt down in front of the feedbox under which Jemima had hidden her nest.

"Hello, Jemima Puddle-duck," Libby said, putting out her hand to stroke the duck's white feathers. "How are you and your eggs today? Are they ready to hatch?"

"We are all eGGstremely well, thank you," Jemima quacked, in a brave but quavery voice. *"I can already feel the dear little duCK-luCKlings scratching about in their eGGshells.*

I am QUite sure we shall be hatching shortly."

Rascal frowned. But Kep had said there weren't going to be any ducklings. Was Jemima imagining things? She'd always been a bit daft anyway — Miss Potter had called her a "simpleton" for being taken in by the fox. Had she gone clean barmy-brained?

"What were you telling me about those eggs?" he asked Kep worriedly. *"If they're not spoilt, what's wrong with them?"*

"Afraid I'm not at liberty to say, old chap," Kep replied in an apologetic tone. *"I promised her — the duck, that is — I'd keep it under my hat."* His face became dark and gloomy. *"Take it from me, though, Rascal. Don't pin your hopes on ducklings."*

Rascal leaned forward. *"But if not ducklings, then what?"* he persisted.

Feeling Rascal's eyes on him, full of a sharp curiosity, Kep turned away to look out the door, giving no answer. Outside in the barn lot, all was in order. The mother pig had retrieved her piglets and was oinking softly to them, the hens clucked to the chicks who crowded noisily around their feet, and Kitchen mooed affectionately to her spring calf. Beyond the enclosure, in the green meadow, the Herdwick sheep grazed with their spring lambs, now grown to a quite respectable size, and the brown mare watched tolerantly as her spry colt raced uphill and down. It seemed to Kep that the whole world burgeoned and blossomed with maternal enterprise, just as it ought. All was natural and right, each animal reproducing its own kind in the great chain of being, every mother caring for her own offspring exactly as every mother should.

Kep shivered. But behind him in the barn, in that hidden place under the feedbox, something was amiss, out of order, untoward. And Kep — who enjoyed a supreme confidence in his ability to tell right from wrong — was sorely perplexed. He had always prided himself on his intelligence, too. Even after Jemima told him that she had taken her eggs from another's nest, he had been confident that he could help her. After all, nature always followed predictable, orderly patterns. Given the right temperatures and the right amount of time, eggs hatched into baby birds. How hard could it be to find out what sort of birds these were meant to be?

But the collie could hardly believe his ears when Jemima told him where she had gotten her eggs. In his experience, eggs would simply not be found where she said she had discovered them. But Kep, who could not bring himself to doubt her, felt a deep sympathy for the duck, whose patient perseverance had won his respect. So he went down to the spot where she said she found her eggs, under a low-hanging willow tree, behind a fringe of ferns near a big rock on the sandy beach along the northern shore of Esthwaite Water, below Willow Bank Cottage.

Kep located the beach on Feswyke Inlet. He found the overhanging willow, the ferns, and the rock, and when he looked up the hill, he could see the half-hidden chimney of Willow Bank Cottage. He was in the right place, he was sure of it. But although the dog investigated the entire area thoroughly, using both his eyes and his sensitive nose, he could find no trace of the spot where Jemima had found the eggs (for that's what she had told him) half-buried in a shallow depression in the sand.

This had made no sense at all to Kep, for he had never met a bird who cared so little for her helpless babies that she did not build a nest to keep them safe, but simply scooped out a bowl in the sand. Kep was a collie, however, and collies are clever enough to know that there might be a thing or two in the world that they *don't* know. Somewhere out there was a bird who preferred to lay her eggs in a sandy bowl, and Kep had assigned to himself the task of finding her.

And then what? Since he was in charge, Kep had given some serious thought to answering this question. He would turn detective. He would investigate the scene of Jemima's crime — the place where she had stolen her eggs. He would locate the real mother. And when he did, he would tell her who had custody of her eggs — but only on the condition that she would allow Jemima Puddle-duck to continue to hatch them. Assuming of course that she was not a predator, the mother bird might be permitted visitation privileges while the hatching continued. In fact, if Jemima agreed, perhaps the two might take turn and turn about until the job was done.

And what would happen when the ten eggs hatched? Ah, there Kep had devised what he felt to be a brilliant solution, worthy of King Solomon. Ten was quite a large brood of babies, too many, really, for a single mother to rear on her own. He would divide the lot in half and give five birds to each mother, allowing each to fulfill her maternal destiny — assuming that the babies were not predators. If they were, the natural mother should be given full custody of the entire brood the moment they hatched, and sent on her way. Although he felt a deep sympathy toward the duck, he could not put other barnyard birds in jeopardy just to satisfy her obsessive need to be a mother.

Kep felt quite proud when he thought of his plan. So, even though he had failed to find the nest, he began looking around for the bird, who had likely been searching everywhere for her eggs — or perhaps she had already given up hope. She would be very glad when he told her that they were safe.

There were, of course, any number of birds feeding on the lake. There were ducks of several species, both surface-feeding ducks and diving ducks, all of whom looked to be promising possibilities. So he went to the water's edge and barked out a polite inquiry to the flock of ducks swimming in the water a little distance out into the lake.

"Excuse me, but is anyone acquainted with a mother duck who has mislaid a clutch of ten fine eggs? If so, would you be so kind as to tell me where I might find her?"

If the ducks knew the answer to Kep's question, they were keeping it selfishly to themselves, which was not very cooperative of them. Ignoring the collie, they went right on with their feeding, turning heads-down tails-up among the green rushes along the lakeshore, and having quite a fine time of it indeed.

Undeterred, Kep trotted up and down the beach, barking much louder now, loud enough for Captain Woodcock to hear him at Hawthorn House, which was just up the shore. But still the ducks paid no attention. Finally, he waded out into the knee-deep water and barked in thunderous tones, with all the energy he could summon. And this time the ducks only flew away, along with the terns and gulls and a pair of herons that had been stalking through the weeds. In fact, Kep would have been quite alone on the beach, if Jackboy Magpie had not flown past and shouted down at him, *"Roister-doister cloister noister!"*

By which Kep understood that his barking was disturbing the peace of the placid lakeside, so perhaps he had better desist, at least until he could think of a way to get the ducks' attention. Anyway, a collie is never without his list of things to do, and there were other tasks Kep had to attend to. So he had gone back to Hill Top, not quite discouraged yet (collies are never discouraged by anything), but definitely troubled.

He had not solved the mystery of Jemima's eggs, and his failure was disheartening.

Beside him, Rascal cleared his throat, bringing Kep back to the present *"But if not ducklings, then what?"* he said again. *"What sort of eggs does Jemima have?"*

Kep sighed. What sort of eggs, indeed? Swans' eggs? Goose eggs?

Hawks' eggs?

Or eagles'?

He closed his eyes and shuddered.

23
Miss Potter Goes to London

Once she was settled in for a stay at the farm, Beatrix always hated to go back to London, even if only for a few days. Usually, she was called back because she was needed at home. Her mother had gone to bed with a cold and required her to manage the servants, or her father required her to manage her mother (who was at times unmanageable by any power on earth). Or both the Potters were bored and resented their daughter's absence, so she was sent for. She must immediately leave off whatever she was doing at the farm (it couldn't be very important, anyway) and come directly home to amuse them.

But Mama and Papa were on holiday at Ulverston, and with any luck, would not require Beatrix's attention for another fortnight. So this time, she was going up to London on some necessary book business. She needed to talk to Mr. Harold Warne about the proofs of *The Roly-Poly Pudding* (which would be published in October) and about the Jemima Puddle-duck doll she had patented the year before and which ought to be going into production shortly. More uncomfortably, she also had to ask Mr. Fruing Warne about her overdue royalty payment. When Norman was alive, her monthly cheques had been punctual, and she could always count on an extra bit if she needed money for the farm. Lately, though, the payments had been slow and irregular, and she needed money to pay for the installation of some water pipes at the farm.

Beatrix planned to go up to London on Wednesday, stay at her parents' South Kensington home overnight, then call at the Warne offices on Thursday morning and at the home of Mrs. Moore (her former governess) in the afternoon, which would bring her back to the farm on Friday. Early on Wednesday morning, she took the ferry across Lake Windermere and caught the train, arriving at Bolton Gardens in time for a late tea.

Since most of the staff had accompanied the Potters to Ulverston, Beatrix had her tea in the pleasant third-floor room that had been her childhood nursery, then her schoolroom, and was now her painting studio. It was rather nice to be alone in the big house, she thought, as she sat down with her tray beside the fire. The place was quiet, peaceful — not usually the case when her parents were in residence and disagreeable bickering was the order of the day.

But while her meal and the fire were comforting, Beatrix was troubled by thoughts of Bertram, who by now was back at his farm in Scotland with Mary, his wife. His wife! Beatrix had not yet got used to the idea, so for now, she was resigned to feeling anxious and fidgety whenever she thought about it, the way you feel when a storm is brewing and you're not quite sure whether it's going to blow over or blow your house down and you along with it.

She was not troubled by the marriage itself, for her brother certainly had the right to marry whom he pleased, just as she should have had the right to marry Norman. But Bertram's lies distressed her — that, and the fact that he hadn't been strong enough to stand up for himself and what he wanted. She was glad he had told her, yes, but the revelation had shifted part of the guilty burden from his shoulders to hers. Really, she thought in exasperation, one ought always to be open and honest about things, no matter how ugly and unpleasant.

Being party to a secret — especially a potentially disastrous secret that could blow the family apart — gave her the nervous fidgets.

And of course, there was tomorrow's visit to the Warne offices in Bedford Street, which was bound to be yet another unpleasantness. Going there was like opening a raw, painful wound. Even though Norman had been dead for three years, it still seemed that he should be waiting to greet her with a smile and an affectionate word. And she felt his absence as keenly as she had his presence.

Norman had been the youngest of the three brothers who managed the publishing company founded by their father, Frederick Warne. It had been Norman who offered to publish *The Tale of Peter Rabbit* ("the bunny book," he called it with a chuckle) and had insisted that her illustrations be printed in color, despite the extra expense. It was Norman who encouraged her to think of ideas for more books, until she was writing and drawing two a year. And it was Norman who invited her to participate in the entire production process, not only writing and drawing and correcting the proofs, but helping to choose the paper, the end papers, the book bindings and cover designs — all the little details that turned each book into a miniature work of art, perfectly sized for a child's small hands. Beatrix always felt that her success was as much Norman's as hers, a product of his sympathetic and thoughtful guidance. She had loved him for it, and she missed him still, missed him more than she could possibly say.

But tomorrow, she would be meeting with Harold, the older Warne brother. The two of them had not been particularly close when Norman was alive, and that had not changed. In Harold, she often felt a subtle resistance to her ideas, and he certainly did not pay as much attention to business as Norman had. Beatrix was fond of Harold's family, and she had no intention of leaving the publishing house to which Norman had devoted himself. In fact, she had even made arrangements to bequeath her copyrights to the company in the event of her death. Still, it would be nice to feel that one's concerns were attended to without having to raise one's voice or stamp one's foot, she thought. And she certainly wished that her royalty payments were more dependable.

But the meeting at Warne's turned out to be cordial enough. She gave Harold her final corrections to *The Roly-Poly Pudding*. They discussed her scheme for *The Tale of the Flopsy Bunnies* (a sequel to *Peter Rabbit* and *Benjamin Bunny*) and the general outline of the Ginger and Pickles tale, which she was already sketching out as a Christmas present for Harold's little girl, Louie. They also talked about the patented Puddle-duck doll, which was being made up to see whether it could be economically manufactured without losing its charm. And before she left, Fruing, the middle Warne brother, gave her a cheque for fifty pounds and promised the same amount in October and December.

Leaving the office with the cheque in her pocket, Beatrix was pleased. Things didn't cost as much in the Lakes as they did in London, and the fifty pounds would take care of the waterworks she was planning, with a bit left over to add a new cow to the herd. As she stopped at a pleasant tea room for a salmon mayonnaise, a scone, and a cup of tea, she was looking forward to the afternoon, which she planned to spend with Annie Moore, her friend and former governess. She had a copy of *The Tale of Jemima Puddle-Duck* to share with the Moore children, and Miss Burns' package for Mrs. Moore. When she had finished her lunch, she hailed a cab and set off for Wandsworth, where Annie lived.

The afternoon was a delight. Annie was only three years older than Beatrix, but she had made her own way in the world before Mrs. Potter hired her as Beatrix's governess. Two years later, Annie married Edwin Moore and started her family, which now amounted to eight children. Beatrix visited when she could, often carrying a basket with a rabbit or a pair of guinea pigs, and when the youngsters were ill or she was away on holiday, she wrote them letters, some of which she had made into books.

Today was a special treat, for Noel was home for a visit. He was the boy for whom Beatrix had written the picture letter that later became *Peter Rabbit.* Stricken with polio at nine and left with a limp, he was now grown to a handsome young man who hoped to become an Anglo-Catholic priest. Four of the girls played for Beatrix — Freda on the piano, Norah the cello, Joan the viola, and Marjorie the violin — while Eric told her about his plan to become a civil engineer and travel the world, like his father. And then Beatrix took her four-year-old goddaughter Beatrix on her lap and read *Jemima Puddle-Duck* aloud to her and six-year-old Hilda, promising to send them a copy of the *Roly-Poly Pudding* when it came out in the fall. When Annie opened the package Beatrix had brought from Tidmarsh Manor, it turned out to be a set of linen napkins that Caroline had embroidered in cross-stitch — proving, Annie said with a laugh, that Miss Burns was properly educating Caroline in the art of being a lady. To which Beatrix replied tartly that she hoped fine sewing was not the only thing Caroline was learning from Miss Burns. "A little botany would be nice," she said, "not to mention geography."

Altogether, it was one of the most enjoyable afternoons Beatrix had spent in a long time. When she left to go back to South Kensington, she was still smiling, remembering the young Moores' bubbling energies and their mother's pleasure in all their accomplishments. But there was a sadness in her, as well, for she and Annie were very nearly the same age. If things had been different, she, too, might have had children and a loving husband.

Of course, Annie had a hard time making ends meet, and her husband (who might have been more loving and less argumentative) was often away from home, leaving her to raise the children by herself. It was not an altogether enviable situation, and Beatrix, who had always been a solitary person, did not *really* want to exchange places with her friend. If she had children, she wouldn't have her books. If she had a husband, she wouldn't have the farm. It was as simple as that.

But she paid a price for those treasures. Annie had her brood, and Bertram his wife, and here she was, alone. She sighed. Was this how it was going to be for the rest of her life? Would her books and her farm and her animals have to make up for human companionship, for support, for love? But when she heard the self-pitying undertone in that question, she shook herself and stopped it off at once. It did not do to spend one's energy pondering life's imponderables. She hailed a cab to take her back over the Thames.

A few blocks from home, she let the cab go and made one more brief call, leaving a copy of her book in Gilston Road for a little boy who was too ill to be sent away to school. The bell at St. Mary The Boltons had just chimed five when she started home, but a slow drizzle — chilly for August — was dropping a pall of mist over the streets and the afternoon was already as bleak and gray as winter twilight. Golden light spilled graciously from the windows of houses, and Beatrix could see people inside, setting out tea things or tending fires or simply sitting, reading. As she walked past St. Mary's churchyard, she thought of families and warmth and companionship, and it was all she could do to push back the self-pity. She put up her umbrella and began walking faster.

Now, both you and I know that every so often some incredibly bizarre things happen in this remarkable world of ours. In fact, if you are inclined to believe in the Folk (or fairies or elves or angels or any other supernatural being you fancy), it will not seem strange to you that occasionally these beings intervene in our lives, and even though we cannot see them, direct us in the way they mean us to go. And sometimes, if we are very obstinate or pig-headed or simply not paying attention, setting us on the right path takes a bit of muscle and a hard shove or two.

However that may be, it was at just this point in our story that the Folk may (or may not) have intervened. You see, St. Mary's is built on what had once been a farm and market garden called The Boltons, set in the midst of lush green fields. There was nothing left of this rural landscape, nothing except for three hawthorn trees, already old when the farm was young. At the very moment when Beatrix walked under those ancient hawthorn trees, she found herself, quite without thinking, turning into the churchyard and taking the path that goes through it, so that she came out on the far side of the church. (I daresay you have done such a thing once or twice in your life: You were so busy with your thoughts that you did not notice where you were going, and suddenly waked to find that you had taken a wrong turn and gone quite out of your way.)

That is what happened to Beatrix, who was surprised to find that she had not walked past the church but through the churchyard and out the opposite side. And then her glance fell on someone she knew, and she was even more astonished. This girl trudging along the sidewalk on the other side of the street, her arms filled with packages and a dark woolen shawl thrown over her head, could not possibly be —

But she was.

Yes, indeed, she was Emily Shaw, our Emily, whom Beatrix had last seen serving as Lady Longford's maid at Tidmarsh Manor, the very same Emily who had abruptly left her post and gone to work at Hawthorn House, and then, as Caroline had reported, to London, where she was now employed at Miss Pennywhistle's. The very same Emily (if Beatrix had only known it, which of course she did not) who had written a letter to her friend Deirdre, back in the village.

Call it coincidence or fate (or the intervention of the Thorn Folk), as I said, some remarkably odd things happen in this bizarre world of ours.

Beatrix stood for a moment, hesitating. She had lived a sheltered life, it was true, but she was an avid reader of the newspapers and no stranger to the social problems of her day. A girl who had left her village and employment in the Lakes and ventured to the city might have done so because she had made up her mind to go and see the world, and was happy to be out and about in such a lively place as London, where the streets and alleys were full of amusements and diversions. A greeting from an acquaintance might be a very welcome diversion.

On the other hand, Emily Shaw might have come to the City because she had something to hide. If that were the case, she would not be pleased to be greeted by someone who recognized her. She might even think she was being spied upon — and Beatrix, who valued her own privacy so highly that she had for years kept her journal in a secret code, understood that motive. Perhaps she should simply walk along home and let Emily go about Emily's private business.

But Beatrix was by nature curious, and she truly wanted to know why Emily Shaw had come to London. Almost before she realized what she was doing, she had crossed Gilston Road, dodging a horse-drawn lorry and a motor car with an annoying horn, and was walking only a few paces behind the girl. Had Emily come to work? Had she found a position, a place to stay? Was she living with someone — a lad, perhaps? If so, she would not be the first young girl whose heart's dream had drawn her away from hearth and home, to follow after someone who seemed to offer her everything she had ever hoped for. And she would not be the first, or the last, to discover that a heart's journey can be a sad and weary journey, not at all as it was imagined to be.

And then Beatrix's curiosity was overtaken by sympathy, for as she drew closer, she saw that Emily's dress was thin, her shoes poor, and her shawl skimpy. Worse yet, the girl had no umbrella, and the mist gleamed wetly on her shawl. And that was the very moment at which the heavens chose to open and send the rain down as if it were being poured out of a pail. (More fairy business, this?) Emily flinched, pulling her shawl up over her head in a futile effort to keep from being truly soaked. Beatrix stepped forward, holding her generous umbrella over both of them.

"Hello, Emily," she said. "The afternoon is very wet, I'm afraid."

Emily's head jerked around and her eyes widened incredulously. "Miss . . . Miss Potter!" she stammered. "How . . . what . . ."

"When I am not at the farm, I live just down the street and around the corner," Beatrix said. "At Number Two Bolton Gardens, with my parents. They're away on holiday just now, so I'm staying there by myself tonight." She smiled in a friendly way. "Are you living in this neighborhood now?"

"I . . . I —" Emily swallowed, and went silent. A moment after, in a low, reluctant voice, she said, "I have a place as an upstairs maid. At Miss Pennywhistle's Select Establishment."

"Oh, yes. Miss Pennywhistle's," Beatrix said. "I know it."

It was a grim place, one of dozens of similar boarding establishments all over the City that accepted the daughters of Army officers and government officials who were obliged to go to India and did not want to take their children with them. French was offered in such places, and music, and the history of English kings and queens, and fine sewing and sometimes art, but not much in the way of real education. Beatrix had sometimes seen a crocodile of Miss Pennywhistle's girls, holding hands and walking two by two down the street, under the watchful eye of their headmistress. The sight had always made her glad to be educated at home, where her governesses had generally allowed her to follow her own unconventional interests.

Miss Pennywhistle's could not be a very congenial place and Beatrix doubted that the "select young ladies" enrolled there were pleasant to the servants. Still, Emily had a situation, which meant that she also had a bed to sleep in and food to eat and was earning something — not much, probably, but something. And judging from the parcels in her arms, she was running an errand for her mistress.

Knowing this, Beatrix should have gone on, but it was raining so hard that she was loath to leave poor Emily without an umbrella. Impulsively, she said, "My house is quite nearby and I was just on my way home to tea. Would you have time to stop for a cup, Emily? You needn't stay long, of course

— and I'm sure I can find an umbrella that you may take with you when you leave."

For a moment, Beatrix thought the girl was going to say no. And then she turned her head, looked up with tear-filled eyes, and said, so low that Beatrix could barely hear her, "Oh, yes, Miss Potter. Oh, yes, please."

24

THE FOX, THE DUCK,
AND THE SHOT IN
THE NIGHT

I hope you have not forgotten the fox, even though it has been a good while since he appeared in our story. When we last saw Reynard Vulpes, he had been to dine with his friends at The Brockery. There, he had learnt Jemima's whereabouts — inadvertently, as it happened. Young Thorn had let it slip that she was confined to the barn, where she was sitting on a nest of eggs. And the look on Bosworth's face had told the fox (who was as clever as they come and could read other animals like a book) that the badger feared that his intentions were dishonorable.

Were they?

Perhaps. Or perhaps not. Who knows? Certainly not Reynard, for like many of us, who understand others better than we understand ourselves, the fox was not at all sure how he felt about Jemima. She was the duck who got away, a distasteful fact that certainly sharpened his appetite. Worse yet, she and that wretched collie — and Miss Potter, too, come to that — had made him look an utter fool. Word about the misadventure had traveled far and wide, and even farther, now that Miss Potter's book had achieved best-sellerdom. No question about it — the surest and most satisfactory way to redeem himself would be to raid the barn, snatch Jemima out from under the collie's nose (Miss Potter's, too), and eat her and her eggs on the spot, leaving a pile of bloody feathers and broken shells in testimony to his superior hunting skills. Reynard had no doubt that Jemima would taste just as good as the countless other ducks he had eaten. Foxes ate ducks. What could be simpler and easier than that?

But this particular truth, as truths often are, was complicated. The embarrassing fact of the matter was that over the course of the duck's visits to Foxglove Close, Reynard had grown almost too fond of her — not as a duck to be sauced or stewed or sautéed and served up at table, but as a duck who appreciated his talents as a gourmet cook, a duck who would laugh at his stories, a duck with whom he might enjoy an interesting dinner-table conversation. Reynard's solitary life was beginning to pall. He wanted company. He wanted companionship. He wanted . . . well, to be honest, he wanted Jemima.

But this was an unconventional, unorthodox, and even unnatural thought, so the fox (much as you or I, when confronted by some inexplicable paradox within ourselves) preferred not to think it. Instead, he made his way to Hill Top Farm the next morning (that would be Wednesday), where he lurked in the bushes and waited and watched as the animals went about their business. He saw the Herdwick sheep and their lambs, the Galloway cows and their calves, the mother pigs with their piglets, the hens with their chicks — all models of maternal domesticity. He also saw Mustard, the old yellow dog, napping in the sunshine beside the barn door, and Kep the collie patrolling the barnyard boundaries. There was no sign of Jemima, who was no doubt penned up, as Thorn had said, in the barn.

So the fox went off to find luncheon, which he did with the help of a young and inexperienced rabbit whom he met on the bank of Wilfin Beck. Then he retired to Foxglove Close, where he drank a cup of Turkish coffee, enjoyed a pipe of his favorite tobacco, and caught up on the newspapers. He napped until the moon floated up over

Cuckoo Brow Wood, at which time he took himself down to the barn, where he crept along the outside wall, sniffing until he came to a point directly behind Jemima's secret nest.

Ah, here she was! He stopped, closed his eyes, leaned against the wall, and inhaled deeply, smelling her scent — the fragrance of warm duck feathers, that unmistakably sweet-sour odor that spells d-u-c-k. This odor (which might have offended some delicate noses) was like attar of roses to our fox, who stood stock-still, inhaling deeply. Whether this was an emotional response or simply hunger, we are not permitted to know, but it is certainly true that he found the scent entrancing.

But the fox did not linger long in sweet enjoyment of Jemima's perfume, for the next moment, he heard the sound of barking. Kep the collie was rounding the corner of the barn at a gallop, shouting and snapping his teeth. Deciding that prudence was the better part of valor, Reynard took to his heels. Anyway, he now knew what he had come to find out: the whereabouts of his duck. His reconnaissance mission was a success, and he could call again when the dog was out on other business. (And yes, you are right to notice that the fox thought of the duck as "his," although in what sense he is using the term is not entirely clear.)

Of course, one creature's odiferous stench is another creature's perfume, so we should not be surprised that while Kep had found Reynard's scent "filthy," the duck had quite a different reaction. She had been dozing and dreaming on her nest, as she did much of the time (hatching is a boring business, after all, especially if it is too dark to read and you are not allowed a candle). In her dream, she was back at Foxglove Close with her dear friend, the sporting gentleman. He was offering her a whole plateful of the most exquisite Turkish Delight, and when she had eaten it, he escorted her to her own private boudoir, which was furnished with soft pillows spread with paisley shawls.

But now she is wide awake, no longer dreaming, and suddenly aware of the scent of . . . was it? Can it be? Yes, she is sure of it! The heady odor that hangs around her like a delicious fog is the favorite cologne of Mr. Vulpes, her very own sandy-whiskered sporting gentleman!

Now, Jemima knew very well that it would be smart to forget the fox, but his gracious charm, his delightful wit, his generous warmth all lingered in the duck's romantic heart. And even though Kep had made it brutally clear who Mr. Vulpes was and what he had wanted of her, none of the collie's warnings or admonitions made any difference. The truth — the irrefutable, indisputable truth (which she should have been ashamed to admit, but was not) — was this: that she cared for Mr. Vulpes. She yearned to leave her nest and these stupid eggs and run away with him. And why else would he have come, if it were not to fetch her?

Who knows what foolishness this simpleton duck might have got up to that night if it had not been for Kep the courageous? His barking awakened old Mustard, who had been sleeping just inside the barn, and both dogs were chasing the fox around the garden, howling and baying and making a furious noise. Mustard could not see very well in the dark, however, and blundered into the cucumber frame, adding the smash of breaking glass to the general clamor.

All this fracas woke Winston the pony, who began to mutter imprecations against rude fellows who stayed up all night, romping and roistering about the garden while respectable working animals were trying to get their sleep.

On the rafter over Winston's head, Chanticleer the rooster also awoke. Thinking that he had somehow slept through the dawn, he raised his voice and announced with authority that the day had begun. (Why he thought this, I don't know, since it was still pitch-black outside, but there's a rooster for you.) Mrs. Boots and Mrs. Shawl, who knew exactly what time it was and that it was *not* time to get up, began to cackle with loud vexation, telling Chanticleer exactly what they thought of inconsiderate roosters.

Upstairs at the Jenningses' end of the Hill Top farmhouse, the barking dogs and crowing rooster and cackling hens awakened Baby Pearl, the youngest Jennings, who began to scream at the top of her baby lungs. Mrs. Jennings, in her hurry to comfort her daughter, knocked over the bedroom washstand, breaking the china pitcher and basin into smithereens.

At nearby Tower Bank Arms (which is very close to the Hill Top farmhouse, as you know if you have ever been to the village), the windows were open on this warm August night, and the Barrows (father and mother and two small Barrows) were asleep upstairs. Mrs. Barrow heard the barking, the crowing and cackling, the crashing of glass and china, and thought that a thief must have broken into the pub through the scullery window. She roused Mr. Barrow, who got up and fetched his bird-hunting gun from the closet whilst she ran to fling herself over the bodies of her children, to protect them from their horrible fate.

Now, Mr. Barrow is a crack shot, and no one brings home more red grouse or pheasants in season than he. He has even won prizes for his shooting at the Hawkshead sporting competition held each year in April, so it must not be said that he is unskilled with his gun. But having never confronted a burglar before, he was understandably nervous (as I daresay you or I would be, in the circumstance). He tripped over his pyjama leg and fell flat on his face. His shotgun discharged, the thunderous blast blowing the glass out of the pub's front door and frightening Tabitha Twitchit and Crumpet, who were innocently hunting voles under the rosebushes in the Buckle Yeat garden next door, and startling the clan of bats who lived in the Buckle Yeat roof. The cats, thinking that Mr. Barrow was firing at them, cried out in alarmed protest and climbed up the beech tree. Mrs. Barrow, thinking that the burglar had killed her husband and that she and her children were next to be slaughtered, added her voice.

And since this is a village and each house is cheek-to-jowl with its neighbor, the alarm was instantaneous. Up Market Street at

Croft End Cottage, Constable Braithwaite was startled out of a pleasant dream (we shall not report its subject) by the shattering roar of Mr. Barrow's shotgun, followed by the ear-splitting shrieks of female and feline voices. Fearing the worst, the valiant constable sprang out of bed, pulled his trousers on under his red flannel nightshirt, and ran at top speed down Market Street to the pub, brandishing his truncheon and shouting "Stop, thief!" loudly enough to frighten off the most foolhardy of villains and waken the soundest of village sleepers — which of course he did. The thief (that is, the fox, who had come calling on Jemima) was nowhere to be seen, but all along Market Street, people were waking up, jumping out of bed, and hurrying to their windows to find out who had been shooting and who had been shot.

And when at last the constable returned up the street to Croft End, he had to answer the questions everyone shouted at him out their windows, until the village was finally satisfied that there was no danger. No one had been injured, and the only serious casualties seemed to be a cucumber frame, two pieces of Hill Top china, and the front door of the pub. Still, it was a full half hour before Market Street had gone back to its slumbers and Mr. Barrow had persuaded Mrs. Barrow that she and the two little Barrows would not be murdered in their beds.

When the hurly-burly began — and especially when she heard the roar of Mr. Barrow's shotgun — Jemima had been very frightened for the fox's safety. But as the cacophony abated and Kep's barking and Mustard's baying sounded fainter and farther away, she knew with relief that Mr. Vulpes was safe. He was very fast, he knew the lay of the land better than any dog, and there were any number of dens where he could find refuge. Mustard would never even see his back, and not even Kep was fast enough to catch him.

Winston went to sleep, Chanticleer settled back on his rafter, the hens stopped clucking, and there was silence at last. Jemima heaved a heavy sigh. If she were allowed to choose, she would leave off this tedious undertaking and follow her friend. But she could feel the new life stirring beneath her. Soon there would be ducklings. She would be a mother, and she could not, must not, *would not* abandon her babies in pursuit of her own pleasures.

But after what had happened tonight, Jemima was now beginning to think outside of her nest. She would not be a mother forever, for it was in the nature of ducklings to grow up and leave her with an empty nest. Once her babies were hatched, it would be only a matter of hours before they were running about the barnyard. In only a few short weeks they would be completely on their own, ready to join the rest of the Puddle-duck flock. Oh, they would come back to her now and then to show off a new accomplishment, or to consult about a particular social problem, or just to tell her they loved her. But basically, they would be their own ducks, with their hopes and their own dreams, and she would be free to have a life of her own, at last. At last!

Jemima took a deep breath, stretched her wings, and resettled herself on the nest. She would prove to Kep and the Puddle-ducks, and especially to Miss Potter, that she could be a good mother, even though it meant denying herself, momentarily, at least.

But as soon as her obligation to her ducklings was satisfied, she would be responsible to no one but herself. She could fulfill what she now admitted was her heart's dearest wish: to be with her own dear sporting gentleman, the one in green tweeds, with beautiful sandy whiskers.

25
CAPTAIN WOODCOCK
LEARNS THE LATEST

The shotgun blast in the night was not the only thing the village had to discuss on Thursday morning, and by Thursday noon, all the various bits and pieces of gossip had been neatly sorted and conclusions reached, proving once again that there is nothing like a village for managing everyone's affairs.

There was both bad news and good news, certainties and uncertainties, and something for everyone.

The bad news was that Miss Woodcock was to marry Major Kittredge and adopt Flora, the foundling infant. There was great dismay over this, because it was widely felt that the major's reputation was forever tarnished by his decision to marry that London actress, and that poor Miss Woodcock, who was widely acknowledged to be the nearest thing to a saint most people had ever met, would be tarred by the same wicked brush. In the general opinion, this marriage was a monumental mistake.

The good news was that Captain Woodcock was to marry Miss Potter. Cheers were heard when this got abroad, although not perhaps for the reason one might think: that everyone wished the couple well and desired their marital happiness. Instead, it was generally believed that the reins of Hill Top Farm belonged in a man's hands, not a woman's — and what more capable hands than those of Captain Woodcock?

It was also felt to be good news that Elsa Grape (a proud person who would never in the world allow herself to be managed by Miss Potter, when Miss Potter became Mrs. Woodcock) was going to work at the vicarage, where the vicar had been in serious want of managing for some time, witness the hems of his trousers and the elbows of his sweaters and the sad want of sweets at the vicarage tea.

But far as the ancestry of the foundling infant was concerned, the village was still in doubt. Some said (darkly, with a frown) that the mother was a gypsy and the father was the major, and Miss Woodcock ought to have a care how she threw her life away on a man who didn't deserve it. Others suspected that the mother and father were *both* gypsies, and that Miss Woodcock ought to have a care about taking in a gypsy child, since it was bound to bring her nothing but grief. None were quite certain how the gypsy (or half-gypsy) child got to Miss Potter's doorstep: some blamed the gypsies themselves, while a few of the older folk insisted that the Folk surely had a hand in it. But whilst there was a great deal of uncertainty about Flora's ancestry, the village had a very firm opinion as to her future. Gypsy children did not belong in the village. She should be sent to the parish workhouse, to grow up with the other foundling children.

Captain Miles Woodcock, who never paid the slightest attention to village gossip, was quite unaware that his marital destiny, and that of his sister Dimity, had been decided. He was, however, anxious to confirm what he had learnt from Hawker in the garden at Hawthorn House, and find out whether anyone in the village knew which of the local girls had just gone off to London. In his own mind, he was calling this problem "The Case of the Missing Mother," and felt he had resolved it quite nicely. Baby Flora was the daughter of a servant girl who had given birth to her at Hawthorn House and had then run off to London, leaving the infant behind. All he had left to find out was her name.

The captain had intended to look further into the matter on Tuesday evening but was prevented by an unexpected bit of business that took him off to Manchester. So it was Thursday night before he could drop in at the Tower Bank to see what he could learn. The pub — the front door of which had been recently and hastily repaired — smelt of fried fish, strong malt ale, and tobacco smoke. Men crowded around the bar, around the backgammon table, and around the dart board, and every so often a cheer would go up. The evening was off to a rousing start.

"Hullo, Cap'n," said Lester Barrow cordially, swiping the bar with his cloth. Lester was a hefty man whose red plaid waistcoat barely buttoned about his middle. "Good evenin' to ye, sir."

Miles sat on a stool and put his elbow on the bar. "What happened to your front door?"

Lester Barrow ducked his head. "Bit of an accident with a shotgun," he muttered. "Had a prowler last night."

"A prowler?" the captain asked, frowning. As the King's justice, he felt he should be aware of any breach of the peace — although of course he had been away from home the previous night and had thus missed out on the general melee.

"Well, not to say a prowler exactly, sir," said Lester Barrow, reddening. "T' missus *thought* it was a prowler, only t' constable reckoned it to've been a fox or t' like, up at Hill Top. T' dogs went through a cucumber frame, and the Jenningses' washbasin got tipped, and t' missus thought it was t' scullery window bein' broke."

"Ah," Miles said, only rather dimly understanding. "Well, then. I'll have a half-pint, if you please." He leaned forward, lowering his voice. The villagers were terrible gossips, the men as much as the women, and he wasn't anxious to call attention to his investigation. "And some information."

"If I've got it," Lester said, pouring the ale and sliding the glass across the polished surface. He raised his own glass in salute. "Congratulations, sir," he added with a sly smile. "We're all for it."

"Thank you," Miles said, wondering vaguely why he was being congratulated. "P'rhaps you might know a housemaid who went up to London a short time ago, in Puckett's cart. I mean," he corrected himself, "that she took the cart to the ferry. I assume that she went by train to London."

"Puckett's cart, eh?" Mr. Barrow raised his voice over the din of voices. "Auld Puckett! Hey, Puckett! Get thisel' over here, man. T' cap'n wants a word."

Miles winced, not wanting his request made so publicly. But a wizened old man dressed in brown sacking was turning away from the darts board, squinting through the tobacco smoke. It was Puckett, who had previously worked in the charcoal pits but resorted to driving his cart for hire when he fell off his roof and broke his leg.

"A word?" Puckett piped, in a high, thin voice. "T' cap'n's not goin' to arrest me, is he?"

This question provoked raucous laughter among the darts players, who seemed to find the idea exceptionally funny. They elbowed each other, guffawing. "T' cap'n aims to make thi license that auld cart, Puckett," one said. Another added, "Puckett's goin' to be fined for carryin' contraband hither 'n' yon, like t' auld smuggler he is."

"He wants to ask somethin' verra important, Puckett," bellowed Mr. Barrow over the clamor. "Git thisel' over 'ere, old man."

At the word "important," a hush fell over the crowd, and curious heads turned in Miles' direction. So much for carrying out his investigation in private, he thought rue-fully. He motioned to Lester Barrow to refill the old man's half-pint, and said, in a low voice, "I understand that you conveyed a certain serving maid down to the ferry one morning recently. Going up to London, she was — or so I'm told."

Old Puckett drained his mug thirstily, put it on the bar, and wiped his gray mustache with the back of his gnarled hand. "Aye," he allowed. "That I did, sir." He scowled. "Bad bus'ness, her goin' to Lon'on. Told her so, I did. Said, 'Girls got no business in t' City.' But her didn't listen." He shook his head sadly. "Females nivver listen to me. Fer as they're concerned, I'm jes' an auld man laid up wi' a gammy leg.'"

"Who was she?" Miles asked. "What's her name?"

"Name?" The old man lifted his brown cap, scratched his head, and glanced craftily at his empty mug. "Name? Well, now, I —"

Miles sighed, resigned. "Another half-pint," he said to Lester Barrow. When it was brought, he picked up the mug before Puckett could grasp it, holding it just out of the old man's reach.

"Her name," he said firmly.

"Ah," said Puckett. He pursed his lips, frowning. "Well, then. If I remember a-reet, her name was Em'ly." He put out his hand for the mug. "Em'ly," he said again, louder.

Miles moved the mug away. "Emily who?"

The old man frowned. "I doan't know, now, do I?" he said crossly. "Who keeps a tally of t' village girls?" He pushed his thin lips in and out, regarding the glass. "Must've come from Hawthorn House, though. 'Twas Hawker who carried her bag to t' road and put it on t' cart."

Well, thought Miles, at least they were speaking of the same girl.

"Em'ly from Hawthorn House?" asked a deferential voice at Miles' left elbow. "That 'ud be her ladyship's Em'ly, I do b'lieve, sir. Em'ly Shaw." The speaker was another man, not so old and stooped as Puckett, with the tanned face and hands of one who worked out of doors. Miles knew him by sight: Matthew Beever, gardener and coachman at Tidmarsh Manor.

"Emily Shaw, you say?" Miles asked in surprise. He'd had a brief acquaintance with the girl in the previous year, when she testified as a witness in the trial of a woman who had made an attempt on Lady Longford's life. A pretty girl, and intelligent, if flighty. But all girls her age were flighty, he supposed.

"Aye, Em'ly Shaw," said Matthew Beever.

He shook his head. "Naughty, her was," he said darkly. "Verra naughty. Carryin' on wi' that gypsy lad. Girls nivver come to no good, goin' on that way."

At last they were getting someplace, Miles thought with satisfaction. "Tell me," he invited.

Pressing his lips together, Beever glanced at old Puckett's glass and then up at Miles. Miles signaled to Lester Barrow. Thus fortified, the gardener spilled the story.

Emily Shaw, while she was still in Lady Longford's employ, had been seen walking out with a lad from the gypsy camp. One of the other servants had reported this, which had led Beever to keep a close watch. When he found them talking together late one evening behind the barn, he had summarily banished the boy and had forbidden Emily to see him again.

"Sent 'im packin', I did," he reported gruffly. "Heard he went south to work in t' hops fields, and not a minute too soon." He shook his head. "Girls that age got no sense. Her'd been mine, I wud've whipped her. Them gannan-folk are nivver up to no good."

Miles didn't hold with corporal punishment, although he understood Beever's concern. Still — "You don't know whether things went any further than talking?" he asked.

"Who knows?" Beever peered up at Miles from under bushy gray eyebrows. "But when her up and left that fast, I sez to Missus Beever it didna look reet t' me. Leavin' Tidmarsh where her was known and gan to Hawthorn House — leastwise, that's what her said. Sounded fishy to me. Hawthorn House's stood empty these last years, since t' Thorn Folk curst it. Why 'ood her want to gan there, if not to hide hersel' away?"

The Thorn Folk. Miles made an impatient noise. One would think someone as sensible as Beever would see how ridiculous it was to further those old superstitions. "So you think the girl —"

"Who knows?" Beever said again. He glanced regretfully into his glass, then up at Miles, who shook his head. "Ah, well," he said, and drained the last drop. "Gone up to Lon'on, has her? I doan't wonder." And with that, he stood up.

"Thank you," said Miles, feeling that the evening had not been a loss. Between Beever and old Padgett, he had made a little headway, after all. He now knew the name of the girl who had worked at Hawthorn House, and who (presumably) had pawned the cornelian signet ring. But one important piece of information was missing. "You have no idea where in London she might have gone?" he asked.

Beever shook his gray head, then brightened, thinking of something else. "Congratulations, Cap'n." He offered a rough hand. "Her's a fine lady, I sez. Betimes a bit short in her manner. Not one to suffer fools. But fine, all t' same. Good luck, sez I, and so does t'missus."

Miles shook the proffered hand, very confused as to pronouns. Who was the mysterious "her"?

"Congratulations?" he asked. "What's this about, Beever?"

Beever broke into a loud laugh, which was echoed by old Padgett and Lester Barrow, on the other side of the bar, and by those who had gathered around them.

"What's this about?" Beever gasped, after a moment. "Why, Cap'n Woodcock, 'tis about yer weddin', that's what."

"My . . . wedding?" Miles asked inarticulately. "What wedding?"

"Yer weddin' to Miss Potter," Lester Barrow said, grinning. "T' village has been talkin' of nothin' else — except, o'course," he added, "your sister's weddin'." He sobered. "There's talk o' that, too."

"My wedding to . . . to Miss Potter!" Miles

felt his mouth drop open.

"Why, aye!" said Mr. Llewellyn, of High Green Gate Farm. Llewellyn was Miles' near neighbor, and rented part of his pasture land. "Aye, and grand news it is, too, Cap'n! 'Tis good that a man gets charge o' Hill Top at last. Miss Potter's fine in her way — I doan't say a word agin' her. But her spends too much time in Lon'on, and t' farm suffers fer it." He leaned forward and said, with a confidential air, "Tha'll take good care o' her affairs, I'll warrant. And if tha decides to sell that parcel on t' other side of t' Kendal Road, why, I'd have an interest."

And even Mr. Jennings, Miss Potter's tenant farmer, held a positive view. "I'll be pleased to work fer thi, sir," he said, shaking Miles' hand vigorously. "Not that I doan't like Miss Potter, but it's just not t' same, workin' fer a lady."

By this time, Miles was so completely confounded that he hardly knew how to answer. He made one or two starts, but barely got his mouth open when he was congratulated by Henry Stubbs, the ferryman, followed by Roger Dowling, the joiner, and Mr. Skead, the sexton at St. Peter's — all offering their jubilant congratulations. It was clear that the match met wide approval throughout the village.

And then it got worse. Lester Barrow — a man who was so parsimonious that he would skin a flea for a ha'penny — began handing out free half-pints. Mrs. Barrow appeared with several bowls of roasted chestnuts, and the men in the pub gathered around, glasses upraised, and began to sing "For he's a jolly good fellow." This was followed by three resounding huzzahs, so loud that the glasses rattled behind the bar.

At last there was a moment's silence, and Miles raised his hands.

"Thank you," he said, conscious that the men of the village had just paid him — still an outlander, even though he had lived there for some fifteen years — an enormous compliment. He could only be grateful, but he had to nip this rumor in the bud, if that were possible. "However, I must tell you that your congratulations are completely undeserved. While I admire and respect Miss Potter to the greatest degree possible, we have not agreed to marry. I have no idea how this tale got started, but I ask you to help me put paid to it, here and now."

The silence was so profound that we might have heard a mouse cough, had there been a mouse in the corner. Then old Padgett said incredulously, "Her's turned thi down, sir?" Wide-eyed, he appealed to Beever. "Miss Potter's turned down our cap'n?"

"The question has not been asked," Miles replied, with the awkward feeling that whatever he said would only make matters worse. "Someone has been spreading untrue gossip."

Henry Stubbs leaned over to old Padgett and remarked, wisely, "He's sayin' that congratulations are primmy chure." Henry's hold on the English language was almost as slippery as that of his wife Bertha's. "He's sayin' they ain't pronounced it yet. They're keepin' it unner their hats." This produced another cheer from the gathered crowd.

Miles was floundering now, confused and uncertain. "It is not my intent to ask the question," was what he meant to say, but even as he formed the words, he bit them back. The idea had suddenly struck him, like a bolt of lightning accompanied by a tooth-rattling clap of thunder, that asking Miss Potter to marry him might not be such a very bad thing, after all.

And with the thought came a great happiness and surprising lightness of spirit. Why, the idea was exactly right! Miss Potter would suit him admirably. She was of an age to know her mind and be settled in her choices. For a woman, she had eminently good sense, and to top it off, she had her own fortune and property. As for himself, he found her attractive, sweetly serious, even tender. He could surely be of help to her with her farm responsibilities, and she would be able to manage Elsa Grape much more strictly than did Dimity. They would be very comfortable together. Yes, indeed, it was a wonderful idea, a perfect idea. Why hadn't it occurred to him before this?

"Tha'rt sayin' the property across t' road won't be for sale?" Mr. Llewellyn asked, in a tone of great disappointment.

Miles smiled. "I am only saying, gentlemen, that this is not yet the time for celebration." Feeling quite pleased with himself, he turned to Lester Barrow and added, "Another round of drinks, Mr. Barrow. On my account, if you please."

He was making his way to the door when little Mrs. Barrow plucked his sleeve. "I just want to say," she said nervously, "that I'm pleased to hear 'bout Miss Woodcock and t' major. I know what everybody is sayin', that she's throwin' hersel' away on someone who doan't deserve her. But I person'ly think t' major's a fine man, and verra brave to give his arm and his eye to his country. I wish 'em both t' best, I truly do, and t' babe as well, poor bairn."

Miles frowned. "Pardon me, Mrs. Barrow. What exactly is it that you have heard about my sister and Major Kittredge?"

"Why, that they're to be married," she said, looking flustered. "Everybody in t' village knows it. They mean to take t' babe to live with 'em, too — t' gypsy babe who was left with Miss Potter."

There was a sudden hush as everyone in the pub turned to hear his response, but Miles scarcely comprehended. He felt as if he had been slapped in the face, or (more accurately) struck over the head with a cricket bat.

Dimity had gone against him? It could not be allowed!

"Rubbish!" he declared. "My sister knows I would never permit such a thing." He looked around at the assembled throng. "Never, do you hear! Never!"

And with that final lordly pronouncement, he brushed past Mrs. Barrow and through the door, slamming it shut behind him.

Now, you and I, from our modern vantagepoint, know how unfair (and usually futile) it is to attempt to impose our opinions on another, particularly where matters of the heart are concerned. But at the time of our story, this was a lesson that many people — including our own cool-headed, thoughtful Captain Woodcock, so admirable in so many ways — had yet to learn. Outside in the dark, this representative of the King's law and order stood for a moment, breathing deeply of the clean, smoke-free air, shaking his head to clear it.

Dimity and that . . . that Kittredge fellow! What in the world could she be thinking? Why, the man's reputation was utterly tarnished. It could never be redeemed! If Dimity married him, she should have to accept a share in his humiliation. And the idea that she would adopt that foundling child, that *gypsy* child? The whole business was out of the question, and the sooner he set her straight, the better.

He pushed his hands deep into his pockets and strode home in a violent temper, the pleasure that had risen inside him when he thought of marrying Miss Potter all but blown away by the storm of anger that raged in his head and his heart.

Meanwhile, back in the pub, the villagers' assessment of the situation was undergoing rapid revision. Miss Woodcock was not going to marry the major after all, because the captain would not permit it. The captain and Miss Potter would be married at some future date, but for the present, their engagement was a secret, which meant that Elsa Grape would probably stay where she was, and the vicar would have to find someone else to manage his hems and elbows. As to the fate of the foundling infant — well, it now seemed virtually certain that she would be sent off to the parish work-house, where she belonged.

Yes, indeed. There is nothing like a village for managing everyone's affairs.

26
MISS WOODCOCK
TAKES A STAND

Major Christopher Kittredge, quite unaware that anyone other than himself and the woman he loved might have taken an interest in their possible marital arrangements, had spent the past two days in London, dealing with his banking and property affairs. This activity was challenging, because the major was the last of the Kittredges and had inherited a number of family properties that required his attention.

But this challenge was as nothing compared to the challenges of the heart. All the while the major was telling his bankers this and his estate agents that and his business managers the other thing, his mind was full of Dimity Woodcock and the recollection of how willingly she had come into his embrace, how easily and sweetly she had said yes.

But the sweetness of Dimity's yes was mixed with the pungent bitterness of her no, which was what the major tasted in his mouth as he took the train to the Lakes, arriving late on Thursday evening. Things changed when he got back to Raven Hall, however, where the butler handed him the cream-colored envelope that had been delivered just a few hours before, from Miss Woodcock.

The major held it in his hand for a moment, hardly daring to breathe. Was she offering him a ray of hope, a slender thread of possibility? Or was she telling him that no was the final answer? If that was it, perhaps he would leave Raven Hall and go back to the Army — if the Army would have him. One-eyed, one-armed majors weren't in great demand these days.

At last he could stand the suspense no longer. He tore open the envelope and read the note inside. (He did not read it out loud, so we will have to wait to find out what it says.) Then, although his dinner was already growing cold on the table, he called for his horse and rode as if the devil were after him through the night to Tower Bank House, reaching the village just about the time the men in the pub were congratulating the captain on his marriage to Miss Potter. In fact, the major rode past the pub very shortly before Captain Woodcock quit it in a deplorable temper, having learnt that the village expected his sister to marry the major.

When Christopher was shown into the library at Tower Bank House, he went straight to the sofa where Dimity was sitting and folded her into his embrace, from which I think we can gather that her no had become a yes. He had already kissed her once and was about to kiss her again when her brother came striding down the hall and burst into the room. Feeling awkward (as I have no doubt you would, too, caught in a similar circumstance), Christopher sprang to his feet.

"Good evening, Woodcock," he said, in as pleasant a tone as he could manage. "Nice to see you again." Of course, it was *not* nice to see him, as you can imagine, for the major would much rather have continued kissing his lady-love than engage in conversation with her brother — especially since he could see the anger written across the brother's face.

"You!" the captain shouted angrily, making a fist. "What are you doing here, Kittredge?"

Christopher wanted to say that he was kissing Woodcock's sister and enjoying it enormously, thank you very much. But this was clearly not an appropriate reply, under the circumstances. He was fumbling for other words when Dimity rose from the sofa, her pink silk skirt rustling.

"Major Kittredge came at my request, Miles," she said in a conciliatory tone. "I wish you would not —"

"This is my house," the captain growled, drawing the battle lines. "Get out, Kittredge. You're not welcome here."

The hair rose on the back of the major's neck. He had not expected such an open declaration of war so soon, even before he'd had a chance to declare his intentions, which were decidedly honorable. (The major could not be expected to know that the captain had already heard about the proposed marriage and had just announced to the assembled male population of the village that he would not permit it to happen. This was truly unfortunate, of course, for once a man like Captain Woodcock has made a public declaration, he cannot take it back without seeming to lose face.)

"Out!" the captain thundered, as the major tried to think about the least provocative way to say that he hoped to claim the captain's sister's hand in holy matrimony.

Clearly dismayed at the sudden turn this conversation was taking, Dimity stepped into the fray. "It is my house, too, Miles," she said. "I asked Major Kittredge to come so that we could discuss our plans to —"

"I won't hear of this," the captain said, turning away. His voice was shaking. "I appeal to you, Dim. No, I order you. Send him away. Now. This minute. To ally yourself to him is to link your name with shame and disgrace."

Christopher looked down at Dimity. She was pale, and he could feel her trembling. What would she say? What would she do? She loved him, he knew. But Miles was her brother, after all, the highest authority in her life. She had lived with him for a very long time, and had accustomed herself to being governed by his wishes. Had she ever in her life said no to him? Could she now?

Dimity squared her shoulders. When she spoke, her voice was soft but astonishingly firm. "I know this is painful for you, Miles, but you *must* hear it. Major Kittredge has asked me to marry him and I have agreed."

The captain turned, his fists clenched, his feelings written on his face in hard, angry lines. "You cannot do this, Dimity. You know how strongly I disapprove." His eyes went to Christopher, then back to his sister. "This is not the man I want you to marry. He is not the sort of husband you deserve." His voice broke. "He has been married before. His reputation is disgraceful."

Christopher opened his mouth to speak up in his own defense, but stopped. What could he say? Woodcock was right. He had made an ass of himself, marrying a woman who had deceived him, a woman who was already married. It was a stigma he would carry to his grave. Did he have any right to ask Dimity to share his shame? Wasn't he being conceited and selfish? His better self spoke up and answered the question bluntly. Yes. Yes, of course he was being conceited, fiendishly so. And unforgivably selfish, too. But all the same —

"And I'm not the only one who feels this way, Dimity." The captain held out his hands in appeal. "I've just come from the pub, where I was told flat out that everyone in the village is against this marriage. They say you are throwing your life away on a man who does not deserve it. They say —"

"Wait a minute," Christopher said, by now thoroughly confused. "How did the village get into this? I've just learnt about it a little bit ago."

"The village always knows everything, Christopher," Dimity said practically. "One can never keep anything secret."

"They say you are going to take that baby,

too!" the captain said in an anguished tone, as though he had been saving the worst until the last. "That *foundling.*"

"Miles!" Dimity exclaimed heatedly. "Every baby deserves a home, and parents who love it. And who more than a foundling?"

The captain's face twisted. "Well intentioned, I'm sure. But her mother is a servant, and her father is a gypsy who's gone south to work in the hops fields. Not the sort of child you can be proud of, Dimity."

"So you've found the parents?" Dimity asked, half-fearfully. She swallowed. "Is it likely that they'll want the baby back?"

"I've no idea," the captain said. "But the child is a gypsy. You don't want —"

"Well, I don't see that being a gypsy makes any difference," Christopher said, trying to be logical. "As long as the parents are willing to renounce their claim, of course. There's enough room at Raven Hall for a dozen children. And we will hire a nursemaid, so there will be no extra work for Dimity." His better self reminded him that he was still being conceited and selfish, and that perhaps the lady had changed her mind, in the face of her brother's outspoken opposition. "That is, if she still agrees to marry me," he said, more tentatively.

Dimity looked up at him, her eyes shining. "Of course I do, Christopher," she replied. "I'm not going to change my mind." She turned to look directly at her brother. "I don't care a fig what the villagers are saying, Miles. And while I love you and will be forever grateful to you for giving me a home, I don't care a fig what *you* say, either."

"Dimity!" the captain exclaimed, astonished. "You can't mean that!"

Dimity looked down, biting her lip. "No, I don't suppose I do, not really. What you think matters very much to me, Miles. I —"

"There you are, then!" said the captain triumphantly. "You've been a dear sister, Dimity, and we've always got on quite well. You've always done what I wanted, haven't you? What I suggested," he amended in a different tone, as if "wanted" might have been a bit too direct.

"I've always done what you've wanted, because it's been something I wanted, too," Dimity replied. "We have never disagreed." She hesitated. "Except about little things, of course, like the rose-and-ivy wallpaper in the front hall, and whether to hire a new gardener or carry on with Fred Phinn until he can't pull weeds any longer."

Christopher's heart sank. Was she saying —

Dimity reached for Christopher's hand. "This is different, Miles. You and the village may say whatever you like, but Christopher and I mean to marry. We have not yet discussed a date, but I hope it will be within the next few months."

The next few months? Christopher felt his heart leap up within him again, and it was all he could do to keep from shouting with joy. The next few months! The best he might have hoped for — if he dared to hope at all — was a year, perhaps even two. But a few months! By thunder, there were things to do! A wedding to be planned, a honeymoon to be arranged, changes to be made at Raven Hall —

"I cannot believe you would act against my wishes," the captain said sourly, shoving his hands into his pockets.

"It is very hard, Miles," Dimity confessed in a low voice. "I wasn't sure that I could do it. But when Beatrix asked me to imagine living my life with Christopher and then imagine my life without him, I knew what I had to do."

The captain looked up sharply. "You discussed this . . . this private matter with someone outside the family?" His eyes grew dark. "With Miss Potter?"

Christopher was taken aback. He knew

who Miss Potter was, of course. She was the sharp-eyed, sharp-witted lady who had unraveled the mystery of the woman he had thought was his wife. Now, it seemed, he was even deeper in her debt, if it had been her counsel that led Dimity to agree to marry him.

"Why, yes, of course I discussed it with her," Dimity replied defiantly. "And I'm glad I did, for she could advise me out of her own personal experience. Her parents forbade her to marry because they felt the man she had chosen was not worthy. She didn't want me to go through my whole life regretting that I had not stood up for myself." She slid a glance at Christopher. "For us," she said firmly, and Christopher felt his heart warm.

"Us" was a beautiful word, he thought happily. Perhaps the most beautiful word in the language. Such a small word, but so full of meaning, so rich with significance, so —

"But that is the very reason why you must not be swayed by her advice!" the captain exclaimed heatedly. "She can scarcely be objective." He appears to have forgotten (although I am sure that you have not) that just thirty minutes ago he had been thinking with pleasure of Miss Potter's great good sense, with the thought of marrying the lady. Now, perhaps, he is reconsidering.

"Nevertheless," Dimity replied, "she was helpful. If it had not been for her —" She stopped. "I am sure that you don't mean to be patronizing, Miles. I know that you have a deep respect for Miss Potter — and for me. I know how much you love me, and how much you want to make me happy."

The captain blinked. If we were to open his head and peer inside, we would no doubt find it rather like a laundry tub full of a confused welter of swirling thoughts swishing this way and that, but dominated by a stunned incredulity. How could it be that his docile, always-agreeable sister was acting contrary to his wishes? From their earliest years together until the present day, he could remember no time when she had not been deferential, when she had not followed his lead, when she had refused to do what he wanted. This — this *refusal* was something straight out of one of Ibsen's dramas, out of *A Doll's House.* What had got into her? Had Miss Potter somehow infected her with a modern view of feminism and female rights?

With a start, he heard Dimity say, in a voice he hardly recognized, "Now that the matter of our marriage is settled, Christopher and I should like to have some time alone. We have things to discuss."

Miles swallowed. He hated to capitulate. He hated the thought that the village would know that Kittredge had bested him. And most of all, he hated the thought of his sister marrying the man. But he had to face the fact that he had no real authority over her. And even if he had, even if she agreed to do what he said, she might hate him forever.

He took a deep breath and put out his hand to the major. "I suppose this calls for congratulations, then," he said stiffly. He narrowed his eyes. "You will be good to her, Kittredge. If you're not, I shall drag you out and thrash you within an inch of your life."

"I will be good to her, Woodcock," Christopher said. "If ever I fail in this resolve, I give her leave to come straight to you and tell you so." Thus, locking eyes, the two men shook hands.

Dimity kissed her brother on the cheek. "Thank you, Miles," she whispered. "You have made me very, very happy."

"Well, then," the captain said, assuming a heartiness he did not feel. "Before I go off and leave you two alone, we should drink a toast. Dimity will have her usual sherry, I suppose. Whiskey for you, Kittredge?"

Christopher looked down at Dimity. "I'll join Dimity in a sherry, I think."

Dimity lifted her chin. "I believe I should like a whiskey," she said.

27
MISS POTTER TAKES CHARGE

When we took leave of Miss Potter, she had just met Emily Shaw on the street and invited her to stop in out of the rain for a cup of tea. Number Two Bolton Gardens was only a few blocks away. Since the servants were gone, Beatrix took her shivering guest to the kitchen, which was nicely warmed by the fire in the range. She put Emily in the warmest chair, hung up her wet shawl to dry, brewed tea, and set out bread-and-butter and cheese, along with some tea-cakes she had bought for herself.

The girl was rather pretty, Beatrix thought, now that her cheeks were turning a brighter color. Her fair hair fell forward over a serious face, and her gaze was thoughtful. She was not much like the flibbertigibbet Lady Longford accused her of being — although perhaps her recent experiences, whatever they were, had brought her a new maturity.

Emily ate as if she had not eaten well for

the past few days, and after a few minutes Beatrix got up to renew the supply of bread and cheese. When she sat back down, Emily said, with a nervous laugh, "I suppose tha'rt curious to know what I'm doin' here in London, miss."

Beatrix busied herself by slicing the cheese — a mild yellow cheese that she had brought from the farm. "I am, rather," she admitted candidly. "I'm a curious person by nature, and I love stories." She didn't look up. "You don't have to tell me, Emily. But if you do, I should rather hear the truth."

The silence went on so long that Beatrix decided either she had offended Emily or that Emily had nothing to tell. The fire crackled pleasantly, and in the upstairs hallway, the tall clock wheezed and began to strike the hour: four hollow bongs, solemn and dignified, fading into silence.

As if this were a signal, Emily raised her head and listened until the clock had finished striking. Then, in a torrential spill of words in which facts and feelings were so confused and incoherent and tangled up with one another that Beatrix could scarcely make it all out, she related what had happened, first at Hawthorn House and then at Miss Pennywhistle's. And as she spoke, she began to cry, her sobs making it all the harder to understand her.

Beatrix listened, at first with surprise and then with a growing wonderment as she tried to fit the pieces of this puzzling, perplexing story together. The more she understood, the more astonished she became, until she was almost dumbfounded by the series of adventures and misadventures that Emily was relating. How had these things happened? How could a tiny baby be treated with such disregard? How could a mother give birth and then simply go on with her life as though nothing had happened? These and other questions tumbled through her mind as she listened, until at last Emily seemed to have got to the end of her tale.

"And now I'm not sure what to do," Emily concluded miserably, wiping the tears from her eyes with her sleeve. "I've made so many mistakes, I don't know where to start makin' amends. There's t' babe, o' course, but what can I do about her now? I don't want to stay on at Miss Pennywhistle's, because t' girls are so cruel and t' work's so hard. But if I leave, Miss Pennywhistle won't give me a character, and without a character I can't get another place." She gulped back a sob. "And I can't go back to t' village, 'cause o' what people will say."

"I see," Beatrix said quietly. There were so many questions still to be asked about the baby, but she doubted that Emily had the answers. In fact, there were several things that Emily could not know, since they had happened after the baby left her care. She didn't know, for instance, that Miss Woodcock now had custody of the baby, or that the blue hand-woven cover had been traced to the midwife, Mrs. Graham, who could now be questioned about the baby's birth.

And Beatrix herself didn't know (for Captain Woodcock had not yet had the opportunity of telling her) what you and I know: that the signet ring found in the baby's basket had been traced to Hawthorn House, and that the captain had already learnt of Emily's interrupted friendship with the gypsy lad.

Emily looked around the kitchen, taking in the shining pots and pans hanging from the rack, the gleaming range and scrubbed pine work table, the dresser full of china. She turned to Beatrix, a question in her eyes. "Dusta think I could get a place here, miss? Wudsta be willin' to speak for me?"

"I suppose I could, yes," Beatrix said slowly. As it happened, the upstairs maid had given notice the day before her parents left on holiday. When the family was once again at Bolton Gardens, a search would have to be made for her replacement. Hiring the servants was Beatrix's job and was not something she looked forward to with great enthusiasm. If Emily was willing to take the post, Beatrix might be willing to hire her — as long as the present perplexities could be resolved. "Would you like to work here?"

Emily pondered this for a moment. "Yes," she said slowly. "London isn't t' place I thought it 'ud be. I'd rather go back to t' village, but I doan't have a place there. And I'm sure people are sayin' bad things about me. I'd be very grateful to work for you, miss," she said humbly. "If it was possible."

Beatrix saw the opportunity Emily had presented her. "Be that as it may," she said sternly, "you must appreciate that we cannot consider your employment until these other matters have been resolved. For that, you shall have to return to Miss Pennywhistle's. *And* to the village. Not to stay, necessarily. But to straighten things out."

Emily turned pale. "Must I, miss?" she whispered. She looked down at her hands, twisted in her lap. "I was hopin' that perhaps I wouldn't have to —"

"Indeed you must," Beatrix said firmly. "None of us can go forward until we have faced up to the past." Then, relenting a little, she added, in a softer tone, "I will come with you, if you like."

Emily nodded. "Yes, miss, please. Oh, please." She closed her eyes, the tears trickling down her cheeks, and murmured brokenly, "What would've become of me if you hadn't seen me walkin' down the street and took charge?"

"You mustn't hope for too much," Beatrix cautioned. "Things may not turn out happily, you know. A serious crime has been committed, Emily. The law must come into it, I am afraid."

Emily was sobbing again, her shoulders shaking. "I've made such a horrible muddle of things, Miss Potter. I promise to do better. I really do!"

Beatrix thought fleetingly of the impertinent bunnies, who were always getting into trouble and promising to do better, without much effect. "I fear that we all make that promise from time to time, my dear." She gave Emily a steady look in which rebuke was mixed with sympathy. "It's a pity we can't keep it."

And with that, Beatrix fetched her umbrella, and she and Emily, once more burdened with her parcels, set out through the chilly rain.

None of the select young ladies were in evidence when Beatrix and Emily arrived at Number Three Lime Tree Place. To the maid who opened the door, she said, very firmly, "Miss Potter and Miss Shaw to see Miss Keller. Privately, please."

They were allowed inside, and within three or four minutes, ushered up the stairs to a second-floor schoolroom. Palely lit by high windows that afforded no view, the room had a high ceiling, a bare wooden floor, four mostly bare walls (one bore twin photographs of King Edward and his mother, Queen Victoria), and a single fireplace with what remained of a small fire. It contained three rows of student desks and benches, a teacher's wooden desk, a blackboard, a rack of rolled-up maps, and a globe. It was a chilly, desolate room, smelling of chalk dust and damp soot, and Beatrix, shivering as she looked around, thought that it was not at all conducive to creativity or real learning. If a student managed to think an independently creative thought in this place, the poor thought would likely shrivel and die for lack of nourishment.

The door opened and a woman stepped

through. Her face was plain, her dark hair twisted into thick coils on the top of her head. She wore a tailored white blouse with a narrow navy tie and a neatly gored navy serge skirt — the uniform, Beatrix guessed, of the school's instructors. She carried herself rigidly, as if to ward off any possible adversity, and there was a wary look about her, reminding Beatrix of an animal fearful of a trap. Her dark eyes, large and intense, went immediately to Emily.

"Why are you so late, Emily?" she demanded sharply. "Cook sent you out hours ago! Miss Pennywhistle will not be pleased to hear that you have been dawdling about your errands." Her gaze flicked to Beatrix, taking in her proper hat, her trim brown jacket and skirt, her gloves. "And who is this, if I may ask? Have we met?"

Beatrix introduced herself. "I reside not far from here with my parents," she added, "and also in the village of Near Sawrey, where I understand you recently went on holiday."

Miss Keller's lips thinned. "I see," she said warily. To Emily, she said, "You may take those parcels to the kitchen now, Emily. Cook will be needing them."

Emily looked at Beatrix, who nodded soberly. With an air of relief, as though she was glad to escape hearing what she knew was about to be said, the girl quickly left the room, not looking behind her.

"Shall we sit down?" Beatrix said, and suiting the action to the words, pulled out a student chair. "I am sure that you are curious as to what I have come about."

Miss Keller sat down, narrowing her eyes. "I must caution you not to believe anything Emily Shaw may have told you. The girl has a habit of making up fantastical stories. She is not to be trusted."

Beatrix gave a small cough. "Is that right? Emily's tale did not seem particularly fantastical, except in one respect. In fact, it corresponds very nearly to what I already know to have occurred. But perhaps I should tell you what she has said, and you can correct any misstatements."

Beatrix related what Emily had told her. And then, since Emily had not known the whole story, added a summary of the events that occurred after she herself opened the door and found the baby on her doorstep.

With each sentence, Miss Keller's face grew paler and paler and her eyes wider and wider, and by the end her face was dead white and she was fighting tears. She fumbled for a handkerchief in the pocket of her skirt.

"I didn't know!" she cried. "Emily told me nothing of this!"

"She was afraid," Beatrix said simply. "She thought you would not believe her. And of course she had no idea what transpired after she came away."

Miss Keller blew her nose into her handkerchief, sat up straighter, and set her mouth in a hard line. "Well, I hardly see that I can be blamed for anything that happened. I made every provision, took every care. When I left to return to London, all the arrangements were settled." She lifted her chin. "And I cannot see why any of this is your concern, Miss Potter. If you think that you can come here and —"

"I have made it my concern because the child was left on my doorstep," Beatrix said in a caustic tone, "which surely entitles me to have a share in the proceedings. In any event, this matter must be settled without delay. I must ask both you and Emily to go back to Sawrey with me tomorrow. If we take the earliest train, we shall be in the village by teatime."

"Impossible!" Miss Keller exclaimed. Her manner was heated. "I have an important position here. I cannot simply go and come on a whim. My students need me. And Miss Pennywhistle would not permit —"

"This is not a whim," Beatrix interrupted. "It is an urgent necessity, and moreover, it is a weekend. If Miss Pennywhistle is reluctant to permit you to take a short leave, I shall be glad to explain what is behind your request. When she understands the significance of this matter, I am sure she will —"

"Tell Miss Pennywhistle!" Miss Keller exclaimed shrilly. Her hand flew to her mouth. "Oh, no. No, no — that won't be necessary."

"Well, then," Beatrix said in a decided voice, "we are agreed. We three shall be going to the Lakes tomorrow." She rose and went to the door, paused, and turned. "Emily tells me that she wishes to give in her notice here, effective immediately. She will be staying with me tonight. I shall send for her bag later this evening." She fixed Miss Keller with a steady look. "And I shall call for you in a cab at seven tomorrow morning, Miss Keller. I trust you will have made your explanations to Miss Pennywhistle and be ready to join me."

Miss Keller, obviously seeing that she had no choice, closed her eyes and nodded.

28
JEMIMA TAKES STOCK

You can well imagine Kep's weary frustration when he returned to the barn after chasing the fox. His paws were sore, and one ear had been ripped open when he tried to quarry Reynard under a thorn bush. But before he went off to have a bit of a lie-down and recover himself, he knelt down to peer under the feedbox in the barn to make sure that Jemima was safe.

Yes, there she was, safe and sound, asleep on her nest with her head tucked under her wing, the very picture of a domestic duck. Gazing at her fondly, Kep thought that he would never have predicted that silly, harum-scarum Jemima would be so responsible. He shook his head sadly as he went away, thinking how dismayed and distraught she would be when those eggs hatched and whatever-it-was came out.

Jemima, however, was only pretending to be asleep. When she peeked between her wing feathers and saw Kep watching her, a hot resentment welled up inside her. She understood that the collie had to do his job, but she was vexed that he had chased her fox away. What business was it of his if she enjoyed a few moments of pleasurable company? She deserved a few distractions while she did her duty, didn't she? And she was tired of Kep's constant surveillance, tired of his watchful eyes, scrutinizing her every move. Hatching eggs was a simple job that any duck could do by herself. It required no brains, no creativity, no imagination, only the willingness to apply one's feathered posterior to the nest, day after day after tedious day.

As you can see, our Jemima has had a change of heart, which is perhaps not surprising, in the circumstance, for direct experience can teach us a great deal that anticipation and expectation cannot. When Emily went to London, for instance, she found the City to be very different from the fairyland of her imagination. And now that the duck has had a full two months to reflect and take stock, she has to admit that the Puddle-ducks were right after all. There is nothing magical about hatching eggs. It is a boring, humdrum business, much better left to Bonnet, Boots, and Shawl, who aren't very bright and have nothing else to do. If she had known just how long this was going to take and what was involved, she would most likely have elected to try something else — adoption, perhaps.

To Jemima, the day (this would be Thursday, if you are marking your calendar) seemed to drag on forever. Hatching must be imminent, for she could feel movement beneath her, the insistent scritch-scratch of duckling feet and the tippy-tap of duckling bills, signaling that her babies were at least ready to emerge from their long (too, too long!) confinement in their eggs. Every ten minutes or so, she got up to check on their progress, gratified by the tiny cracks she could see in the round white eggs. She quacked some soft quacks of motherly encouragement and then applied her ear to the eggs, hoping to hear baby quacks in response. But not a peep could she hear, not a sound, nothing but the impatient scritch-scratch and the tippy-tap of babies, anxious to come out and explore the wide, wonderful world.

But they didn't. Thursday's hours were just like Wednesday's hours and Tuesday's, and all the previous hours of all the previous days, which seemed to stretch endlessly, back to the beginning of time. Jemima had long since finished knitting the yellow shawls, which lay folded in readiness beside the nest. And she had read every single one of the romances she had brought with her, and read them again, and yet again, until she was bored with the silly stories and wishing she had borrowed a few Sherlock Holmes, which might at least have engaged her intellect.

As Thursday night turned into Friday morning, all Jemima could do was doze and dream of the day — THIS day, it was devoutly to be wished! — when her eggs would have hatched, her ducklings would have been successfully reared, and she could pursue her own independent life, far from the constraints of nests and eggs and baby ducklings.

She would be free, a free duck, able to take wing and fly in whatever direction she chose.

And she had a pretty clear idea what direction that would be.

29
Miss Barwick
Delivers

If you will remember, the village had been a-buzz all day Thursday with the news of two impending marriages. Miss Potter was to marry Captain Woodcock and Miss Woodcock was to marry Major Kittredge. There were two consequential corollaries of these matrimonial matters: Elsa Grape would go to the vicarage, and the foundling gypsy babe would go to Raven Hall.

Captain Woodcock, however, greatly altered these understandings. When he put in his unexpected appearance at the pub on Thursday night and announced in no uncertain tones that he was *not* going to marry Miss Potter (at least in the foreseeable future) and that Miss Woodcock was absolutely *not* going to marry Major Kittredge ("Never, do you hear!" he had exclaimed angrily. "Never!"), it was fairly evident that the village would have to regroup and reconsider.

As I am sure you expected (if you are at all wise in the ways of villages), the men went straight home from the pub that night and told their wives about the captain's extraordinary pronouncement, after which the couples discussed the situation long into the night. So you will not be surprised to hear that, as the next morning's cheerful sun rose over Claife Heights and smiled benevolently down across its favorite cluster of tidy houses and gardens, everyone in the village already had formed an opinion (some had two or three!) about these various marital misfortunes.

In the kitchen at Hill Top Farm, Mrs. Jennings had served Mr. Jennings his usual breakfast of eggs, black pudding, and tea, and was now preparing breakfast for Miss Potter's pigs: ordinary pig-slop for most of them, but a special pig-pail with two boiled eggs and a cup of fresh milk, still warm from the cow, for Miss Potter's favorite pig, Aunt Susan. With regard to Miss Potter's pending marriage, Mrs. Jennings was disappointed, while Mr. Jennings was still hopeful. The captain had not said they *would not* marry, just that they would not marry *now.* And whilst Mr. and Mrs. Jennings respected Miss Potter and thought that she was doing her best by the farm, they shared the general feeling that it would be better if a man had overall charge. Men always had a better notion of farming than ladies, especially a London lady like Miss Potter, who had never even lived on a farm before she owned one.

Down the hill at Tower Bank Arms, Mrs. Barrow was cooking breakfast for the inn's two overnight guests: eggs (boiled and poached), sausages, broiled kidneys, mushrooms (baked for twenty minutes, with a knob of butter and some pepper, according to Mrs. Beeton's recommendation), along with toast, muffins, tea, coffee, and cocoa. But Mrs. Barrow was an efficient cook, so in the midst of her duties there was plenty of opportunity to share last night's news with the kitchen maid, Ruth, who was an ardent reader of romances.

Ruth concurred with Mrs. Barrow, believing that Major Kittredge would make a fine husband for Miss Woodcock, and that it was a rotten shame that t' village was so set against it and that t' captain wouldn't let 'em marry. And as for Miss Potter, Ruth expressed the heartfelt view that there couldn't be anything more gratifyin' than a romance between that dear lady and t' captain, for Miss Potter's hopes had been blighted once already, poor thing, when her parents wouldn't let her marry t' man she loved. Having thus agreed, Mrs. Barrow served up the breakfast and Ruth carried it in.

Across Market Street, at Anvil Cottage, Sarah Barwick (who was known throughout the village as an early bird) had already finished the morning's baking and was loading her bicycle basket for her bakery customers: two extra loaves of bread for Belle Green (Mrs. Crook had weekend guests — a pair of cyclists from Kendal), scones for the Wilsons in Castle Cottage, teabread for the Skeads at the post office, and Cumberland sausage rolls for Captain and Miss Woodcock at Tower Bank House. Miss Barwick was one of those "rational thinkers" who felt that women should have more freedoms, that they should take full charge of their lives, and that they should refuse to be bound by other people's expectations. Her costume was the outward expression of this inward belief, for her working kit was a pair of corduroy trousers, cut full for maximum comfort and suited to pedaling her bicycle in even the dirtiest of lanes.

She had already heard the Thursday news about Miss Woodcock's engagement with a great deal of pleasure, for Dimity had mentioned her hopes and Sarah — who counted herself a very good friend — was happy to hear that they had been realized. She greeted the announcement of Miss Potter's engagement with a little frown, however. She thought she knew Beatrix rather well, and her friend had not said one word about her engagement. What's more, Sarah had not seen any indication of a special feeling between Beatrix and the captain when the three of them had met at the fête at the previous weekend. If Beatrix had been at home, of course, Sarah would have dropped everything and popped straight up to Hill Top to ask if it were true. But Beatrix had gone to London and wouldn't be back until late on Friday, so the confirmation — or the denial — would have to wait.

Since Sarah did not have a husband to carry the news home from the pub, she hadn't a clue as to the previous evening's events until Hannah Braithwaite, on her way to the village shop for a box of soap flakes, stopped to tell her. Miss Potter's wedding would be delayed (but only slightly, since the captain was clearly eager to have it done as soon as possible, and everyone agreed that it was a highly desirable match). Miss Woodcock's wedding was off completely, now and forever more, amen.

"Off?" asked Sarah regretfully.

"Off," said Hannah. "My husband said t' cap'n was positively neg'tive." She leant forward and lowered her voice. "She's not to have t' babe, neither. T' cap'n doan't want his sister rearin' a gypsy child."

"Well," snorted Sarah, "I'd say that's a pity, I would, indeed."

Thinking very hard thoughts about the captain, she got on her bicycle and rode off. She loved Dimity, but she did wish that her friend had more backbone and would stand up for what she wanted. Where her brother was concerned, Dimity practiced a doll-like compliance. She was too accommodating, too ready to do the man's bidding, too much of a mouse. It was awful to think of her being forced to give up her heart's one true desire, just to satisfy her brother's narrow-minded worry about the major's reputation.

Now, Sarah herself had never been one to carry tales — in fact, she despised gossip and rarely repeated it. But as she went round the village, delivering her baked goods first to one house and then another, she could not help hearing gossip. And this morning, there was plenty of it, everywhere she stopped.

At Belle Green, Mrs. Crook understood

that Miss Potter was sadly disappointed that her wedding to the captain would have to wait a month or so (and well she might, since the captain was the best catch in the district). And of course, Major Kittredge had felt much chagrined when he discovered that the captain refused to allow him to marry Miss Woodcock, as well *he* might, since marriage to a good woman was the only way he could redeem his blackened reputation, and Miss Woodcock was a woman beyond peer, who could redeem the devil himself, if she had to.

"Oh, poor Miss Woodcock," said Tabitha mournfully, from her vantage point on the outer window ledge. *"And so sad for the major, who is really a very nice man."*

"I told you so, didn't I?" Crumpet said cattily. She was sitting in the pot of rosemary below. *"I told you that Captain Woodcock wouldn't let her marry someone who has been married before, even if it wasn't a real marriage."* She sniffed sarcastically. *"And I suppose you'll want me to believe that you knew all about Miss Potter and the captain."*

"Of course I knew," Tabitha lied. The truth was that she had spent all day Thursday cleaning mice out of the Belle Green barn, and as a consequence had heard no gossip at all. But she wasn't going to give Crumpet

the satisfaction of knowing that.

Crumpet twitched her tail. *"Bet you didn't know a thing about it,"* she said.

"Bet I did!" Tabitha cried, showing her teeth.

"Didn't!"

"Did!"

"Let's not go into that again, girls," Rascal barked from the kitchen stoop. When Miss Barwick came out to get on her bicycle to make her next delivery, he was right on her heels, with the cats following after, eager for more news.

When Miss Barwick arrived at Castle Cottage, Mrs. Wilson told her that the major was so angry about the rejection of his suit that he had decided to rejoin the Army, although what the Army would want with a one-eyed, one-armed major, Mrs. Wilson was sure she didn't know. As to Miss Potter's wedding, Mrs. Wilson had heard that it was only delayed by a few days, until the captain could arrange the sale of some of Miss Potter's land (the bit across the Kendal Road) to Mr. Llewellyn, who'd had his eye on it when that lady bought it right out from under him. Which was not a neighborly thing to do, but very like Miss Potter, who seemed to feel that she was entitled to every parcel of land that came up for sale.

"That's odd, that is," said Rascal. He and the two cats were waiting for Miss Barwick just outside the Castle Cottage door. *"Miss Potter fancied that meadow particularly. She wanted it for her Herdwick sheep. I'm surprised to hear she's selling it."*

"She's doing it because she wants to please the captain," said Crumpet, swatting a fly.

"And how could you happen to know that sentimental trifle?" inquired Tabitha scornfully. *"You're making it up."*

"It is not a trifle," Crumpet replied in a definitive tone. She narrowed her eyes. *"And I am NOT making it up!"*

"Are!" squalled Tabitha.

"Am NOT!" yowled Crumpet.

*"Girls, GIRLS, **GIRLS!**"* barked Rascal.

"Scat!" cried Mrs. Wilson, coming out of the door with her broom, and so they did.

At the post office, Miss Barwick handed over the loaf of teabread (Mr. Skead's favorite, which Mrs. Skead could not be bothered to make, because it took too long to soak the fruit in the tea, and the dough had to be set to rise three times). In return, she got the Anvil Cottage post and the news that Miss Potter and the captain had decided not to wait any longer than necessary and would be married just as soon as the banns could be published and the sale of one or two pieces of property arranged. Elsa Grape had already discussed her new employment with the vicar and was right this minute packing her bags in anticipation of Miss Potter's taking command of the kitchen and housekeeping. Miss Woodcock, sadly, was prostrate with grief at her brother's refusal to allow her to marry, whilst Major Kittredge, who knew better than to try to get the Army to take him back, had told his staff that he was joining the French Foreign Legion.

"The French Foreign Legion!" yipped Rascal happily. The animals were sitting on the path, waiting for Miss Barwick to come out. *"I'll offer to go with him. Every officer needs a keen, quick-witted dog to carry his kit. And I've always fancied a trip round the world."*

"I'm sure the vicar is happy that Elsa Grape is coming to do for him," Tabitha remarked. *"She's a much better cook than Mrs. Thompson — her Yorkshire pudding is especially fine."* She frowned. *"But I wonder how Miss Potter and Miss Woodcock will get along in the same house. I know they're friends, but —"*

"If you ask me," Crumpet said wisely, *"the captain won't want two women living with him. He will probably go to Hill Top Farm, and let his sister have Tower Bank House."*

"*Nobody asked you, Crumpet,*" said Tabitha.

Crumpet's tail began to swell. "*I have a right to my opinion, don't I?*" she asked hotly.

"*As long as you don't force it on the rest of us,*" Tabitha growled. "*We don't need your silly speculation.*"

"*It's not silly!*" Crumpet defended. "*It's a perfectly logical solution to a —*"

"*It is* very *silly,*" Tabitha said. "*A silly speculation from an exceedingly foolish cat who —*"

"*Here comes Miss Barwick with her post,*" Rascal put in hastily, before Tabitha could say another word. "*Let's see where she's going next.*"

30
DIMITY DEALS WITH EGGS

There was one item left in Sarah Barwick's basket: a packet of four Cumberland sausage rolls for Captain and Miss Woodcock at Tower Bank House. Sarah parked her bicycle outside the kitchen door and knocked, with some trepidation. She didn't want to disturb the house if Dimity was indeed ill. On the other hand, if Elsa Grape (a temperamental sort of person at best) was really packing to leave for her new post at the vicarage, the sausage rolls might save Dimity some work, when it came to luncheon. She was not the best of cooks.

But to Sarah's surprise, the door was opened by Dimity herself. She was wearing an apron smeared with egg yolk, and she had a spoon in her hand. "Why, good morning, Sarah," she said happily, stepping back. "How nice to see you. Oh, are those the sausage rolls? Thank you so much for bringing them. Miles will be delighted."

"You're welcome, I'm sure," said Sarah, now rather puzzled. Dimity seemed to be bubbling over with good cheer this morning, when by all rights she ought to be crying her eyes out. She sniffed. The kitchen smelt of lemons. "You're making lemonade?"

"Lemon curd," Dimity said happily, pushing the brown hair out of her eyes. "Miles is very partial to it." She made a little face. "Although I must say, it is not as easy as Mrs. Beeton claims. It wants to go all lumpy."

Sarah saw behind her on the work table a confusion of pots and bowls, a scattering of caster sugar, several nearly nude lemons, broken egg shells and a puddle of rich yellow yolk, a large tin grater (much abused), an egg beater (likewise), and a butter crock. Mrs. Beeton's famous cookbook lay facedown in what looked like more egg yolk. On the floor, there were several lemons, a broken egg, and a few bits of butter. And on the kitchen range, a double boiler, from which a little curl of steam arose.

Sarah suppressed a smile. When Dimity indulged in cookery, it was disastrous. Elsa Grape had been known to forbid her the kitchen, because of the amount of mopping-up required afterward.

"And do you have time for tea, dear?" Dimity went on gaily. "If you do, we might as well have it here in the kitchen, since Elsa has gone to the butcher's shop in Hawkshead."

Ah, thought Sarah. That explained it. When the cat was away, the mouse could cook up some lemon curd. Well, if cooking made Dimity feel better, she should by all means do it, regardless of the consequences. Anyway, she looked quite charming this morning, her cheeks flushed, her eyes bright, her brown hair in untidy ringlets at the edge of her white collar. If Dim was grieving over the demise of her dream, her grief could not be read in her expression.

"Yes, of course, I'll have tea," Sarah said, handing over the sausage rolls. "You're the last stop on my route this morning. Elsa's at the butcher's? I thought the boy came round three times a week."

"He does," said Dimity, dropping her spoon and the packet of rolls into a drift of sugar. "There's no dealing with him, though," she confided, fetching the teapot and two cups. "No beef, ever, only lamb, no matter how I beg and plead. And Miles tries to be brave and pretend it doesn't matter, but of course he's sick to death of lamb. It's deplorable. So I have sent Elsa to the butcher, with instructions to be very stern about beef and pork." She took down a plate. "Will you have a scone?" She laughed a little. "Although I'm afraid that's rather like carrying coals to Newcastle, isn't it? I'm sure you've baked two batches of scones this morning, and sold half already."

"True enough," Sarah admitted, "but you know I always say yes to Elsa's. Her scones are better than mine, although you mustn't tell her that." As Dimity bustled about, she sat down at the table, pushed the grater and the egg beater aside, and took out a packet of cigarettes. Smoking, along with the trousers and the bicycle, marked her as a New Woman. "I'm glad to see you looking so chipper, Dim," she ventured. "I heard you were ill."

Outside on the stoop, Tabitha breathed a sigh of relief. *"Miss Woodcock is obviously quite well. Lucy Skead didn't know what she was talking about."*

"Ill?" Dimity laughed lightly, tossing her head. "My goodness, wherever did you hear that? I've never felt better in my life." She pushed an ashtray in Sarah's direction. "You see before you a happy woman."

"Happy?" barked Rascal. *"After what she's been through?"*

"Happy?" Sarah frowned. "Actually, I

didn't imagine you would be taking it like this. Everyone says you're prostrate." She lit her cigarette. "Well, not everyone, exactly. Lucy Skead said it, and Lucy always has the last word. I thought maybe you'd been knocked flat by the latest about the major."

Startled, Dimity looked up from pouring the tea. "Latest? What latest?"

Sarah put on Lucy Skead's high-pitched, rattling tone. "That he can't have you and the Army won't have him, so he's gone and joined the French Foreign Legion, poor man."

"As I said, I'll be glad to carry his kit," Rascal put in. *"I'm ready at a moment's notice."*

"The Foreign Legion?" Dimity threw back her head and laughed, long peals of laughter. "Dear me! Is that what people are saying?" She set down a plate of scones. "Oh, poor Christopher!"

"That's what Lucy Skead is saying," Sarah replied. She cocked her head curiously. "It's not true, then?"

"No, of course it's not true." Dimity sat down, leaned forward, and heedless of egg shells and sugar, put her elbows on the table. "Christopher and I are to be married, Sarah. And if Baby Flora's parents can't be found, or if they don't want her, we're taking her to live with us." She beamed.

"There. Now wish me joy, for I shall be joyous, I promise. Christopher and I are to live happily ever after, just as in the fairy tales."

"Married?" Crumpet cried.

"Married!" Tabitha shrieked.

"No Foreign Legion for me," Rascal said, and hung his head.

"Married!" Sarah exclaimed delightedly. "That's wonderful, Dim! And oh, yes, yes, yes, I wish you all the happiness in the world, crammed into the hugest basket and overflowing, and every joy your heart could ever possibly hold. But the villagers are saying —"

"I am sure they are saying all manner of silly things," Dimity replied, with a dismissive toss of her head. "I understand from Mr. Phinn — he actually deigned to pull a few weeds for me out of the pole beans this morning — that Miles may have made an injudicious remark or two at the pub last night."

Sarah tapped her cigarette ash into the ashtray. "Yes, I think he may have done," she said with a wry smile.

Dimity smiled blissfully. "But whatever he said, and whatever they think, it doesn't matter, Sarah. Christopher and I have settled it between us, and with Miles. You would have been proud of the way I stood my ground. I was very strong-minded, exceedingly so. In fact, I don't know if Miles quite knows what to make of it. I told him that Christopher and I intend to be married, with or without his blessing. And that is that."

"Dimity Woodcock, you are a treasure!" Sarah cried, clapping her hands. "Congratulations and best wishes and all that rot. No, seriously. I'm thrilled down to my toesies. To think that the mouse found the courage to roar at the lion!" She sobered. "I hope your brother wasn't too deeply hurt."

Dimity sighed regretfully. "He's not terribly pleased. But he'll come round, I'm sure of it. He will be friends with Christopher yet, just you wait and see if he won't." Her mouth set in a determined line. "Anyway, I cannot let my brother live my life for me. If I couldn't see that for myself, Beatrix made it very clear."

"There," said Tabitha, quite serenely. *"It was our Miss Potter who helped her see the light."*

Sarah put out her cigarette and took up a scone. "I daresay that invoking Bea's name made it easier for your brother." She looked around at the mess Dimity had made of Elsa's clean kitchen. "How is our Elsa taking it?"

"Elsa?" Dimity laughed. "With remarkable grace. She doesn't like the idea of my raising the baby — a gypsy child and therefore not fit to live with proper folk. But she's glad to have me gone and out of the way. She'll have Miles all to herself, the way it was before I came here."

"All to herself?" Sarah blinked.

"Well, yes. She's been with him for a very long time, you know."

"Yes, I know, but —" Sarah paused. "She's said to be going to the vicarage. She hasn't given in her notice yet?"

"To the vicarage!" Dimity exclaimed anxiously. "I knew the vicar was looking for someone to come in and do for him, but I never imagined that Elsa would leave Miles. Heavens above! What will he do? And why would she?"

"It's all on account of Bea, I think," said Sarah. She smiled. "Of course, I'm just spectacularizing, as Bertha Stubbs says, but I'm sure that Elsa doesn't relish the idea of taking orders from our Miss Potter, who will certainly have her own ways of doing things here."

"Taking orders from — ?" Dimity asked. "You're saying that Miles and Bea —" Her eyes widened and her hands flew to her mouth, as the light suddenly dawned. "You're telling me that they are going to be married? My brother and . . . and Beatrix Potter?"

Sarah stared. "You didn't know?"

"Of course I didn't know!" Dimity squealed. "Miles is always so closed-mouth about his personal affairs. He'd never discuss anything like that with me. But I couldn't be happier, of course. Beatrix will be wonderful for him. I've been thinking and scheming and plotting how I could get him to see that it is a perfect match, and all along he . . . and she —"

"The thing I don't understand," Sarah said slowly, frowning, "is why Bea hasn't mentioned it to me. Not a word. Not even a syllable. Has she said anything to you?"

"No, but then she mightn't. She's a very private person, you know. Most likely, she and Miles have decided not to tell anyone, hoping to keep it to themselves as long as possible."

Sarah nodded. "That's certainly true. Well, it's out now. The village is talking about nothing else — except that you are prostrate with grief, of course, and that the major has run off to join the Foreign Legion."

Dimity rolled her eyes. "Christopher will be so amused when I tell him," she said. "But what shall we do about Miles and Bea,

Sarah? We ought to surprise them."

"We should have a party," Sarah said, finishing her scone.

"We should, indeed!" Dimity exclaimed, and then laughed delightedly. "What am I thinking? We *are* having a party, tomorrow night. And Miles was positively insistent on inviting Bea."

"Well, then, that's when they are planning to make the announcement."

"I am sure you're right," Dimity replied. "Originally, there were to be just four of us — Miles and Bea and Mr. Heelis and I. But I have invited Christopher, so there will be five." She gave Sarah an intent look. "But that will leave poor Mr. Heelis as odd man out. You must come, Sarah, and then we shall be six."

"I?" Sarah flushed. She was not used to parties, which required dressing up and minding her manners. "I really don't think —"

"Of course you do! You like Mr. Heelis, don't you?" Dimity frowned. "I don't mean it in a silly way, Sarah. I just mean, you wouldn't mind sitting beside him and making dinner-table conversation with him, would you? Mr. Heelis is very shy, but I'm sure you can draw him out, with your easygoing manner. And he is really very sweet."

Sarah thought for a moment. Will Heelis had been very kind to her when he helped resolve the legal tangles when Miss Tolliver bequeathed Anvil Cottage to her several years before. She had seen him since on one or two other legal matters, and he was always courteous and attentive. If ever she fancied a man —

"Well, then, yes," she said, suddenly making up her mind. (We must not inquire too deeply into all the factors that went into this decision, although I suspect that Mr. Heelis' previous courtesies might have been a part of it.) "If you want me, I shall come — although I'm afraid I haven't a thing to wear." She looked down at her trousers and laughed. "I do have dresses, of course, but I don't have any party frocks."

"Oh, that's easy," Dimity said. "We're of a size, you and I. You can look through my closet and borrow anything you like." She clapped her hands. "Oh, I'm so glad I've made the lemon curd, Sarah! We shall have it for dessert, with Elsa's sponge and —" She stopped suddenly, sniffing. "What's that smell?"

Sarah, who was wondering whether Dimity might allow her to borrow her pink silk dress with the velvet ribbons and ivory lace, lifted her head and took in a deep breath. "It smells like something's burning," she said, and glanced quickly at the ashtray into which she had stubbed her cigarette to see if she had set something afire.

"Burning!" Dimity jumped up and ran to the stove. "It's the curd!" she cried in dismay. "I was supposed to be stirring it. It was already lumpy, but now the lumps are *burnt!*"

Sarah got up and went to the stove to look. "Some housewife you're going to make," she said, shaking her head with a laugh. "Although when you're married and living at Raven Hall, I don't suppose you'll ever have to go near the kitchen." Raven Hall was fully staffed, with several cooks and kitchen maids. "Just as well," she added. "I hear that the chief cook is a true terror."

"But I should learn to cook," Dimity said, very seriously. Her brow was creased. "Every wife ought to know how to make tea and breakfast, in case of necessity."

"You might not want to start with lemon curd, though," Sarah said, "especially if you're going to forget to stir it — although it's my fault, too. I kept you busy talking. If you want to make another batch, I'll help."

411

"There aren't any eggs left," Dimity said disconsolately. "Elsa had a dozen when I started, but I broke several when I tried to separate the yolks from the whites, and then two or three rolled off the table and went smash on the floor. There aren't any lemons, either."

"Yes, I see," Sarah said, glancing down at the floor. "Well, I have plenty of eggs I can let you have, if you want to try again, and lemons, too. But we'd better clean up this mess before Elsa comes back from the butcher shop. You know how she feels about your cooking in her kitchen."

"I'll clean," Dimity said promptly, reaching for the mop. "You go get the lemons and eggs."

"P'rhaps I wouldn't have liked the Foreign Legion," Rascal said, watching Miss Barwick roll her bicycle down the garden path in the direction of Anvil Cottage. *"It's always seemed like an exotic idea, but the life might not have suited me after all."*

"So!" Tabitha stood up and arched her back, twitching her tail victoriously. *"Well, what do you say to all this, Miss Know-It-All? Our Miss Woodcock is marrying her major, regardless of the captain."* She looked around. *"You were wrong, Crumpet. Admit it! Crumpet!"*

412

But Crumpet was not there. She had thought of something urgent she had to do at the other end of the village and had gone off to do it before the morning got a minute older.

31
AND MORE EGGS!

Dimity Woodcock and Sarah Barwick were not the only ones in the village who were concerned with eggs that morning.

Jemima Puddle-duck had not spent a restful night. The occupants of some of her eggs seemed to be in a spirited mood, and she had been repeatedly roused from sleep by violent tremblings and tumblings and pushings and shovings beneath her. She got off the nest several times to try to puzzle out what was going on. Was this normal egg behavior? Did ducklings always act like jumping beans when they were getting ready to come out of their shells?

But Jemima was completely inexperienced when it came to eggs, since (as you know) the Jennings boy had stolen the ones she laid in the garden and the fox-hound puppies had eaten those she laid at Foxglove Close. And because she had kept the current batch secret, she could hardly run to one of the other Puddle-ducks to ask. They probably wouldn't be able to advise her, anyway, since they had as little experience of eggs as she did. And asking Mrs. Boots or Mrs. Shawl or Mrs. Bonnet was completely out of the question. She refused even to speak to those snobbish creatures.

So she would simply have to be patient and hope for the best. She checked to make sure that the yellow knitted shawls were handy, as she understood that ducklings were rather damp when they came out of the egg, and she didn't want them to catch cold. Then she settled back on the nest, put her head under her wing, and fell into an exhausted sleep, although she was startled awake every so often as one of her restless eggs nudged her uncomfortably hard. If it was this difficult to bring offspring into the world, she thought resignedly, it was a wonder that the race of Puddle-ducks had not died away altogether!

Deirdre was also concerned with eggs that morning, but in a slightly different way. When the eight little Suttons sat down to breakfast, each of them had eaten a poached egg with their toast and tea. The two grown-up Suttons had eaten four eggs between them (with sausages and oat biscuits), so that the dozen eggs Mrs. Pettigrew had begun with at half past six were all gone. The tapioca pudding that was wanted for nursery tea required four eggs, so more had to be obtained. Mrs. Pettigrew gave Deirdre a basket and instructed her to stop at Hill Top Farm on her way back from the post office and ask Mrs. Jennings for two dozen.

So at twenty past ten that morning, Deirdre, accompanied by two of the young Suttons (Libby and Mouse), presented herself at Mrs. Jennings' door with the basket. When Mrs. Jennings went to the cupboard to fetch the eggs, she could find only sixteen. And since she was in the midst of washing the floor (Friday being Cleaning Day throughout the village, as Monday was Washday and Tuesday was Ironing Day and so on, all by general understanding), she told Deirdre to go down to the chicken coop and fetch the other eight herself.

As the two little girls went into the barn, Deirdre went right to the nests to collect the eggs. Luckily, most of the hens had got their egg-laying over with early that morning and gone into the garden to look for bugs, so she found seven eggs without once getting her hand pecked by an angry hen. It was only when she got to the last nest that she found Mrs. Shawl still sitting on it, with her feathers puffed up in a ruff round her neck and a scowl between her eyes. Risking a stab, Deirdre put her hand underneath and pulled out a warm brown egg. She was putting it into her basket when Mouse gave a loud shriek. The cry so startled her that she dropped the egg and broke it.

"Now see what you've done, you c-c-careless g-g-girl," Mrs. Shawl cackled crossly. *"All the hard work I've g-g-gone to, laying that g-g-gorgeous egg, and not a thing left to show for it. Well, there won't be another until tomorrow."* And with a huffy *harrumph!* she jumped down and ran off to join her sisters in the garden.

Deirdre hurried across the barnyard and into the barn, where she found Libby and Mouse on their knees and elbows in front of the feedbox, peering at Jemima's nest.

"What is it, Mouse?" Deirdre asked anxiously. "What's wrong?" She was suddenly aware of the sound of a duck quacking — loud, hysterical quacks punctuated by deep gulps and sobs and squawks.

Libby looked up. Her eyes were big as saucers, and she could barely speak. "Jemima's eggs!" she whispered. "They're hatching!"

"They're hatching," Mouse said, "But they're not —" She gulped. "They're not ducklings!"

"QUACK!" cried Jemima frantically. *"My darling duCKluCKlings! They're —"*

"Not ducklings?" Deirdre scoffed, getting down onto her knees and peering under the feedbox. "Don't be a silly Mouse. What else could they be? What —"

And then she saw what Mouse was looking at, and her heart almost stopped.

Jemima had fallen into an exhausted sleep sometime in the wee hours of the morning and slept until Chanticleer began to crow on the rafter overhead, getting the day off to a rousing start. By this time, all the eggs were moving about with violent jerks, as if they were billiard balls with their own internal means of locomotion. And when Jemima put her head down close to the nest, she could hear a constant gnawing sound, like something crunching.

"QuaCK-quaCK?" she inquired softly. *"What's going on in there, my sweet little duCKluCKlings? It must be terribly tedious, cooped up in those teensy eGGs. I do so wish you would hurry up and come out. I have your names ready, so who will be First?"*

And she did know their names. She had puzzled for quite a long time over what to call her ten ducklings. She had thought of

418

naming them for colors, such as Fuchsia, Chartreuse, Scarlet, and so on, but since they would all be yellow to start with and white when they grew up, colors might confuse them. She had also thought of naming them for herbs — Sage, Parsley, Thyme, Basil — but feared that this might give Mrs. Jennings ideas about holiday dinner, which wouldn't do at all.

And then it had suddenly come to her, a very simple solution, in a flash that seemed almost of genius. She would call them First, Second, Third, Fourth, and so on, in the order in which they emerged from their eggs. And as each came out of its shell, she would give it a name, a motherly kiss, and a little yellow shawl, to ward off chills.

But the eggs made no answer to Jemima's maternal inquiries, so she did what she had done every morning since she had begun this task. Very tenderly, she turned them over with her bill, noting with pleasure that the cracks were definitely widening and that some even seemed to be chipped, as if the duckling inside had a tiny hammer and chisel and was chiseling his way out. Now, that was progress, she thought. Real progress! Today, without a doubt, she would finally introduce First, Second, Third, and the others to the world.

And with that happy thought, Jemima climbed back onto her nest, settled down, and tried to take a nap. But her sleep was troubled by more stirrings and scratchings and scrapings and scuffings beneath her, and by a very bad dream, a ghastly nightmare, that kept going on and on and on. In her dream, she was dozing on her nest when she heard the unmistakable sound of an egg cracking. Filled with excitement, she jumped up to see what was going on in her nest.

And when she did, she saw something so horrifying, so absolutely appalling, that she could hardly believe her eyes. Three of the eggs had cracked open and the creatures inside were pushing their way out.

But they weren't ducklings!

No, they were goblins!

Or if they weren't goblins, they were trolls or gnomes. They were malformed and misshapen, with gnarled, scaly humps on their backs, and legs with talon-tipped claws, and preposterous heads like snakes, and lidless eyes and beaklike snouts that gaped open and shut soundlessly.

Worst of all, they had no feathers!

Jemima shrank back, frightened half out of her wits. After all this work, all these many days of sitting numbly on her nest, she had hatched monsters! devils! demons! Her heart was truly broken. But she had promised faithfully, so she had no choice but to kiss each ugly, scaly creature as it lurched out of its shell — First, Second, Third, Fourth — and drape the beautiful yellow knitted shawls over their bizarre bodies. She watched, horror-struck, as the monstrous creatures — Fifth, Sixth, Seventh, Eighth — swarmed over the nest and out onto the floor — Ninth and Tenth, here they came! — dragging their pretty shawls through the straw. She shrieked and cowered in a corner of the wall and —

And then she woke up, and it wasn't a dream at all. There were ten grotesque goblins or hump-backed imps or misbegotten devils — God Himself only knew what they were! — crawling over the nest, across the floor, creeping, scurrying, hurrying, and she was crowded against the wall, babbling and quacking and crying.

Jemima Puddle-duck's long-dreamt-of motherhood had become a nightmare.

Deirdre could hardly believe what she saw. The panic-stricken duck was cowering against the wall with her wings over her eyes, quacking frenziedly. All around her feet, large brown beetle-like creatures were crawling out of broken eggs, crawling over the edge of the nest, crawling out toward the light, crawling and crawling and crawling. But they didn't have six legs, like a beetle, or eight legs, like a spider. They had just four, and a tail. Four stumpy legs, with tiny toes that sported spiky toenails. They wore half-walnuts on their backs, with overlapping scales, like armor. Their mouths were hooked beaks, gaping wide and snapping shut, and their bright eyes had no lids.

"Monsters!" Jemima shrieked piteously. *"I've given birth to QUACK gargoyles! to QUACK QUACK* **dragons!** *QUACK!"*

"Spiders!" Mouse cried. "Jemima is hatching spiders!"

"No, they're beetles, Mouse," said Libby. She made a face. "Big, ugly beetles!"

"They're not spiders," Deirdre said. "They're not beetles, either. And they're certainly not ducklings." She crawled under the feedbox and picked up one of the creatures off the floor, holding it up. "Look, girls. They're tortoises!"

"Tortoises?" Libby and Mouse echoed blankly.

"No!" cried Jemima, aghast. *"You mean, after all my QUACK hoping and watching and waiting, all my QUACK dreaming and knitting*

and naming, I have been sitting on a QUACK nest of QUACK QUACK

REPTILES?"

32
TORTOISES?

Libby, almost over her fright but still much puzzled, looked up at Deirdre. "What is a tortoise?" she asked. "Is it some sort of comb?"

Now, I'm sure you know what tortoises are, and turtles, too, for you have read books and watched films and gone to zoos and seen a great many creatures as you traveled the world. But please don't think it strange that Libby and Mouse have never seen a tortoise, for the truth is that there are no native tortoises (who are land creatures) or turtles (who are amphibious) in the entire Land Between the Lakes — indeed, in all of England and Scotland. This may come as a great surprise to Americans, for our lakes and rivers are full of turtles (who are glad to dine on ducklings, when they can catch them) and our fields and woodlands are home to many tortoises — in fact, I have a box turtle (who is really a tortoise, but that's another story) living in my garden at this very moment. I'm glad to have him, too, or her — I have not closely inquired as to gender — for box turtles feast on insects that might otherwise feast on my vegetables. Every garden could use one.

"Do you remember Mr. Alderman Ptolemy Tortoise in Miss Potter's book, *Jeremy Fisher?*" Deirdre asked. "They are reptiles that carry their house around with them." (At the word "reptile," Jemima gave another horrified *QUACK!*) "When a tortoise wants to go home, all it has to do is pull its head and legs and tail indoors and shut the windows." The baby tortoise obliged, so that Deirdre held nothing in her hand but a very curious shell, sturdily constructed and neatly covered with what looked like scales, arranged in a symmetrical fashion. "People use tortoise shells to make combs and hairpins and shaving brushes," she added.

Jemima was crushed. *"Do you mean to tell me,"* she wept, *"that I have been sitting on a collection of QUACK combs and hairpins these whole two months?"*

Libby frowned. "Is a tortoise anything like the Mock Turtle?"

"Very good!" Deirdre exclaimed, who just read the children "The Mock Turtle's Story" from *Alice in Wonderland.* "They are quite like the Mock Turtle, I should think, although there is nothing very 'mock' about these." She put the little creature down. "These tortoises are quite real."

" 'The master was an old Turtle,' " said Libby, quoting the Mock Turtle. " 'We used to call him Tortoise —' "

" 'Because he taught us'!" Mouse piped up, and both girls giggled.

Kep came running full-tilt into the barn, and skidded to a halt. *What's all this noise?* he barked. *What's going on here?*

"Look, Kep!" Libby exclaimed, pointing. "It's a tortoise! Jemima hatched it!"

Tortoises, Jemima whimpered hopelessly. *All my darling duCKluCKlings have turned into QUACK combs and hairpins!*

Kep stared at the small black creatures crawling erratically through the straw on the barn floor. *Tortoises?* He put a paw on top of one and watched as it promptly retracted all its extremities, like a mechanical toy. *Never heard of 'em.* He bent down and sniffed. *Don't smell like much. Do they bark? Do they bite?*

Mouse picked up one of the babies and turned it upside down, squealing with delight as its head and legs and tail disappeared. "But where did they come from?" she cried excitedly. "How did they get into

Jemima's nest?"

"And whose *are* they?" asked Libby — a question that has no doubt occurred to you, too. For if there are no tortoises in England, how can there be tortoise eggs?

Of course, you and I and Kep could answer the first of Mouse's questions, for we know that Jemima found the eggs half-buried in silt along the shore of Eeswyke Inlet, at the edge of Esthwaite Water. Thinking they were duck eggs, she took them home with her. I'm not sure how she did it, but I like to imagine her carrying the eggs to the barn in her poke bonnet — in twos and threes, probably, for all ten at once would have been more than a mere duck could manage.

"As to where they came from," Deirdre said importantly, "I believe I can answer that question. But perhaps it is better to show you." And with that, she began scooping baby tortoises into her basket, along with the eggs.

"Wait, Deirdre!" Kep barked, alarmed. *"Stop! Hold on! Cease and desist! You cannot take Jemima's babies!"*

"Indeed she can," Jemima said grimly. *"I give her leave to take every single one of the horrid QUACK creatures. I want nothing more to do with them. Two whole months QUACK*

of my life, and I've hatched shaving brushes! QUACK QUACK!"

At that moment, Mrs. Jennings, who had finished cleaning the floors in her house, came into the barn with a pail to get some fresh milk from Kitchen the cow. "What have you found?" she asked Deirdre, seeing the children on their hands and knees.

Deirdre stood up and held out her hand, palm up. "It's a tortoise," she said, wisely failing to mention that the duck had hatched it, and that there were others.

"Eek!" cried Mrs. Jennings, putting her hands to her face, much affrighted. She had never seen a tortoise and was deathly afraid of scaly things. "Get it out o' here!"

"Are you sure you don't want it?" Deirdre asked earnestly. "Perhaps it belongs to Miss Potter."

"T' foul creature doan't belong to her nor to me, neither!" said Mrs. Jennings. "Take it straight away. And if there be others, take them, too. Now!" Skirts flying and pattens clattering, she ran out of the barn, in such a hurry that she forgot entirely about the milk.

Deirdre looked at the little tortoise in the palm of her hand, its legs and head and tail tucked inside its shell, and then at the other babies, scurrying around under the feed-box.

"I think we had better take them to their mother," she said.

"By all means," gritted Jemima. *"Find the unfortunate QUACK creature and give her babies baCK!"*

"Their mother?" Kep barked in a wondering tone.

"But who is their mother?" Mouse asked.

"And where does she live?" Libby wanted to know.

"Come along and I'll show you," Deirdre said.

Since I (and I hope you, as well) would very much like to know the answers to both these questions, we will go with Deirdre and the two little Suttons. And since Kep wants to know, he's coming along, too.

But Jemima, even though Kep politely invited her, declined. She had already had quite enough of tortoises, thank you very much. And now that she was free of her maternal responsibilities, she had other matters to attend to. I suspect that these had to do with her friend, the sandy-whiskered gentleman.

Miss Potter always said that Jemima Puddle-duck was a simpleton.

33

THE TALE OF HORTENSE THE TORTOISE

Deirdre, Kep, and the two young Suttons walked up the Kendal Road, turned left at The Garth, and went downhill in the direction of Esthwaite Water until they reached a large complex of buildings known as Esthwaite Farm. Deirdre led her little group down a path to Willow Bank Cottage, where she knocked at the door and asked for Mrs. Allen. When the maid asked what they had come about, Deirdre said, "Please, miss, tell her it's about tortoises."

Now, if someone appeared at your door and announced that they had come about tortoises, I daresay you would be tempted to send them straight away. But Mrs. Allen, when she heard this, dropped everything and hurried to the door. This lady had a great interest in the subject, you see, because she happened to be the owner of quite a few exotic pets, including two fine leopard tortoises that her great-uncle Roger had brought back from Africa many years before. These tortoises, named Hortense and Horatio, were still young when Great-Uncle Roger found them in a cage in a noisy, crowded market in Botswana. Admiring their brown and yellow carapaces and feeling that two such handsome tortoises deserved better than to end their days as hairbrush handles or bracelets or earrings, Great-Uncle Roger bought them for a shilling each and shipped them to England, where they took up residence in the conservatory in his garden, near Brighton. Great-Uncle Roger enjoyed his tortoises for ten years before he fell ill and died, and something had to be decided about the future of Hortense and Horatio.

And that future might be a protracted one. Tortoises can live a long time, if they manage to survive the hazards of hatchlinghood. Eagles and owls and frigate birds gobble them readily, and eels and crocodiles and mongooses (or is it mongeese?) snap them up in their vicious jaws. Once successfully grown to dinner-table size, they are also prey to humans, who fancy the tasty meat that is locked up in the great cupboard of their shells, and the shells themselves, which are turned into all manner of useful and decorative objects. A leopard tortoise who somehow manages to escape these various predations may grow to the size of a large china wash basin, weigh in the neighborhood of thirty to forty pounds, and live for more than sixty years.

After Great-Uncle Roger's death, the leopard tortoises of our tale made their home with his daughter, who had a house next door to The Elms in the village of Rottingdean, near Brighton. You may recall that The Elms is the house in which Mr. Rudyard Kipling resided while he was writing the novel *Kim.* In fact, Mr. Kipling enjoyed visiting with Hortense and Horatio, for he had written about a tortoise named Slow-Solid in one of his *Just So* stories — the one called "The Beginning of the Armadillos," in case you want to go and read it — and was rather fond of the creatures. I daresay that if Mr. Kipling had known that Hortense and Horatio were in want of a home, he would have taken them to live with him, and there would be no tortoises in our story.

But to tell the truth, it is not easy for two very large tortoises to find a good home. Hortense and Horatio had several other adventures (I do not know what they were, so I cannot relate them) and were at last given into the custody of Mrs. Janet Allen

(Great-Uncle Roger's great-niece), who lived at Willow Bank Cottage, at Graythwaite Farm. The tortoises traveled by train to the Land Between the Lakes and took up residence in the Willow Bank greenhouse, where they were very comfortable. Mrs. Allen, a matronly lady above middle age, was possessed of several interesting creatures, including a spider monkey named Spiffy, a parrot named Admiral Nelson (who gave commands in great nautical style), and Timothy the Tegu lizard. She became quite fond of Great-Uncle Roger's tortoises and took great care to provide them with everything their hearts could desire: collards, kale, cabbage, parsley, dandelions, mustard greens, and corn, with grated carrots, zucchini, and a chopped apple for variety. She made sure they had clean hay and fresh water, and gave them pleasant weekly soakings in a large pan filled with warm water. (She had read that leopard tortoises enjoyed these long baths.) They lived in the greenhouse, but spent time in the garden on bright warm days, foraging in the grass.

As time went on, Mrs. Allen noticed that the two tortoises were quite opposite in temperament. Horatio was a phlegmatic tortoise who liked to sit under a vine and wait for dinner to be served, after which he would shut himself up in his shell and have a nap (or perhaps he read the newspaper or did the crossword puzzle) until it was time for dinner the next day. Hortense, on the other hand, was far more adventuresome. She was inclined to wander, specially when she had it in mind to lay eggs, which, in the manner of tortoises, she buried in a hole she had dug for that purpose.

Now, most female tortoises, I am told, give little thought to the health and well-being of their offspring, leaving them all alone to get on with the business of hatching and to fend for themselves in the great world. But Hortense was made of different stuff altogether, and (like our Jemima) had an intense personal desire to be a mother, a desire so strong that one might almost call it an obsession. She did not want to leave the raising of her young to others, intending instead to watch over them and rear them carefully. She had not had any success, however. It seemed that, just when she got into the mood to lay a clutch of eggs — in Great-Uncle Roger's conservatory, or in the garden at Rottingdean — something always happened to disrupt her life. It was exceedingly trying.

So when Hortense settled in at Willow

Bank, she began to think once again of motherhood. She decided not to leave her eggs in the garden, where they might be inadvertently dug along with the potatoes and turnips. Hence her occasional sorties along the shore of Esthwaite Water (such as the time she was found by Miss Potter and Miss Potter's brother Bertram and returned to Mrs. Allen, who was very glad to see her). But being a tortoise, Hortense had by nature a smallish brain, and so even though she was determined to be a good mother, she could never quite remember where she had left her eggs (which she always took care to cover). When she went back to check on their progress, she could not find them.

But even if she had remembered, it wouldn't have mattered, for I am sorry to say that Hortense's eggs were no safer in the meadow and along the lakeshore than they would have been among the turnips and potatoes in the garden. They were promptly dug and eaten by foxes and badgers and other such predators, while the few hatchlings who survived were quickly gobbled up by the fierce eagle who lived along the shore and was always on the lookout for lively hors d'oeuvres.

Now, when she was told by the maid that a young person had come to see her about tortoises, Mrs. Allen was immediately apprehensive, thinking that Hortense might have wandered away again. But when she saw what Deirdre had in her basket, amazement took the place of apprehension.

"Why, these are baby leopard tortoises," she cried in astonishment, taking one up and examining the pattern on its shell. "Where in the world did you get them, my dears?"

Deirdre hesitated. Then, thinking she probably ought not to reveal Jemima's part in the affair, said, "We found them in the Hill Top barn. Do you suppose they belong to Hortense?"

"At Hill Top?" Mrs. Allen asked. "Then they must be Miss Potter's tortoises. I know she is very fond of animals — perhaps she has a tortoise."

"But Miss Potter is in London just now," Deirdre said, "and Mrs. Jennings was very upset when she saw these. She told us to take them straight away."

"Well, then," Mrs. Allen said, in a practical tone, "if Mrs. Jennings doesn't want them, I'm sure I do. And if Miss Potter wants them back, or some of them, please tell her that all she has to do is ask." And with that, she led the way to the small greenhouse in the corner of her garden, where Hortense and Horatio were basking on a pile of fresh hay in the morning sunshine. A moment later, Deirdre was tipping the ten tortoises out in front of them.

Now, tortoises are not by nature demonstrative creatures. Horatio was not at all impressed by the sight of ten miniature versions of himself crawling under his nose and over his shell, so he immediately shut up shop. But Hortense let out an astonished hiss.

"My eggsss have hatched!" she cried in an excess of ecstatic recognition. *"My babiesss have come home to their mother! What joy! What blissss! What a sssweet sssurprisse!"*

And with that, we shall leave Hortense to the care and enjoyment of her large and unruly brood, entirely unaware of the vital role in her hatchlings' survival that had been played by Jemima Puddle-duck of Hill Top Farm. That dedicated, indomitable duck devoted two full months of her life to service as a surrogate mother, keeping the tortoise family safe from the predations of all those creatures who enjoy eggs for breakfast just as much as you and I do.

And now that the full story of the duck's heroic efforts is known, I hope Mrs. Allen will tell it to Hortense, and encourage her to write Jemima a thank-you note.

34
CAPTAIN WOODCOCK
CONCLUDES

It was Friday evening and Captain Woodcock was at his desk in the library at Tower Bank House, staring out the window at the darkening evening and trying to sort his disorganized thoughts into some sort of order. His efforts were thwarted by the disturbing wails of the foundling infant, crying in an upstairs bedroom. He could hear his sister's footsteps, as she paced patiently back and forth, trying to lull the baby. Did Dimity truly intend to take the child into this unfortunate marriage she proposed with Kittredge?

Miles dropped his head into his hands and ran his fingers through his hair. Surely she couldn't be serious, on either score. Surely she would think better of —

He stopped. That way lay only certain frustration. He knew his sister well enough to know that when she had given her word, as she had to Kittredge, she would keep it.

Unless something extraordinary happened to prevent it (another unsavory episode of Kittredge's past revealed, for instance), she was as good as married right now. Better to concentrate on finding the child's mother — Emily Shaw, he now knew her to be, the servant girl who had left her place at Tidmarsh Manor and gone to work for a temporary employer at Hawthorn House — and force her to take her baby back.

The conclusion the captain had reached certainly seemed clear enough to him, and if you had been sitting in his chair, it might seem just as clear to you. The girl (the very same who had pawned and redeemed the cornelian ring on the desk in front of him) had given birth to the baby. Then she had left it at Hill Top Farm, with the hope that Miss Potter might raise and educate it. And having abandoned her baby, the mother had gone to London, where she could disappear from view as surely as a stone tossed into Esthwaite Water.

But Miles felt sure he could find the girl. He had friends in London, at New Scotland Yard and in the Metropolitan Police. He would ask them to be on the lookout for her. She was bound to surface, sooner or later, probably in the commission of some crime. A village girl, thrown onto her own resources in a city as large as London, alone, friendless — yes, she was bound to be involved in some sort of criminal activity. When this occurred, the police would detain her until he could bring her back to take possession of her baby. The child belonged with its mother, no matter who or what she was, and not with Dimity. And with this thought, Miles was satisfied, for he knew it to be the only logical conclusion to this sad circumstance.

He took a sheet of paper and his pen and wrote rapidly for three or four minutes. Then he smiled with a grim satisfaction and signed and dated his letter, putting it into an envelope and tossing it into the basket for the next day's post. There. With luck, the girl would get herself on the wrong side of the law within the fortnight and be back in the village the week after that.

And having satisfactorily disposed of the baby's mother, the captain thought once again of his sister's marriage. Was it not possible that Kittredge had got to Dimity at a weak moment? Perhaps she was not as certain as she seemed to be. Perhaps, given enough time, she would come to her senses and repent. In that event, his best course of action would be to delay the marriage as long as possible, without seeming to be deliberate, of course. He would not want his sister to think that he was keeping her from her happiness.

How to do that? The easiest thing would be to invent a business transaction that would take him away at certain critical times — at the reading of the banns, for instance. This would delay the business by a fortnight or two or even three. And during that time, perhaps Dim would come to her senses and see what a foolish mistake she was making, especially if, in the meantime, Will Heelis let her know how he felt about her.

Miles brightened. Yes, by Jove, that was it! When Dimity saw that her choice lay between solid, respectable Heelis and that rogue and rotter Kittredge, she would certainly see the light. So tomorrow night's dinner party, at which both men would be guests, was critical. He should have to speak to Will ahead of time, to make sure he understood the importance of acting promptly and decisively. Seize the bull by the horns, so to speak. Strike while the iron was hot. Faint heart ne'er won fair maid.

At that, he frowned, for he was not sure that Will was the sort to seize or strike. Will was not a man of faint heart, exactly, but he would prefer to watch and wait, to allow things to develop over time — all well and good when there *was* time. But in this case, time was jolly well running out, and Heelis would have to be made to understand the urgent need for action.

But there was more, and here Miles was getting to the heart of things — to *his* heart, as it were, and to Miss Potter. For the idea that had come to him in a brilliant flash at the pub the previous night had stayed with him all day, nudging him from moment to moment, reminding him that there were important things in this world besides property rights and legal affairs and breaches of the peace. There was love, by thunder. Love! The quiet, reassuring love of a woman who was mature enough to know her mind, wise and witty enough to be a fitting companion, and so sweetly comforting that she would light a lamp down all the years they would spend together.

Yes. Yes, indeed. Miss Potter would make an amiable wife, the best in the world. And Captain Miles Woodcock, being a man of action (a man who could seize a bull by its horns and strike while the iron was hot), knew just how to proceed. As soon as she returned from London, he should ask her at once to marry him. Well, not at once, perhaps, for he would not want such an important matter to appear as if out of the blue. He would need a little time for court-ing. A little time to get her used to the thought.

Then, having gained the lady's consent, he would introduce himself to her parents, announce his intentions, and ask for their blessing. There was that old business of Miss Potter's earlier engagement, of course, but that was past and done, and he felt confident that the objection her father and mother had raised against her previous choice — that he was not a gentleman — could not be raised against him. With any luck, he could win the lady's consent and her parents' approval and be married by Christmas! Of course, it would come as an enormous surprise to Dimity, although he could not imagine that she would object. If she did, what matter? He was going to fol-low his heart in this, and that was that.

The baby had by this time stopped cry-ing, Dimity had stopped pacing, and having sorted and organized his chaotic thoughts, Miles pushed back his chair, lit his pipe, and reached for his book. He was well into the latest of Sir Arthur Conan Doyle's adventures of Sherlock Holmes when the doorbell rang. He waited for a moment, expecting Elsa Grape's footstep in the hall, and then remembered that she had gone out for the evening. So he put his book down and went to answer the door himself. You can well imagine his surprise when he discovered that the lady of his heart was standing on his very doorstep.

"Why, Miss Potter!" he exclaimed. "How good to see you. And how very kind of you to call this evening." He opened the door wider. "Please do come in and have a cup of tea! Dimity will be very glad to see you." As he was himself. She was very pretty, with her hair curling softly in the damp, her cheeks flushed, her eyes very blue.

"Thank you, Captain Woodcock," she said gravely, "but I'm afraid that this is not a social call." She stepped aside, and he could see that there were two others with her, a younger girl and a woman of nearly Miss Potter's age. "I should like you to know Miss Emily Shaw," she said, gesturing to the girl. "And Miss Rowena Keller. We have some important news for you regarding the baby."

"The baby?" He blinked, and then understood. Emily Shaw was the girl for whom he had asked the police to search — and here she was, in the company of Miss Potter!

"The baby," Miss Potter repeated, looking past him. "The baby that Miss Woodcock is holding at this very moment."

Miles turned. Dimity had come down the stairs and was standing in the hallway, the infant in her arms.

"Oh!" cried the younger girl with great excitement. "It's Flora!" And with that, she pushed her way into the hall and ran to Dimity. "Oh, please, miss," she pleaded. "Oh, please, do let me hold her!" And before Dimity could say a word, she had seized the child. "Oh, dear little Flora, you dear, dear thing," she murmured, pressing her cheek against the babe's. "I am so sorry for all I have done!"

Dimity's face whitened. Miles saw her sudden look of anguish and knew it for what it was: inconceivable, inconsolable loss. Flora's mother had returned to claim her, and Dimity would have to give up the child she had come to love as her own. The look completely unmanned him, and instead of feeling glad that his problem had been solved, he felt a sharp, sudden stab of guilt, as if it had been he himself who had ruined his sister's hope of maternal happiness.

Struggling to regain his equanimity, he turned to face Miss Potter. "You've brought the baby's mother, then?"

"Yes." Miss Potter took off her gray kid-leather gloves and folded them into her pocket. "You offered us tea, Captain. I think we should all be glad of a cup, as the story may take some time."

"I'll leave you," Dimity said in a voice choked with emotion. She looked at the girl, still clutching the baby. "Shall I take Flora upstairs, or —"

"Elsa is out this evening," Miles said. "Would you be so kind as to bring some tea, Dimity?"

"And then I wish you should join us, Miss Woodcock," Miss Potter said, in a tone of deepest sympathy. "This matter involves the baby's future welfare. I think you must hear it."

Miles saw his sister gulp back tears. "Very well, then," she whispered. "The kettle's on. I'll just get the tea." She fled.

Miles found himself, to his own very great surprise, wishing fervently that Miss Potter had not used whatever magic she had used to find and fetch the baby's mother. It had broken Dimity's heart.

He sighed. "Shall we go to the library, then?"

35

MISS POTTER TELLS A STORY

It took only a few moments for Dimity to bring the tea tray. When they were all supplied with the necessities, Captain Woodcock turned from Beatrix to the girl holding the baby.

"I think it is time that the truth is told. The whole truth," he added sternly. "And nothing but the truth."

Beatrix sighed, wondering if it was ever possible to tell the *whole* truth about anything, especially about something as complicated as this affair. But one had to try. "I very much agree," she said. She looked encouragingly at Miss Keller, who was sitting next to her on the sofa, tense and rigid, her hands clasped in her lap. She had cried a good deal in the train, and her eyes were still very red.

"Miss Keller?" she prompted, when a moment went by and nothing was said.

Miss Keller wore a furtive, tightlipped

expression in which fear and an awareness of guilt were mixed. She looked, Beatrix thought, the way a chicken looks when a hawk hovers overhead. "You tell it, Miss Potter," she muttered, and put on a half-hearted effort at haughtiness. "You're the one who insisted."

Beatrix sighed. This unpleasantness would be over so much more quickly and easily if only people would do as they should. But that was probably too much to ask.

"Very well, then," she said, and turned to the captain. "Here are the facts as I understand them. Miss Keller has for several years been employed as an instructor at a select establishment for young ladies in London. When she discovered that she was to have a child, she knew that she could not keep both the baby and her employment. Her employer has always insisted on the strictest of moral standards and would certainly discharge her if she was found out."

The captain leaned forward. "Just a moment." He looked from Emily Shaw, who was tenderly holding the baby, to Miss Keller. "You mean to tell me that *you* are the mother of this child?"

Miss Keller pressed her lips together, stared defiantly at him, and said nothing. On the other side of the room, Dimity

Woodcock gulped, audibly.

Beatrix put her hand on Miss Keller's arm, leaned close, and spoke in a low voice. "As I told you, Captain Woodcock is a Justice of the Peace. I believe you should answer his question."

"I am the child's mother," Miss Keller said, without expression.

"And who is the father?"

Miss Keller looked down at her hands. "He is dead."

Beatrix cleared her throat. "Miss Keller — that is the name by which she is known at her place of employment — tells me that she and the man in question were married in secret, at Gretna Green. A few days thereafter, her husband was killed when the motor lorry in which he was a passenger went over a cliff in Wales. He left his widow without funds. This is why she had to retain her post at the school, and why she had to have the baby in secret."

"I see," said the captain, and Beatrix knew from his tone that he suspected that the story was not true. She hoped he would not demand to see a marriage license, for that would serve no useful purpose and would only further alienate Miss Keller. He seemed to reach the same conclusion, for after a moment he said shortly, "Well, then, go on."

"Thank you," Beatrix said and resumed her story. "Miss Keller, not wishing her situation to become known, wrote to her uncle, a certain Captain Villars in Calcutta, asking to have the use of Hawthorn House, which he owns."

"Hawthorn House!" interposed the captain. "Of course! You are the lady I learnt about from old Hawker!"

Miss Keller looked at him but said nothing.

"Captain Villars agreed that she should take the place," Beatrix went on, "and Miss Keller settled herself there. She hired a cook-housekeeper, Mrs. Hawker, and Miss Shaw as her personal maid. She did not go out, except for short walks in the garden. She preferred that no official record of the birth be made and she wished everything to take place in secret, so she avoided consulting with Dr. Butters. As the time of her confinement grew near, she obtained the services of Mrs. Graham, a local midwife."

"Why, that's the person we met at Longvale Farm!" Dimity exclaimed. "It was her mother who wove the blue coverlet!"

"Exactly," Beatrix said. "Mrs. Graham assisted at the birth, which occurred without complications. But she did more. She agreed to take the infant as her own child. Having made this arrangement, Miss Keller returned to her post in London as soon as she was able, leaving the child in the care of Miss Shaw, who remained behind."

"So you see," Miss Keller put in defensively, "I committed no crime — except, perhaps, for the minor matter of failing to register the birth. I did not abandon the child. I arranged to have her cared for by a loving family. I even left a valuable ring, which could be sold to provide for her welfare, and promised to send additional funds as necessary."

"Ah, the cornelian signet ring," the captain murmured. The initials R.K. — Rowena Keller.

Miss Keller lifted her chin. "Yes. It was all working out just as I planned — until Mr. Graham came home and spoiled everything."

"Spoiled everything?" Miles asked, but Miss Keller had lapsed back into a sullen silence.

"Mr. Graham apparently felt that three girls were enough," Beatrix said dryly. "Had the child been a boy, he would have agreed, or so he said. Mrs. Graham was obliged to return the baby to Hawthorn House, but by that time, Miss Keller had already left for London, and Miss Shaw, who had accepted Miss Keller's offer of a place in London, was preparing to follow."

"So if Miss Keller had already gone, it was Miss Shaw who abandoned the baby at Hill Top Farm," the captain said, pursing his lips.

"No," Beatrix replied. She had debated how best to tell this part of the story and decided on a recital of the bare facts. "The baby was taken from Miss Shaw by an elderly person who appeared at Hawthorn House, abducted the child from its cradle, and subsequently left it at Hill Top."

"I knew nothing of this, of course," Miss Keller said energetically. "When Miss Shaw arrived in London, she gave me to understand that everything had gone as planned, and that the child was safe with the Grahams."

Emily bit her lip. "I didn't think you'd believe me."

"Is it true?" the captain demanded. "The baby was taken from you?"

"Oh, yes, sir," said Emily, raising her eyes. "She was. I swear it, on my honor. T' lady — t' person moved so fast that I couldn't have stopped her, no matter how hard I tried!"

"Well, then, who was this person?"

"I doan't know, sir. An old woman is all I kin say, sir. I'd nivver seen her before. She —" Emily swallowed. "She was strange."

"And you really expect us to believe in this 'strange old woman'?" the captain asked, clearly disbelieving. "Wasn't it *you* who abandoned the baby at Hill Top Farm, so that you could go off to London in pursuit of your own pleasure?"

"Oh, no, sir!" Emily exclaimed, shaking her head violently. "It was t' old woman as did it, sir! Wrapt up in all manner of odd shawls and scarves, she was. And she moved very fast." She appealed to Beatrix. "Isn't that right, Miss Potter?"

"If the captain will recall," Beatrix said carefully, "I reported that I myself saw such an elderly person disappearing over my garden wall, immediately after I discovered the baby. Miss Shaw's description tallies with my own observation. But as to the woman's identity —" She gave a little shrug. "I couldn't say. Perhaps she was one of the gypsies."

She and Emily had discussed another possible explanation, one that involved the legendary Folk. Beatrix might be a grownup, but she had never quite given up her childhood belief in fairies, for in her personal opinion, there were some things in the world that simply did not admit of any other explanation. Still, she knew without asking that the captain was not of the same mind (or rather, his heart was not going round to the same tune, as one of her favorite writers had once put it). So there was no point in suggesting that Flora had been taken by one of the Folk.

"There may be other explanations," she went on, "but that seems to be the most logical. As to why a gypsy woman should take Flora from Hawthorn House and leave her at Hill Top, I'm afraid I have no explanation."

"I see," the captain said, although Beatrix understood from his tone that he did not see at all. He frowned at Emily. "And it was you who took the ring to be pawned in Hawkshead, Miss Shaw?"

Emily nodded, at the same time that Miss Keller spoke. "You know about that?" she asked in surprise, and then lapsed back into silence, apparently regretting the question.

"Miss Keller has told me that there were periods when funds were in short supply," Beatrix said. "She applied to her Uncle Villars for help, but it took some time for the money to arrive from India. In the meantime, she sent Emily with the ring to be pawned."

"That seems to answer every question but one," the captain said, with the air of a man who has almost cleared up a very substantial mess. "What's to be done with the child?"

"I'm sure I don't know," said Miss Keller crossly. "I no longer consider myself responsible. I made every necessary arrangement. I cannot see that I have any obligation —"

Dimity stood, cutting her off. "Major Kittredge and I would like to adopt Flora," she announced in a tone that brooked no dispute. "We are to be married soon, and both of us are anxious to give her a proper home." She looked at Miss Keller with a mixture of defiance and dislike. "She will be loved and cared for as our own."

"Oh, Miss Woodcock!" Emily cried. "Oh, miss, that's wonderful, truly it is! How fortunate for little Flora!"

Miss Keller gave a cough, which Beatrix thought signaled relief for herself rather than gratitude for Dimity's offer. "Well, then, that settles it, doesn't it?" she said crisply, with a gesture that might have been a washing of hands.

"Not so fast," the captain said, speaking in what Beatrix thought of as his Official Tone. "There are several things that must be done, Miss Keller. First, you shall see that your child's birth is properly registered. And then you shall sign an affidavit, before witnesses, stating that the infant's father is deceased, relinquishing your maternal rights, and giving your permission to the proposed adoption. Is that agreed?"

Beatrix caught the look of surprised gratitude that Dimity cast on her brother and thought she understood what was behind it. Apparently the captain had reconsidered his opposition to the marriage — at least, his public opposition. Privately, he might try his best to work against the idea, but he was not going to voice any open opposition.

"I suppose," said Miss Keller, in a hard tone. She cast a look at Flora, still fast in Emily's embrace, and put on a softer smile. "It's not that I don't want to be a mother," she said, "or that I don't feel my obligation fully. It's just that I cannot, in my present circumstance, care for a child. I'm sure you understand."

Beatrix thought that no matter how daunting the circumstance, she could never have given up her own child. And she did not trust Miss Keller's smile, for it seemed contrived and false. However, that was neither here nor there. Once the birth was registered and the affidavit signed and witnessed, Miss Keller would have nothing more to do with Flora. She would belong to Dimity and the major, who would do their best to be good parents.

Miss Keller stood. "If that is all, then," she said, "I will be off. I've taken a room at the inn for the night." She pulled down her mouth. "I had expected to return to London tomorrow, so I should like to get this official business over and done with as early as possible."

"I shall see what I can do," Captain Woodcock said.

Reluctantly, Emily handed back the baby to Dimity. "I'm so glad to know Flora'll have a good mum and dad, miss," she said, in a subdued voice. "I cared for her best as I could, y' know. Wisht I'd done better."

"I'm sure you did very well," Dimity said. She hesitated, and Beatrix read what was in her friend's mind, and very much approved. She smiled as Dimity added, "If you are not set on returning to London, Miss Shaw, I might be able to offer you the post of nursemaid — here at Tower Bank House at first, and later at Raven Hall. On a trial basis, of course," she added. "To see whether it suits."

"Nursemaid?" Emily exclaimed incredulously. She clasped her hands, her face wreathed in smiles. "Oh, miss, I should love to stay with Flora, and you, too." Then the smiles vanished. "But Miss Potter said I could work for her, in Lon'on. I was thinkin' I wouldn't come back here. I'm afraid people may b'lieve that I —"

"As long as Flora is safe and cared for," Beatrix interrupted, "it shouldn't matter what they believe. Anyway," she added reassuringly, "Miss Woodcock and I can set them straight. As to Bolton Gardens — that might be arranged later, if you still wish it."

"Well," said the captain, "everything seems to be settled."

Dimity's glance at her brother brimmed with happiness. "If you'd like to begin our arrangement tonight," she said to Emily, "we can put a cot in Flora's room for you."

At Emily's delighted "Oh, yes, please, miss!" Miss Keller stood, with a loud harrumph that said more plainly than words what an appalling mistake Emily was making. "I shall be off," she said haughtily. "Captain Woodcock, I shall expect you tomorrow."

When Miss Keller had gone, Dimity took Emily and Flora upstairs, leaving Beatrix with the captain, who offered sherry. When Beatrix declined, he poured a glass for himself, shaking his head.

"Miss Potter, I am constantly amazed by your powers. How in the world were you able, in all of London, to locate Emily Shaw and Miss Keller?"

Beatrix smiled and related the circumstances. "There, you see, Captain Woodcock? It was sheer happenstance." It was probably wise of her not to mention her suspicion that the Folk had intervened in the business, for the captain would never admit the possibility. (You and I, however, know that it was when Beatrix walked under the hawthorn trees at St. Mary's that she found herself turning to cross the churchyard, which brought her out at a point where she could not fail to see Emily. If we like, we can speculate that these ancient hawthorn trees — at least as old as the thorns at Hawthorn House — were home to some of the London-based Thorn Folk, for hawthorns are hawthorns, wherever they may grow.)

The captain nodded. "And why do you suppose Miss Keller wanted Emily Shaw in London? I should have thought the girl might be a threat, given what she knew about the baby."

"I wondered that myself," Beatrix said. "I think, however, that Miss Keller believed it was safer to have Emily where she could manage her with threats — and perhaps rewards — of her own. At a distance, Emily would be beyond Miss Keller's control."

"I see. Well, be that as it may, we are in your debt once again." The captain seemed to hesitate. "I wonder — I thought perhaps . . ." He slid her a sidelong glance. "Would you be interested in motoring to Ambleside with me on Sunday afternoon, Miss Potter? We could have a bit of a look round and afterward stop to eat at a little teashop I know there. It's quaint and very pleasant, and the drive is enjoyable."

Beatrix thought swiftly. She liked Captain Woodcock, who struck her as an interesting and thoughtful person, and someone she might like to know better. But she had spent several days of her precious time in London, and there were a great many things she wanted to do before she had to go away again.

"Thank you very much," she said regretfully, "but I'm afraid I shall have to say no. I'm truly sorry. But I have so little time to spend at the farm. I feel as if I am snatching at every minute as it races past."

"That's all right, then," the captain said in a reassuring tone. "I'll ask again."

Beatrix nodded. It did not occur to her to wonder why he was asking.

"But you *are* planning to be with us for dinner tomorrow night," he went on.

"Oh, yes," Beatrix replied. She smiled. "It looks as if we have something to celebrate."

"What? Oh, yes." The captain looked glum. "My sister's engagement."

"And the baby," Beatrix reminded him.

He looked away. "Yes, that. I must say, Miss Potter, I am relieved that the baby my sister is intent on adopting is not a gypsy baby. I am grateful to you for identifying the real mother."

Beatrix only nodded, although within herself, privately, she thought that it was rather sad that Captain Woodcock could focus only on who the baby was not (at least so far as he knew) rather than who the baby was: a beautiful infant with a promising future in a family who would love and cherish her. And it was really too bad that he could not be pleased that his sister had the courage to follow her heart.

Perhaps she was not so sorry, after all, for declining his invitation.

36
DINNER AT TOWER
BANK HOUSE

Miles had intended to speak to Will Heelis before the dinner party on Saturday evening, with the hope that he could persuade him to declare his feelings to Dimity promptly and decisively. But he was thwarted by Will and Kittredge coming in together, in a jovial mood. They had met one another on the road, and Kittredge had told Will that he and Dimity were to be married.

So the cat was out of the bag, and Miles knew that he would have to give up any idea of matching his sister and Heelis. Will was every inch a gentleman and would never think of poaching on another man's territory. What was more, Will seemed genuinely pleased to learn of the engagement. But that was because he *was* a gentleman, Miles thought darkly, and too kind and beneficent to risk looking ahead to the unfortunate consequences that were bound to come of this marriage.

Will Heelis, for his part, was delighted to learn about the engagement. He had always liked Christopher Kittredge (who was a client as well as a friend) and he was a great admirer of Miles' sister, a sweet lady, although perhaps a little too much under her brother's thumb. But perhaps he ought to revise that estimation of her, for according to Kittredge, she had faced her brother's outspoken disapproval with great courage. Will was also pleased to hear that the fate of the foundling baby had been settled to everyone's satisfaction — and the baby's great advantage. And if he had understood correctly, Miss Potter had played an important role in the business.

Ah, Miss Potter. Yes, indeed, Miss Potter. Strange, how she always seemed to have a hand in whatever village puzzle needed resolving. She was certainly looking very pretty tonight, he thought as he joined the group in the library and caught sight of her sitting on the red velvet sofa. She was dressed in a modest blue silk blouse and neat gray tweed skirt, her chestnut hair smoothed back, her china-blue eyes bright and observant.

Now, if this were a romance, we might note that Will's heart leapt up and clicked its heels at the sight of Miss Potter. But it isn't, and it didn't, quite, although perhaps it beat just a little faster than it usually did (although Will did not seem to be aware of this). He admired Miss Potter, whose little books were a great favorite among his nephews and nieces, for he had some idea of the concentrated effort and attention to detail required to produce so many very fine books. What's more, he had represented her in the purchase of one or two small pieces of property in the last year, and had found that attention to practical detail was as much a characteristic of the businesswoman as it was the artist. Added to that, he liked her quick, sharp wit and her straightforward manner. She was comradely and comfortable and always made him feel as if they were meeting person-to-person, rather than woman-to-man.

Will was not one for small talk and usually found parties difficult. But tonight, he really wanted to know how in the world Miss Potter had managed to find that baby's mother. It must have required some sort of serious sleuthing. So he went straight to the sofa, sat down beside Miss Potter and asked how she had managed it. With interest, he listened to her intriguing tale, then stayed to talk about other matters until dinner was announced, at which time his host appeared to take possession of Miss Potter and Will (who felt a brief disappointment at this) was instructed to escort Sarah Barwick to the dining room.

Miss Barwick, in a gay mood, was looking unexpectedly feminine in a pink dress decorated with tiers of gauzy ruffles. Will found her so amusing and entertaining that he forgot his disappointment, especially since Miss Potter was seated directly opposite. Dinner passed more quickly and pleasantly than he might have expected. And at the end of it, when Miles officially announced the engagement of his sister (in a brusque and offhand way that Will thought ungracious), Will himself stood and proposed a toast.

"To the future bride and groom," he said, holding up his glass. "We wish you health, happiness, and joy, now and forever." He was rewarded with Dimity's grateful smile and Miss Barwick's fervent "I'll say amen to that," which made everyone chuckle — everyone but Captain Woodcock, that is.

On the other side of the table, seated at the captain's elbow, Beatrix also felt sad for Dimity at her brother's obvious lack of enthusiasm. He was so clearly unhappy about the way things had turned out that

Beatrix almost felt sorry for him — but not quite sorry enough to try to brighten his glum mood. So she had passed the dinner hour mostly in silence, doing what she often did at such gatherings, observing others. It was heartening to see Dimity and the major with their heads together, so deeply engrossed in each other that they almost seemed unaware that anyone else shared their table and so much in love that it shone like a dazzling light in their faces.

And it was amusing to see Sarah Barwick with Mr. Heelis, for Sarah was livelier than usual, and Mr. Heelis flatteringly attentive. Beatrix could not help the small sigh that escaped her. Well, well. She had been wrong when she thought it was Dimity to whom Mr. Heelis was attracted. It was Sarah, gay, mischievous, energetic Sarah — who, for all her protesting that a man would limit her independence, was clearly attracted to Mr. Heelis. They were a handsome pair, Beatrix thought, for Sarah's fun-loving lightheartedness offset his quiet, steady demeanor, and his physical height and strength complemented her lithe and boyish figure.

Beatrix looked down at her plate, aware that she should be happy for Sarah, for whom a match with Mr. Heelis would be a very good thing indeed. She would not have to work so hard to support herself. Like Bertram, Sarah would have someone to care for and someone who would care in return, someone to share the good times and bad. And as the days became months, and the months became years, the two of them would grow closer and dearer and more devoted. Fortunate Sarah, Beatrix thought. Fortunate, oh, fortunate Sarah.

And because Beatrix was who she was, she looked up at Sarah and smiled.

37

THE PROFESSOR CONCLUDES

On a fine late-August evening, a week after the dinner party at Tower Bank House, our friend Bosworth Badger came out of the front door of The Brockery. He stretched his forepaws high over his head, bent over and touched his toes (not an easy trick, because of his stoutness), straightened, and took three deep breaths, casting an appreciative glance across the valley to the hill beyond.

On warm summer evenings, after dinner, Bosworth likes to take a cup of tea and a plate of sweet somethings to the porch outside his main entrance, where he can enjoy a last glimpse of the sun, dipping like a huge round slice of orange into the lemon-and-lavender clouds behind the great purple fells. The badger sits in his wicker rocker and makes notes for the next day's entry in the *History,* where he records all of the important events in the Land Between the

Lakes. These are not just animal events, of course (although there are many of those), but human events, as well, for animals have a great interest and stake in what humans do in the land that they all have to share.

This evening, Bosworth had jotted two notes. One had to do with a happy event — happy to his way of thinking, at least, although he understood that there were those who were not so pleased. *First reading of Miss Woodcock's and Major Kittredge's banns,* he wrote. *Wedding scheduled for early October, to be celebrated at St. Peter's.* The second seemed to him much less happy, although again, there were those who felt otherwise. *Baby Flora's mother officially resigns her claim,* he wrote.

He put down his pencil with a sigh. It was unnatural, this business of being a mother one minute and not the next. Badgers did not do things that way. A mother badger had her babies and raised them until they were old enough to go out on their own. She would be aghast at the idea of handing one of her cubs to another mother badger to raise. He shook his head. He would never understand how such a thing could have happened, nor did he want to try, since he was only a simple badger and the motivations of Big Folk were entirely beyond his comprehension.

A sudden shadow blackened the sky overhead and descended directly onto the ground in front of him. "Hullooo," it said, in a hollow voice.

"Hullo to you, Professor," said Bosworth, pleased to see his old friend. For the shadow was none other than Professor Galileo Newton Owl, D.Phil, a very old, very large tawny owl who lived in a great hollow beech tree at the top of Cuckoo Brow Wood. The professor was well known and widely respected for his studies in astronomy (his specialty was celestial navigation) and applied natural history, especially where it concerned small furry creatures with distinctive tastes. His nocturnal field trips took him across all of the Land Between the Lakes. Nothing much happened that was beneath his notice, so to speak.

Bosworth hefted the teapot. "Two cups left," he announced, pouring one for his friend and refilling his own. "Haven't seen you here for some time."

This was the case, for while the professor regularly extended invitations to his earthbound friends to join him for dinner or dessert-and-coffee in his beech-tree apartments (and had even put up a ladder), Bosworth rarely accepted. Houses that swayed from side to side in the slightest breeze made him seasick. Might as well live on a houseboat in the middle of Lake Windermere. The Sixth Rule of Thumb kept him from openly criticizing his friend's living and dining arrangements, so he simply declined. And although the professor occasionally called at The Brockery, he felt cramped and claustrophobic belowground, so the two friends usually met out of doors.

"I've been out of town," the professor said, accepting the cup the badger handed him. "Visiting my cousin, Old Brown. The one whooo lives on the island, youoo know."

Ah, yes. Old Brown was the owl whose annoying encounter with the saucy Squirrel Nutkin had been immortalized by Miss Potter. "I hope you found him well," said Bosworth, pushing the plate of Parsley's macaroons forward with his paw. He knew they were the professor's favorite.

"Very well, yes, indeed," the owl replied. He accepted a macaroon and added sugar and lemon to his tea. "But he tooold me something I found exceedingly difficult tooo credit. It concerns the fox whooo lived at Foxglove Clooose and a certain duck from Hill Top Farm. Have yoooou heard this tale?"

The badger chuckled. "Yes, we've all found it hard to understand. But it is true

— or at least, it has been reported as true by a number of individuals, all of whom claim to have a certain knowledge of it."

Bosworth had learned a long time ago that truth was often a matter of point of view, and that it was better not to believe a thing, particularly a thing that seemed at first hearing to be incredible, until the report had been corroborated by multiple sources. This one had. He had heard it first from Jackboy the Magpie. Since Jackboy's reports were garbled and easily misinterpreted, he had sought confirmation, which had come first from a passing hedgehog and then from a trusted observer, Felix the Ferret. Felix had escaped from his master and gone to live under the bridge at Wilfin Beck, where he could keep a close eye on all the neighborhood comings and goings, especially those of the rabbits in the nearby warren.

The professor snapped at his macaroon. "What this wooorld is coming tooo, I don't knooow," he muttered.

"It is certainly strange," admitted the badger. "We entertained that fox here some days ago. He expressed a great interest in the duck's whereabouts, especially after he heard that she was sitting on a nest of eggs. I assumed that the fellow had the usual foxy sort of interest. I wouldn't have been surprised to hear that he'd raided the barn and had her and her eggs for dinner." He rolled his eyes. "Little did I know."

"Sooo it's truooe, then," the professor said gloomily. "The fox has run off with the duck, and they have set up housekeeping in some unknown place."

"Perhaps it is more accurate to say that the duck has run off with the fox," said Bosworth, "or that they have run off together. If you happen to hear any news of them, I should like to know, for the record. I've noted the fact of her absence, but I'm reluctant to attribute it to a romantic involvement until there is some proof."

"Romance." The professor rolled his eyes. "Well, I suppooose there have been odder things. Cats whooo kept company with dogs, and mice who fancied cats. I even knew an owl whooo adopted a mouse tooo keep his address booook for him. One hopes the fox and the duck will be happy together, although one doubts it very much." He helped himself to another macaroon. "Old Brown never quite gets his stooories straight. There was something about the duck's eggs hatching into dragons."

"Dragons," chuckled Bosworth. "Actually, they hatched into tortoises."

"Tortoises!" The owl opened both eyes

very wide.

"Indeed. The duck apparently took them from the nest where the mother tortoise deposited them. The hatchlings have been returned to their proper parent."

"Pity," murmured the owl. "I've had tortoise eggs ooonly once, when a friend obtained some that had been imported from the Orient. Quite tasty. I would love to have sampled these."

The badger nodded regretfully. Eggs were a taste that he and his friend had in common, and had he found these in the right condition, he would likely have made quick work of them. "However," he added, "I understand that the infant tortoises are doing quite well under the care of their mother. And I just heard this afternoon that Hawthorn House is to be sold, so there is some hope that it will be refurbished and lived in once again."

"I wonder," said the owl thoughtfully, "how the Thorn Folk will view that outcome."

"Perhaps the new owners will plant some hawthorns and the Folk will return," the badger remarked. "Anyway, all's well that ends well."

"I suppooose," the owl echoed. "Although I am amazed by the quantity of strange things that gooo on while I am not here."

"It has been an interesting few weeks," Bosworth agreed. "Will you have another macaroon, Owl?"

"I believe I shall," said the owl thoughtfully. "Macaroooons are among my favorites."

And with that, I believe we must conclude.

HISTORICAL NOTE

By 1908, the year this story takes place, Beatrix Potter must have been feeling pleased with all she had been able to accomplish. Already, fourteen of her little books had been published, including *The Tale of Jemima Puddle-Duck,* which came out in August of that year. (Our Jemima presumably saw or heard of it while Miss Potter was still working on it.)

But while her books were selling well, there were frustrations. As Beatrix tells Bertram in Chapter Nine, she had been pursuing various licensing possibilities for character toys and dolls, games (she designed a board game herself), and china. She had an entrepreneurial instinct and seems to have had a great many merchandising ideas. But she was frequently disappointed, for Harold Warne (who had taken over the administration of her work after Norman's death) does not seem to have shared her merchandising enthusiasms. The French and German translations dragged on (neither was actually published until well after the war), the Puddle-duck doll took so long to get into the stores that Beatrix worried about imitations, and she was not happy with the licensing of the china. It was not the first time there had been difficulties. The publisher had failed to obtain a timely American copyright for *The Tale of Peter Rabbit,* and the book entered the public domain — an error that Carol Halebian has called "one of the most costly errors in publishing history." This mistake allowed for the unauthorized appearance of Beatrix's work, beginning in 1904, when Henry Altemus published the first pirated *Peter,* with non-Potter illustrations. This was only the beginning, as many such copies and imitations were to follow.

Progress at Hill Top was perhaps more to Beatrix's liking, and certainly more under her control. By the summer of 1908, her flock of Herdwick sheep had expanded to more than thirty, there were nearly a dozen cows and some fourteen pigs, as well as chickens and ducks (including the irrepressible Jemima). Beatrix came as often as she could and stayed as long as possible, busying herself with the livestock, attending estate sales and buying furniture for the farmhouse, and trying to catch up with her sketching. We don't know for certain when Bertram told her about his secret marriage, but the conversation may indeed have taken place as I have fictionalized it here, when Bertram had come for the holiday and they were both away from their parents.

I have also fictionalized Beatrix's visit to her former governess, Annie Moore, whom Beatrix visited on many occasions, often taking her animals with her. When the Moore children were ill or when she was away on holiday, Beatrix wrote them newsy letters, some of which she turned into books — most notably, *The Tale of Peter Rabbit,* written to Noel, and *The Tale of Jeremy Fisher,* to Eric. To Freda, Beatrix gave the original exercise book containing *The Tailor of Gloucester.* Two of the girls, Norah and Joan, visited Beatrix's farm in 1912, and after Beatrix moved to the Lake District, she always sent a warm Christmas greeting and a fine, fat turkey for the Moore table. You will find photographs of the Moores and reproductions of Beatrix's letters to the children in Judy Taylor's fine collection, *Letters to Children from Beatrix Potter.*

And so we come to *The Fairy in the Oak,* mentioned in Chapter Twenty. Beatrix wrote this fairy tale in 1911 for two New Zealand children. (It is included in Leslie Linder's *A History of the Writings of Beatrix Potter*, pp. 351–56, and in Beatrix's *Fairy Caravan*.) The story, she writes, was told to her by the man who built the stone wall in her orchard (if you have visited Hill Top, you have walked past this wall). This same man had helped to take down the oak, "the finest tree for miles around — and that oak did not want to leave the place where it had grown." But eventually, the evicted Oak Fairy found herself a new role in life, when she went to live in the bridge that her oak had been used to build. She is content, Beatrix says, because her strong oaken bridge is used by the children on their way to school or play and by the farm wives with their baskets. And sometimes, the Oak Fairy herself comes out to lend a helping hand:

The patient plodding horses bend to the
    easier road;
and Something leads them over, and helps
    to lighten their load.
It wears a duffle grey petticoat and a little
    russet-brown cloak;
and that is the end of my story of
                    The Fairy in the Oak.

RESOURCES

Halabian, Carol. "Peter Rabbit Piracies in America," In *Beatrix Potter in America,* edited by Libby Joy, Judy Taylor, and Ivy Trent. Beatrix Potter US Studies I. Papers presented at the Beatrix Potter Society US International Study Conference. The Eric Carle Museum of Picture Book Art, Amherst, MA, November 2005.

Lear, Linda. *A Life in Nature: The Story of Beatrix Potter.* London: Allen Lane (Penguin UK), and New York: St. Martin's Press, 2007.

Linder, Leslie. *A History of the Writings of Beatrix Potter.* London: Frederick Warne, 1971.

Potter, Beatrix. *Beatrix Potter's Letters.* Selected and edited by Judy Taylor. London: Frederick Warne, 1989.

Potter, Beatrix. *The Journal of Beatrix Potter, 1881–1897.* New edition, transcribed by

Leslie Linder. London: Frederick Warne, 1966.

Potter, Beatrix. *Letters to Children from Beatrix Potter.* Selected and edited, with introductory material, by Judy Taylor. London: Frederick Warne, 1992.

Rollinson, William. *The Cumbrian Dictionary of Dialect, Tradition and Folklore.* West Yorkshire: Smith Settle Ltd., 1997.

Taylor, Judy. *Beatrix Potter: Artist, Storyteller and Countrywoman.* Revised edition. London: Frederick Warne, 2005.

RECIPES FROM THE LAND BETWEEN THE LAKES

MR. VULPES' TURKISH DELIGHT

Jemima Puddle-duck is not alone in her love for Turkish Delight, a candy that was often presented by Victorian gentlemen to the ladies they were courting. It is probably best known as the seductive confection offered by the White Witch to Edmund Pevensie in C. S. Lewis' *The Lion, the Witch and the Wardrobe.* There are several versions of this recipe; this is Jemima's favorite.

1 lemon
1 orange
2 cups sugar
1 1/4 cups water
4 tablespoons unflavored gelatin
1/2 cup toasted nuts or candied fruit, chopped fine (optional)
2 tablespoons confectioners' sugar
1 tablespoon cornstarch

Peel the lemon and orange. Scrape the pith from the peel and cut it into strips. Squeeze the juice and strain it. Dissolve the sugar in half of the water over medium heat. Add the strips of lemon and orange peel and the juices. Bring the mixture to a boil and simmer over low heat for 15 minutes. Remove from heat. Stir the gelatin into the hot liquid and allow to set for 5–10 minutes. Strain the mixture into a bowl and add nuts or fruit. Pour into a shallow pan and let it set for 24 hours. Cut into 1-inch squares. Sift the confectioner's sugar and cornstarch together onto a plate. Roll the candy squares in the mixture. Store the squares, layered and dusted with confectioners' sugar and cornstarch, in closed containers.

PARSLEY'S POTATO PANCAKES WITH MUSHROOM FILLING

Potatoes were a staple food in the Land Between the Lakes. Everyone grew them, everyone ate them at every meal, and every cook had a repertoire of family favorites. Parsley's rich pancakes are made frittata-style, with leftover mashed potatoes, and filled with mushrooms. The quantities given are for one large pancake. Double or triple as necessary.

Pancake

2 eggs, beaten
1 cup mashed potatoes
1 tablespoon grated onion
salt and pepper to taste

Filling

2 tablespoons butter or margarine
2 green onions, finely chopped
1 clove garlic, minced
1 1/2 cups mushrooms
1 tablespoon fresh parsley, minced
1/2 teaspoon dried thyme
salt and pepper to taste
parsley for garnish

To make the pancake, beat the eggs into the potatoes and add grated onion, salt, and pepper. Set aside.

To make the filling, heat the butter in a small skillet and sauté the onions and garlic until soft. Add the mushrooms and cook for 5 minutes, then stir in the parsley, thyme, and salt and pepper.

To cook, heat butter in an 8–10″ skillet, and pour in the potato mixture. Cook until nicely browned on bottom, then turn and cook. Spoon on the mushroom mixture, fold, and serve. Garnish with parsley sprig. Serve with sausage and Jane's currant buns.

JANE CROSFIELD'S GLAZED CURRANT BUNS

Buns

1 package dry yeast
1 1/4 cup milk, scalded and cooled to room temperature
3 3/4 cups flour
1 egg, beaten
1/4 cup sugar
1/2 teaspoon salt
1/4 cup melted shortening
1/2 cup currants (raisins may be substituted)

Glaze

2 teaspoons cornstarch
2 tablespoons cold water
3/4 cup boiling water
granulated sugar
cinnamon

Preheat oven to 350 degrees. To make the sponge, dissolve the yeast in 1/4 cup milk. Add to the rest of the milk, and pour into a large bowl. Mix in 2 cups flour, beating until the sponge is smooth. Cover and let rise in a warm place. When light, stir in the egg, sugar, salt, shortening, currants, and 1 3/4 cups flour and mix to a soft dough. Knead until elastic, cover, and let rise. When doubled in bulk, turn onto a board, roll out

1/2″ thick, and cut into rounds. In a greased baking pan, set close together or separated, depending on whether you'd like a soft or a crusty bun. Cover and let rise. When doubled in bulk, bake about 25 minutes at 350 degrees.

To make the glaze, make a paste of the cornstarch and cold water. Add to the boiling water in a small pan and simmer 10 minutes. About 5–10 minutes before the buns are done, brush the cornstarch mixture over the tops and dust thickly with sugar and cinnamon. Return to the oven until done.

SARAH BARWICK'S TEABREAD

This traditional teatime favorite comes from the Borrowdale area and is served throughout the Lake District. Anvil Cottage, where our fictional Sarah Barwick lives and operates her bakery, really did house a bakery. From 1911 on, it was operated by Mrs. Green and then by her daughter Mollie. Until recently, Mollie Green had a tearoom in the front parlor.

3 cups raisins and currants, mixed
1 1/4 cups strong black tea
3/4 cup brown sugar
1 egg, beaten

2 tablespoons margarine or butter, melted
1 3/4 cups flour
1/2 teaspoon soda
1 teaspoon cinnamon
1/2 teaspoon cloves

Preheat oven to 350 degrees. In a large bowl, soak the raisins and currants in the tea for 6–8 hours. Stir in the sugar, egg, and margarine or butter. Sift together the flour, soda, cinnamon, and cloves and mix into the sugar-egg mixture. Pour into a lightly greased and lined loaf pan and bake at 350 degrees for 60–75 minutes, until top springs back from a touch. Cool in the pan for 5–10 minutes, then invert onto a wire rack. Slice.

DIMITY WOODCOCK'S LEMON CURD

Traditionally, lemon curd is spread on scones at afternoon tea, but you can also use it as a tart filling or spread it between the layers of trifles or cakes. Dimity used caster sugar (so called because the grains are fine enough to pass through a sugar "caster" or shaker). If superfine sugar is available, use it — otherwise, plain sugar will do. Do remember to stir.

4 large egg yolks
2 large whole eggs

3/4 cup sugar

1/2 cup fresh lemon juice (don't use bottled juice)

4 tablespoons unsalted butter

grated zest of 2 lemons

Beat together the egg yolks and the eggs in a medium bowl. Put the sugar and lemon juice into a small, heavy-bottomed saucepan. Stir in the eggs. Cook over low heat, stirring constantly with a wooden spoon, until the mixture thickens and coats the back of a metal spoon, about 8–10 minutes. Pour the curd through a fine strainer to remove any lumps. Cut the butter into four pieces and add a piece at a time, stirring until smooth. Stir in the zest. Cover the surface with plastic wrap so a skin doesn't form. Cool completely before using, or refrigerate for up to 4 days. Makes 1 1/2 cups.

GLOSSARY

Some of the words included in this glossary are dialect forms; others are sufficiently uncommon that a definition may be helpful. My main source for dialect is William Rollinson's *The Cumbrian Dictionary of Dialect, Tradition and Folklore.* For other definitions, I have consulted the *Oxford English Dictionary,* second edition (London: Oxford University, Press, 1989).

Awt. Something, anything.
Betimes. Sometimes.
Bodder. bodderment, boddering. Trouble.
Character. Recommendation from an employer.
Dusta. Doest thou, do you?
Ga, gaen, gang. Go, going.
Gammy. Lame, injured. "Laid up wi' a gammy leg."
Gannan-folk. Traveling people, gypsies.
Goosy. Foolish.

How. Hill, as in "Holly How," the hill where Badger lives.

Laid on. Installed.

Nawt. Nothing.

Off-comer. A stranger, someone who comes from far away.

Pattens. Farm shoes with wooden soles and leather uppers.

Reet. Right.

Sae. So.

Seed wigs. Small, oblong cakes, like tea cakes, flavored with caraway seeds.

Se'nnight. Seven nights, a week. A contraction similar to fortnight, fourteen nights, or two weeks.

Stook. To set up in sheaves.

Trice. Very quickly, all at once, "in a trice."

Trippers, daytrippers. Tourists, visitors who come for the day.

Turf. A slab of earth, with the grass left on it, sometimes used to construct small temporary huts.

Up to London. In nineteenth century railway schedules, "up trains" always meant trains traveling to London, "down trains" traveling away from London, regardless of the direction.

Verra or varra. Very.

Wudsta. Wouldest thou? Would you?

Yoller. Call out, yoo-hoo.

The employees of Thorndike Press hope you have enjoyed this Large Print book. All our Thorndike and Wheeler Large Print titles are designed for easy reading, and all our books are made to last. Other Thorndike Press Large Print books are available at your library, through selected bookstores, or directly from us.

For information about titles, please call:
(800) 223-1244

or visit our Web site at:
www.gale.com/thorndike
www.gale.com/wheeler

To share your comments, please write:
Publisher
Thorndike Press
295 Kennedy Memorial Drive
Waterville, ME 04901